Praise for the Weird Girls series

"One of my favorite books/series . . . so much action, so much violence and, oh, the lust radiating off of our heroes . . . I definitely recommend this series for lovers of all things paranormal and awesome."
—*USA Today*

"Robson's blend of smart-alecky wit, good old-fashioned romance, and suspenseful episodes of fighting off evil spirits form a paranormal thriller that will make pulses pound."
–*Publishers Weekly*

"[With Robson's] edgy, witty and modern style of storytelling, the reader will be drawn deep into this quirky paranormal world. . . . Strong pacing, constant action and distinctive, appealing characters—including a gutsy heroine—will no doubt keep you invested."
—*RT Book Reviews*

"A healthy dose of humor, a heaping dash of the supernatural, and a pinch of mystery all laced with a heavy dollop of action . . . Robson knows how to combine all the best ingredients to keep her readers hooked and begging for another hit."—*Fresh Fiction*

"...Robson's supernatural tale will leave readers clawing for the next installment." —*Booklist*

"Jam packed with action, suspense, kickass girls, hot guys, humor and all out weird girls, this series has me coming back for more and more." –*Night Owl Reviews (Top Pick)*

"I was blown away by the depth of passion, humor, and creativity in this story...If you are a fan of powerful, sarcastic heroines and cross-over urban fantasy / paranormal romance stories, I highly recommend *Of Flame and Light.*" – *Grave Tells Romance*

"I fell deeply in love with Cecy Robson's sharp, funny dialogue, hilarious characters and brilliant world building." – *Book and Movie Dimension*

"When you begin, reading *Of Flame and Light* the rest of the world will slip away. Action-packed with heart, growth, and supernatural awesomeness." – *Caffeinated Book Reviewer*

"Cecy Robson created this amazing world full of characters that will make you laugh, love and cheer for the sisters that have always been called weird. Not to mention shifters that will knock your socks off." – *Under the Covers Book Blog*

"You will laugh, you will cry and you will seriously want to yank Genevieve by the hair so hard that you get a hand full of nothing but roots. In short- go one click this series and binge read until you get to *Of Flame and Light...*" - *The Reading Cave*

"There is something about Cecy's writing that grips me and holds me to the page...I'm so in love with these sisters and characters. can't wait for more books!" – *My World in Words and Pages*

By Cecy Robson

The Weird Girls

A Curse Awakened (novella)

The Weird Girls (novella)

Sealed with a Curse

A Cursed Embrace

Of Flame and Promise

A Cursed Moon (novella)

Cursed by Destiny

A Cursed Bloodline

A Curse Unbroken

Of Flame and Light

The Shattered Past Series

Once Perfect

Once Loved

Once Pure

The O'Brien Family Novels

Once Kissed

Let Me

Crave Me

Feel Me

The Carolina Beach Novels

Inseverable

Eternal

Infinite (coming soon)

of
Flame
and Fate

A WEIRD GIRLS NOVEL

CECY ROBSON

Cover design © Sarah Hansen, Okay Creations LLC
Edited by Gaele L. Hince of BippityBoppityBook.com
Formatting by BippityBoppityBook.com
Content editing by Sue Brown-Moore of DaVinciKittie.com

This book contains an excerpt from Sealed with a Curse, the first full-length novel in The Weird Girls Urban Fantasy Romance series by Cecy Robson. The excerpt has been set for this edition only, and may not reflect the final content of the final novel.

Published in the United States by Cecy Robson, LLC.

ISBN # 978-1-947330-01-6

Dedication

To the "weird girls" of the world: Don't be afraid to be different and allow that difference to shine

Acknowledgements

On May 1st, 2009, I decided to write a book, just to see if I could. That book would eventually become Sealed with a Curse, the first novel in the Weird Girls series.

The first person to believe I "had something" was my husband Jamie. The second was my friend and mentor Susan Griner. The third, fourth, and fifth were Valerie McMullen Secker, Crissy McMullen Roth, and Maria Hanley. The sixth was my agent and now best friend, Nicole Resciniti.

I don't know who followed next. But you all did and stood by me, even when I wasn't sure Celia, Taran, Shayna, and Emme would continue their journey. So when the tigress roars and shows her claws, when the feisty hothead throws her sarcasm and flame, when the perky one skips forward to stab the bad guy in the heart, and when the sweet one soothes your ailing heart, know that they do so because of you.

Thank you for believing. You have my heart.

To my team Kimberly Costa and Kristin Clifton. I found you because you were fans of my work. Now, I'm a fan of yours. And to Gaele Hince, you get me. Even when I'm not certain I "get" myself.

Chapter One

I'm shoved into a cold room where a band of bloodsucking fiends tear off my clothes. Their long nails graze my skin as their master watches, his cold gray eyes glinting with malice.

"Son of a bitch," I say, smacking Edith Anne's hand away when she cops a feel. "The demon's in my leg, *not* my tit!"

There's something you don't say every day, but then that's why humans are safe in the world and weird gals like me are stuck with demons burrowing under their skin.

"Just making sure," Edith adds with a wink.

I'm ready to punch her in the face, except I'm too busy cringing at the thing crawling beneath the length of my shin, its spindly insectoid appendages stretching the skin as it curls up and over my knee cap.

"Get it out of me!" I screech, growing nauseous with each numbing tug it creates beneath the underlying tissue.

"We're trying," Agnes Concepcion snaps, like I'm somehow inconveniencing her by having an evil being claw its way through me.

Her tiny plaid skirt smacks against my hip as she shoves me into a massive glass and tile shower. Three other vamps, dressed like naughty Catholic schoolgirls (don't get me started) follow us in, bottles of champagne tight in their grips.

"What the hell?" I ask, kicking as if I can somehow shake this thing loose, and certain the booze is to celebrate my grisly death.

Bottles of champagne open with a pop, the naughty Catholics pouring the bubbly over my breasts, back, and ass. This isn't real. This is something out of a bad porno and somehow I'm the star.

But as the fluid reaches my thigh the lump with the creepy legs bounces, pulling at the muscle it's crawling over, squirming to the left then right, trying find its way around the torrent of liquid they're pelting me with.

"Don't let it reach her heart," Master Vampire Misha Aleksandr orders from the opposite side of the bathroom.

"What's it going to do to my heart?" My head whips back and forth when none of the vamps answer. "It's going eat my freaking heart isn't it?"

"Don't be ridiculous," Agnes mutters, adjusting her tiny librarian glasses as she angles the bottle she's holding.

"Okay . . ." I begin.

"It needs your heart to nest and lay its eggs," she explains.

"*What?*"

"But yeah, then the hatchlings will munch on your heart like raw steak," Edith adds. She reels me around when additional vamps swoop in with cases of wine, drenching my chest with more alcohol.

She seems to be having fun. I'm mostly trying not to hurl and wondering how the hell this happens to me.

Agnes is more focused. She drips the wine just above the demon, forcing it back down my leg. "*Quiesco,*" she says, her tone as sharp and commanding. "*Quiesco.*"

My body shudders as the demon scurries downward. Its movement doesn't hurt, surprising since I think it has pinchers, but the yanking motion is unnerving, like getting stitches while under anesthesia. My head flops forward and my vision starts to swim.

"I don't feel good," I mumble.

Agnes slaps me, the sting of the strike causing my eyes to whip open. "Don't fall asleep." She slaps me again when my eyelids flutter and close. "Taran, the poison the demon is spewing is numbing your skin and making you drowsy, if you succumb to it the alcohol won't work and the demon will take you."

Again, her palm whips across my face. "Stay awake so we can cut this thing out of you."

I slap her back, knocking her glasses askew. "I'm awake, damn it."

She smirks because she hits harder and maybe because she likes it, too. She returns to my leg when the vamp behind her hands her another bottle of champagne. "*Quiesco*," she whispers against my leg, her breath hot against my cooling skin.

My head falls forward as I start to go under. This time, Edith smacks me.

"God damn it," I hiss, my right arm quaking and threatening to release my flame.

"I was just taking my turn," she replies defensively.

Her gaze locks on my arm. She eases away as a spark of blue and white escapes from my fingertips, giving me and my power ample space as the surrounding vamps shower me with alcohol.

"Master," Agnes says, ignoring us as she concentrates on my thigh. "It's settling. I need the knife."

"The wolves are bringing it," he replies.

"The wolves?" I ask. Okay. Now I'm wide awake.

The doors crash open as a pack of *weres* in human form stomp in, the exception being an immense, midnight-black wolf with a white left paw who leads them. His lips peel back, exposing a row of pointy fangs as he growls at the vampires surrounding me. But it's the man storming forward with dark almond eyes and a six-inch dagger in his hand that gives me pause.

"Hi, honey," I say, giving him a little wave.

Funny thing, he doesn't wave back. His gaze swoops

over my naked body. "Hold her," he snarls, ramming the knife into my thigh.

Reality shoves aside the shock of having the man I love stab me in the leg. Like a heated blade through butter, he slices through the skin and muscle, creating a diagonal line and spraying blood across the glass shower walls. I expect pain, scorching white-hot pain, and to lose my blood supply in large volumes. But like the creepy crawly beneath my skin, I just feel that wretched pulling and grabbing.

My bleeding trickles to a stop just as Gemini's hand plunges deep into the incision. The image is so graphic and brutal my stomach lurches. I'm seconds from passing out. The vamps on either side of me are the only thing keeping me vertical. But when my focus latches onto the hilt of the dagger, and I realize it's a femur—a *freaking femur*! — my body immediately slumps.

Of course, that's not the worst part.

The tangle of bodies, limbs, and faces, carved around the hilt twitch, as if seizing, breaking free of what's holding them to slither. Oh, and it gets better. The mouths open, singing one messed up version of *O Fortuna*.

"Jesus Christ," I gasp, my body trembling violently as their slowly amplifying voices echo across the room.

Agnes grips my jaw, yanking my face toward her. "Taran, get it together before you set this whole place on fire."

I wrench my head free. "Don't you think I'm trying?!"

I bite back a curse, and a few more, when something scampers toward my right butt cheek.

It doesn't get far. Gemini thrusts his hand deep, wrenching a large, *screeching* lump from my leg, exciting the minute faces continuing to sing and slide along the hilt. Their voices crescendo and their bodies writhe with glee. I don't get a good look at the demon impaled by the dagger, and I don't want to. I only see enough to realize I was right about the spindly legs and pinchers.

Gemini carries the shrieking demon to the sink, ignoring the way the long cluster of centipede legs kick out and clutch

4

blindly at the air. I wish I could ignore it. But those things you can't unsee? I've seen plenty in my twisted, messed up life and this is one more to add to my list.

Gemini holds out his free hand. Without asking, a vamp drops an open bottle of vodka into his palm. Gemini pours the vodka over the demon, stunning it and causing the legs to fall open like petals—nasty petals covered with blood, pointy grippy ends, and little bits of me.

With a turn of his wrist, he drops the demon into the sink. It falls with a sick plop.

Agnes's weight abruptly pulls off me when she stands and hurries to the sink. She flicks a lighter another vamp tossed her and drops it on top of the demon. "*Ad infernum,*" she tells it, sending it back to hell.

The vamps step away from me as the flames spray up to lick the ceiling. The exception is Edith who remains on her knees, clutching my leg between her breasts and sealing my wound with several fast and enthusiastic strokes of her tongue.

"*Get away from her,*" Gemini demands. His voice is more beast than human, setting off an orchestra of snarls from the rest of the pack.

Like a very hungry dog with a bone, Edith doesn't want to let go. Gemini doesn't give her a choice. From one breath to the next, he rips me from her, wrapping me in a blanket someone hands him and carrying me away.

"Taran," Misha calls.

Gemini and I glance at him. "I'll see you soon," he tells me with a smile and an all-too playful wink.

The midnight wolf at our side answers with a powerful snap of his jaws, not quite loud enough to overshadow the inhuman growl from my mate, nor the choir in the knife, which is evidently having the time of its cringe-worthy existence.

"Babe," I begin, touching his shoulder.

My touch is usually enough to soothe him, or at the very least keep him from mangling the closest prey. Hey, sometimes that's the best I can hope for. To his credit, he hasn't eaten anyone, yet.

He reels, rushing forward, his insane speed and strong movements propelling us down the long hall. I don't see the splendor of Misha's estate, and barely feel the bounce of Gemini's feet as he leaps down the grand staircase. I'm too busy pressing against him and attempting to soothe his livid beast even as I struggle to calm my fragile nerves.

I can feel Gemini fighting not to *change*, my fear urging his beast to appear. During times of stress and unparalleled danger, two wolves are better than one. They can protect and fight with graceful lethality. But the danger is over, and right now, I need the man to soothe me, not the wolves who bite.

I'm tough as railroad spikes, aggressive as a fighter going for the championship belt, and as powerful as most preternatural beings we encounter. That doesn't mean I don't get scared. Me and fear are old friends, lovers, and sometimes enemies, and over the past few days fear has paid several visits, reminding me it's never far away.

I rub my cheek against Gemini's chest. Just as my presence manages to keep him from munching on vampire limbs, his warmth and the familiar way his body curls around mine reminds me I'm safe.

The moment we're outside, a frigid wind streams across Lake Tahoe, breaking through the thick pines and sending an army of goosebumps marching down my spine. Gemini leaps from the stacked stone steps, landing beside his black Mercedes SUV. He places me in the passenger seat, slamming the door closed with enough velocity to rattle the interior cabin.

My guess is he's a little pissed. He tosses me a glare. Or perhaps, a lot pissed.

His midnight twin wolf hops into the rear when Gemini throws open the door, sniffing the top of my shoulder. "I'm fine, sweetie," I assure him.

I take a moment to stroke his large head before clicking my seatbelt in place.

Gemini pauses, likely sensing my touch through his twin. The midnight wolf turns back to look at him and whimpers. I think he's sad, but then I realize Gemini is calling him back. From one leap to the next, the wolf dissolves into Gemini's exposed back, returning home and once more becoming part of Gemini's soul.

This time, when Gemini closes the back door, it's less forceful. Yet his anger remains.

Another *were* approaches carefully, keeping his gaze lowered as he opens an old piece of leather fabric stained with wine-colored splotches. Gemini drops the knife in the center of the cloth, growling words I don't understand as he folds each corner over the knife, muffling the mouths that continue to sing.

"Get the knife back to the Den," he orders, securing the knife with twine.

"Do you want us to follow you back?" the *were* asks.

"No," Gemini tells him. "The Elders need to settle the knife and seal it in the vault. Otherwise, it will need to eat and search out prey. I don't want to spend the night hunting demons to feed it, or tracking it if it flees."

If *it* flees . . .

Apparently, I'm not the only one disturbed be this news. The *were* straightens. "How long do I have to get it to the Elders?"

"Not long," he answers, tightly. "*Go.*"

And he does, breaking into a run and peeling away in his truck.

Gemini slips inside. I place my hand on his shoulder. "Tell me you were kidding about a knife, partial to breaking into creepy songs, running amuck in Lake Tahoe in search of demons to eat?"

He frowns. "Why would I joke about something like that?"

Humor is apparently lost on the Guardians of the Earth. I blame it on all the scary things they're forced to mutilate, oh, and possibly global warming.

He and his twin growl at the pack of *weres* gathered in front of us. I pull up the blanket covering me as they scatter. *Weres* are used to being naked around each other in human form, but I'm not a *were*, and because of it, they've never seen me naked.

Until tonight, cause, don't I know how to put on a show?

The next set of growls from him and his twin have them all hopping inside their vehicles and cranking the engines. The lights from the cars in front of us cast a gleam against the angles of his face, sharpening the menace plaguing his features.

He's angry, and he should be. As a non-*were* different rules apply to me, one of them being they shouldn't stare at his naked girlfriend.

He powers across the blue slate-lined double driveway, causing the dusting of pine needles covering it to stream past the window. I wait until we clear the wrought iron gates at the entrance to the compound before placing my hand on his thigh. But it's not until we pass the miles of stone wall surrounding Misha's property that I speak again.

"That probably looked pretty bad, huh?" I ask.

He clenches his jaw tight, enough to strain the cords along his neck. "Which part? The part where I find you surrounded by vampires pouring champagne over your naked body?"

"Um . . ."

"Or do you mean getting the call that a parasitic demon has infested your leg and is attempting to make your body its nesting ground—then watching it try and claw its way to your heart?"

"Ah . . ."

His steely eyes cut my way. "Or perhaps you're referring to the she-vamp licking your thigh in a way I should only touch you?"

Yeah, he's a little irate. I start to defend Edith, but she is Edith and those were some pretty suggestive licks.

"Baby," I say.

"Don't." He huffs. "Nothing you say changes the fact that you're working for the leeches."

"You know why I'm doing it," I tell him. I groan when he all he does is stare ahead. "I have to protect my sister."

"No, *I* have to protect her, *and you*," he fires back. "I can't do it if I don't know where you are."

"I didn't mean to run off, but we needed the relic of Dirpu." He narrows his stare. "Well, we did," I insist. "And FYI, I totally snagged it. It was in Egypt."

"I know," he snaps. "Reports of fire raining down in Giza was my first clue to your whereabouts."

"That was an accident," I say, pointing at my right arm. Its stark white appearance glows like a strobe at the mention, lighting the dimness of the cabin and blanching the rest of my olive skin. "You know how she gets when . . ."

"Your life is in danger?" he offers when my voice trails.

I press my arm against my belly, stroking it with my other hand. My right arm is a combination of magic I was born with, and magic as old as time. My left is all me, my original fire and lightning.

I have complete control over the power radiating through my left arm. My right, not always, especially when she's angry.

"It happens, Tomo," I add quietly.

He stiffens at the sound of his real name. When we're alone at night, or at times when I want to feel close to him, it's the name I use instead of the nickname he goes by. I don't feel close to him now, not with his anger erecting an invisible wall between us. But I want to.

I love him. I don't want to go back to how we were all those months we were apart, miserable, hurt, and bitter. It took so much for us to reconcile. The last thing I want is for something else to drive us apart.

"It only happens when you're in places and situations you shouldn't be," he says.

He's still angry, but his quieting voice assures me he doesn't want to be. "The relic of Dirpu opens portals to the demon domain," I explain. "I couldn't chance the Dark Legion seizing it once its location was leaked." I twist to better see him. "Try and understand, whatever evil is threatening to rise could have used it to summon a warrior demon, an evil spirit, or something just as deadly to kill Celia and her baby. I can't let that happen."

He pulls onto the highway leading back to Dollar Point. "Was that how the leeches spun it?"

"What?"

We're driving fast, too fast. He eases his foot off the accelerator as we round the curve and Lake Tahoe comes into view.

"Taran, at last count there were two-thousand, seven-hundred, and thirty-eight documented relics of power. At least half can open portals, a third can summon darkness, and close to eighteen can bring on Armageddon and divide the sun in half." He glances at me. "Did the vamps happen to mention that?"

No. But holy shitballs. I cross my arms, the motion turning off the fluorescent bulb that is my right arm. "Well, now there're one less to worry about."

He punches the gas, accelerating up the hill. "You can't go after every relic that presents itself—no one person can—which is why my pack works as a team to secure each that's located. How do you think we found the dagger?"

I knit my brow. "Are you talking about that fucked-up singing knife?"

He scrunches his face. "Don't insult it, it can hear you."

"*It can hear me?*" I glance out the window in the direction of the woods, then back toward the lake where the moonlight streams rays of silver light across the gentle waves, waiting, just waiting, to hear O Fortuna begin to play. "You're not kidding, are you?"

He shakes his head slowly. "The Dagger of Aberlemno sees all, knows all."

I still. "Please tell me it's not one of those things that can split the sun."

"It's not."

My shoulders slump. "Oh, good—"

"But its brother can."

Its brother can. *Awesome.*

I keep my comments to myself, obviously. God forbid I piss off the knife, its evil fork brother, or whatever the hell.

"This world is messed up."

"I know, Taran," he agrees. "Which is why I need to spare you from it."

"It's too late to shut my eyes and pretend the boogie monsters don't exist, love."

Again he quiets, the intensity in his watchful eyes growing more severe. "You can't keep doing this, Taran," he says. Regardless of the brewing anger overtaking his form, he eases the SUV around another curve. "Not to yourself. Not to us."

"I'm not trying to hurt us," I add.

"But you are," he tells me. "When you disappear without telling me where you're going, and what you're up to, you're betraying my trust and our relationship."

"That's not my intent," I say, hoping my tone reflects how bad I feel.

He sighs. "But it's the result."

I've hurt and likely embarrassed him. But the road to hell is paved with good intentions, and once more here I am, adding another flat stone and taking a step closer.

"You wouldn't have let me go," I point out.

I'm not trying to be difficult, nor am I anything close to defensive, at least not this time. When it comes to the bad guys, my role in the secret world of the supernatural has always been muddled. That changed when my sister became pregnant with the first of several children prophesized to rid the world of a new evil that's rising.

Without meaning to, Celia became a target. As a result, I delegated myself to stand in front of her, doing my best to shield her from the encroaching arrows.

I don't want to die. If I'm being honest, I'm scared shit-less. But I'm more scared of losing Celia, and what will happen if the Dark Legion succeeds in killing her babies before they have a chance to be born.

Gemini meets my gaze, it's brief, but more than enough to silence my thoughts. "You're right," he says. "I would have found a way to keep you."

I stroke my right hand when she twitches. She does that

when deep emotions rile her and her power awakens. It's the reason why fire rained down in Giza and the Sphinx is now sporting a new tan. It wasn't my intention to mar a monumental treasure, but when you're fending off another curse, inadvertently wake a skeletal army (also, not my fault), and unleash the skin burrowing demons protecting the relic you need, everything goes to hell and things get blown to shit.

"All those times you left to fight during the supernatural war, you ignored my pleas to stay," I remind him.

"I didn't ignore them," he says. "As a *were*, I'm sworn to protect the world, and because of it, I was obliged to leave you."

"And I'm obliged to protect my sister," I remind him.

"It's not the same thing," he says, his voice gruff. "You're being used. Can't you see that? The vampires have the means to ghost you around world, not for the earth's or the Alliance's gain, but for theirs. Each relic is power they accumulate to do as they wish, regardless of what the rest of us need or desire."

"I know," I say quietly. "But whatever relic I find doesn't just go to any vampire."

"No," he says, his voice lowering. "It goes to one of the most powerful in existence." He looks at me. "As the only known vampire with a soul, Misha will one day be unstoppable."

"He will," I agree, lifting my face in his direction. "But the only reason he has a soul is because Celia returned it, giving him back some of his humanity, as well as his heart."

"You're giving him too much credit," he counters.

"And you're not giving him enough," I press. "He loves her, Tomo, and because he does he'll protect her, using the relics if it comes down to it."

"Is that what he told you?" he asks, hints of his anger returning.

"He didn't have to. I just know he will." I ignore his growing anger, keeping my voice calm. "You can't dismiss what Misha and Celia have been through."

"Do not insult my alpha by comparing his matehood with

Celia to whatever affections that leech feels toward her."

"That leech helped save her life." The memory of that day causes my eyes to burn and my arm to twitch. "She wouldn't have made it without him and the fate of the world would already be decided."

"It doesn't absolve him from all those times he risked her life and now yours. I won't have you working for him, Taran."

He's tapping into his inner beast. I have an inner bitch and she's just as effective. "And I won't have my sister in danger. Not if I can help it."

"By putting out fires better handled by *weres*?"

I shrug. "Every bit helps."

"Not when all it helps are the vampires."

"Gemini, do not let your hate for the vamps cloud what I'm trying to do for Celia, Aric, and their baby." He doesn't budge, which only frustrates me more. "After what they've been through, they deserve some peace and happiness."

"Not at your expense!" he growls. He pulls into our neighborhood, slamming down the parking brake in front of our house just to glare at me.

I glare right back. "I'm not going to let her die," I say. "Not if I can help it." I swing open the door and step out, fumbling with the blanket as I limp forward and a sharp sting tears up my thigh, burning my skin.

Chapter Two

Here's the thing about being a badass, you have to walk the walk and talk the talk. The talk, I think I have down. The walk, not so much. Holy shit. My leg is pulsating, as in throbbing, and pounding, and taking on a life of its own. I grip it, uselessly trying to stop the swelling spreading up to my ass. Each pop and pull against my skin feel like a boil pushing through, following the same path that demon took when it tried to burrow its way to my heart.

I trip over the blanket that smells like wererat, causing my boobs to spill out, just in time for our evil neighbor Mrs. Mancuso to step out onto her porch. Christ, it's like she waits for me.

"Taran Wird!" she shrieks. "Are you naked?"

"No, I have a fucking blanket."

Considering I have boils the size of quarters scattering along the length of my leg at warp speed, it's the best comeback I have.

Gemini appears out of nowhere, wrenching me into his arms to keep me from falling on my face, but not quite managing to keep the girls in.

Flashing my boobs doesn't upset Mrs. Mancuso. No. Not

at all.

"You are naked!" she screams at me.

"No, shit," I snap, gathering the blanket closer.

Of course, Mancuso doesn't stop there. "Take your disgusting body and your even more disgusting suitors elsewhere!"

"I did. Your son-in-law says, hello," I fire back.

"You *whore*."

Gemini hoists me in his arms. "Damn it, woman, don't you have children to lure into your gingerbread house!"

It's the last comment I manage before the quickly forming boils singe like fire against my skin and I coil in anguish.

Gemini launches us up the wooden steps. "Taran," he says. "The demon's venom is fading."

I know it is. He doesn't have to tell me. Another wave of pain claws its way up my chest, the agony making me curl into Gemini's chest.

Mrs. Mancuso is still yelling, still name-calling and her support hose likely still in a bunch. For once I don't care. My leg and butt are spasming out of control, causing the rest of my body to quiver.

I gasp, struggling to speak. "What's happening?"

"The demon's venom numbs its prey to allow it to nest," he explains. His feet pound against the wood floor as he races me back to my room. I make out the picture of my sisters and I in the hall, but not much more. "Now that it's fading, your body is reacting to all the damage it caused."

What feels like an ivy of thorns digs into my skin. I bite down, not wanting to scream or fire up my arm. But I'm already plenty pissed and so is Sparky. Heat spreads the length of my limb, making it jerk. I clutch it to me when Gemini grunts.

"Don't," I tell her. "You'll hurt him."

It seems ridiculous for me to speak to my arm as if she's an entity in and of herself. But as much as my right arm has become a part of me, she's not the original.

The original was eaten by a crazed werewolf.

15

"Easy," I whisper against the skin, trying to stay calm and keep her calm as well.

She responds for the moment, just a moment. But that's not how she'll stay.

My new arm was created from a combination of *were* magic as old as the earth and my matehood with Gemini. It, I mean, *she's* different, maybe even weirder than me and my sisters.

My head spins as another rush of pain builds, this one stronger than the last.

I'm in my bathroom, I think. Voices echo around me. Celia is here, so is Aric. They groan, coughing.

"Parasite demon?" Aric asks.

"Yes," Gemini replies, his voice tight.

"Oh, God," Celia says, sounding sick.

"Celia, I need you to leave," Aric tells her. "The smell can't be good for you or the baby."

"Where's Emme?" Gemini asks.

"She's coming."

It's the last thing Celia says before she disappears. Gemini growls low and deep. "Where *is* she?"

"Easy," Aric says, his voice barely below a snarl. "She'll be here soon."

With me hurt, both are on edge, their beasts close to pushing through their human counterparts and taking charge.

"I'm turning on the water," Aric says. "I mean your mate no harm."

In the world of humans, and under similar circumstances, one man wouldn't have to reassure another this carefully. But *weres* are more beasts than human when their mate is injured, and the need to protect them overshadows reason.

If Celia was present, Gemini's wolves would recognize her as Aric's lover and Gemini wouldn't take offense to having another alpha male so close. But she's not. She's trying to find Emme. At least, that's what I hope.

Another strong stab of pain pelts through my leg, sharpening as it intensifies and making me whimper.

I scrunch my face, my nails digging into Gemini's arm

when he goes ballistic and his twin wolf punctures through his back. The wolf snaps his fangs, just barely missing Aric's face.

"Babe, don't," I stammer.

I lift my arm to stroke his face when an odd red light swarms my line of vision, blinding me.

Growls thunder, the pure viciousness within each beating against my ears. More wolves arrive. I think I see Koda but I can't make out the others. My pain escalates, making me scream.

My right arm shoots out, detonating power like a cannon and ripping me from Gemini's hold.

"No!"

What sounds like a mound of bodies, collide. I think I'm blowing things up and I'm terrified I've set the house on fire, but then the red light is replaced with a pale yellow one and the pain searing through me abruptly stops.

With each breath I take, a cooling sensation seeps through my lower back and spreads along my leg, easing the tension and extinguishing the pain.

"Her right leg," Gemini says, his voice bordering on murderous.

My youngest sister's voice is quiet and calm, bringing peace. "I know, I can feel it. Just a little more."

She trembles, her small hands trailing down my cheek.

"What's wrong?" Gemini says.

"There are . . . holes," she tells him.

"The demon made them when it borrowed through the muscle," Gemini explains.

Emme's light fades slightly, because yes, his comment is as nasty as it sounds. But then the glow intensifies against my eyelids and her need to heal grows urgent.

I force my eyes open as her light fades. My sisters surround me, including Celia who couldn't seem to stay away, her long brown and gold waves brush against my forehead as she peers down.

"Are you okay?" she asks.

"Sure," I say. "Why wouldn't I be?"

It's a stupid response, of course. I'm just excited I didn't burn the house to the ground. Believe it or not, I've blown my share of buildings to bits.

Celia exchanges glances with Shayna. I didn't even know Shayna had arrived. Her large blue eyes blink back at me and her sleek black ponytail bounces as she speaks. "Dude, you had a demon digging its way through your body, toward your heart, to lay its eggs. That's like, *epic*, even for you."

"It happens," I mutter.

My comment earns me collective growls from the wolves.

Emme's hands slip away. Sometimes, she doesn't have words for me. Shayna, always has plenty. "I know you've had a rough night and all, T, but try not to upset the furries. They don't like evil things especially when they're trying to hatch other evil thingies inside you. You know what I mean?"

"Understandable," I agree. I lift my head, but even that seems like too much of an effort, the muscles along my neck feeling more like tight rubber than anything that belongs on my body.

Koda and Aric are restraining Gemini close to the door, their muscles bulging as they struggle to keep him in place.

"Why are you holding him?" I ask.

They ease their grip, not that my beloved appears any less irate. "Gemini, didn't take your pain well," Celia explains quietly. "He settled with us here, just not as much as we'd like." Her husky voice softens as she speaks to him. "How are you?" she asks him.

He doesn't reply despite that I know he heard her. She doesn't push, and thankfully, Aric doesn't push him to answer.

There's a towel around me, one of the thick white ones from the linen closet near the door. I hold it against me as I peel my sticky back from the cobalt blue tile that makes up my bathroom floor.

Celia helps me into a sitting position, her inner tigress giving her freakish strength even in her delicate condition.

"Thanks, Ceel," I tell her, my attention staying on

Gemini. "I'm all right," I assure him.

He shakes his head slowly, the tendons along his dense frame taught and stressed. "The only reason you're alive is because the parasitic demon was male, and males can only nest in the heart. Had it been a female, your body would be riddled with malevolent eggs."

"Oh." I swallow hard when my stomach lurches.

Celia clasps her mouth. "Are you sure it was a male?"

"Yes. It had four penises as opposed to two."

Koda and Aric nod, agreeing and seemingly satisfied that the creature with four penises was less harmless than the one with only two.

My sisters may or may not have gagged, and I may or may not have joined them.

"This isn't going to happen again," Gemini tells me.

"No, kidding," I say. "I'll be damned if I step foot in Egypt again."

Cracking jokes and my gift for sarcasm have saved me from falling apart more than once in this twisted world. I'd rather bitch and laugh than cry or scream in fear any day. *Weres*, bless their snarling and growling little hearts, don't have much of a sense of humor. Aric and Koda glare. Gemini grows alarmingly still, menace dripping from his body like sweat or maybe even blood.

"Ah," Celia begins, her attention shifting between me and Gemini. "Why don't you give us a minute? We're all a little wound up."

I'll give her that.

I think if anyone else had asked, a resounding "no" followed by several snapping jowls would have commenced. But since learning of Celia's pregnancy, and more so now that her baby bump is pronounced, the beasts lurking within our lovers are tamer in her presence. They don't want to upset her and do their best to keep her calm. One by one they leave.

Gemini is the last to go, edging away slowly, but not before casting me a look that assures me we're not done arguing yet.

"T," Shayna says. "Gemini is totally pissed. I thought his

head would split in two and tiny versions of him would rush out, waving swords."

"I was thinking the same thing," I agree. Okay, I wasn't. But far be it for me to throw shade on Shayna's awesome visual.

I try to stand, except all I manage is to bend one knee. Celia lifts me with pretty much the same effort she'd lift a toothbrush. Speaking of which . . . I start forward, eyeing my toothbrush as if it can somehow scrub the nasty demon experience from my teeth. I stumble forward with my first step, griping the white granite countertop when my legs give out.

Ceel clasps my arm, steadying me. "Don't be so quick to move," she warns. "If you'd like, I can help you to bed."

"I don't think that's a good idea, Ceel," Shayna says, scrutinizing me closely. She points somewhere near my right breast. "Whatever that is smells demon-ish." She shakes her head. "Trust me, evil never washes out of sheets."

"Good to know," I say, inching closer to the cool granite counter. My legs tremble, feeling wobbly. Somehow, I manage to straighten and not fall on my face.

Celia holds tight as I adjust the towel around me. "I'm okay," I assure her.

She releases me slowly, her gaze on mine. "You don't seem okay," she says.

She has a point. I cling to the edge of the counter and reach for a washcloth in the dark wood cabinet below. Shayna hops on the counter beside me and Emme lowers herself to the edge of my large bathtub.

"Rough day," I admit.

"You've been gone for three," Celia reminds me.

"Most of it was traveling. It was only the acquisition of said object that more or less sucked."

"Is Misha okay?" I nod, noting how she sighs with relief. "What about the others?"

"Two recently *turned* vamps didn't make it," I say, remembering how they were running beside me and how abruptly they vanished when we rounded the bend. "Elise and

Dillon." I wash my hands, noting how much energy the simple task seems to take and how brown the water turns at the base of the sink. I sneak a glance at Celia. "Did you know them?"

"Not as vamps," she admits.

Shayna stiffens. "So you knew them as . . . *food*?" she asks.

I already know the answer and don't bother to wait for a response. Instead I focus on brushing my teeth.

"They were favorites among his older vamps," Celia responds. She plays with the ends of her hair. "I remember them begging to be *turned*. Misha denied them more than once. He wasn't sure either would survive the process. I suppose they did."

"Until they didn't," I add. I finish brushing my teeth. "I suppose they didn't read the fine print. There's more to being part of Misha's keep than good looks and kissing ass."

"If they were so new, why would Misha take them on a mission this soon? Especially one so dangerous?" Shayna asks.

Her husband and mate Koda, like most *weres*, hate vamps. Koda is more audible in his hatred, and his distrust of them has rubbed off on Shayna.

Celia leans against the counter and crosses her arms. "Newly *turned* vampires aren't like newborns Shayna. They're strong and formidable, and required to prove themselves to their master. And as much as they become a part of his family from the moment they're created, they're the first to be sacrificed."

"That's like, *so cold*," Shayna says.

"It's not about being cold. It's a hierarchy that exists among vampire clans. Misha would rather risk the life of a new vampire than one he's grown to care for and trust."

"That doesn't make it any less right," Shayna counters.

"I'm not saying it is," Celia says, keeping her cool. "But it's their way. Vamps are loyal to their masters at all costs, or else. Just as *weres* are loyal to their packs."

"That's different, Ceel," Shayna argues.

"Is it?" Celia asks. "Each species would die for their kind and their leaders, even when their leaders may not be righteous."

Good Ol' Sparky gives me an involuntary twitch, making me almost lose my balance. She's not happy, probably because one of those non-righteous *weres* ate her predecessor.

"Sorry," Shayna offers.

I don't miss how she forces her attention away from me and Celia. I may have lost an arm, but Celia lost far worse.

In the quiet that follows we surrender ourselves to our thoughts, none of them good, and maybe some worse than others.

Quiet isn't something that we welcome when we're together. It's too lonely and dark there. Perhaps that's why Emme, our light, is the first to speak.

"There was a lot of damage to your leg," she says. She keeps her head down and tucks a strand of her wavy blond hair behind her ear. "It took a lot for me and your body to heal you. You'll need to eat and rest soon to recoup your energy."

"I know. But I'm too wired to sleep and the last thing I want is food."

I slip my toothbrush back in the holder, trying not to focus on my out of control hair in the mirror. The hair wins, giving me pause and letting me really see how ragged I appear. My dark waves are coated with leftover desert sand and blood. My dark blue eyes are streaked with ugly red lines from lack of sleep. Dry blood coats my legs, reminding me of the smack down with the demon and that sing-song knife, too. Man, the last seventy-two hours have sucked. Yet they don't compare to the fear I feel every time I think of something happening to Celia.

I should be used to the danger. All of us should. Except none of us signed up for this shit, and if anyone deserves a smaller helping it's Celia.

Regardless of all the madness and muck I encountered, I smile at Celia's pregnant belly. There's a *baby* growing inside of my sister, a little miracle that brings me a kind of happiness I've never quite felt.

I've never been goo-goo, gah-gah, over babies, and I've never wanted any children of my own. But I'll admit, my ovaries gave a little twitch when I learned she was expecting.

"Taran, I don't want you working for Misha."

Oh, and there goes my smile. "You did," I remind her.

"That was different," she tells me. "Everything's changing, and too much is wrong with the world."

I run cool water over the washcloth. "Ceel," I say, wringing out the excess. "You joined vamp camp during the biggest supernatural war to ever transpire."

"It was a dangerous time," she admits. "But as bad as it was, this is worse."

I dab at my cheeks. "Why? Because you're carrying the first of what might be many kiddos to tip the scales on the side of good?"

"No, because I won't be able to keep you safe. Not this time, Taran."

The extent of her vulnerability hits us harder than it should. Celia was always the protector. Always. But I was a close second and it's time for me to step up to the plate.

It sounds ridiculous in a way. When the ancient power of Tahoe began luring supernatural beings into the area, and said species began losing their shit—first the witches to power, and second the vampires to a supernatural plague—I was the first to pack our things and throw them in the car. I begged my sisters to leave and tried to convince them to flee someplace safe.

Our problem is, we've never been safe.

Through no fault of our own, us Wirds were born "weird". We were cursed with magic meant to kill us. Well, peeps, the curse backfired, making us different from all races of human and supernatural, stronger than most beings in existence, and ultimately targets.

"Don't you worry about me, Ceel." My gaze falls to her belly. "Worry about you and junior."

"Not at your expense," she tells me.

She echoes Gemini's words, not that I need to hear them. It's not that they don't affect me. But like with Gemini, I don't want to argue with Celia. So I ignore her words as best I can, despite how each plea slaps me across the face and demands I pay attention.

Gemini, makes it a little easier. He returns, his rage as evident as it was when he left. He leans against the wall, the intensity behind his aura threatening to chip the tile.

I toss my stiff, disgusting hair. "You'll excuse me, won't you, girls?" I ask. "I need to tidy up and look good for my man."

Emme scurries out as if she can already picture us naked. Shayna throws her arms around me, hugging me fiercely. "I'm glad you're okay." She pauses, whispering low. "Next time, you're taking me and Em with you."

She exits quickly, her ponytail swinging merrily behind her.

Celia is the last to leave. I know she wants to talk me out of helping Misha, and beg me to keep my distance from the vampires. After all, I gave her the same speech when she left us to be with them.

I'm ready to offer a little sarcasm for the road and to pique her smile. But the sadness in her features shuts my mouth and drives an extra pang of guilt straight into my heart. I shouldn't have left without telling them. Except sometimes, you do shitty things to keep those you love safe.

"Don't do anything stupid," she tells me. "Not for me, not for anyone."

"Oh, you know me," I reply.

She shakes her head, walking away and pulling the door behind her.

The door barely finishes clicking shut when Gemini's deep and graveled voice unveils his displeasure and draws my focus. "We need to talk."

His anger and frustration appears to have doubled since leaving the room. Anyone else would think twice about contradicting him. Except I'm not just anyone, not to him.

"No," I respond. "That's not what we need." I pull off my towel and let it fall at my feet as I walk to the shower.

With a sigh filled with too much stress and way more

exhaustion, I lean in and turn on the water, adjusting the temperature before stepping inside. Swirls of black, brown, and red, splatter along my feet as the water drenches my skin and hair. The red and brown are a mix of sand and blood. The black . . . Christ, it could be demon poop for all I know. I don't want to guess, and am glad I took Shayna's advice against soiling my sheets with evil.

I reach for my shower gel and loofa, working fast and scrubbing hard. Whatever is painting my skin this awful color, I just want it gone, and half-wish I could apologize to my drain for all the gross chunks it's had to swallow since we first moved in.

The water isn't yet clear and I haven't quite finished washing my body when Gemini steps into the shower with me.

Brown muck and bits of leftover DNA still cover my back. Yet he embraces me, loving me and offering forgiveness I probably don't deserve. "I don't want anything to happen to you," he murmurs, curling against me and stroking my chin carefully.

"I know."

It's what I tell him. But as I think about the fate of the world, and how it all comes down to my sister's babies being born, I don't believe there's a choice. Someone has to live. And that someone is Celia.

Chapter Three

I like shoes.

Pretty shoes.

The taller, the better.

At only about five-foot three, they make me feel statuesque.

My only gripe, they're hard to run in.

And right now, I'm running pretty damn hard.

"Excuse me. Pardon me. *Pardon me.*" Shit. "For the love of God, move out of the way!"

I'm in Reno, the Nevada side of Tahoe. We don't come here much. Sure it's close to home and has a lively nightlife, and yes, there are beautiful forests and stunning attractions nearby. But too many times my love and his furry friends have found partially eaten body parts in those woods and more than a few of the attractions have been splattered with blood and innards as a result of supernaturals gone wild.

Humans chalk them up to gruesome homicides committed by psychopathic serial killers.

I wish I was that naïve, strolling through life believing monsters don't actually exist.

Instead I'm running down the sidewalk past one of too

many casinos and snaking around far too many bodies.

The flashing lights strobe against the vampire I'm chasing, setting his white dress shirt aglow and bleaching his skin. It's not a good look for him, and despite my cute giraffe print open shoulder flouncy dress, it's probably a bad look for me, too. I don't do sweat well, and right now, I'm bathing in it, my back is drenched and the fabric of my dress clings to my skin.

My stilettos pound against the sidewalk as I jet after him. His stride is easy, using a tenth of the muscle I am. If he wanted to, he would run, and I wouldn't be able to catch him. His pace is fast enough that I can't shoot a bolt of lightning into his back or set him ablaze without striking some poor unsuspecting tourist. But it's slow enough to make sure I follow. If I had any doubt, the glance he tosses me over his shoulder squashes that doubt to bits.

Yeah, this leech wants to lead me into a trap, and maybe take a bite. But Gemini is the only one I let bite me, and his nibbles tend to be south of my neck.

My phone rings. I answer it only because I see that it's Shayna.

"Dude. Where are you?"

"Virginia Street," I say, struggling to speak and breathe, and freaking run.

"Still?" she asks.

"It's a long damn street," I stammer, winding around a crowd of people emptying out of a club.

"Do you still have eyes on your guy?"

I sigh, wondering what spy movie she swiped that term from. "Yeah, sure," I mutter.

Until I don't.

"Shit," I say.

"What's wrong? Did you lose him?" Shayna asks.

I scan the area, taking a moment to catch my breath. Shayna inherited a little bit of her mate's essence. It's enough that she can heal, albeit at a much slower rate, and more than enough that she wouldn't struggle to catch up to a vamp like I am.

"Yes," I admit. I adjust my dangly purse against my shoulder. "What about you? Are you still at the club?"

"Yup. The eagle has landed. She's in the nest and watching the eggs."

I assume she means she hasn't left the club. "What about the other vamp, is he still there?"

There's a pause. "Didn't you hear me? The eagle is in the nest—the *nest*—and she's watching the eggs."

"Shayna, I don't know what that means. Please speak a language I can understand."

"You're cranky."

I'll give her that. "Is the vamp there or not?"

"Uh-huh, I'm looking right at him," she says slowly.

"Does he see you?" I ask carefully, noting how she quiets.

"Now he does . . . I think he picked up my scent."

"What?" We were seated in the upper tier of the club, with an entire dance floor of gyrating bodies separating us. Magic gives off a certain aroma, earthy and primal for *weres*, stormy and dangerous for witches, and sex and candy for vampires (I know, but I don't make the rules). My sisters and I being different, give off totally unique scents. According to Gemini, we smell like power. I'll take it. I just don't like those we're trying to follow to know it, too.

"Shayna," I say. "How can he possibly scent you?"

"I don't know. But he did."

"My guess is he's about to bolt." I glance up. "I'm next to El Dorado. Don't go after him by yourself. Take Emme and—"

"Wait, Emme isn't with you?" she asks.

I stop moving. "No . . ."

"Oh, no," she says.

"Oh, shit," I say.

A wall of men step in front of me. All with long beards; all wearing lumberjack chic attire; all full of themselves.

"Hey, baby," one of them says, stroking his beard suggestively. "Looking for a good time?"

"Looking to chop wood?" I fire back. "Fuck off, Paul

28

Bunyan."

"Oh!" his friends yell.

I hurry around them as Shayna speaks fast. "T, Emme chased after you when you followed your vamp out of the club. I saw her step out and into the foyer. Didn't you see her??"

"No." I look behind me. "And I don't see her now. Let me try her cell. You stay with your vamp. If we can't find her, his friends have her, and we're going to need them to tell us where she is."

Where Emme is soft words and gentle motions, Shayna is all perk and lightning fast. She doesn't sound perky now, and if the vamps do have Emme, they're going to get acquainted with Shayna's super reflexes and pointy weapons very soon.

Her tone reflects the seriousness of the situation. "I'm on it. He won't lose me."

No. He won't. "Be careful," I tell her.

I don't wait for her goodbye, immediately calling Emme as I move further down the street. Cars honk their protest when the convertible in front of them doesn't move, earning an irate middle finger from the driver, despite the half-dressed blonde, laughing and cuddling against him.

I continue forward, snaking around a group of senior citizens chatting away. Emme's phone rings against my ear, each dragged out tone making me more anxious. My right arm shudders, firing a warning. I turn in a circle, scanning the perimeter. But all I see and feel are humans.

"Call me," I say, when the voicemail picks up.

I adjust my elbow length cream-colored gloves, wondering if Sparky picked up on something I didn't. I lift the phone again and send Emme a message using the voice to text feature.

Where are you?

Again, my arm shudders. Again, I'm thinking it's not a good sign. "Okay, girl," I say. "What are you trying to tell me?"

I pass the casino and a mime juggling on the street. I also edge around a drag queen whose on-point makeup more than rivals mine. I'm not certain where I'm headed, all I know is that for now, forward is my only option.

Shayna can't track like a *were*, but whatever bit of Koda she has in her, is enough to recognize some scents. She can scent my aroma enough to find me if necessary, but only if I don't stray too far from the El Dorado.

The thing is, I may have to stray far.

I ease my way forward, my instincts and my arm, warning me something isn't right.

My thumb slides along the back of my phone as I walk further away. I steal a glance at it when it vibrates, hoping it's Emme only to see Shayna's text.

The vamp is on West 4th and Evans.

Which means she is, too.

Damn it. This was supposed to be a simple grab and dump. We grab the two vamps and dump their asses back at Misha's.

Ordinarily, I wouldn't have taken this assignment, not so soon after Egypt, and not when Gemini is still so pissed. But I only promised him I wouldn't leave the country, not the state.

Vamps . . . they're not the cuddliest creatures you'll ever meet. They go crazy and evil without a master to ground and control them. I think it's safe to say no one wants crazy and evil vampires running around. So here I am, fending off drunks, racing past drag queens, looking for the bloodsucker I need to take down, and hoping to God he doesn't have my sister.

I try Emme again, my blood going cold and every hair on the back of my neck standing on end when I catch the weak sound of her *Angel* ringtone. I look ahead, the sound growing weaker and appearing to move away from me.

Shit. Shit. Shit.

I call for backup, not that it stops me from edging toward where the sound disappears. Trap or not, the bastard who has Emme is going to tell me where she is.

Tonight's backup is in the form of a naughty, and very slutty Catholic schoolgirl. Thankfully, Agnes Concepcíon is as smart as she is trampy.

"What?" she says when she answers.

Hey, I never claimed she was nice. "I need you here."

"Is your prey in custody?"

"No. Both took off, one has Emme."

"I'm coming—*fuck*."

What sounds like glass breaking erupts on the other end before the line goes dead. Okay, not just dealing with two rogue vamps here. My arm involuntarily jerks. I clutch it to me, knowing she's getting ready to react, with or without me.

Except I don't see anything, nothing but wall to wall tourists and promoters trying to lure them into the clubs. "Not yet," I tell her, trying to soothe her.

I wait until I'm sure she's not going to lash out, and hit Emme's number again. I freeze in place when the line rings and the familiar ringtone sounds louder to my left, down an alley, because why the hell not?

I scan the long narrow space separating the buildings. A small bulb fixed above a closed door is the only source of light. I make out a dumpster further down and what might be a boarded up window on the opposite building.

My right arm jerks, warning me, as if a desolate, dark alley isn't enough of a clue that something is lurking in the shadows, waiting to eat me.

I shove my phone into the exterior pocket of my purse, careful to place it with the mic sticking out, and adjust the chain-link strap so it crosses my chest like a seatbelt.

With a curse, and few more colorful mutterings, I step into the alley.

In a creepy movie, what I'm doing would be considered suicide. It's the scene where the young woman, crazy enough to trek into known danger alone, would meet her gruesome death. Here, it's survival; mine, my sister's, and anyone these vamps have targeted.

I strip out of my gloves, left first, then right, dropping them as I walk. Fashion doesn't mean shit when your sister's life is in danger. Besides, these vamps know we're not the humans we pretend to be.

Sparky flares like a light beam with the next step I take.

Her glow isn't as fierce as it can be, broadening enough just to show me what's ahead, like the rat that races in front of me, and his friend who follows. I cringe, though given what's waiting for me, rats aren't so bad.

My vision sharpens as my body responds to the preternatural magic. He's close. Either I'm moving toward him, or he's moving toward me.

I glance around, but I don't see anything. I only *feel* him. "Siri," I say. "Call Emme."

"Calling Emme," Siri says, her voice oddly vacant in the bleak surroundings.

The further I venture, the more the alley becomes its own separate world far away from the strip. Dingy and gritty, it shows the underbelly of the city that spellbound tourists prefer not to see, the dirty side that reeks of sin and feeds on innocents.

The cell phone ring sounds through the leather fabric. But it's the familiar ringtone of Emme's phone to my right that has me turning left.

That's right, *left*.

I'm not stupid. When evil lures you one way, you go the other.

My problem is, I never could outrun evil.

The vamp I was following soars from his spot high against the building, the sharp nails he used to fix himself to the brick, raking against my throat as he slams me into the opposite wall.

"Looking for me?" he asks.

Pain shoots down my spine and I can barely breathe. My heart pounds wickedly against my ribcage as I try not to panic. Fear is like an aphrodisiac to vamps, and this vamp is deriving more pleasure from me than I want.

"As a matter of fact, I am," I say, struggling to speak.

He's not trying to kill me. Not yet. If he was, Sparky would have detonated him like a piñata. That doesn't mean he didn't hurt me or that he's allowing me to move. I can barely breathe, my lungs clenching with the need to draw a full breath.

The fingers of his opposite hand skim down my cheek, the motion and greed in his dark ravenous stare churning my stomach. "My, you're a pretty thing."

My right arm shudders. She doesn't like him touching us either. "Where's my sister?" I bite out.

"The blonde?" he doesn't wait for me to answer, gripping my throat tighter. "You don't need to worry about her anymore."

His voice drifts as his chin lowers to where my power builds. He jerks when he realizes what's happening. But it's too late. That familiar zing charges through me as my lightning releases, sending bolts of blue and white in a swirl of sparks down the length of my metal purse strap, jolting the vampire and hurling him across the alley.

Brick dust explodes in a thick cloud when his body strikes the opposite building. I snatch him up by his throat with my right arm when he falls forward, the power within it making my limb outrageously strong. "I asked you a question, *where's my sister?*"

His eyes widen, but his shock is only brief. Long nails stab against my skin. I barely feel the pointy tips. As lethal as his dagger-like fingernails are, they're no match for the magic protecting my arm.

I lift him higher and fire another bolt to snag his attention. His legs rattle and his feet fling out like snapping sheets. "You think you're the one in charge," I tell him. I give him another squeeze, my fury helping me ignore the ache wringing my throat. "You're wrong."

His stare shifts to the side, alerting me someone else has arrived half a second before he's wrenched from my grasp.

A stream of warm blood splashes across my chest. Gemini leans with his back against the wall, gripping the decapitated vampire's head by his long, messy hair. I should be used to decapitated vampires. I should be used to a lot of things. Except I'm not completely desensitized, *yet.*

I beat down the splash of acid burning its way up my throat. "I need him alive," I say, swallowing hard. "His friends have Emme."

"No. We do," he replies. Every muscle strains against his dark gray T-shirt as he pushes off the wall and tosses the head aside, marching to where the vamps body is desperately trying to crawl away.

The body can't see where it is. It only senses danger, leaving a streak of red as it scuttles across the concrete.

Gemini kicks it over, bringing down his heel into the chest. With a sickening crunch the sternum cracks and ash explodes in a small mushroom cloud.

There's a plus to killing a vamp, no traces that he ever was, when he goes. The downside is, whatever blood spills pre-death stains like a murder scene, which is why I won't be wearing this dress again.

I bat at the stain. What hasn't soaked through as blood has already turned to ash. "She's okay?" I croak, trying to hide my injuries and very much avoiding eye contact.

"She's fine," he says. His superior vision hones in on my neck the moment I tilt my chin. He rushes forward, lifting my jaw gently. "You're hurt."

"No, just a few bruises," I assure him.

"They could have been more," he says, his voice gruff.

He has a valid point. If my arm didn't possess all the mojo that it does, that vamp would have killed me and tossed aside my broken body. But I don't want to agree, and I definitely don't want to argue, not when his features turn feral and I sense the essence of his beast caress my skin.

"You said you were going out with the girls," he reminds me.

"I was," I say, keeping my voice gentle and casual, like he didn't just break a vamp in two. "And we did."

"*No*," he responds, his expression seething with ire. "You went hunting."

I clutch his wrists. "Baby, I know this looks bad—"

"Dude!" Shayna grinds to a halt at the other end of the alley, her sword out and a decapitated head swinging merrily in her opposite hand.

Perhaps "merrily" isn't the best word seeing how the head is snapping its fangs and trying to bite her.

I groan. I have a way of leaping from bad to worse, straight into a pool of trouble where I can do little more than doggy paddle around the edge.

Shayna's focus bounces from me to Gemini. "Um, hey, Gem." He doesn't answer. She looks down the street and away from us. "Koda's here. Isn't he?"

"He is," Gemini replies. "I think I should warn you, he's about as happy as I am."

So, likely homicidal.

"The wolves have Emme," I say, hoping to ease her mind and lessen our current dilemma. Nothing lifts a mood like a thwarted kidnapping. Yay, us.

She lifts her arm. "I'm guessing we don't need him?" she asks, pointing at the head with the tip of her sword.

"*No*," Gemini answers.

She sighs, her shoulders slumping. "I'll go find the body."

Like a little kid being sent home, she marches back in the direction she arrived, leaving me with Gemini. His hands fall away as I ease away from him. I walk to the opposite end of the alley, retrieving Emme's phone and thanking God Almighty she's not hurt.

"I'm sorry," I begin. "I wasn't trying to upset you."

Gemini isn't looking at me, his rigid stance is turned in the direction of an approaching vampire wearing a very tiny plaid skirt.

Agnes's white shirt hangs in tatters, her lacy red bra poking through the strips of fabric as she struts forward. "This wasn't our fault," she says, ignoring me to speak to Gem.

"No?" Gemini counters. "Then why the hell are me and my pack picking up your fucking mess?"

I stiffen, hurrying to his side.

Agnes has no status in the supernatural world outside of Misha's keep. Gemini does, although you'd never guess by the way she answers him. "We were informed of two rogues. Our master acted well within his rights—"

"Your master acted without informing the Alliance," Gemini growls. "Placing my mate and her family in danger!"

I step between them when Gemini's shoulders roll forward. He's ready to attack and so is Agnes. Her nails elongate in succession with her fangs, "You don't know who you're dealing with."

"No, *you don't*," he snarls.

"Gemini, stop," I urge. "I won't have you fighting with Misha's family."

"Then she needs *to stand down*," he replies, his voice morphing from primal to deadly.

I've seen my lover angry and vicious and know his statement is no longer a warning. It's a proclamation of death, irrespective of which hierarchy of supernatural it offends.

My hand grips his shoulder as my head whips back. "Back off," I tell her.

She scowls, her anger turning on me.

Celia maintains a title and position within Misha's family that affords her the right to order and lead them in his absence. I don't have anything like that and am simply trying to avoid her re-death. Gemini is furious, and if he's acting within Pack duty, he can legally strike her down.

"Agnes," I say, digging my nails deeper into Gemini's shoulder. "Stand down, *now*."

I don't think she's listening to my pleas as much as she realizes Gemini is ready to destroy her. His eyes lock on her, the steel and ire in his gaze forcing her to obey and edge away.

Not that she's done talking. "Your mate works for my master out of choice. She came willingly as did her sisters."

"Not anymore. Tell your master as Second in Command to the Squaw Valley Den Pack, he is hereby summoned to meet with the Alliance and disclose any and all information surrounding the vampires you were hunting."

She frowns. "They're rogues," she informs him. "More than we anticipated, yes, but nothing more."

"You're wrong. If your master gave a damn about anything aside from himself he would have known, we would have told him, and none of us would be here."

Her nails dissolve within her fingertips as she watches

him closely. "As Chief Advisor to the House of Aleksandr, I accept your request."

"We expect him, not you."

"Very well," she says, not that she's happy.

She turns on her heel, halting in place at the sound of Gemini's growl. "One more thing."

She stops, her spine stiffening when she hears him stalk forward, his voice unbearably rigid. "I swear on my honor that if you *ever* risk my mate's safety again, I'll kill you *and* him."

Chapter Four

Gemini pulls off Virginia Street, taking a side road that leads into a modest part of town, far away from the glitzy lights. My hand slides along the armrest. I'm not one to fidget, but keeping my hand on the armrest keeps it off my throat. I don't want to bring more attention to my bruises there, or to the ones likely lining my back. Gemini doesn't need another reason to make due on his threat.

I lean back into the seat and try to relax my breathing. I'm not thrilled with what he said to Agnes, how he swore to kill her and Misha if he felt my life was at risk because of them. As one of the most powerful masters in existence, I don't want him and Misha fighting, ever. I can't be sure who would win, and neither deserves to die.

"Baby, I'm sorry," I tell him.

He rolls to a stop at a light. "You're always sorry, Taran. That doesn't stop you from acting any time the vampires snap their fingers."

"It was a simple snag and dump," I say, speaking softly. "Two vampires, three of us. We didn't think anything could go wrong."

"But it did."

"I know it did. But as an Alliance member, it's my duty to protect."

"No," he says. "Your duty requires you to help the Alliance as a whole, should your powers be needed. That's not the same thing as being the leeches' go-to."

I open my mouth and quickly shut it. I'm not going to win this one, not with the bruises scattered along my body.

"Why did he call you?" he asks, speaking of Misha. "If it was so simple, why not just send his own?"

"His vampires are known by face and by scent, they bear his mark. We don't. We had the best chance of rounding them up and assuring the human populace would stay safe."

Gemini doesn't budge, his focus intense and straight ahead.

My words release carefully. I'm not blind to his anger nor can I dismiss the damage the vamp inflicted. "You said they weren't regular rogues," I remind him. "What did you mean by that?"

"The Alliance has learned that the Dark Legion isn't just targeting Celia." He squares his jaw. "They're recruiting rogue vamps in addition to lone *weres* and witches."

"For an army? Like before?"

"No," he says. "As Assassins. They're trying to infiltrate and wipe out the most elite in our circles. Earlier this week, one of Genevieve's bodyguards killed a witch who tried to poison her."

Genevieve is Tahoe's head witch, absurdly beautiful and as powerful as an encroaching tornado. I know from personal experience. More than once our magic has clashed, and more than once we've come close to blows.

"We would have dismissed it as an isolated incident had our former Elder in Colorado not been ambushed during a hunt early today."

"By another *were*?" I guess.

"No. By several young witches who'd camouflaged themselves as trees."

My eyes widen. Having had my stint in witch school, assuming another form is a torturous undertaking that takes a great deal of strong magic.

"Why?" I ask. "I mean, I get that the elite are more of a threat than the average supernatural. But their supreme strength and abilities makes them more lethal and dangerous. They're not exactly easy targets."

"They're not easy targets," he agrees. "But the assassins are formidable. From what we've learned, they're not willing to fight alongside the Dark Legion, but they are willing to take their money and do their dirty work."

"Was the Elder harmed?" I curse at the stoic way Gemini nods.

"He gained the upper hand and killed the witches who attacked him, but he didn't walk away unscathed. He's healing slowly, not as rapidly as we hoped or expected."

I flex my hands when I realize how hard I'm clenching them. "That means the injuries he sustained were laced with curses."

"They were," he replies. "Another *were* wouldn't have survived the attack, and if he had, the magical damage the witches inflicted would have finished him off." His stare cuts my way. "Genevieve took the poison, her protection spells and the speed in which her bodyguard reacted were what saved her. Otherwise, we would have lost her."

My fingers trail involuntarily to my throat. The vamp who attacked me was absurdly fast. There was more to him than either me or my arm were ready for.

I pause when a thought occurs to me. "The Elders and the Head Witches were targets," I say. "What about the master vamps?"

"Uri was attacked an hour ago."

"*Misha's master?*" He nods. Holy shit. Even I try not to piss him off. "Why? Going after Uri is like going after a world leader."

Only silence greets me. "Just tell me," I urge. "Why are only the best being stalked?"

His breath releases in a huff. "Because regardless of our differences as *were* and witch, and our continued distrust and conflicts with the vampires, all in the Alliance agree on one thing: Celia must be protected in order for her children to live and fulfill the prophecy."

His response pisses me off. "They're trying to make it easier to kill Celia."

"Yes. But there's more. Given the amount of magic being used and the degree of strength the assassins possess, we've concluded the Dark Legion is being led and empowered by shapeshifters."

I almost lose what's left of my dinner. Shapeshifters are born witches. They spend their lives making blood sacrifices to their deities in exchange for the ability to assume whatever form they wish. They carry the power of hell within them and are almost indestructible. Almost. But as strong as they are, and as much as I believe Gemini, too much of his theory doesn't make sense.

"How can the shifters lead something of this caliber?" I ask. "For the most part, they seem mindless. Grunting and repeating words over and over, completely disconnected from reason and their human counterparts."

"Don't mistake their lack of speech for lack of communication or intelligence," Gemini warns, the tension in his tone appearing to encompass every part of him. "They're as calculating as they are wicked, and can communicate through and with their neophytes."

"What the hell is a neophyte?" I ask.

"A witch close to becoming a shifter, strong, dark, but still human." His hand opens and closes as if trying to shake some of the tension free. "They're spearheading the rise of the Dark Alliance and using the power of the shapeshifters to reinforce the assassins' potency."

"How?" I ask.

"Blood," he answers simply. "The blood of a shifter is laced with dark magic conjured in the depths of hell itself. Drinking it feeds the magic within them."

"But you've attacked shifters, and it didn't make you any stronger," I point out.

"No," he agrees. "But shifter magic is closely related to witch magic since that's how they're born. While it can make

41

a witch stronger and more dangerous, it makes us sick."

"What does it do to vampires?" I ask, wondering exactly how much crap we're actually dealing with.

"Both witches and vampires are closer to humans than we are. It makes them more lethal as you saw for yourself. The effects however, are temporary," he explains. "A few days, perhaps a week at best."

I quiet. "Long enough to kill an Elder, a master, or a head witch," I reason.

"Exactly."

"I have to protect Celia," I say without thinking.

"No, I do," he snaps. I start to argue, only for him to cut me off. "No more, Taran. You can't work for the vampires and you can't engage in anything that jeopardizes your safety."

"But if I can help Celia—"

"The best way to help her is by staying alive. You can't help her or her children if you're already dead."

My right arm trembles with the need to release flame, rattling my entire body. The look Gemini pegs me with is forceful, challenging. He's ready for the fight he anticipates between us. Except I'm not raring to go toe-to-toe. Not with him. I'm furious over the shit hand we've been dealt, and all the crap cards that keep coming.

His gaze softens at the sight of my quickly forming tears. "I don't want her to go through this," I tell him. "Celia needs her chance at a normal life and so do her babies." I pause, the weight of my words making it hard to speak. "She's never going to have it, is she?"

"I'm not sure. Not with everything her children and Aric's are destined for."

He pulls along the curb and puts the SUV into park. The steering wheel groans beneath his grip, the metal within it bending, revealing the extent of his frustration, but also another emotion I can't quite place. "When I first learned of the curse placed upon you and your family, so much about it didn't make sense," he says. "The curse not only kept you alive, it granted you these unique powers, making you beings of magic when nothing but human blood raced through your veins. Why? Why would magic so vile and dark work in your favor rather than kill you as it was conjured to do?"

I often wondered that myself. I tilt my head, listening closely. My lover isn't asking me a question, he's working through his thoughts, applying reason to the unreasonable.

"I think this Darkness that's rising had been centuries, perhaps even millennia in the making. And I think those who nourished it wanted to prevent good from winning at all costs." He reaches out, stroking my cheek, his touch breathtakingly gentle given the ease he used to kill that vampire. "You are that good. You and your sisters, as is Aric given his supremacy among our kind." He sighs, appearing sad. "But you were just the start. Aric and Celia's children will be the ultimate end."

The tear that falls slicks a line down my cheek. "Do you think they'll make it?"

I've always counted on Gemini's optimism. Today, it doesn't come. "I can't be sure. Not with everything coming at us, and not with our numbers dwindling as they are."

Another tear, another breath that releases too harshly.

"That doesn't mean we should give up, my love," he tells me. "It only means we should fight smart. They need us, Taran. Aric, Celia, their children. They need all of us." He wipes my cheek with his thumb. "So don't rush to meet death. Choose your battles wisely and we'll cheat it together. That way, maybe we can have our chance at happiness, too."

Maybe. Happily Ever After is a concept completely foreign to me. But I'll take the opportunity for a happy for now.

I start to tell him when he looks past me, frowning. I turn around to see what caught his attention, jumping when I see who it is.

Emme walks toward me. The best way to describe her is that she resembles Carrie. *The Carrie.* The one who had a bucket of pig's blood dumped on her at prom and went supernatural windmill on her graduating class.

The only difference is Carrie was less bloody.

On either side of her stand members of Gemini's pack in human form. I throw open the door and hurry toward her, stopping just before I reach her. "Are you all right?"

"I've had better evenings," she admits, her voice quiet.

"What the hell happened?" I ask, circling her. Christ, it's like she fell into a large vat of red and orange paint.

"I didn't want you going after that vampire alone," she says, casting a hesitant glance in the direction of the wolves eyeing her. "I tried to follow you, but was trapped within the crowd on the dance floor. By the time I made it outside, you were far down the street. I tried to chase after you, but someone swiped my purse and threw a pillow case over my head. I was shoved into a car and . . ." She makes a coughing sound, like she's gagging. "I couldn't see. I knew I was in trouble and did my best to picture pulling heads from shoulders with my *force*."

Emme's telekinesis is no joke. Still, I blink back at her, stunned. "I guess it worked."

"Not exactly," the wolf to her right interjects. He clears his throat. "She ripped them in half. Down the spinal column," he adds, painting a brighter and more gruesome picture. He makes a zigzag motion with his hands. "Only jagged. Not smooth."

"Definitely not smooth," the wolves around him concur, nodding.

To kill a *were*, you have to either decapitate him, or detonate his heart with cursed gold bullets. To kill a vamp, more specifically an old one; their head must be removed and the heart destroyed. Based on the sight before me, Emme missed the heart and probably the head too, leaving the vamps to spurt body fluids like a hydrant.

"There were chunks," the first wolf says.

"Lots of chunks," his buddies agree.

"Had to scoop through them just to get her out," the guy to my left adds.

"Um," I reply.

He points to Emme's stomach. "You see that, that's bile. I'm guessing two, maybe three livers' worth."

"You think?" His friend takes a sniff. "It smells more like small intestine to me."

"Okay, we get it," I say, holding out a hand and trying to stop them. I'm sure this is regular dinner talk to the midnight streakers, but seriously, I could have gone without the visual. And so could poor Emme.

Beneath all the red and orange my very petite sister is probably a nice shade of green. I'm ready to hurl, and I wasn't even there!

I cover my mouth with my hand. "You ripped them apart," I say. "Literally."

She makes a face. "I sort of panicked," she offers, apologetically. "I was pulling and stretching skin and bone." She starts gagging. "But they were the wrong kind of skin and bone."

I'm picturing lots of crawling organs trying to rejoin as Emme continued her ripping frenzy. It's awful. It's twisted.

And it's what kept her alive.

"Screw them," I tell her. "I'm just glad you're okay." I hug her against me, trying not to cringe when she feels wet and spongy.

"Eww" the wolf next to me says.

"Really?" I ask. "After the chunks, *this* is what grosses your ass out?"

"Taran," Emme says carefully. "You're hurt."

She may not have noticed the bruises, but she feels them with her healing *touch*.

"I'm all right," I tell her. In truth, I could be better. My throat is sore and scratchy, and it hurts to swallow, and when I move, the throbbing along my spine grows more pronounced. But I don't want to upset Gemini further. He's already angry enough.

Emme holds me closer. "Here, let me just help you." Her head falls against my shoulder. "It will feel good to help, instead of harm."

"Okay," I say, her comment making me sad.

Emme doesn't have a cruel bone in her body. That doesn't mean she hasn't killed or that her hands aren't stained with the blood of our enemies. It only means she's had to fight harder to keep her innocence and hang tight to her kindness. Like the rest of us, she pushes through the nightmares as if they didn't come, and does her best to live with sins she never meant to commit.

My eyes scrunch closed as I feel her power work through me. I don't realize how bad I'm hurt until something cracks along my lower back and the soothing sensation of her *touch* stretches across my right hip.

Gemini steps forward, straightening when he sees what she's doing, and how much time she takes to heal me. His gaze drifts my way, the anger he demonstrated earlier flashing briefly across his watchful stare.

I'm sure we'll discuss the dangers of chasing a vampire down a dark alley in more detail later; that conversation never gets old. For now, his attention strays to Emme. "Why isn't she bathed and dressed?" he asks his wolves.

I release Emme, although I admit I get a little stuck.

The bile sniffing wolf approaches Gemini, keeping his head lowered. "The Elders don't want us using the safe houses until they're checked for possible sabotage. They request your presence, along with your mate and her sister at the Den."

"All right," Gemini says. He extends his arm. "Come on, Emme. I have clothes you can use."

"Thank you," she says, her head bowing as she passes the wolves. It must have been difficult being alone with them. While they wouldn't hurt her, she like the rest of us aren't Pack. If it weren't for our mates and our positions within the Alliance, none of us would be allowed at the Den.

Emme, unlike Celia, Shayna, and I, doesn't have a mate. The longer we associate with the *weres*, the more it seems to impact her and the way others within the Pack view her.

She slips inside Gemini's ride, gasping when her shoe leaves a mark. "I'm sorry."

"Don't be," he tells her. "It'll come off."

I can't agree. I don't think they make cleansers that remove liver stains. And if they did, it was probably invented by a werebeast with plenty of samples.

"Let me help you," I offer, frowning at the scrutiny the *weres* peg her with. I pause when I catch the two wolves in front watching her with interest. I wish I can say that's a good thing. Except I'm not sure another beast is what Emme needs in her life.

Gemini shuts her door, turning to look at me. I touch his hand when I sense his lingering frustration. "We'll talk about us later, okay?"

"Fine. There's definitely more to say."

His voice seems barren of emotion, though my guess is there's a lot brewing beneath. "What's wrong?" I ask.

"Not now," he says, stroking my cheek lightly. "We have to go."

I follow him to the rear of his SUV. All *weres* keep extra sets of clothing in their vehicles. With all the *changing* they do, it's a must. I'm sure Gemini's packmates offered Emme clothes, but like me, she's not going to strip in front of just anyone. *Weres* are comfortable being naked around each other. We're not.

I slip into the back when Gemini passes me a pair of sweatpants and a T-shirt. Emme is going to swim in these, but it's better to look slightly awkward than to continue wearing what she is. If anything, I'm ready to do her a favor and set the clothes she's in on fire.

"Come on," I say. "Let's get you out of these clothes."

I try and unzip the back of her dress, grimacing when the damn zipper gets stuck on something thick and slimly.

"What's wrong?" Emme asks. "Is something on me?"

"Honey, everything is on you," I say, cringing when I break through the sticky bits and see how much is left. "Try to pull it off from the front."

She keeps her back to me. For lack of better terms, her back is moist. Very moist. *Seriously moist!*

"Can we stop somewhere?" I ask. "A motel or something just so she can get a quick shower?"

"There's no time," Gemini says.

I try and unsnap Emme's bra when she struggles. Yeah,

that's pasty, too. But as much as I want to rid her of all these gross clothes, Gemini's vacant tone momentarily keeps me in place.

"Taran, is something wrong?" Emme asks me.

Her eyes are rammed shut. She's likely terrified of what's soaking through her bra and what I might tell her it is.

"Not at all, sweetie," I insist. I'm grateful she can't see my face when I peel her out of her dress, especially when something *plops* down her back. Thankfully that's the worst of it, and super props to Gemini for keeping large black garbage bags in one of the seat compartments. I won't ask why he needs bags this large. He is *were* and I've been grossed out enough.

"Gemini, could you pass me my purse?" He drops it in my hand. "Thanks, love."

I reach into the larger compartment where I keep a tiny container of hand sanitizer. Honolulu Sunshine, doesn't that sound nice? Well, it smells even nicer! I lather my hands and Emme's. It works so well to remove the nasty bits of leftover vamp, I slather it on her face then use tissues to dab her face somewhat clean.

We're on the highway back to Tahoe by the time Emme is finally dressed. Like I thought, Gemini's clothes are too big on her. But she's warm, and safe, and alive. I'll take it, especially with all the danger we've learned of tonight and following Gemini's proclamation that we may not survive it.

As Emme settles, Gemini explains the suspicions the Alliance has about the Legion and how the shapeshifters are likely the opposing force leading them. When he's done, I leave Emme to her thoughts and crawl into the front passenger seat. Totally illegal I know, but just as Gemini is calmer when I'm near, Sparky and I do better with him beside us. His hand slides over mine and he gives it a squeeze. I look up at him, smiling as much as I can, considering our rather eventful night.

"Who was called to the meeting?" Emme asks. "Was it just the leaders in the surrounding territories?"

"No. Alliance members from all over the world have

been summoned," he replies.

Again, the way he speaks makes me take notice. "Like who?" I ask.

Tension gathers along his shoulders. Apparently, I asked the winning question. "Babe?" I press.

"Those highest within our supernatural circles." The apologetic look he shoots me and the words that follow send chills down my spine. "Including Destiny."

Chapter Five

Trudhilde Radinka aka Destiny.

I first met her in vampire court a few years ago. The same day we met Misha, in fact. We were charged with unjustifiably killing one of Misha's keep, a big no-no unless the vamp tries to kill you first or he directly challenges you to some stupid duel.

The court was packed with beings with sharp nails and fangs, deliberated by vampires older than dirt, and brought forth by Misha who will one day strike the most powerful master dead. Their collective power raked against our skin and pierced our bones, demanding blood and torture.

But it was Destiny who scared the unholy shit out of me.

Forget that she dresses like a six-year-old who found a chest stuffed with clothes accented in polka dots, zebra stripes, feathers, and roadkill fur. Destiny is different. No, she's flat out bizarre. You know some of those freaks who walk around, those you suspect collect shoeboxes stuffed with Barbie doll legs and dust bunnies who resemble celebrities? Destiny is their leader and she wears that crown proudly.

Once every century an especially gifted baby girl is born from a union of two powerful witches. She is given the name of the original and most powerful soothsayer of all time. But it's her insane ability to accurately predict the future that earns her the nickname Destiny.

She's who decreed Celia and Aric's children would rid the world of evil, sticking to her guns even after Celia was told she could no longer bear children.

I glance behind me as we reach the base of Granite Chief Peak, expecting her to pop out of the rear wearing a zebra-striped fedora. "Of all the supernaturals out there," I mutter.

"She's not so bad," Emme says. She squirms as the first of many magical defenses leading up to the Den press against us. "She's just a little unique and quirky."

"Unique and quirky are good words," I agree, rubbing my arms and trying to shake the mix of witch and *were* magic we're doused with. "So are outlandish and alarming."

It's not that I don't like Destiny. Frying my brains to goo in vamp court aside, she's nice enough, always waving and smiling like we're besties. And if it wasn't for her and all the clout she carries beneath the weasel fur she wears, Celia wouldn't be under the protection she is, and her future children would be seen as mutts not saviors.

Gemini's SUV barrels up the path, slinging mud from last night's rain against the windshield and tiny pebbles pitter-patter beneath the undercarriage. I frown when I realize something doesn't make sense. "Wait a minute. Why would someone target Destiny?"

"Why wouldn't someone target her?" Emme questions softly. "She's hailed as royalty among witches and is held in high regard across the supernatural spectrum."

Gemini smirks. He knows what I mean. "Because you have to be a real dumbass with a death wish to mess with Destiny. I get that her name is figurative, but it's literal too, given that her predictions, and those of her predecessors, are never wrong."

"Pardon?" Emme asks.

"She can 'see' anyone trying to kill her," I elaborate further. "And because she can, she can obliterate her assassin long before he thinks about taking her out."

My "weird" magic gives me glimpses of the future. They're always graphic and tend to revolve around chaos and dismembered body parts soaring through the air. They also pop out of nowhere and usually haunt me for months. I don't think Destiny has that problem and would bet she can summon her visions at will.

"There's a lot we don't know about Destiny," Gemini adds. "And a great deal more she and her predecessors have kept hidden. What we do know gives us just a hint of her strength. It's what's kept her, and others like her, safe throughout history."

"I figured," I add. "Disastrous taste in clothes aside, she's not stupid. Personally, I think all the bells, whistles, and funky fur are to distract from all the mojo lurking beneath."

"Agreed." He eases along the road, easily avoiding a large ditch. "There are countless legends surrounding Destinies. All warn that an attempt to kill Destiny seals your own fate."

"You can't kill Destiny?" Emme asks.

"It seems that way. All documented attempts throughout history were foiled, and every assailant who tried met a strange fate."

"What constitutes a strange fate?" Emme asks.

He glances at the rearview mirror.

"Never mind," she adds quickly. "Maybe I don't want to know."

"But maybe you should," he tells her gently. "Have you ever heard of Draco the Athenian law maker?"

"No," Emme replies. I shake my head too.

"Unbeknownst to the humans he served, he was a warlock and among Destiny of Aegina's biggest critics. It was rumored he hired a merc to kill her in 620 BC. The night of the assassination attempt he went to a theatre, likely to make himself visible so he wouldn't be named a suspect." His gaze flickers to me. "He never made it out of that theatre."

I'm picturing something gruesome involving a sharp weapon. But Gemini did say "strange fate" and he doesn't disappoint.

"He was showered with coats and hats from grateful citizens. So many he was smothered to death."

"All right, that's messed up," I agree.

"There's more."

"There always is," I say, steeling myself.

"When his guards peeled back the layers of clothing in an attempt to rescue him, they found the hired assassin on top of him with his throat slit."

"Mmm," I say. But what I'm really thinking is *damn* what a freaky way to go!

"In 455 BC, Aeschylus, Athenian author of tragedies, and brother to the local head witch, sent a band of marauders to ambush Destiny of Athens en route to Troy. He was furious with Destiny following her prediction that he would die by a flying object, convinced she was trying to intimidate his sister into surrendering her territory."

I hold out a hand. "Let me guess, that Destiny made it out unscathed didn't she?"

He nods. "The creek that ran through his property turned red from the blood of the marauders found stacked like stones up stream."

"What happened to him?" Emme asks, hesitantly.

"He was killed by a tortoise dropped by an eagle. Most believe the eagle mistook his bald head for a rock it needed to shatter the tortoise's shell." He shakes his head. "I don't think that's true."

Neither do I. Death by tortoise is some messed up comment to chisel into your headstone. "What about Destiny of Athens?" I ask. "Did she take his sister's territory?"

"No," he says. "A different witch did when she died of grief following her brother's death." He stomps on the gas as the road grows steeper and narrows. The rows of sugar pines thicken, shadowing the ravine below. "These stories are just the beginning and grow more violent in the middle ages."

"Do they all involve witches?" I ask. "It seems to me that's the running theme here."

"No, some involve vampires and *weres* who saw her as threat or viewed her as competition." He shoots me a look.

"We all have blood on our hands."

"We do," I agree. If history has taught me anything it's no race has been exempt from cruelty. "But as much as Destiny falls under the witch umbrella, she doesn't embrace the world of covens and spells." To my knowledge, she wasn't required to attend "witch school", unlike me who was forced to (although I'm not a witch) just to keep Sparky from burning us alive. "And the spell-wielders don't exactly embrace her. I've never seen any witch from any coven run up to her like an old friend, happy to see her, and glad she arrived."

"I know. It's one of the reasons I feel bad for her," Emme adds quietly. "She's invited to all these exclusive events and interacts with the most prestigious members of supernatural society, but it's only because of her power and her title of Destiny. I don't think she has many real friends or genuine relationships."

"I don't think so either," I agree. "Except for Tye." I laugh when I turn to look at Emme, knowing she's blushing. "You remember Tye don't you?"

Gemini takes a sniff, likely picking up on Emme's sudden shyness. "What don't I know?" he asks.

"Oh, it's nothing really," she says.

"Just that she made out with the son of the president of the North American Were Council," I add, ignoring her attempts to silence me. "No big deal, right, Emme?"

Gemini rubs his jaw, chuckling as he straightens his SUV. "When did this happen?"

"Malaysia," I say, laughing.

His grin fades as he inhales deep. "That wasn't Tye," he murmurs.

"What?" I turn around, but Emme's found someplace else to look. I'm dying to know who she was with. I was certain it was Tye. But something about the way she curls inward makes me back off.

"Ah, so getting back to Destiny," I say, unable to keep the worry from my tone. "Seeing how anyone who has ever opposed her kind dies in some tripped-out way, she should be safe. Between her powers and what history has shown, it's like she's impossible to kill."

"But she's not," Gemini says. "It's true that no one has ever succeeded in killing a Destiny. That doesn't mean she can't be killed. We can't assume she's safe nor can we abandon her without protection."

"I suppose you're right," I say, thoughtfully, remembering the shifters and how they're feeding the assassins their blood. Some prick could try and off her. Destiny, while not exactly normal, is very human, and God knows she has a heart.

I roll my shoulders when another wave of magic pushes through me. The defenses are similar to the ones surrounding our house and capable of blowing any threat to smithereens. But the ones around our house are welcoming since we're a part of it.

Mate or not to the second in command, and sister-in-law to a pureblood Leader, my sisters and I still don't feel welcomed, and these magic wards reflect their dislike.

I lean back into the comfortable leather seat, thinking matters through and trying to come to grips with it all. Normally, it takes forever to get up the mountain. Tonight it doesn't take long enough. I hate what's happening—the greed, the constant battle for supremacy that wages between "us" and "them"—there's no end in sight, not even with the exorbitant amount of loss on both sides.

My eyesight sharpens and my nerves go on edge the moment the stone fortress that surrounds the Den comes into view. I don't see the *weres* stalking in the shadows along the perimeter, but my body and magic sense their presence.

"They're friendly," Gemini assures me when he glances in my direction and catches sight of my eyes.

What he means is they're part of the Pack. Friendly is a loose term around here and not one I'd ever use to describe a *were*. The fact that they're prowling outside Den walls is indicative of their need to protect and readiness to kill.

I blink several times, trying to clear the unusual way my irises blanch when preternaturals draw too close. But it's not until Gemini strokes his hand gingerly against my cheek that I finally settle. It's not that I think the *weres* would attack me unprovoked. It's more that I recognize we'll never quite fit in, regardless of how hard we try.

We reach the tall wrought iron gates at the main entrance. Slowly and gracefully they part, allowing us through and onto the hundred acres of land secured behind the fortress. As the tree line breaks further up the road, the sea of lush green grass that usually greets us by day opens to waves of inky black.

Each blade of grass glints with silver, illuminated by the full moon pushing through the cluster of clouds stretching across it. I expect the usual, young *weres* in their beast forms racing along, their large paws indenting the thick sod as they practice tracking those who threaten the earth.

I never told Gemini how much I like watching the young *weres*. Their energy during their lessons is a perfect blend of innocence and excitement, and the thrill of the hunt, that's something altogether different. They want to be the good guys, and are enthusiastic about learning their duties. I don't know another species like that, I suppose that's why I have such a strong respect for them.

Tonight, that enthusiasm and innocence is gone, replaced by a sense of seriousness I wish they didn't have to know so young. It's no longer playtime, too much shit is going down. I catch traces of their eyes as Gemini careens forward, their large bodies huddled along the taller stalks of grass and slinking through the thick forest in silence.

"The kiddos are out late," I say.

"They've been pulled for watch," Gemini says. "Every student will be required to work in shifts for the next few weeks. Perhaps longer depending on what happens next."

Even with all the magical booby-traps and protection spells the property has been saturated with, and the older *weres* skulking outside the Den walls, it's not enough. The Alliance isn't taking any chances.

I only hope they don't take any chances when it comes to Celia.

"Did you know?" I ask, my voice unusually quiet. "That

any of this was coming?"

"We're always suspicious when something occurs out of the ordinary," he says, reaching for my hand. "And as a whole, *weres* tend to be more paranoid, given what our species has been exposed to." He kisses my hand. "But whatever doubts remained vanished following the assault against Genevieve."

"And the attack against Uri was the final nail in the coffin," I reason. "Seeing how high his rank and how insanely dangerous he is, I'm sure that put everyone on edge."

"It did," he agrees, his voice lowering as we pull into the main campus.

The Den originally resembled a fancy ski resort catering to those of lavish means. Since the war, and everything that happened in between, what originally was designed to be a school for werewolves expanded, becoming a safe haven for *weres* of all species

A large fountain at the center of the campus seamlessly joined the new buildings with the old, and small paved streets separate each block. I was worried when the expansion began that the area would lose its elegance and prestige. But the *were* who designed it wanted to stay true to the original vision, maintaining its beauty as well as its opulent reputation.

Three-story buildings, adorned with stone steps that lead to wraparound porches with stout granite pillars and outdoor fireplaces, line each row. The landscaping is subtle, not that it needs much. A few shrubs here, a tree there, and sculptures made from boulders and petrified wood strewn in between. Just as the vamps have their share of wealth so do the *weres*, and they're not afraid to shine a spotlight on all they've accrued throughout the centuries.

Ordinarily, there aren't many cars lining the streets. The majority of residents park in the underground garages that double as reinforced bunkers in case of an invasion. Tonight, a parade of Hummer limos and high-end cars that must have had a bitch of a time burning rubber up the steep mountain path hug the curb, their presence showcasing just how many have gathered seeking protection and adding to the heaviness drifting in the cool night air.

Gemini parks behind a familiar limo with BYTEME plates. "Are we late?" I ask, stepping out.

"Looks that way," he answers, glancing up toward the center building. "Emme, come with us and stay to my right."

Ordinarily, Gemini and I walk into the Den grounds holding hands. It's something he prefers since he claimed me to remind others who I am to him. He doesn't like how the stares of males, and sometimes females, linger on my face and body. And with everything that's happening, I also think he worries about who may try to harm me in an attempt to hurt him.

"It's all right," Emme says, shutting the door. "I don't mind walking behind you."

No, she doesn't, which is why Emme is the sweetest person who's ever walked the earth. She never wants to be perceived as intrusive, nor does she need to be coddled. She is, however, non-too confident in her getup and likely wants to run and hide.

She yanks up the waistband of her sweatpants, creating a bulge along her midsection and fanning out the borrowed long-sleeved T-shirt she's wearing. I think she was trying to improve her appearance, only now her slight frame has an odd shape, similar to Tweedledee and Tweedledum, only way cuter.

I think.

Her nose crinkles when she lifts her sleeve and she takes a whiff. God bless her. Honolulu Sunshine cleaned off our hands and her face, but the scent of entrails lingers and her hair is well, "crunchy".

A deep growl has her jumping and me whipping around with my firing arm out. Blue and white flames ribbon around the length of my arm, sending sparks to trickle against and char the sidewalk. The knuckles of my left hand cracks, my lightning ready to nail whatever threatens us, if my fire doesn't burn it to ash first.

"Gemini," I say, widening my stance as I look around.

"It's all right," he murmurs.

Regardless of what he claims, the muscles along his back stretch, threatening to split his shirt in half and allow his twin wolf to leap out. He scowls, looking up, the intensity in his stare rivaling the heat in my arm.

From the roof a brown wolf leaps like liquid fur, landing before us with his haunches raised and his gums peeling back from his jowls.

My arm shuts off, recognizing Bren long before I do. "What the hell is your problem?" I ask.

I glance around, certain he must be growling at another wolf behind us. But the only one behind me is Emme.

She averts her gaze. "No," she whispers.

"No what?" I question.

"She's not speaking to you," Gemini answers. He sidesteps in front of Bren, keeping him from Emme. "She's not hurt and she won't be. You have my word I'll keep her safe."

I breathe a sigh of relief. Bren tends to be protective of me and my sisters, especially Emme. He probably scents the vampire blood still soaking her body and is stressed about what happened to her.

I step forward only to startle when he snaps his fangs.

"Not tonight," Gemini fires back, his voice as deep as the growls Bren greets us with. "She needs space and we need to get inside."

I don't see Bren move, his motions too quick. Gemini does, shoving his body between him and Emme when Bren lunges to the right.

"Bren," Gemini snaps. "We need to portray a united front. I'm going to ask you one more time to keep your distance from her. If you don't, the Pack won't allow you anywhere near her."

Emme wrings her hands. "Bren, go," she says, her expression breaking. "We'll talk later."

It's not Gemini's threat that makes Bren back down, it's the way Emme appears to splinter. As I watch, I can sense pieces of her fall away like shards from a once glorious piece of crystal.

Bren's growls fade away, and from one moment to the next, he's gone.

"What was that?" I ask, turning to Emme.

It takes her too long to answer. "He doesn't want me hunting."

That's nothing new. Like I said, Bren has always been protective. But this wave of protectiveness isn't directed at me, or Shayna, or Celia. Not this time. This time, it's all about Emme.

"No, he doesn't. But that's not why he's pissed." I take in her demeanor and how she seems to pull away. "Emme, what's going on?"

Emme meets my face, saying nothing all the while appearing to hold too much back.

"Just tell me," I say.

Gemini's fingers trail to my lower back. "Now isn't the time," he says, the way he grips my hip giving away the severity of the situation despite his gentle hold. "A lot is happening between the *weres* and how Emme is perceived," he explains. "It's firing Bren's defensive nature."

He focuses on Emme. "I need you to stay beside me," he tells her. "And you're not to leave with another male unless it's me, Aric, or Koda. Females are fine, but not other males. Am I clear?"

It's often hard for me to keep my trap shut. This is one of those moments, and if it weren't for how Emme seems to withdraw further, I would be demanding a lot more than I'm getting.

"All right," Emme agrees just above a whisper.

"Let's go," he says.

I glance at him, hoping he'll give me a clue to what's happening. He keeps his stare ahead. He's trying to keep Emme from appearing alone and vulnerable. I know that much. Except there's more to it based on Bren going all animal.

Two *weres* in human form guard the double front doors leading into the main building. I recognize them from last year's graduating class. They nod to Gemini and open the doors, allowing us through. The viciousness in their deep-set eyes alert me of their anger and how they're prepared to maul anything that tries to get past them.

But the way they regard Emme is entirely different.

I was already tense, but all this heaviness soiling the air is doing little to soothe me and Sparky. I mutter a curse when she starts to quiver. Gemini reaches into the pocket of his jeans and pulls out my gloves.

"Here, take these."

"I'm not trying to hide who you are," he adds when I reach for them slowly. "But I am trying to keep as much attention off you as I can."

"All right," I say, realizing he only means to keep me safe.

We pass through the large foyer and continue down a long corridor paneled in dark wood, our steps the only noise in what should be a building busting with activity and magic.

I tug on my gloves as we walk, stretching my fingers through them. "I didn't know you had them."

His focus locks onto the entrance to the ballroom ahead. "I found them when I first entered the alley. They slipped my mind when I saw the *situation* you were in."

"I had it under control."

He looks at me.

"Well, I did," I mumble.

"With that logic so did Emme," he says, jerking his head in her direction. "And we see and smell where that led her."

"You can smell me?" she asks.

She could smell herself when she pressed her sleeve against her nose, and likely reasoned it was only because she's close to the source. Personally, all I smell is Honolulu Sunshine, having lathered it on her like she was covered with bile, because hey, she sure as hell was.

I glance at Gemini, knowing his nose scents a lot more than my sanitizer.

"My apologies Emme," he says.

Emme's panic-riddled features whip my way. I know what she's thinking, the room is going to be packed with supernatural noses. They'll scent her, and see her, and good *Lord*, no wonder he wants her so close to him. He's the best line of defense she has.

"It's not a big deal," I say, in true pa-shaw fashion, lying through my damn teeth.

She covers her face. "Yes, it is," she moans.

The doors part ahead of us. I think it's some spell. I don't know the extent until we close in.

I don't see the *weres*, not at first. Their appearance slowly taking shape as I near, starting with the blurry images of their outlines seconds before their large shapes fill in.

Two hulking men wait on either side of the door, wolves the size of buffalo standing guard at their sides. They scowl when they see us. However, it takes the gray wolf with smooth dark fur sneezing and thrusting her tongue in disgust to make me realize they're not exactly angry.

Like the *weres* at the front doors, they smell Emme, and like them, they don't think my hand sanitizer did the trick. If anything, it's like all the glop she was doused in is burning its way through their snouts.

"Is it that bad?" I whisper.

"No," Gemini answers.

He's lying. Obviously.

I stop in the doorway. The massive room, surrounded with floor to ceiling windows that unveil a sky littered with stars, appears to be under construction. Several tools, ladders, and piles of lumber are strewn haphazardly across the large expanse and the skeletal remains of broken furniture rest against the far walls.

"Keep walking," Gemini says.

I do, my eyes widening as the piles of lumber and remnants of construction vanish, and a large group of supernaturals slowly come into view.

The room has been disguised and altered with a cloaking spell. A *formam mutatio* spell if memory serves. Anyone who manages to get through the wards and guards will only see a room in the process of being fixed, not the magical muscle hidden within it.

Yet once we're in, the magical muscles collectively flex, tracing like points from an arsenal of daggers across my skin, not enough to hurt, just enough to show me how easily they could puncture my flesh.

Uri, Misha's master is close, as are the Pack Elders, and Misha himself. I feel them. Genevieve, Tahoe's Head Witch, is here, too. Her magic like the others is strong enough to drip like warm blood against my skin. But even if I couldn't feel her power, I'd know she was here. No one else could have cast a spell of this magnitude so quickly.

Some of her coven linger just a few feet away, huddled closely and speaking in hushed voices. I nod as I pass them, trying to be polite. Ordinarily I'd stop and chat. But these are extraordinary circumstances and no one is in the mood for friendly conversation.

Seated at a large granite table along a raised platform are Celia and the Pack Elders. Aric stands directly behind Celia, his arms crossed and his expression as dark as the five o'clock shadow lining his jaw. Celia is saying something I don't quite hear, and she doesn't quite finish. She and Aric turn in our direction, their eyes widening when they fix on Emme.

A cluster of *weres* and witches loitering beside an elaborate buffet quiet as we near. I assume it's because Gemini has arrived or because they sense my magic. It's not until we're almost to them that I realize they barely notice us. Oh, no, they're attention is all on Emme.

The *weres* lower their plates stacked with prime rib, fruits, and bread as we reach them. The witches mostly clasp their mouths, their faces blanching. It's bad enough Emme looks like a hot mess. She reeks of one, too.

Witches have a way of sensing suffering and death, and likely sense all the damage Emme inflicted on the vampires. The *weres* sense more than that, their noses wrinkling, and more than a few walking away and leaving their food behind.

"Oh, *God*," Emme squeaks, covering her face.

"It's not you, it's them," I say.

I look to Gemini who regards me as if I'm crazy. "Isn't it, love?" I ask through my teeth.

"Yes," he mumbles. "Of course."

Damn, he's a terrible liar when it counts.

The wall of bodies ahead of us, some more or less human, others in beast form, part, giving us ample space as we make our way toward the raised platform where Celia appears worried and Aric is close to losing his cool. I'll give us this, we know how to make an entrance.

And so does Destiny.

A spray of black, white, and hot pink feathers pop up over a crowd of very uncomfortable looking witches. The witches spread out, their medieval, crushed velvet gowns elegant and lovely, the exact opposite of the little number Destiny is sporting.

Oh, and when I say "little", I'm lying.

Picture a zebra pantsuit, as painful as it sounds, and throw in a pair of polka dot hot pink boots. I know what you're thinking, they don't make that shit. I'm sure "they" don't. Destiny, being the little creative stinker she is, must have dropped a few grand on the boots only to staple black leather circles to them. Don't believe me? I can see the staples from here, fixed to the center of the dots so the edges flap like birds with broken wings as she races toward me.

She hangs tight to the pink cowboy hat on her head, the spray of feathers on the front fanning out like a giant turkey's ass.

"Taran!" she says, waving madly with her free hand. "You didn't get eaten!"

I point at her and make this clicking sound with my tongue. "Not yet, girl."

She throws her arms around me. "It's great to see you, and Celia, oh, and Shayna, too." She hooks a thumb. "Shayna is outside," she says, dropping her voice. "But I'm afraid she and Koda are fighting. Something about a vampire head, and finding her standing over the vampire's writhing body." She thinks about it. "Or was she writhing and the vamp's body standing?" She shrugs. "I couldn't hear well over his growls."

"Yeah, ah, rough night," I say, glancing at Gemini who is unusually quiet.

His stare is intense and glancing ahead to where Aric appears to be arguing with the Elders. I can't hear what's being said, but we both see enough to know Aric isn't happy.

"Where's Emme?" Destiny asks, looking past me.

I turn to where Emme is standing directly behind me. She offers Destiny a wave. "Hi, Destiny," she says. "It's nice to see you."

Destiny, bless her fashion faux pas heart, keeps her smile. "Wow. Look at you," she says. "I'd hug you, but I don't want to get anything on my new outfit."

"I'll bet," I say.

Her smile softens. For what has to be the second time since I've known her, I get a peek at the human beneath all that crazy persona. "I really want to thank you, for stepping up and having my back. It means a lot."

Gemini and I exchange glances. Like me, he doesn't seem to know what the hell she's talking about.

That's when the crazy persona that is Destiny returns with a vengeance. "Haven't you heard?" she squeals, jumping up and down and clapping. "You're my new bodyguard."

Chapter Six

I pat her shoulder, trying to reassure her and hoping not to piss her off. That brain zapping thing she does is for real, peeps, and I'm not going through it again. "I'm sorry, but I think you have me confused with someone else."

"No."

I smile. At least I try to. It's hard to smile with the amount of zebra stripes currently blinding me, and because something, a *really bad* something, makes me think she's telling the truth.

"That's not possible," Gemini says, his voice trailing as Aric and Celia approach.

Both of Celia's hands are wrapped around Aric's arm and she's leaning close to him. It's something she always does when he's close to losing it. Awesome.

Aric's tight stare shifts to Uri, Misha's maker and the granddaddy of all master vamps.

I'd noticed his presence when we walked in, you can't *not* notice power that potent. But I'm not a fan of Uri, and didn't bother to seek him out. I do now, mostly because Aric makes it a point to check on him.

Uri is seated a few rows down from where we wait. He's

infamous for three things: his strength, the array of young, studly, and shirtless men always at his side, and his capes. That's right, capes. Money and influence evidently affords you the right to dress any way you damn well please. Tonight his cape, a deep green one with speckled fur along the collar is draped over the chair.

Genevieve bends in front of him, tending to his face similar to a makeup artist applying the finishing touches to a Broadway star set to take the stage. It's not until he turns to the side that I realize Uri's face is covered with holes!

They're oozing, burrowing deep into the muscle and partially exposing his skull. "Jesus," I rasp, my shock and disgust forcing me to take a step back.

"He's had a bad night, too," Destiny says, her voice sad.

She must have a better relationship with Uri than the rest of us. Celia can't stand him, writing him off as a cold, cruel leader, and master manipulator. "Misha is getting too powerful," she told me in a whisper. "It won't be long before Uri tries to kill him so he can take that power for himself."

I agreed, and it scared me senseless. Misha is Celia's friend. If Uri goes after Misha, Celia will rise to protect him.

Since I first met Uri, an inner voice warned me to stay clear. Despite those stupid capes he flaunts like his young lovers, he emits danger like a coiled cobra. I'm not afraid of him. I'm just aware that snake can strike, and if he does, especially against my family, so will I.

The young men Uri feeds from stroke him lightly, speaking words of adoration. The one closest to me is crying those thick awful tears that form when your soul is falling away in pieces. All of Uri's lovers are like that, completely enamored with him, desperate for his attention however piddly.

It doesn't mean anything. Not to Uri. Whatever fondness he has is always fleeting. They'll bore him soon enough and he'll move on to the next few men who peak his interest, not caring about the broken hearts he leaves behind.

For now though, they're with him, and whether he'll ever admit it, he needs them. He's trembling horribly, and close to seizing. Whatever spell was cast continues to burn its way through the tissue, causing him pain he otherwise would not openly show. Pain, hell, *any* display of vulnerability in the presence of other preternaturals will get you killed by the one waiting to take your spot.

My gaze skitters around the room and to the other vamps loitering nearby. Like Uri and Misha, they'll always be young and beautiful, the *turning* process gifting them with immortality and eternal beauty for the simple price of your soul. None are masters. The few who were met their demise years ago, leaving Misha to command the entire west coast, a position he won't abandon without a fight.

Gemini leans into me, his warm breath teasing my skin. "Don't get involved," he warns, his lips skimming along my ear as he whispers. "Not our pack, not our fight."

I nod. Like me, he senses the vampires' restlessness. Newly *turned* vamps or those new to a keep are like ravenous hyenas. They'll attack those they perceive as weak, their primal and predatory instincts often overriding their common sense. Magic eating holes into his face or not, Uri is deadly.

And so is Misha who stands directly beside him.

Ire claims Misha's stance like armor. It's so severe, even his most trusted vampires are afraid to draw near. His long blond mane is pulled back in a silver clip. It's his "battle hair". He's ready to destroy anyone who threatens his master.

Celia has often questioned Misha on whether the loyalty he demonstrates to Uri is extended back to him. Misha has never responded either way, not because he doesn't know, but because I think he does.

"If Misha is ever going to take Uri out, this is his moment," I murmur, knowing Gemini can hear me.

Misha's head swivels in my direction, his narrowing eyes alerting me that he heard me loud and clear. Damn these vamps and their super senses. "I'm only saying what everyone else is thinking," I reply in that same hushed tone.

"He won't. Not now," Gemini responds, well aware Misha can hear him and not giving a rat's ass. "He'll wait for the right time."

My comment annoyed Misha, but all Gemini's words do is trigger that wicked smile Misha is known for. I'm not sure why Misha smiles then. It could be good. It could be sucky. Either way I'm not returning it. I may be his merc for hire. That doesn't mean I'll jump aboard the Misha death train should it decide to run off the tracks.

Destiny who has been unnervingly quiet, and a little too smiley, adjusts her cowboy hat just right. The whacky feathers poised on top release a snowfall of black, white, and hot pink plumage. "She's beautiful, isn't she?" she asks.

I don't have to guess she's looking at Genevieve, the head witch. When I first met Genevieve, I mistook her for a vamp because she's seriously that good looking. Her long dark hair is gathered in a bun that's supposed to look like she pulled it up in a haste, yet somehow adds another air of elegance to her already spellbinding appearance.

The loose strands that escape Genevieve's bejeweled hair pin fall along her sapphire eyes and porcelain skin, skimming her cheeks as she treats Uri's wounds.

"Oh, but you're pretty, too," Destiny adds, giving me a playful nudge. "A real looker."

"Ah, thanks, there, Des. You . . ." I give her the onceover, trying to think of something nice to say. "You have a nice smile."

"Super thanks." She cups her hand, pretending to whisper. "But betcha it's not as nice as Genevieve's."

I'm sure nothing is, given her awe.

Genevieve scrutinizes Uri's face, her yellow amulet streaming rays of bright sunlight as she fills Uri's wounds with what resembles spackle. She mumbles a chant, her lips soft as she moves them, but her magic forceful, driving the curse that struck him out of his system.

As her light withdraws so does his trembling. All at once he slumps forward, his boyfriends barely catching him in time.

Misha doesn't move, keeping his arms crossed and watching Uri closely as Genevieve withdraws.

I straighten. "Is now the right time?" I whisper to

Gemini, noting that in spite of his stance, Misha is geared to attack.

Gemini doesn't respond with words. He clasps my elbow and Emme's leading us away.

I don't think I manage to fully shift my weight when the first of several vampires attack. Misha snatches two up by the throat, his movements too quick to register.

With a simple squeeze, and a hiss that chills me down to my soul, he caves their larynxes inward. Ash drifts out in a haze, coating the air with murder just as something flies over my head.

Like a bowling ball being thrown against granite, a head strikes the opposite wall, cracking the skull and caving it inward.

Emme rams into me as she leaps away from a decapitated torso, flipping like a fish out of water toward us.

"What was that?" I say, watching the torso flop past us.

"A torso," my beloved replies.

I let out what I hope is an easy breath. It's not. Seriously, what the hell?

"I mean what happened?" I ask instead.

The torso explodes in a billow of ash. "Misha willed his leeches to die," Gemini explains.

Emme and I exchange glances. "He can do that?" I ask.

"Being their master and given his power, yes," he says, his dark expression split between disappointment and relief.

"And what about that?" I ask, pointing to whatever is crawling away from the corner. A werewolf munching on what looks like a chicken wing steps over it. He doesn't care. It's vamp bits.

"Arm," Gemini answers. "She was torn into five pieces."

"By Misha?" I ask, wondering how exactly he managed to pull that decapitated rabbit out of the hat.

"No," Gemini says, his unease evident as he turns toward Destiny.

She keeps her smile. "It's not nice to attack those who are weak. Don't you think?"

I try to nod and fail. The best I can do is not put more

distance between us.

The pull of Genevieve's mojo has me turning toward her. She's looking at the vamp standing in front of her. The vamp isn't moving, only because Genevieve isn't letting him. He falls apart. Literally, his petrified body parts splintering down the middle and crumbling as they strike the wood floor.

I don't think this vamp went after Uri. He went after Genevieve believing she was distracted. His mistake. Genevieve doesn't miss a thing.

"Thank you," Uri mumbles, his speech slurred.

I think he's talking to Misha, who he often refers to as "his son", or maybe Destiny who could be some freak second cousin twice removed for all I know. But they *only* killed a few vampires. Genevieve healed him.

She quietly observed the violent exchange between the vampires, failing to respond until she was imperiled. As much as she willingly cured Uri and lifted the curse bestowed upon him, I don't think Genevieve would have shed a tear had the opposing vampires succeeded in killing him.

She passes the wooden bowl filled with the goo she used to treat his wounds to one of her "sisters" and irritably wipes her hands with a towel another offers. Her coven responded to the threat upon their leader, they just weren't as fast or ruthless as Genevieve. "Don't thank me, Uri," she answers him flatly. "Just do the right thing."

She walks away in a huff, briefly acknowledging us with a tilt of her head. "Gemini, Sister Taran."

"Hey, Vieve," I answer, my tone grave given the carnage.

Gemini acts as if he doesn't see her, his spine stiffening as Aric stalks forward with his arm around Celia. He's wearing a black T-shirt and jeans. My sister is in a navy maxi dress. I think she chose it for the dark color and how the dress falls loosely at her sides, camouflaging her pregnancy. She dresses like that a lot. I think it's her way of shielding her child. But the way the soft material gathers around her belly, there's no hiding the little one growing inside her.

Misha looks up as they pass, ignoring the vampires brushing the ash from his Armani suit. Celia shakes her head, letting him know she can't talk right now and warning him to keep his distance from Aric.

Everyone is on edge.

Except for Destiny who beams at Celia's approach.

"Hey," she says when only mere feet remain between us. "I told Taran the great news."

"And I told her she must be mistaken," I sing.

Aric and Celia only tense further.

"No . . ." I say when they reach me.

"Taran," Celia begins.

"*No, way,*" I insist, my attention lobbying between she and Gemini. Emme steps aside, giving us room, but also trying to keep the focus off her and her disheveled state. I get it. Everyone's upset enough. But if Celia is trying to apologize, apology not accepted because what the hell? "I'm supposed to be protecting you," I remind her.

"She's not doing this," Gemini says, his comment spilling over mine.

Aric tightens his jaw. "It can't be helped. Not with everything that's happening."

"Destiny is not *pack*," Gemini says. "Nor is she *were.*"

Destiny takes this moment to fluff her feathers. Well, why not?

"That doesn't make her less valuable," Aric says, his attention flickering to Celia.

I pace in circles, muttering a few curses before whipping back and ramming my hands on my hips. "You think she'll protect Celia if we need her to?"

"Why wouldn't I?" Destiny asks, appearing confused. She motions to Celia's. "Those babies are coming, it's just a matter of time." She smiles softly. "They have to, the world won't survive without them."

When it comes to a baby being born, everyone should be all a flutter, expecting only the good things babies bring: cuddles and kisses, intermixed with promises for the future. But this child is different, burdened with a destiny he doesn't yet know.

The heavy task my sister's child will bear quiets us all,

surging our fear, but also feeding our hope. This baby is special, and so are his siblings, they have to be if evil itself doesn't want them born.

The silence lasts only briefly. There's too much to say and more to do. "We can't count on the vampires," Aric tells us.

"No shit," Gemini snaps, his anger altering his generally calm disposition into something fierce.

"Watch it," Aric warns. "I'm not happy about this either."

"Then why allow it?" Gemini fires back. "If this was Celia, you wouldn't have it."

"Not wanting it and being able to stop it are two different things. Neither matter because bottom line, we don't have a choice," Aric counters, his light brown irises flashing with resentment. "From now on, all the wolves from the Squaw Valley Den Pack are assigned to Celia. Genevieve's Coven and the Coven of Versailles will be protected and watched by the Chinese Imperials."

"Who are the Imperials?" Emme asks.

She blushes, embarrassed about interrupting, but recognizing the severity of the situation.

"The Chinese Imperial Coven," I answer, glimpsing at how Gemini's focus doesn't waver from Aric. "They're masters of magic and practitioners of sacred and mystical martial arts."

"Mystical martial arts?" she questions.

"Yes. Kind of like the *Crouching Tiger Hidden Dragon* version of the broom humpers," I explain.

A passing witch glares my way. "I'm sorry," I offer. "But that's the best way to describe them."

"They're recluse and secretive," Aric elaborates. "For the most part, they keep their distance from other witch clans, presenting themselves only during times of unrest or when they feel they're most needed."

"They were the ones entrusted with securing Asia during the last war," Gemini adds.

Emme tilts her head gingerly. "If they can secure an

entire continent, why aren't they watching Celia?" she asks carefully.

"Because physical prowess and magic aside, they're not *weres*," Aric replies.

In other words, he doesn't fully trust them to watch our girl.

Gemini's frown burrows deep. "Are the Imperials coming here? Or are we seeing both covens to China?"

Aric rubs the scruff of his five o'clock shadow. "The Imperials are en route and should arrive by morning to escort the covens to a secret location in Europe. We won't know where they are, but both Ines, the Head Witch to the Coven of Versailles, and Genevieve have sworn a blood oath to return should we *call* them." He makes a face. "The vampires are the only ones unwilling to lend us their full support. Uri and Ileana Vodianova have acquired protection of their own and are fleeing somewhere across globe. The remaining American masters, in addition to those in Canada, and Central and South America have already disappeared. Misha is the only one who agreed to stay and offered his help should we need him."

No wonder Genevieve was so angry. Instead of forming a united front, the vamps have once more chosen to save their own billion dollar backsides.

Except for Misha, who will never abandon Celia.

Chapter Seven

"The only one unaccounted for is Destiny," Aric says, turning in her direction. "Someone has to watch her, given her position and title. Tye offered, but as son to our president, he's under guard as well."

"I don't want Taran assigned to anyone," Gemini interrupts. "I want her watched *by me*."

Celia leans closer to Aric. I mirror her motions, taking Gemini's hand and keeping my body close. More times than not, she's managed to soothe Aric's wolf this way. And while I'm not normally so intimate in public, I think it's time I start given the circumstances.

Aric's voice is harsh and leaving absolutely no room for argument. "Based on Taran's position as an Alliance member, her resourcefulness, and her skills, she was chosen to guard." Gemini starts to argue. "It's either Destiny or Misha. Those are our only choices seeing that he is the only vampire who has agreed to stay."

So it's between a freaky zebra striped wall or a hard place with fangs. Nice.

I don't like this. But as bothered as I am, I'm counting on

Misha to protect Celia at all costs. He owes her as much. I'm also counting on Destiny's sense of loyalty. She tore into the vamp who attacked Uri for "not being nice". If I protect her, I'll earn her loyalty, increasing the chances for Celia's survival and that of her babies.

That said, *damn*, this is a pussy assignment. No way in hell is anyone going to go after Destiny.

She loses a little more plumage from her cowboy hat when she jogs awkwardly in place. "Sorry," she says. "New boots and I have to break them in. Otherwise, I'm going to look funny walking in them."

"Yeah, we wouldn't want that," I agree.

Aric starts to speak, stopping suddenly when Destiny switches to jumping jacks. "The guy at the boot shop told me this helps, too," she adds when we all gape.

I pinch the bridge of my nose. Yeah, no one's going after this little dickens.

"This is the best I can do," Aric tells Gemini.

Gemini digs his fingers through his hair and steps away. He's not quite on board. But I am. I have to be.

Destiny does a little shimmy and some odd movement with her hand, similar to what I do when I have an itch on my back and can't quite reach it. "Babe," I say, edging toward him.

He meets my face when I embrace his waist. It's the first time today that I've had the chance to hold him close. He realizes as much, dropping his arms to circle my back. "I don't like this," he says, his thumbs brushing over my hips.

"I don't either. But Destiny needs us, and we need her to help keep Celia safe." I reach up to stroke the smooth hair of his goatee. "She's not an easy target and she's a friend." He looks at me. "Okay, ally," I clarify.

I peer around his large body to see what sort of boot-breaking-in-calisthenics she's doing now. She stops in the middle of her toe-touches and offers me another enthusiastic wave.

My lips stretch into a smile and I wave back. This time, my smile isn't forced. For all Destiny makes me nervous, and despite that I've often questioned her stability, she's not mean. Another dismembered arm crawls away from its hiding spot under a nearby table. I crinkle my nose. Well, that is if you don't piss her off.

"I can keep her safe, and me as well," I assure Gemini, cringing as Misha's vamps swarm the remaining body parts and tear into them like piranhas. "You know I can," I offer, startling when I hear a wet crunch.

"It's not that I don't trust your strength, I just don't trust what's happening," he tells me.

"I know," I say, lifting up on my toes to kiss him. My lips meet his only briefly. He's conceding for the moment, but he's not happy about it.

He releases me slowly, turning back to our small group. Aric nods, but that's all. I know he's grateful for my help, yet out of respect for Gemini, he'd prefer not to involve me.

He kisses Celia's cheek, whispering something I don't quite catch. "Don't worry, love," she says. "Just do what you have to and I'll see you tonight."

She steps carefully away and toward Emme, except like always, Aric doesn't appear to want to let her go.

"Emme," she tells her when his hands finally pull away. "Why don't we go back to Aric's chambers? You can shower there and change out of these clothes."

"I'd like that," she says.

We grimace when she has to peel her sticky feet free from the floor. As she walks, her tiny flats make an odd squeaky noise. Christ, we didn't clean her feet and she likely has vamp parts stuck between her toes. I'll be sure to set her shoes on fire, too. What can I say, I'm a hell of a gal.

We march across the wood floors, avoiding the scuff marks created during the altercation and the mounds of ash from the now re-deceased attackers. I don't know who the poor sap is assigned to floor mopping duties, but he's going to fucking hate us.

My vision sharpens as we pass the cluster of supernaturals gathered closest to the door and my arm gives an involuntary jerk. There's so much mystical energy, the communal power pokes at my skin and riles my arm's magic. I think she sees them as competition. I only hope she's wrong.

"Who are all these beings?" I ask Celia.

"Royalty," Destiny answers. I hadn't noticed her follow. "Oh, I'm sorry. Do you mind if I tag along?"

"Not all," Celia says, shooting me a poignant look.

Oh, yeah, I'm supposed to be watching her. Tee-hee, silly me. "Just stay close to me, kid," I tell her, making a show of standing in front of her.

I pause, glancing over my shoulder at Celia. "Wait a minute, shouldn't someone be with you?"

She purses her lips. "Oh, they will be. Don't you worry about that."

The moment we step through the doors, wolves in beast form surround us, their four hundred pound bodies creating a wall. Their stares are alert and some lick their jowls, already anticipating what their enemies' blood will taste like pouring from their fangs.

We keep pace with Celia, Emme's squeaky shoes outrageously loud along the dark corridor.

"I take it when we're done they'll follow us home?" I ask.

"I'm not going home," she says, her expression growing sad. "We're staying at the Den in one of the new buildings." Her long wavy hair brushes against her shoulder when she turns to look at me. "So are both of you, as well as Shayna."

Emme's shoes stick to the floor with every step she takes, between that and all the squeaking, no way are we sneaking up on anyone. "Why are we staying here?" Emme asks.

"Because you're our family and Aric wants to keep you safe."

"That's sweet," Emme says. "But as an Alliance member, shouldn't I be assigned to guard duty as well?"

"Aric argued against the Alliance assigning you a post, Emme," Celia replies. "They agreed to his request."

"What about Shayna?" Emme asks.

Celia's gaze flickers to me as she carefully chooses her words. "He didn't want either Shayna or Taran assigned to guard duty. But he couldn't convince the Alliance. As a compromise, she'll be helping Taran watch Destiny."

"But not me," Emme states slowly.

"No," Celia answers.

"Is it because they're mated and I'm not?" Emme questions, shedding light on what Celia doesn't say.

"No, sweetie," Celia tells her. "It's because of who they're mated to." She glances at me, apologetically. "As second in command, Gemini holds an elite position in the Pack, as does Koda, being Aric's Warrior. Due to Alliance numbers being low, mates of high-ranking *weres* who possess supernatural abilities are now required to assist the Alliance. If we were human, we'd have an out. But here we are."

I glance behind me as we step outside. It's close to midnight, and the temperature has dropped significantly since we first arrived. "Is that why Koda and Shayna are fighting?" I ask. "She wants to help, and he doesn't want her involved?"

"It's one of the reasons," Celia says. "He wasn't happy when he found her carrying that decapitated vamp head around like a purse." She narrows her eyes. "You were supposed to go out for dinner and drinks, remember?"

"We had a drink," I offer, not that it does anything to appease her.

"Before or after you hunted the vampires baiting you?" she asks. She doesn't wait for another smartass response. "They tried bringing the head in for questioning. It's all they had after the Pack killed the other vamps they tracked. But the stupid thing kept trying to bite them on the ride up. The moment they reached the base of the mountain, the wards blew him to ash."

"Oh," I say. "All over Koda's new Yukon?"

"Yes."

"Yikes," I say. Since meeting us, Koda hasn't had much luck with his vehicles.

"But it's Shayna's safety that has him most upset. That, and the lying," she adds, shooting me another dirty look.

Why am I always the one in trouble? "I didn't make her lie, and honestly, it's like that woman can't wait for a fight . ."

My voice fades when something appears to make sense. "Wait a minute, is Shayna going all wolf?"

"The Elders don't think so, I mean not to the point where she'll *change* and go furry. But they think that the wolf essence that was passed to her has stirred a primal need to hunt." Celia rolls her eyes. "Based on his growls, Koda would prefer she gather."

"She gathered that decapitated head rather nicely," I say, thoughtfully.

"Would you stop cracking jokes? None of us are amused," Celia tells me. "Koda was already livid when he arrived, but he completely flipped out when Aric told him Shayna would help guard Destiny."

"It's going to be a real party!" Destiny squeals, clapping her hands. "Like a sleepover that never ends."

Yee-ha.

We cross the street. The pads of the wolves' heavy paws barely making a sound, unlike me in my heels and poor Emme. "What about you?" I ask as we hop onto the next walkway. "Is your inner tigress itching to hunt?"

"She's itching to hunt, prance, frolic, you name it," Celia says. "But pregnant *weres* aren't allowed to *change* since it's too traumatic on the fetus. I'm not *were*, but Aric doesn't want to take any chances."

Celia can also *shift* underground like sand through colander and surface unscathed. Aric probably doesn't want her doing that either seeing how her body breaks up into minute particles. "It's better to be safe," I agree.

"It is," she says. "But I can't make my tigress understand. She wants to run for miles like we used to." She motions between the walkways separating the houses and toward the forest. "Aric is hoping she'll be more content here since there are more places to openly roam. I guess we'll see."

Celia wants to comply and keep Aric from worrying. Yet the way her bare arms gather around her belly assure me she'd prefer to be home. She doesn't have a lot of good memories of the Den. How could she? For too long the *weres* attempted to pry her and Aric apart, angry that his pure bloodline would be ruined by mating with my non-*were* sister. It was a horrible time for them, causing deep scars that will never heal. Just because she's finally welcomed doesn't erase the damage that was done.

"You're going to love being my bodyguards," Destiny says, bouncing along, her giant spray of feathers fluttering in the breeze. "I have so many fun things planned."

"Like shopping for new clothes?" I offer.

"How did you guess?"

"I just know you *love* your outfits," I reply through my teeth.

"I do, but that's just the start. I booked dinner reservations at the Fawn and Pheasant and arranged for a helicopter to take us."

"Yeah?" I ask. It shouldn't surprise me. All the higher ups in the magical world possess some serious cash. I never exactly understood how they acquired all that money, be it dues or investments. Whatever the way, it's not in short supply.

"I also have front row seats to see Johnny Fate later this week. I'll get two more, for you and Shayna," she tells Emme.

"Johnny Fate," I say, slowly. "Isn't he that freak who tours with all those loud and obnoxious garage bands?"

"He's not a freak," Destiny says.

"Yes, he is." I huff. "Believe me, I know a freak when I see one . . ." My voice trails when I realize who I'm speaking to. "Sorry, girl."

"For what?" she asks, appearing confused.

And cue the crickets.

I clear my throat and try to help Celia up the stacked stone steps when we reach the building. That goes over as well as you think. She hisses at me, her hormonal inner kitty apparently tired of being placated.

Destiny continues as if uninterrupted, and as if I didn't come close to losing an eye. "Taran, please. I'm dying to go. There's something about Johnny that just calls to me."

"Calls to you?" I ask.

"Yes."

Her eyes develop a vacant stare. I watch her closely, wondering why she seems to slip away. "Are you feeling well?"

"Of course," Destiny replies, her enthusiasm returning with a vengeance. "Just tired and excited to meet Johnny."

I'm not sure I believe her.

She smiles, appearing delighted just as another pair of wolves appear in human form. They open the doors, encouraging us to pass. "Thank you," Celia tells them. She starts to head in, but the *weres* who escorted us refuse to leave. "As mate to your alpha, I thank you for your service and dismiss you to your remaining duties," she adds.

They bow, retreating slowly and watching her as the doors shut.

Celia isn't one for attention and I can tell she's uncomfortable. She presses her back against the door, looking past the long winding staircase to where three more *weres* wait. "I'm sorry I hissed," she says. "It's been a long time since, you know."

"Had sex?" I ask, wondering where she's going with this.

Her face reddens and she glares at me. "I meant had any independence."

"Oh, that makes sense."

She covers her face, allowing her cheeks a moment to cool. When she drops her hands away the humiliation I caused is absent, leaving only her sadness. "I realize that my baby needs protection," she admits. "And that Aric and I aren't enough considering the threats surrounding us. Except it's hard to accept that this is the turn my life has taken. Somedays, I'm so overwhelmed, I just want to flee with Aric and not look back." She shakes her head. "But that's not an option. Nowhere is safe."

She seems close to tears, her sadness so tangible I'm ready to cry with her. But neither she nor I give in.

Emme steps forward, carefully wrapping her arms around her. "I'm sorry, Celia."

Emme's cadaver-ish aroma should send Celia running. Except Celia doesn't move, welcoming Emme's embrace and the kindness she offers.

I gnaw on my bottom lip, wishing she and Aric were enough, that we all were. But this big bad, is really bad. I only hope our combined forces can keep her safe.

"You're going to be okay, Ceel," I assure her. "None of us are going to let anything happen to you or baby Aric." I stroke her back. "Have you eaten lately?" She shakes her head. "Let's get you something to eat, it'll make you feel better."

She nods. Food comforts Celia in a way nothing else can.

Destiny steps in front of us, grinning and simply head-over-hideous-boots happy for what may happen next.

Oh, yeah, that's right, I'm supposed to stay with her.

"When and where is the concert?" I ask.

"Santa Barbara, Friday night," she replies.

"And you're sure you want to go?" I question.

"I really do," she says. "From what I've learned, he has the best voice ever. Mesmerizing, even."

"Mesmerizing?" I ask, something about the word giving me pause and causing my arm to twitch. "Have you ever seen him perform before?"

"Never," she admits. "But I've always wanted to. Something about him has always spoken to me."

"I'm that way with Ed Sheeran," Shayna says, nodding like she understands.

"Ed Sheeran is terrific," Destiny says, approvingly. "But concert goers who've attended Johnny's shows *always* agree on one thing, there's no one else like him."

I'll give Destiny this, she was right.

Chapter Eight

I hold my arms up and out, allowing the security guard to a wave his metal detecting wand and check me for weapons. I'd heard of Johnny Fate, the hard rocker with a cult-like following, but all of it was bad: tearing up hotel rooms, allowing his fans to beat up the paparazzi, and peeing on public property. So am I thrilled to be attending his Champagne and Guts tour? No. If anything, I'm counting on my stilettos being classified as weapons and getting thrown out.

Already, my teeth are rattling from the brain crushing music blaring through the speakers and the lead vocalist's "Help me, I'm on fire" screeching. I'm hoping Emme packed earplugs, in addition to the clear plastic rain slickers in case some asshole pukes on us. Seriously, it's that kind of crowd. Bodyguard duties be damned, I want to save my hearing and protect my cute clothes.

"You a big fan of Johnny Fate?" the guard asks me.

"What?" I ask, plugging my ears when the lead singer of Give Me Death screams the chorus.

The guard laughs. "Don't worry. Write My Name in Blood is on next. They're a little better."

"I'm sure," I mutter, frowning at how he continues to wave the wand over my chest. Christ, it's only seven now and I can't wait for the night to end.

His expression grows smug. "I can get you backstage if you want."

"That's not necessary." He's a big guy, young and very immature. My guess is he was hired for his bulk, not his personality.

"You serious?" he asks.

"I'm not a fan," I tell him, wondering just what he thinks I'll do to get backstage.

"Then what are you doing here, princess?" He gives the wand another wave, this time, closer to my breasts. He's not obvious to anyone close by, but he is to me, the curvy motions he's making is pissing me off. "Tickets are hard to come by, and it's real tough to get backstage."

I'll bet it is.

"I'm here with a friend." I try to smile. "Are we done?"

He shakes his head. "Nope. You have to take off the gloves, gorgeous," he tells me, his tone suggesting he'd rather I take off my panties. "Gotta make sure you're not hiding something I haven't seen underneath."

"Of course," I purr at him. He leans back on his heels, watching me peel off my left glove, his stare dragging down the length of the bare skin. The music shifts, growing louder and more obnoxious, not that it distracts the guard. He smiles, approvingly, his expression eager for more. His smile vanishes as I unveil my right arm, the stark white skin and bright blue veins branching across giving him one hell of a pause.

He coughs into his fist, quickly averting his gaze. "You can step through."

"What's wrong?" I ask, playing dumb. "Don't like what you see?"

He doesn't answer. I'm not the perfect woman he mistook me for. I'm deeply flawed and now he knows it. I sashay by him as I slip my gloves back in place. How quickly women go from beautiful to shit in a lowly man's eyes, and

85

how little he cares who it harms.

I reach for my cell phone waiting for me in the small plastic bin, my fingers sliding over the pretty sparkly case a few times before I think to lift it. I toss the guard a smile over my shoulder. "It's okay, big guy. My boyfriend loves me, no matter what I look like."

If he hears me, he doesn't show it, resuming his wand waving duties. There were several men behind me. I hadn't noticed them. They noticed me. One guy shrugs, speaking to his buddy and not bothering to censor his remarks. "Her ass is nice and so is her body, just have to keep that other shit covered."

Nice.

I shove my phone into the back pocket of my jeans and march toward my sisters, trying not to stomp my tall heels against the walkway. I don't want these assholes to know they hit a nerve. But my feelings aren't as impenetrable as people think. Anger fills me, as does humiliation, and a little bit of shame although I try to beat all three away. I'm still human after all, and sometimes shit hurts no matter how much you wish it didn't.

I fiddle with my silver hoop earrings and run my hand down my sleeveless black tiered top, pausing at the way Shayna eyes those men. The wolf side she was gifted with probably wants to fight and protect. That's understandable. If roles were reversed, I'd fry anyone who treated Shayna this way. Except this was directed at me, making the hug Emme greets me with more difficult to take.

"They don't know anything about you," she tells me. "Including your heart."

I give her squeeze, but don't allow the embrace to linger. I hate feeling sorry for myself. For better and often worse, me and Sparky have worked things out. We know we're stuck together and I think we're both determined to see our lives through.

I hop onto the cement base where a brass statue of a musician has been erected, using the arm to help me balance. Although I examined the map of the venue prior to my arrival,

I want to make sure I know where we are and familiarize myself with possible escape routes.

The sunken arena is outdoors, and very unlike the sport complexes where most concerts are held. A circular concourse makes up the upper level where I'm standing, the beer and food stands positioned every few yards quickly filling with attendants making their way from the security checkpoint.

From my position, I can see the multiple tiers leading down to the stage where an immense, rectangular flat screen takes up the expanse. Several other large screens are perched on either side, showcasing the members of Write My Name in Blood as they bang their heads to noise they've convinced themselves is music. Don't get me wrong, I like rock. I just don't like feeling like my skull is being beaten with one.

I ease my way back to the concrete walkway, taking Shayna's hand when she offers it. "Are we good, T?" she asks.

"The eagle is in the nest and laying eggs," I agree.

"It's all about the eggs," she says, laughing.

Despite my sarcasm, and all my bitching, I'm taking the assignment seriously. In the off chance something should happen, I want to be ready.

"Let's find our seats," I tell her. "I don't want to miss a moment of Johnny."

"Yes, you do," she says, her voice practically inaudible over the music. She points to her ears. "I'm already wearing the plugs. This music, it's too much, my hearing can't take it."

"*My* hearing can't take it," I add, and it's no way as sensitive as Shayna's. Our wolves probably couldn't get within a mile of this place without their eardrums rupturing.

Destiny, doesn't have that problem. I groan when I turn and find her dancing in place, offbeat to Write My Name in Blood's rendition of *Enter Sandman*. The best way I can describe this band is loud. Seriously, that's all I have. According to Bren, Metallica inspired them and Skid Row gave them a voice. Metallica, could have inspired them I suppose, they inspired a great number of metal bands. But any voice Skid Row gave them was quickly butchered and sent screaming.

The screaming continues as the lead singer reaches a crescendo. "Motherfuckerrrrrrrrrrr."

Everyone around us loses it. Me and Emme mostly cover our ears. Destiny, she's part of the "give me more" crowd, the teal feathers she wrapped around the tight-as-sin bun on top of her head bouncing as she head bangs, or jogs in place. I'm not quite sure what she's doing. It could go either way.

"Woo-hoo!" Shayna yells, her fist in the air. "Go, Destiny!"

That's Shayna, always encouraging no matter what's happening, or how bad things look. "She's going to lose all her feathers before we make it to our seats," Emme says.

"Is that such a bad thing?" I ask, taking in the teal plumage already covering her zebra striped boots with green pompoms, and no, the poms don't match the feathers.

We talked her out of wearing a hat and that's about it. Polka dot black and white booty shorts hug her petite hips. And because that's not sexy enough, a tiny lime green bustier is currently cutting off the circulation in her tiny rack.

"It's going to be a warm night in Santa Barbara," I told her. In other words, "For the love of Christ, please wear something else."

"I know," she gleefully responded. "That's why I'm wearing shorts."

She had me there.

The screams on stage end, but not the ones behind us. I jerk around. The security guard and the men who were standing behind me, yank at their clothes. The motions shouldn't be strong enough to tear their clothing free from their bodies, but that's what's happening, leaving the three of them in their tighty whities.

"What the hell?" one of the other guard yells, ordering the rest to stop the line.

"Ants," the guard who checked me hollers. "They're all over me."

I gasp. Armies of ants crawl down their bodies, leaving welts deep into their skin. They swat at their skin, but the ants are immune, marching down their legs and spreading out along the walkway, forcing those trying to enter the venue to give them ample space.

My attention trails to Destiny, who, bless her heart, continues to bounce away despite the break in the music and the looks tossed her way. "Did you do that?"

"No one messes with my bodyguard," she says. She points to the left of the circular concourse. "I smell funnel cake. To the food stands, peeps!"

We drift behind her, following closely. I can't help my smile. In many ways, Destiny still scares me. However, this past week I've seen a different side to her.

For one, she eats most foods with chopsticks.

"It keeps your fingers limber," she claimed.

Really *loves* polka-dots.

"They're like the sun. All big, round, and out there—only black."

And she can't get enough of feathers.

"Everyone needs fun and color in their lives," she insisted.

In the two days since we arrived, we hit every trendy thrift shops in Santa Barbara, only for Destiny to wear the outrageous clothes she purchased to the fanciest restaurants in town.

Girlfriend will never win the fashionista of the year award. But she's a decent person, kind and thoughtful, who looks out for those few she calls her friends. Genuine would be another way to describe her, and perhaps lonely, too. Although she dresses as if she could care less what others think of her, I see how much it hurts her to be different, and I'm not speaking of her bizarre taste in clothing.

Maybe that's why she fiercely protected Uri. He was nice to her and a few months ago hosted her at his castle in Europe. And perhaps that's why she's so nice to us, we're among the few she considers friends.

"Are you all right, Taran?" Emme asks.

"Yeah, just thinking about Destiny," I reply.

Shayna takes the lead, her long ponytail swinging as she

weaves through the crowd. "Come on, dudes," she yells, careful to make sure we don't lag behind.

I like her being the first line of defense, and in this scenario, I prefer to guard the rear. Weapons are Shayna's thing and she uses them well. Nothing with ammo, but plenty of sharp and pointy to make up for it. She can take a piece of wood and transform it into a deadly blade so long as she's holding metal on her body. Tonight, she chose the platinum belly ring Koda gave her, the short red crop top she's wearing and her low riding denim shorts, giving everyone a view of the bling and her thin ballerina build.

The box of toothpicks shoved into her back pocket gave the guard a laugh. I don't think he'd laugh if he knew what she could do with them and am thrilled to pieces she didn't stab him through the eye with one.

But the toothpicks are just a start. The long necklace that drapes between her breasts is her greatest asset, and what she'll convert into a sword if she needs to.

Not that I think she'll need to.

My gaze scans my surroundings. I don't expect anything to happen, but long ago I learned something always does. I stiffen when I realize something is different, my body whipping around when it occurs to me what it is.

"What's wrong?" Emme asks. She sweeps along as I resume my pace, her hands loose over the sundress she's wearing in case she needs to act.

"It's probably nothing," I mutter.

She glances around, expecting something to pounce. "Taran, what is it?"

I angle my chin to look at her. I'm taller than her by a couple of inches, but I tower over her in these heels. She's in sandals, always choosing comfort (and clothes she can easily flee in) over style. Sadly, I can probably run faster in stilettos than she could in her flat shoes.

"There aren't any *weres*," I say.

"That's understandable," she remarks carefully. "The music is awful. My head is already pounding."

"It's not just *weres*," I say. "There aren't any beings of

magic aside from us."

She quiets, realizing where I'm headed. "There aren't many preternaturals left following the war, only about a hundred thousand scattered across the globe. Not to mention, with the new threat, they're being utilized in every way the Alliance can think to use them."

She's not dismissing what I'm saying. It's more like she's thinking out loud.

"I know," I agree. "But even though most *weres* have migrated to Tahoe, and were accepted into the Pack, there are still *lones* out there, and Lesser witches who never made the coven cut. I don't sense so much as a tarot card reader."

"Is that a bad thing?" she asks, taking her time to further inspect our surroundings.

"It shouldn't be," I say, although I'm starting to think maybe it is.

"And you don't sense any vampires?" she presses.

"No, but they stay close to their masters, and the music would be too much for a rogue."

"That's true," she says, appearing nervous. "And no master I know listens to bands like these."

She's right about that.

We're almost to the funnel cake line when a band of men with large chests, lots of tats, and even more piercings stalk toward us. We don't exactly blend. Especially Emme who looks like a little dove amidst a flock of vultures.

The last concert we attended was Pink. I'd say it was a different crowd, one where I wasn't worried about being trafficked or having my kidneys sold on the black market.

The man in front with a row of piercings along his forehead, nose, and chin, fixates on Emme. He makes a "V" with his fingers and flaps his tongue through the center. Yeah, I'd say this is a different crowd than we're used to.

Emme gasps. "Did you see that?"

"I was trying not to," I say, making a face.

She shakes her head. "I'm not sure this was a good idea."

"No," I agree, especially given the odd lack of magical creatures. "But it's what Destiny wanted." I bat away a small plume that breaks away from her hair and reaches my nose.

"You like her, don't you?"

She's only asking because in all honesty, I don't trust many people, not after the way they've treated us throughout our lives. And when you don't trust, it makes it hard to like.

"She's not so bad," I say. "Just a little lonely, like the rest of us."

I almost kick myself for what I say.

Emme's gentle stare trickles with sadness. Her irises are green and similar to Celia's. But where Celia's stare is intense, warning those who draw too close they're about to lose a limb, Emme's is soft, allowing her vulnerability to poke through.

"You still feel alone?" she asks. "Even though you and Gemini worked things out?"

I don't know how to explain what I'm feeling without further diminishing what she's going through. I do my best. "Ever since we were little, it's always felt like it's us, the four of us, against the world. The wolves have made it better, expanding and fulfilling our family more than I've ever believed possible. But despite the security and love they offer, it still feels like the majority are against us." I shrug. "I guess that's why I still feel we're on our own."

"I know what you mean," she says. Her focus trails ahead. "Do you think that will ever change for us?"

My first thought revolves around what Gemini said and his uncertainty regarding whether most of us will survive what's coming. But I can't think that way, not now, and especially not with Emme beside me. She's hope in a sweet dress and sweeter smile. I won't allow her to lose that light in her heart, and damn it, despite the odds, I'm not giving up on us. "I think the best we can do is what we're doing, keep moving forward and fighting the good fight."

There's the smile I so adore. "You're right," she says. "You're always right."

I laugh. "You don't mean that."

"Okay, maybe I don't."

When Emme laughs, my life is a little brighter and her

entire face lights up. Unfortunately, today it casts a spotlight we don't need.

I place my arm around her when a man with a shaved head and a devil's goatee hones in on Emme, his eyes wild. "I want to make you scream," he tells her.

In a strange way, I think he means it as a compliment. That doesn't mean we take it that way. "Back off," I snap. "She's with me."

"She can be with us," he says, holding out his arms. "There's plenty here for both of you bitches." His friends, who likely graze the covers of every sex offender alert in the press, laugh. I don't think they mean to intimidate, they simply do, allowing their size and appearance to speak for them.

I'm not easily intimidated, and I've never had a problem speaking my mind. "Sons of Anarchy called, you didn't get the part. They think you're full of shit, and P.S. you're an asshole."

"Oh!"

I lead Emme forward, glaring at them when they try to follow. One of the guys smiles. He stops smiling when his arm involuntarily lifts and smacks the Sons of Anarchy reject across the face.

The audible skin to skin connection punches through the murmurs of the growing crowd.

That's all it takes for a fight to break out. I look at Emme, my mouth falling open when the corners of her pink lips lift. "They weren't very nice," she says.

"No, they weren't, and didn't you show them?"

Shayna laughs, lifting the long needle she created with her power. As I watch, the silver metal shrinks, reducing in size and returning to its original toothpick form. She pockets it and whirls back around. As much as she was leading, she was still aware of what was happening behind her. That's one of the many things that rock about Shayna, even when you don't think she's aware, she is and she's ready for it.

"Don't worry about us," I tell her. "Keep an eye on Destiny."

Destiny turns around. "Isn't this the best day, ever?"

"You bet it is," I say, not meaning a damn word.

We trudge through the circular concourse and reach the funnel cake line where the space is at its tightest. At least thirty people are waiting in front of us, eager to get their sugar on. Just ahead more people are swarming a pizza and hotdog stand. I'm wondering what the hell this crowd ate, smoked, or snorted to give them the munchies so early on.

I don't wonder long.

An odd outpouring of magic sweeps through the crowd, putting my senses on alert and lifting Sparky in the air.

"What the hell?" I ask, using my other hand to pull her back down.

A woman, who bleached one half of her hair and shaved the rest, rams into me, her eyes wide and fixed in the direction of the stage. "Johnny," she rasps.

"Johnny," someone else mimics. "He's here. *He's here!*"

Johnny Fate's name swirls in awed, hushed tones, the power within it appearing to tame the aggression and unite all who have gathered.

"I can see him." The man who speaks, stumbles forward, knocking into another woman who barely notices. "I can see Johnny."

My attention skips around, wondering how it's possible he can see Johnny. The giant flat screens mounted around the stage aren't visible from where we stand. That doesn't mean I don't believe him.

"Something's here," I say, rubbing my arms irritably. "It's not bad magic, it's strange magic. Different from anything I've ever felt."

I speak quickly, not caring who hears me and wanting to make sense of it all.

"I feel it, too," Emme says. Her expression is almost blank from shock. She looks at Shayna who nods in agreement.

We exchange glances, jumping when Destiny raises her fists and screams. The crowd joins her, losing their shit as the first chord of an electric guitar belts out, ricocheting from every speaker.

Shayna checks her phone. "It's early," she yells. "Too early."

Maybe. But there's more to this than what we're seeing and feeling. "Call the wolves," I tell her, my gaze skimming around the crowd.

Son of bitch. I see nothing, but feel everything.

"What do I tell them?" Shayna asks me.

"I don't know," I say, muttering a curse. "That something's not right. We have to get Destiny out of here."

"Taran," Emme begins, her face paling. "Destiny's gone."

Chapter Nine

I jerk right and then left.

"Where is she?" I ask, yelling to be heard when another chord from a guitar rings out and the crowd bellows with excitement.

"She was just here," Shayna says, her tone reflecting my shock.

The throng of people in line for food and booze push toward us, hungry for Johnny to take the stage. "Don't fight them," I say, when Shayna tries to move against the group rather than with it. "Get to the front of the stage. She's probably there."

"And if she's not?" Shayna asks, holding tight to her phone when someone bumps into her. "Everyone is moving forward, we won't be able to make our way back up."

"Then we'll have to cut through the backstage," I reason. "Whatever it takes, either way we have to find her."

I keep Emme close when what feels like an avalanche of bodies shove us in the direction of the sunken arena.

"What's wrong with them?" Emme asks, her attention bouncing along the rough and tumble crowd.

"I don't know," I admit.

The best way I can describe Johnny's fans are zombie-like, blindly following their hero, with no regard for anything else. They're in a daze, like they need their next fix, and only this rock god can provide them the drug they seek.

"*Johnny.*" The woman to my left cries, falling into her partner who cuddles her close. "I get to see him. I get to see, Johnny."

"I know, baby," her partner tells her, her cheeks damp with tears.

I curl my right arm into me, not only to keep her in line, but also to bring me comfort.

During the British invasion, millions of young women became obsessed with the Beatles. I never understood it, finding all those images of women screaming at the sight of John, Paul, Ringo, and George, disturbing.

Johnny's followers remind me of those women, except it doesn't make sense. They aren't young teen women swooning, dreaming and desperate for love. They're grown men and women better suited for biker bars and brawls.

"Koda, Gemini, and Bren are on their way," Shayna says. "Tye is bringing them in with his helicopter."

Emme stiffens at the mention of Bren's name. I thought they'd made up, but it's like every time they're together, there's this overwhelming tension, and it's been going on for a long time. I think I know what's happening, in fact, I'm sure of it. But Emme and Bren aren't who keep my interest then.

"I thought Tye was under lock and key," I say. The North American Were Council is the governing body for all *weres* in the U.S. and throughout Canada. "As the son to the president, the Alliance demanded his protection."

"Come on, T," Shayna yells. "Tye likes to be coddled just as much as Celia."

"Good point," I say, wondering who Tye had to maul to get free.

"Besides, you know him and Destiny are buds," Shayna reminds me, slapping her hands over her ears when another strum of the guitar follows another, and another, the succession of musical notes growing more frantic.

"Who else is coming?" I yell, my voice competing and failing miserably over the cacophony of sound.

"No one. Everyone else is too far out." Shayna scrunches her face, her small pixie features pained. "Something's way wrong in Rockville, dudes. Let's find Des and get out."

Shayna drops her hands away from her ears. I'm not sure how she's not losing her mind. The noise is killing my hearing, and mine isn't as keen as hers. She removes the long silver chain around her neck and clutches it against her side. Very carefully and covertly, she manipulates the metal and changes it into a sword.

"The magic is getting stronger," Emme says, her attention darting around. Like me, she's expecting whatever this thing is to suddenly appear.

"It's not getting stronger," I say. I keep my gaze away from the mesmerized crowd and in the direction of the stage. "We're just getting closer to it."

We reach the steps leading into the sunken dome. I barely keep from falling when the crowd lunges forward.

Bodies big and small shove me through the narrow opening, and down the first step. No one is checking tickets, the ushers appearing as taken by the music and the presence as the rest of the throng.

I'm squeezed between two large men, cursing when I realize I lost Shayna and Emme. My first thought is to move to the side and into a row, but everyone keeps bustling forward, piling into the front section and anxious to get close to the stage.

The guitarist playing stands near the corner, his fingers flying over the strings. He feels the music, and so do the rows of people raising and lowering their arms, bowing before him.

My guess is he's the one with mojo, the music he's playing a hypnotic melody, snagging those who hear him and refusing to let them go.

I play with the idea of zapping him. Not enough to kill him, just enough to stun him until we get a fix on what's going on. The crowd is oblivious and might not notice. But he's too far away and I can't be certain how those around me will react. It could snap them out of their fog, or harm them in some way and turn them violent.

The latter keeps me from acting, that, and because I can't be sure he's the man behind the magic.

Again, I stagger forward, the fans too eager to care who they trample.

The next person who pushes against me is more aggressive. This time, I don't keep my feet. I fall into the woman in front of me, rushing to stand when the lights go out and the music abruptly cuts off.

Darkness stretches across the arena, and good God, do I feel alone. I can't see anything. All I feel is the mound of bodies closing in, keeping me immobile and making it hard to breathe.

Panic sets in the longer I'm blinded. I tug the cuff of my glove, hoping Sparky will light up and give me a fighting chance. Except no one is fighting, or yelling, or moving.

No. It's time for Johnny Fate to start the show.

The stage explodes with pyrotechnics, reenergizing the crowd as the larger than life Johnny Fate takes center stage. "Santa Barbara," he yells. "Do you crave Champagne and Guts?"

Everyone shrieks at the top of their lungs, banging their heads as the bass guitarists and lead drummer rev up the music, morphing it from a staccato of loud obnoxious noise to a mash-up of classic metal mania and garage band awesomeness.

Johnny Fate's image takes up every super-screen. Some images show just his face, others his full frame. I've never seen him, and didn't bother to look up anything about him. Maybe I should have. Maybe, it would have prepared me for what I see.

His bleached blond hair is cut short all around except on top where a mop of long strands drape to one side, resting against his sweaty cheeks. To my right, I see all of him, his entire upper body a working canvas of tattoos. The only visible part unmarked with ink is his face, the exception being the three blacked-in tears cascading from his right eye.

His arms stretch out, parting the sides of his fringed leather vest and exposing a tattoo of a green serpent devouring a bleeding heart. Across his flat stomach is a mural of his bandmates, their black and white faces inked into a large and eerie image of a full moon.

The tats are powerful, dark, and violent. They don't quite fit someone who is on the small side, and whose bandmates tower over him like overinflated gym rats.

Black leather pants hug what looks like muscle developed just enough to add definition to Johnny's slender legs. He's cute, and I can see why some young, impressionable women would fall for him, but not older women, or even men—especially in this crowd. If the majority were on parole or on probation, it wouldn't shock me. Their response to him does.

I zero in on his arm sleeve tats. One looks straight out of Tolkien's Mordor, desolate darkness without hope. His opposite arm is all jungle, hidden predators lurking in the shadows and behind wide jumbling leaves. I zero in on what might be a rhino, a wolf or two, and a couple of boars.

"This doesn't make sense," I find myself saying. The music is good, bordering on great. Except it's not the rage-filled kind I expect this group of people to fall for. There's a heart rendering melody to it, I feel each tug and pull, like I would my own sadness.

"That's him?" Shayna says.

I didn't see her muscle her way through, she's just there, Emme clutched close to her side. Good, I'm glad she has her. Regardless of her power, Emme's small stature makes her vulnerable in this mad horde.

"T, he is so *not* what I expected," Shayna yells over the music.

Like me, Shayna probably can't get past how young he seems. He can't be older than me, but he's trying to be, embracing a persona that appears forced.

Strip away the overload of ink running along his neck, arms, and torso, and he resembles a softer, slighter version of Justin Bieber, rather than the heavy metal rocker the audience can't get enough of.

The opening melody seems to take forever. Like the Meatloaf songs of years ago, each note is designed to tell a story long before the lyrics unfold. But when Johnny's hands wrap around the mic and he leans in close, and his first words spill across the arena, the energy erupts, detonating in an atom bomb of power.

Unlike the lead singers who took the stage before him, Johnny doesn't screech. He *sings*, beautifully, his emotion and agony stopping everyone in place.

"Your love was meant to heal me.
Your words were meant to cure.
Your arms were destined to embrace me.
You were supposed to leave me pure.
Instead you looked away and sighed.
Leaving me to weep. Leaving me to die."

Every word is like a dagger, stabbing me through the heart, his voice as commanding as Chad Kroeger and his words as poignant as Eminem's, telling a story of a life filled with torment and sorrow.

A few people beside us fall to their knees, clutching their chests and openly weeping.

This is only the first song and their response to his music is not what I expected. No, Johnny, isn't what I expected.

Something in me clicks in a way I don't want it to, sending the urgency I'm feeling out of control. "We have to get to Destiny." I rush forward, pushing people out of my way as I make my way closer to the stage. "We have to get her out of here now!"

"T. *T*, what's wrong?"

I can't explain to Shayna what I don't understand myself. Johnny is different, even more so than Destiny. It's a bad thing, I think. No, not think, *know*.

It's as if a grenade has rolled to a stop at my feet with its pin missing. I don't wait for it to explode. I move fast, desperate to spare us from the blast.

I think Emme and Shayna follow. At least I hope they do. I don't stop to look, dodging around the bodies too large to push through.

The music blares, each beat matching the painful thuds of my heart, and each syllable flowing through Johnny's lips, pulling out memories better left forgotten.

I reach the arena floor when my phone vibrates in my back pocket. I only answer it because I think it's Shayna or Emme.

Gemini's face flash across the screen. "What's happening?" he growls. "I can feel your torment."

"I don't know," I say through my teeth. I'm not a hysterical woman. It's not a luxury I can afford if I want to stay alive. I'm hysterical now, the raw feelings poking through making it hard to stay calm.

"I need you here, okay?" My already fast breaths quicken. "Please come, love. I need you."

"Taran, *Jesus*."

Like me, he probably can't believe I'm this much of a mess, begging him for help. I should get a hold of myself. He's not here and all I'm doing is further stressing him and his beasts.

"Are you hurt?" he asks, trying to make sense of why I'm so upset. "Did someone hurt you or the others?"

"No. We're not hurt—something isn't right," I say. "There's magic, lots of it. I don't know what kind it is. But it's affecting us and everyone around here."

It's as much as I manage. "We're in route," he tells me. "Stay alive, you hear me?"

I nod, although he can't see me, my nervousness propelling me forward and to the first row of seats. My foot hits something hard. I'm not sure what it is, my gaze unnaturally fixed on Johnny as he sings, every deep emotion I've ever felt dripping like honey with each of his lyrics.

The stage, the people, everything falls away, leaving me in a world filled with blinding white light.

Quiet greets me, loud in a way and eerily still, erasing the panic engulfing me seconds ago.

At first, I think I'm dead, and somehow made my way into heaven. But then hell arrives, knocking me hard in the head and reminding me of my sins.

Skulls litter the desolate and burning ground, their charred remains smeared with blue and white ash. Some are human. One is of a beast. There's no life around me, nothing but smoke and what remains of my fire.

It's then I know that I'm in neither heaven nor hell. I'm in the future, my vision forming from stress or panic, or simply the need to fuck with me.

I fall to my knees from the gruesome sight, lifting the skull of the beast at my feet. It's feline, a tiger. Just like my sister.

A sob cuts through my throat as I clutch it to me, its weight unbearably heavy and too much to hold.

I startle awake from my position on the concert floor, Destiny's bleeding body tight in my arms.

Chapter Ten

"Omigod."

My words jumble, my mind trying to take in everything at once. Destiny is convulsing in my arms, blood pooling from her mouth and seeping from her eyes.

Before all this shit, I was a nurse, and thank God. My ingrained training pushes past my shock and forces me to act.

I flip Destiny onto her side, keeping her from choking. "I've got you," I tell her. "You hear me? I have you, just stay with me."

Truth is, I don't have anything. There's a forest of people circled around us. No one sees me, and for certain no one sees Destiny or the blood pooling around her.

"I need help," I yell. "I need a medic here now."

The audience members continue to sway, failing to respond to anything but Johnny. I reach out, grasping the man closest to the stage by the leg. A familiar buzz builds from my core, sending a current of lightning shooting across my arm and into the man.

It's stronger than I intend, making him jump. He slumps forward, gripping the stage to keep from pitching forward. He looks at me, his dazed expression dissolving as his stare falls on Destiny.

"Get help," I yell, when he doesn't move. "This woman is injured."

He backs away. "Holy shit," he says, scanning the area for someone to call.

His mouth opens wide, his stomach tightening as if ready to holler, only for him to become alarmingly still. As I watch, his fear and shock dissolve into confusion. "Get help," I say again. "Are you listening, she needs a doctor!"

His attention flickers to me and then back to the stage where it stays.

"God *damn it*." I say, almost leaping out of my skin when I see Shayna.

She shoves her way through the crowd, pulling Emme behind her. They fall to their knees on either side of me.

Emme's *force* shoves those drawing closer away from us, expanding the small space around Destiny. "What happened to her?" she asks.

"I don't know," I say, trying to push through the images of the skulls flooding my mind. I swipe at my eyes, anxious to forget what I saw. "We have to get her out of here."

"She's seizing," Emme says as if I don't already know. "We can't move her like this." Her small hands slip over Destiny's paling skin, her soft yellow light encasing Destiny all at once.

Emme shakes her head. "I can't stop it," she admits, her voice panicked. "None of her systems are working correctly."

"What's that supposed to mean?" Shayna asks, shoving a woman away who almost steps on Emme.

Emme keeps her eyes closed, the yellow light surrounding her intensifying. "Her heart, her brain function, everything is off."

"Then heal her wounds and let's get her out of here," I urge.

Emme shakes her head and opens her eyes, her expression grave. "There's nothing to heal," she tells us. "There aren't any wounds. It's her body, it's just shutting down."

"*Why?*" I ask.

No sooner do I get the word out than my attention trails to the stage.

Johnny's voice fades, ceasing to sing in the middle of his next verse. The stacked bodies part, everyone appearing confused as to why their legend would simply stop and deprive them of his glory.

But it's the look of horror on his face when he sees Destiny that keeps me from moving. He sees what's happening, except instead of rushing to help, or calling help for her, he backs away in fear.

Fear of Destiny.

I rise slowly. "Get her out of here," I say, my anger punching each syllable. "He's the one making her bleed."

"T . . ." Shayna lifts her arm over her head, the sword she converted elongating in length and sharpening, and the stage lights gleaming against the length. "You can't go after him alone."

Johnny fixes on Shayna's sword, stunned by her ability.

His shock doesn't last. He jumps when he catches my livid expression. "Emme, do you have her?" I ask.

She knows it's up to her to get Destiny to safety. "Yes."

"Good," I say, striking the first person blocking me with lighting.

Johnny drops the mic, backing away and stumbling over the long cables. I storm forward, zapping anyone with lightning who doesn't move out of my way.

"What the fuck?" someone yells.

"Johnny," a woman screams. "Don't leave us."

A chorus of pleas for Johnny to sing rings out, taking over the entire dome, only to turn into screaming when he reaches the rear of the stage and the curtains come crashing down.

Shayna races ahead of me, the inner beastie Koda fed her spirit with making her fast, and that long sword of hers easily parting the crowd when they see it.

Without breaking her stride she leaps onto the stage, her wrist twirling the blade and her steady focus ahead.

An immense security guard runs out from behind the curtain, lifting the mic stand and gripping it fiercely in his wrist. "I'm warning you, lady. You better put that shit away."

Shayna's sword cuts through the air with a *swoosh*, slicing the stand in half and splitting the guard's T-shirt. He glimpses from his exposed chest back at her.

"Dude, that's me telling you to run," she bites out.

He does, but his buddy who thinks Shayna is joke pounds across the floor, racing toward her "Get off the stage now—"

My lightning propels him to the opposite end and straight into more clamoring security guards. The lights and pyrotechnics continue to erupt, illuminating our blatant show of kickass and hopefully disguising it as part of the show.

Shayna pivots, her sword out and away from me as she offers me a hand. "We have to move, T," she tells me, hauling me up.

My attention darts briefly to Emme. She's pushing her way along the side row, using her *force* to carry Destiny as she continues to seize.

"She's not better," Shayna says, reaching for a handful of toothpicks and converting them into long sharp needles. "Whatever magic he's using is no joke."

"I know," I mutter, wondering exactly what he is. "Just stay close. I don't think we can fight him one on one."

We stomp across the stage, ignoring the murmuring spreading along the crowd. Everyone appears confused yet the all-encompassing vibe circling the atmosphere is abandonment. They're lost without Johnny.

Whatever he's doing not only effects Destiny, it infects anyone within his reach. As it is, I still sense that lingering sadness and panic he invoked.

"What the fuck?"

What seems like the entire security team piles onto the stage. Shayna raises her sword and lunges at them, her battle cry resonating against the speakers as she charges.

They don't find her intimidating. The sword is another story. She attacks them in a circle of movement, slicing lines across their bodies and grazing their skin just enough to get their attention.

They may not fear her, but they do fear what she can do with her sword.

I reach the curtain, my body slapping against it as I try to find the opening. About a half dozen swears fly out of my mouth as I fumble down the length, wondering how I missed the divide within the fabric.

The mutterings across the arena grow more intense as does my urgency to find Johnny. They're ready to riot, their need for Johnny piquing their violent natures. Magic or not, this crowd is dangerous, people are bound to get hurt, including us.

The curtains are heavy, the multiple layers overlap making them hard to lift. I'm ready to crawl underneath them when Shayna appears.

"Move, dude," she tells me, swinging her sword.

One, two. She parts the curtains with precise and elegant cuts. I whip off my gloves as we scramble through. Almost immediately, my right arm assumes that eerie glow, casting some light in the pitch-black surroundings, but not enough to prevent me from ramming into a wall.

Sparky lights up, the glow vibrant and showing that it's not a wall I collided against. It's more like I mountain of steroid injected muscle. I look up, past the curly chest hair and nips pierced with silver bars to meet the bass guitarist looming over me in the face.

The hair of his long mohawk skims across my forehead as he curls forward. "You don't belong back here," he tells me, his dull irises laced with menace. "You need to leave our Johnny alone."

I lift my right arm. I don't know this guy. I don't even know Johnny. What I do know is Johnny is doing something to Destiny and he's not getting away with it.

"Get out of my way," I tell him, my arm flaring in awesome swirls of blue and white flames. *"Now."*

Unfortunately, my buddy here isn't as impressed by my pretty fire as I am. He grabs Sparky, his beefy hand crunching through my power and extinguishing the flames. The sheer might he uses forces me down, my knees slamming hard against the floor and making me scream.

Pain and anger trigger my magic, resurging the dwindling embers encasing my skin and combusting it into a raging and burning limb. The guitarist holds tight, not even blinking as my fire burns through his flesh and bone. His arm crumbles off in a kaleidoscope of colors, and still he just stands there.

Behind me, another man screams and Shayna's sword flings away, her vicious strikes cutting the air and creating a high-pitched torrent of sound. I don't dare turn away, my full attention on the guitarist and the creature he becomes. He shakes his head from side to side, his features contorting and morphing into a wolf while the rest of him stands as man.

I wrench away. "What the hell?" I gasp.

Wolves, *real werewolves*, can't change their individual body parts. Only Celia can. Whatever this thing is, is unlike anything I've ever seen.

As quickly as I speak he snags my arm, once more piercing through my magic and puttering out my fire. He hoists me high in the air, his hot breath fanning across my face when he snarls.

I'm thrown toward the front of the stage, the weight of my body smacking against the dense fabric, sliding me along the length and beneath. The barrier it provides keeps me from a direct collision course into the audience, and likely spares my life. That doesn't mean it doesn't hurt like a mother when I crash against the stage floor.

I land on my right arm, the way it curls around me protecting my head. I'm not sure if it was my instinct to do so, or if it was my arm's. Right now, I don't care. I force myself up, grunting as pins and needles radiate down my leg and spine. I stumble forward, my thoughts a scrambled mess as I try to make sense of what's happening. The guitarist isn't human. Neither is Johnny, his unparalleled virtue transmitting across the air like deadly vapor.

My hip throbs as I limp forward. Something rubbery hits me in the head. I turn around only to see what looks like a hamburger patty lying just a few feet away. Something else belts me in the arm.

"What the hell?"

The audience is pelting me with food. *Food.* Ever have a hotdog flung full force against your bare skin? That shit hurts.

I hurry to the side, swearing when slices of pizza, churros, and full cups of beer follow more hotdogs. Johnny's fans are completely coming undone. Yet it's the collection of growls erupting backstage that propel me faster.

What might be a drumstick nails me in the shoulder before I finish squeezing through the small opening. "Christ," I mutter, racing forward only to grind to a halt when I see what's become of Johnny's band.

The guitarist stands idly in front of me, watching the pack of werewolves circling Shayna, even as his body crumples in pieces, disintegrating like a paper mache rainbow.

"You're not biting me," Shayna tells them, her stare intent. "Uh-uh. You only think you are, wolfies."

I lurch forward, my hands out and trembling from the raw energy singeing through my veins. But then something snakes around my ankles, tripping me and wrapping around my form as I fall.

It's not until a long forked tongue flicks my chin that I realize it's an actual snake.

His head shifts from side to side, the markings along his scales appearing painted on. He doesn't bother looking at me, fascinated it seems by the altercation across from of us.

Tattered pieces of clothing lie in piles along the floor, pushed aside by massive paws the size of my head. The wolves narrow the perimeter they formed around Shayna, their movements awkward and stiff, not fluid like real wolves. These aren't normal supernatural beasts. This is whatever Johnny's band was.

I attempt to roll, but the snake constricts, warning me I should stay in place and tightening further when I try to call forth my flame in a rush.

I don't dare move, not yet, not when this snake can squeeze the life out of me. Instead I slowly build a spark deep within me, nourishing it within my core to detonate when the moment is right.

As far as I can tell, there are four wolves, and several other creatures lurking nearby. I can feel them, just as much as I feel this snake coiled around me. But it's Johnny I feel the most, the divination he creates surrounding us and invigorating those determined to protect him.

"Don't move, T," Shayna calls to me. "It won't hurt you unless you threaten it."

"What about you?" I ask, hoping she's right.

"I've already did something threatening."

Which means she's in more danger than me. I take a few breaths, building upon the torch expanding inside me, not enough for the snake to notice, I hope, just enough to expand my power.

Shayna's penetrating blue eyes remain on her targets. "These aren't normal *weres*," she says. "And Johnny is worse than we thought. The moment you're free, find him. All the help I need is on his way."

I know who she means. Koda's howl blasts as loud as a rumbling storm, gathering momentum and speed as he closes in. He's not far, nor alone, my bond with Gemini alerting me he's also near and *really pissed*.

The hilt of Shayna's sword elongates and thins out, forming another deadly blade. She spins, twirling her wrists, slicing the snout of one wolf and stabbing the one who lunges in the eye. Her sinfully quick reflexes force the others who try to advance back, just as Johnny's magic starts to pull away.

He's abandoned his hiding spot and moving fast.

Shayna feels his abrupt retreat. "You have to go, T," she says, whirling her sword as she pivots away, creating more space between her and her attackers. "Can't lose the bad guy now."

She's right, and like a flick of a lighter, I release my fire.

I expect the snake to jerk in agony. But he just looks at his crackling skin, watching it break away in colorful chunks when he tries to constrict.

A man cries out in pain behind the stage. I think it's Johnny. I just can't understand why he's hurting.

The moment I'm free, I roll, away from the lingering flame and to my feet. My right arm extends out, shooting a long ray of lightning into a leaping wolf. He hits the giant flat screen as I swirl around and finish off the guitarist gunning for me.

Another wolf attacks Shayna, materializing from the deep shadows along the dark stage. I don't know how many there are, I just know we have to keep fighting. These creatures are deadly, yet nothing close to mortal.

Instead of burning in my fire, or bleeding from Shayna's strikes, the wolves simply stop being. They fall in shuddering, helpless heaps, breaking apart in colorful ash that floats into the air and drifts idly away. As much as they seem to hurt, none howl or bleat in agony, unlike those terrible cries resonating in the distant.

I lash out, the wolf who charges zipping out of the way so I only manage to torch his paw. His snarls cease and he stops moving, watching with curiosity as my fire eats away at his leg.

These aren't real beings. They're not real anythings.

The shimmer of their fur gives them a slight, animated look, if it weren't for the force the guitarist used against me, and the way the snake coiled around my body, I could have easily mistaken them for visions.

"Shayna," I say, edging closer when I sense more creatures lurking in the shadows. There are too many. We need to get the hell out of here."

"Uh-uh," she says, fear and determination warring in her features. "You need to get out and find Johnny."

The wolves growl at the mention of Johnny's name. "I mean it, T, this guy is bad news."

The urgency in her tone scares me. She's afraid of what Johnny is and what he can do. Shit. So am I.

Another menacing howl, this one closer and more familiar, calls near the entrance to the arena. Koda is almost here. This is my chance to find Johnny.

I back away, in the direction I felt him vanish. But as inhuman as his protectors are, they're not blind or stupid.

The wolf targeting Shayna abandons her to trail me closely, his fangs peeling back and exposing a row of razor sharp teeth.

"Easy boy," I tell him, keeping my firing arm out. As much as I'm willing to defend myself, something about them makes it hard to attack. There's a misery that surrounds them, as gut-wrenching as the lyrics in Johnny's song. Yet while I pity them to some extent, that pity isn't mutual.

Without warning they attack, the wolf shadowing me thrusting his large body forward and clamping down on my arm.

My screams are inaudible over the deafening sound of cracking bone. The wolf who has me digs his fangs deep, the needle-length tips puncturing through the muscle and into the marrow.

I retaliate with a vengeance, and so does my arm, using our collective rage to fuel my fire. Blue and white flame reflect along the wolf's dark eyes. There's no fear, no soul, simply a mindless determination to stop me at all costs.

My fire intensifies, the pain I'm feeling receding as the flames eat through the wolf's snout, breaking his face apart in a spray of bright color. Sweat cascades down my spine like rainfall from the singeing cocoon of energy my small frame has become, it consumes him, tearing him apart. And still there he stands. No pain. No regret. Nothing that constitutes thoughts beyond the need to protect.

The impact of his demise is like an atom bomb of paint, casting multi-colored rays of light across the battleground the stage has become. A wolf speeds toward Shayna. She spins out of the way, moving with a dancer's grace and burying her sword into his neck.

A hard grunt escapes her mouth from the strength she uses. I expect the usual, a head rolling away, a heavy body slumping. But that's not what comes.

She digs her heel in and yanks hard, trying to free her sword when it doesn't finish breaking through. I rush toward her when another wolf closes in, only to be intercepted by another round of beasts.

Two boars with large tusks snort in challenge while the rhino behind them pushes his way between them.

My heart all but bursts when Shayna's needles fly through the air and *our* wolves appear.

Koda's large red body collides into the two boars now littered with needles, thrusting them away from us as they turn on him. She crawls away, scanning the demolished area for a new weapon to transform.

Gemini's twin wolf leaps across the stage, his midnight color fur making him almost invisible in the bleakness. I barely catch sight of him, his speed and heavy build ramming the rhino charging toward me.

Strong arms wrench me out of the way, the familiar hold keeping me from reacting. Gemini pins me to the far back wall, using his body like armor to encase me. "What happened to you?" he says. "Jesus, you're covered with bruises."

"Johnny Fate is some kind of mystic. He hurt Destiny—"

"She's safe." He drags me down the stage and further away from the fight. "Bren and Tye have her and Emme."

He whips around when the rhino tosses his twin across the floor, racing away from me and tackling the large beast.

"Taran, you have to go," Shayna urges, sharpening a symbol from the drum set and transforming it into a medieval axe. "We've got this, get Johnny."

I stagger backward, the increasing screams from the arena helping me gather my resolve. I shoot back stage and down the steps, shoving past a group of scantily-clad women scrambling to escape. I manage to find an exit door when I hear something behind me.

One of the boars, covered with needles and trembling wobbles toward me. He shouldn't be dying, not like this. But here he is, his body disintegrating into a pool of vivid colors.

"Son of bitch," I mutter, throwing open the door and taking off in a sprint.

My heels beat against the cement steps leading up to the rear of the arena. I made it outside, but I don't know where I'm going, and can't predict what may attack next.

People are running everywhere, some wearing headsets, appearing to be part of the crew, others members of the audience, searching for somewhere to hide or flee. I can't imagine what they've seen. Personally, I've seen enough. That doesn't stop me from racing forward, my body alert and seeking that pull from Johnny's magic.

I reach a gated parking lot, my gaze immediately latching onto Johnny's tour bus. A larger than life image of him sprawled across a bed is painted on the side. A crumpled white sheet is the only thing covering his waist and he's making one of those pouty faces that's supposed to be sexy. It doesn't seem right, neither does the image, too sensual for someone who could easily pass for a teen.

The bus's engine is running, the driver's head jerking in every direction as he barks into his radio. I don't bother to raid it or speak to the driver. If Johnny was inside, he'd already be gone.

I walk toward the other cars parked along the lot, trying to get a hit on Johnny's mojo. It's not until I pass a black Lincoln Town car that the tiny hairs along my arm tingle and I get a taste of Johnny's pull.

It's not a lot, just enough. I look toward my left where it's fading, down a beaten path leading to a section of woods.

Damn it. I hate the woods. Nothing good besides Bambi has ever come out of that shit.

I crack my knuckles and lift my hands slightly away from my sides, stalking forward and preparing for anything that could attack. The tension consuming every nerve cell along my body surges with every step I take, adding an extra layer of pain to my throbbing injuries.

The woods, thankfully, aren't very thick, nor are they too far from the highway. I can hear the honking horns and thrumming engines just ahead and to my right. It only takes a few yards for the trees to break and the path to open into a field of dry grass and the spindly weeds thriving beneath scattered rows of discarded plastic cups and crushed beer cans.

Cigarette buds are also a dime a dozen, littering the

ground in front of me, and I have to step over what resembles a broken crack pipe just as the ramp leading into the arena comes into view. Awesome, if Johnny doesn't kill me some amped up addict just might try.

My focus sharpens as Johnny's magic sends my instincts on high alert.

I hear him, long before I see him, hunkering by a large stone and speaking fast.

"I don't know," he says, his voice shaking. "Just get me out of here . . . they took out my band— What? . . . These girls, Drake—No, not groupies—women. Super women or some shit. They took out my band. They're dead. They're Goddamn dead."

His skin is bleached white and dripping with sweat, his tenor voice shrill. "Please, Drake. I know what I said. I'll keep going . . . I swear, I will— Yes, another two years, whatever you want just get me out of here."

Being positively stealth in these shoes, I crunch an old beer can partially buried in the soil.

He whips around, almost dropping his phone when he sees me. "You," he rasps.

I don't know what I expected to see in Johnny. Some defiance, yes. It's what I'm used to. Anger too, it comes with the territory. I don't expect fear, loads of it. But that's exactly what Johnny Fate hits me with.

Like I said, he looks young. But fear makes you either age before your time or leeches your strength, reducing you to a delicate shell close to cracking.

I'll give him this, Johnny does fragile well, his trembling form reminiscent of a lost, wounded bunny who can't find his way home.

I hold out my hands, ready to defend myself or lash out if he strikes. Except all he does is stand there, paralyzed with fear, his body quivering out of control.

"I need you to come with me," I tell him gently.

He takes off like a rocket, a great deal faster than I can run.

"Johnny, wait," I yell.

"Eat shit," the wounded bunny answers.

All right, can't exactly fault him for that one.

I chase him across the field of withering grass, garbage, and varying degrees of drug paraphernalia. With the amount of concerts the arena has hosted, the field has seen better days and more crackheads than a hundred city blocks. I don't want to step on a syringe, in fact, I'm terrified of it. But I'm more scared of what Johnny will do if I allow him to escape.

My legs propel me forward, the muscles of my thighs, burning with how hard I'm running. With the exception of Emme, anyone else on Team Taran would have caught him by now and shred him to confetti. As it is, I'm barely keeping him in my sight.

"Johnny, I'm not going to hurt you!"

It's an absurd thing to say, and I mean every damn word. Johnny isn't a predator. He neither hunts nor stalks, outwardly fleeing and absolutely terrified.

He peels off his leather vest, exposing blotches of reddened skin lining his back. I'm not sure what they are or what he's doing until another creature leaps from his back, enlarging in size and falling with a crash directly in front of me.

I stop dead. The way this thing materialized is almost identical to the way Gemini's twin wolf separates from his human half. Except where Gemini's ability is more of a smooth, liquid motion, Johnny's is abrupt, a missile fired in retaliation and aimed right at me.

I don't move, more dumbfounded than afraid as I take in this massive new threat. It's unlike anything I've ever seen, his build at least seven feet in height and his musculature reminiscent of comic book hero, supersized and overly done.

His head is that of a ram, his legs, too, the hooves stomping aggressively in challenge. But his torso and arms are human, stretching out and bulging as they wait for me to act.

He's making it clear I have to get past him to get to Johnny. But he's not attacking. Like the wolves on the stage, he's *protecting*.

"Johnny," I yell. "You don't want to do this."

"Fuck off," he yells back.

The creature hunkers down, digging his hooved foot into the soil and kicking back the dirt and broken glass.

No more warnings. He's ready to charge. "I don't want to hurt you," I tell it.

Like the wolf who bit me, there's nothing human in him. His stare is void of emotion, almost robotic, and like a robot blindly following commands.

He snorts, his breath visible in the cool air.

I back away. "Stop," I tell it, my arms lighting up in a spray of sparks. "I *don't* want to hurt you."

His head jerks to the side, charging past me.

The force he uses spins me and forces me off balance. I regain my balance in time to see him collide into Gemini.

"No!"

Gemini's human form is dragged across the field, his hands gripping the ram's horns.

The ram plants his hands into the battered soil, using them like paws to thrust him across. Gemini, steels himself, digging in his feet and driving the ram's head to the side, trying to snap its neck.

I don't stand there, I can't. My hand jerks out, the buzzing sensation making it tremble and sending a stream of lightning into the ram's hide.

Johnny's pained scream from behind me has me turning around, he's sprawled on his chest, kicking his feet.

My attention returns to Gemini at the sound of his pained grunts. He has the ram's back, his legs wrapped around his torso in a figure four leg lock. The strong muscles of his arms bulge as he readjusts his grasp over the ram's horns and yanks his neck to the side.

It's only because I know Gemini is okay that I take off after Johnny when he flees into the darkness.

The lights along the highway are the only reason I can see as much as I do. It doesn't take me long to find him.

All I have to do is follow his cries.

Near a mound of withering grass, and close to a smaller

patch of woods, I find the rock star, curled in a ball. Broken brown and green glass litter the ground surrounding him, and what looks like a discarded sneaker, digs into his back.

Less than a mile away, a line of cars battle it out to exit the arena. He almost made it.

Almost.

I walk slowly to him, noting how his skin is an awful shade of gray. Patches of raw skin paint his back, arm, and neck. If I didn't know what happened, and if I wasn't standing directly over him, I would have mistaken them for port wine stains.

As I watch, his spine arches and his head turns in an unnatural direction, his neck snapping with a sick crunch.

"Shit," I say, leaping away.

He rolls onto his back, his eyes wild. "Don't come any closer," he warns through his teeth.

I don't move, observing him carefully and coming to terms with what happened. My gaze moves to his stomach, the definition in his abs brutally disrupted by more patches of raw skin where the inked in images of his bandmates once lay.

Okay. His tattoos come alive. I get it. What I don't get is *how*.

"Stay away from me," he says. He tries to sit up, his chin jerking behind me when someone else approaches.

I don't have to turn around to know it's Gemini, and I won't turn my back on Johnny this time.

Johnny tries to crab-crawl away, the heels of his palms pressing into the glass strewn along the ground. He winces as the shards cut into his skin. But he's badly hurt and barely able to move.

Gemini prowls forward, his animalistic gaze aimed at Johnny.

"Babe, don't," I tell him. My fingers skim lightly over his spine. It doesn't seem like much, but for the moment, it's enough to keep my wolf in place.

Sparks of lightning zing from my fingers when I crack them. "I have him," I assure him.

Johnny's focus darts from Gemini to me. "What the fuck are you?" he asks.

The unearthly growl Gemini releases cements Johnny in place. "The better question is, what the *fuck* are you?"

Johnny opens and closes his mouth, his chest rising and falling as he struggles to speak. I angle my chin to look at Gemini. "You don't know?" I ask. I was certain he would.

He shakes his head. "I smell witch, but witches can't conjure whatever the hell I just killed."

"It was a tattoo," I explain. "His tattoo. The rhino, the wolves, they were all inked into his skin."

"*What*?" Gemini asks.

I point to Johnny's wounds. "I didn't cause those injuries," I say. "None of us touched him. When he went on stage, he was covered with tats. Now all that's left is damaged tissue."

Gemini charges forward, lifting Johnny by the throat and taking a sniff. Johnny flails his arms, his gray skin turning blue.

"Gem, stop it."

He drops Johnny like trash before I can intervene.

Gemini is the reasonable one—the one with the cool head which is why Aric chose him as his second in command. Except he's not so cool when I'm in danger, his beast side accelerating his aggression.

I'm certain he crushed Johnny's larynx, but thankfully Johnny is still breathing, his skin morphing back to gray.

I frown, noting how quickly the color begins to improve. He's still in bad shape, and unbelievably pale, but he is healing.

"He didn't try to hurt me," I say, speaking softly to ease Gem's anger and soothe Johnny's fear. "Not outwardly. If anything, I think he was just trying to defend himself."

My voice fades in the breeze as Gemini's features harden. "What is it?"

The cords along his throat tighten as he swallows hard. "He's a Fate, Taran." His eyes lock with mine. "The male version of Destiny."

Chapter Eleven

Gemini escorts Johnny back in the direction of the arena.

And when I say "escort" I mean he lifts him by the arm and drags his floundering feet across the ground.

"If you try to run, or use your magic against us, I'll kill you," my beloved tells him, flatly.

Johnny rights himself, more or less stumbling forward. He laughs, kind of hysterically, bordering on psychopathic. "You're a werewolf, aren't you?"

His question is odd, as if he's not completely sure. He should be sure, being what he is.

Gemini picks up on as much. "That's right," he replies.

We wait for more of an explanation, not that it comes. You don't have to be a genius to figure out Johnny is terrified of Gemini.

"You've never seen a werewolf?" I ask, careful to keep my tone light.

His attention trails to me. "Sure. Plenty of times. They just don't see me. Right, big guy?"

Gemini's deep growl has Johnny shrinking inwardly. Again Johnny looks my way, this time for help.

"Don't taunt the big bad wolf," I warn. "Unless you want

to be eaten."

I don't realize how far we ran until I see the bright arena lights in the distance, barely visible in the ink black night. I stumble over a rock, swearing when it hits the open toe of my tall shoes.

"Are you all right?" Gemini asks, beating back what very much resembles a smile.

He watched me pack and questioned why platforms are my go-to for guard duty.

"Sneakers are more practical," he said. "In case you have to run."

"Sneakers don't go with my cute clothes, and they can't stake a vampire."

He crossed his arms. "When was the last time you staked a vampire with a shoe?" He thought about it. "When was the last time you staked a vampire ever?"

I didn't have a good comeback then, and I don't have one now. Right or not, I'll never admit my choice in footwear was damn stupid, especially with that smirk he's currently wearing.

"I asked you if you're okay?" he reminds me.

"Fine, baby," I tell him. "Why wouldn't I be?"

"Because you wore those ridiculous shoes instead of practical sneakers," he mutters.

"I'll remember that next time."

"Next time your life is in jeopardy?" he asks, growing annoyed.

There's no point in arguing that my life wasn't in grave peril, seeing how it damn well was. Instead, I shift the conversation back to Johnny where it belongs. "What did you mean by wolves can't see you?" I ask Johnny.

Gemini answers when Johnny clams up. "It means if we passed him on the street, we'd mistake him for a warlock since he only smells of witch magic."

"So what's the big deal if he is a Fate?" I ask. "It's all shits and giggles having Destiny."

Based on the bitterness claiming Johnny's boyish features, and the way he averts his gaze, I asked the million-dollar question.

Gemini's rigid stance alerts me that it's not good news. "Destinies are rare," he says.

"Right, a gifted female born of two witches, once every century," I say, articulating what every supernatural knows as I wonder where he's headed.

"Fates are even rarer," he replies. "There's only been five documented in history."

"Now you have lucky number six," Johnny says, his voice absent of humor.

Gemini tightens his posture, pretty much the same way he does right before he takes a swing. "What's the problem with having Fate and Destiny?" I ask, seeing there obviously is. "Aren't they the same thing?"

"They are, and they're not," Gemini replies, his expression darkening further. "They're not supposed to coexist. They *can't* actually, not in the same lifetime."

"Because they're anomalies?" I ask. That's my guess. But there's more, *obviously*.

"In part," he answers. "But it's what happens when they're together that's the real issue." He releases a harsh breath. "According to mystical beliefs, their powers brutally clash, interfering with the natural balance of the earth and triggering the start of unspoken evils.

I stumble to a halt. "Are you fucking kidding me right now?"

Gemini and Johnny stop in place, frowning. "I'm sorry," I say, holding out a hand. "But I'm sick to death of all this mystical shit. It's always something with you people."

"You people?" Gemini asks, cocking a brow.

I point. "That's right, *you people*. It's always doom, gloom, and destruction, *always*. Whether it's some prophecy saying we'll sprout six tails if we wear green on Wednesday during a full moon while watching Seinfeld or finding some messed up artifact that opens a portal to hell—and don't get me started on that damn singing knife you shouldn't insult or risk having it stab you in the ass while you sleep."

Gemini tries to shush me, I'm guessing about the knife. I

don't, enough is enough. "And now you're telling me the lead singer of some boy band with freak of nature skin is bringing on the apocalypse?"

"I never said anything about the apocalypse," Gemini says. He thinks about it, maintaining that same stoic tone. "At least not at the moment."

"And I'm not in a boy band," Johnny adds, getting pissy.

I ram my hands on my hips. "Oh, now you have something to say?"

He scowls at me, but then something he sees in me softens his brow.

"What are you?" he asks again. "You're not a witch or a beast." He huffs. "And I don't think you sprout fangs either."

"No." I smile. "But I have been known to bite."

Gemini works his jaw, trying not to grin. I've taken my fair nibbles of him. And with his primal side on edge, he remembers when and where.

I keep my voice easy, although by now all I want to do is go home and fall asleep in my lover's arms, comforted by his presence and knowing that I survived yet another hellish night.

What sucks is, that's not an option, and crawling into bed is a goal too far away to see.

We reach the small section of woods, the mounting darkness stimulating my arm to flick on like a night light and set the skin aglow.

Johnny's gaze takes it in, appearing as fascinated as a Star Wars nerd with a new light saber. "Cool," he says.

Damn. If I dropped him in the middle of any college campus, he'd fit right in. This is a kid who should be headed for class somewhere, or talking to his buddies about the next big keg party. This isn't someone who should hold the grand title of Fate. It's too much of a burden and more than someone this young should bear.

I look at Johnny, and the way my arm casts light against his youthful features. "What's going to happen to him?" I ask Gemini.

"That's up to the witches," he replies, his voice low.

Johnny bows his head, that same sense of defeatism claiming him as heavily as before.

I stiffen. "Wait . . . you're not going to kill him, are you?" Gemini doesn't answer me. "Are you?" I press, barely believing it.

"Whether he lives or dies is not my call. Nor is it the decision of the Pack," he replies. He continues forward, leading Johnny down the dark path and toward his impending doom. He stops when he realizes I'm not following. "Taran, we have to get him to the Elders so they may summon the witches."

"So *they* can kill him?" Un-freaking believable. "What do you think they'll do, babe? Burn him at the stake? Drown him? Nothing like a good public stoning, is there?"

He rubs his goatee, muttering a curse. "Ines who leads the French Coven, and Genevieve will decide what's best."

"Why?" I ask.

"Because he's one of them, and as head witches to the most powerful clans, they rule on behalf of their kind."

He takes me in the longer I stand there. "As part of the Alliance, the *weres* will be allowed a say," he adds, his way of attempting to placate me when I don't move.

When he says *weres*, he means the North American Were Council, in addition to Gemini's pack since he was the one who seized him.

"And how will you decide?" I ask.

My chest tightens as his features steel. "I will decide as I always do, in favor of our world, and for the greater good."

The traffic along the highway finally lifts, allowing the caravan of cars to speed up. Their engines roar, the drivers anxious to put space between them and the arena.

I remain still, refusing to move. "He's just a kid," I say to Gemini. "Not a shapeshifter, and not one of their twisted followers." I motion to Johnny. "Look at him, he's barely a man."

Gemini is the logical one, the one who's able to stay reasonable even when I'm losing my mind. For the most part, I welcome his sensibility, it keeps me sane after all. I don't welcome it now. Sometimes, it's not enough to use logic and reason. Sometimes, you need to follow your heart and allow it to guide you to do the right thing.

"He's not just a kid, Taran. He's a young being of power who will keep getting stronger in ways that could potentially destroy us."

"You're acting like he's a villain bent on taking over the world."

The look Gemini hits me with lodges the breath in my throat. "Is that what you think, that he's the new threat the Alliance has been worried about?"

"I don't know," he states, his intensity building with each word. "What I do know is what history has shown us, that when Fates and Destinies appear within the same lifetime, darkness rises and evil is reborn."

"This has to be the most blatant display of over-exaggeration I have ever heard," I insist, turning in Johnny's direction. "I mean, if we're all still alive, their presence can't be that bad, can it?"

"Actually, it can," he replies. "The most devastating earthquakes, cyclones, and tsunamis have been linked to the coexistence of Destinies and Fates. They've also been tied to the appearance of dark ones so savage and murderous, the world has come close to obliteration."

I stop moving. "So you're saying the natural disasters that have occurred over these last two decades, and all the unexplained evil nasties we've encountered are the result of Destiny and Johnny being born during the same century?"

"No."

I sigh. "Oh, good."

"I'm saying they're just the start." He lifts Johnny's arm, his effort minimal but enough to pull Johnny to the tips of his toes. "I can't be sure if he is the new evil we've been anticipating. But the power he possesses could be what feeds the evil and ultimately gives our enemies the upper hand."

"You're assuming he'll go all dark side or allow himself to be used," I point out. "That's not fair, the same could have been said about me and my sisters."

"You're different, and so are your sisters," Gemini snarls, giving Johnny a shake. "Don't allow your sympathy for him to blind you to what I'm saying. There's a reason the witches pass the Law of Death to Second Fates and Destines born."

"Come again?" I ask. "What the hell is the Law of Death to Second Fates or whatever?"

"I can tell you," Johnny says. He huffs, rolling his shoulder and rubbing it when Gemini sets him down. "You don't mind, do you, wolf? This is technically about me."

Gemini doesn't respond, especially when angry tears form across Johnny's eyes. "As per Witch Law, the Destiny or Fate who is born first is revered and takes her or his place among the supernatural royalty," he replies bitterly. "The one born after must be destroyed within the first year of life. Nice, huh?"

So his only mistake was being born. Damn.

"My parents were powerful witches. Did you know that?" he asks. "The way I hear it, among the most badass witches who ever were. They knew what I was when I was born. And because they knew, they ran." He paces in place. "I was raised in Canada, among humans."

"In hiding," I assume.

"No, out in the open," he replies, frowning. "They didn't know what I was, and they didn't care either."

"What happened to your parents?" Gemini asks, his tone even. He isn't as sympathetic to Johnny's situation, but he's always had a pack that's welcomed him.

Johnny rights himself, anger marching like an army of resentful soldiers across his features. "They left me to help fight your supernatural war," he says. "In case you're wondering, they didn't make it back."

Gemini inhales deep, taking a breath. Johnny is telling the truth, if he wasn't Gemini would call him out.

"How old were you?" I ask. "When you lost them?"

"Sixteen," he says.

I almost tell him I was half his age when I lost mine. But I don't know Johnny, and whether or not I can sympathize with him, my guard remains up.

"Sorry to hear that," Gemini tells him. "This way."

He secures Johnny's arm again, this time, using more care. I didn't have to mention my past, he knows it well, just as he knows that's where my thoughts are now. "Taran, we need to return," he says. "The others are waiting and the covens need to be informed of the Fate's presence."

His pace quickens when he senses me follow. I walk behind him with my arms crossed, lost in my memories and how close they mimic Johnny's past.

Johnny glances behind me. "I take it you two are a thing?"

Gemini scowls at him, his grip tightening. "I'm just asking, man," Johnny tells him. "I don't mean nothing by it."

"He's my mate," I say. I hurry to clasp Gemini's hand, affirming our relationship and slightly soothing my wolf's temper.

"But you're not human?" Johnny asks, his voice lowering at the sight of Gemini's nasty glare.

"Not exactly," I reply. "I'm different. Like you." I think about all the tats he brought to life. "Okay, maybe not like you."

The corner of his mouth lifts into a smile. That smile quickly fades away when Gemini snarls. "He's not doing anything," I say to Gemini.

"No, but he's thinking it," he replies. "I can scent his attraction to you."

I edge around him to speak to Johnny. "You never want to give a *were* the impression you're challenging him or threatening his relationship."

This time, Johnny makes quite the effort to keep his eyes off me. "Good to know," he mumbles. "Anything else I might need to know about them?"

"You really don't know anything?" I question.

"I know they don't like my music," he says, his grin returning.

"Which is how you've kept us from finding you," Gemini reasons. "Hire bands that make more noise than music so those like us with sensitive hearing move away from you rather than closer."

He adjusts his hold on my hand, steadying me as I ease through a stretch of harsh terrain. "Makes sense," I concur. "The opening bands were too much for me." I think about it. "Wait, I get how all that loud metal music would keep *weres* and anything with preternatural hearing away, but loud sounds don't affect witches the same way. If anything, they should have been attracted to and sensed your magic. Why not?"

Gemini grinds to a halt and whips Johnny in front of him when he tightens up. "My mate just asked you a question," he says. "I expect you to answer."

I don't like how aggressive Gemini is being with Johnny, and almost intervene. Except I don't want to challenge his beast's authority with prey in his hands, which is how my wolf sees Johnny. I also want to know what we're up against, and as much as I pity him, I can't be certain Johnny is on our side.

Not after the affect he had on Destiny.

"My crowd doesn't do organic," Johnny explains quickly when Gemini gives him a shake. "They're not into nature and they're not what you call granola."

Unlike the witches.

He shrugs free of Gem's hold when he loosens it. "I also don't release my music. It's concerts only."

"So you hide in the open, all the while preventing anything magical from knowing you're there," I reason.

He rubs his shoulder again. "Something like that," he says. He addresses Gemini, careful not to make direct eye contact. "Look, my people aren't going to just let me go. I'm under contract. They'll want to know where I am and who I'm with."

Gem steps forward, looming over him. "If there's anyone left, they'll be dealt with. I assure you, no one will stop us from taking you."

Johnny's face blanches. "Did you kill them?"

Gemini doesn't answer.

"What the fuck?" Johnny says. "They were just people, roadies. They weren't going to do anything to you, asshole."

I force myself between them. From one blink to the next, I'm suddenly off to the side. I barely felt Gemini graze his fingers over my hips when he lifted me, and only mildly felt my feet press to the ground. But here I am, back where I started.

"Tomo," I plead. "Don't hurt him."

Gemini shoves his face into Johnny's, forcing him back. "No human was hurt. Our job as Guardians of the Earth is to protect, not harm. That doesn't mean we'll allow them to harm us, or interfere with our duties. Tonight, those duties involve taking you back to our Den." His gaze turns to steel. "And if you ever insult me again, you'll be eating from a tube in your stomach."

Johnny rises to his full height, attempting to appear tough. But there's no stopping the quiver in his voice or his blanching skin from paling further. "Did you eat anyone?"

"I don't eat people," Gemini snaps, his patience wearing thin.

"Dudes!" Shayna races toward us, skipping to a halt when she sees Johnny and the mere centimeters separating him and Gemini. She lowers the ax she's carrying to the side. "Destiny isn't doing well," she says. "She stopped bleeding, but we need to get her back, like, now."

Behind her, Gemini's twin wolf pads forward. His hackles rise and his feral eyes latch onto Johnny. He growls low and deep, lowering his head as if ready to attack the moment he gets the word.

My knuckles skim down Gemini's spine. "If you allow your twin back inside you, will you be more pissed or will he help you calm?" His narrowing eyes tell me enough. I sigh. "We're not all going to fit."

"Fine," he says.

Like black paint streaming across water, Gemini's twin dissolves into his skin, becoming one all mighty being.

Johnny has had his share of surprises. A wolf, the size of a full-grown tiger merging with a man, was yet another he wasn't prepared for. He backs away, almost falling against the curb.

"Let's go," Gemini says.

Shayna leads us to the closed off parking lot where a helicopter is waiting. The tour bus is gone, so are the other cars parked in front of it. Johnny may have "people" except it doesn't appear they bothered to wait for him.

Bren and Emme stand a few feet from the copter doors, and even further away from each other. Even from here, I feel the invisible wall of emotion between them.

Destiny is sitting on the ground. The bun she fastened on the top of her head is unraveling and barely keeping her long hair away from her pale-as-death face. Her clothes are smeared with blood and she lost all the feathers she painstakingly threaded through her hair. It breaks my heart to find her like this, and while she's no longer seizing or bleeding, she's not in good shape.

"Did Emme manage to heal her?" I ask.

Shayna's ponytail swings from side to side as she shakes her head. "No. Emme says she couldn't. Whatever was happening just seemed to stop." She blows out a breath, fluttering her bangs. "Tye's hoping the witches can help her. He's already alerted the Pack and requested they *call* for Genevieve's return."

"And how is Tye doing?" I ask.

"Not good, T," she says, sounding sad. "Destiny is his best friend."

Yeah. She is.

Tye is crouched beside her, speaking quietly, his chin length blond hair swaying around his chiseled features. Worry tightens his brow, but here he is, doing his best to keep her calm.

He grins and says something that lights up her eyes. A soft smile plays across her face.

Until she sees Johnny.

Lightning crashes, shaking the earth. Shayna whirls around, her jaw falling open. "Was that you?" she asks.

"No, I—"

Another bolt of lightning illuminates the dark night, landing mere yards from where Destiny waits and rattling the earth.

Destiny screams in torment. She grips Tye's arm, her body convulsing in violent waves as dark fluid pours from her eyes.

"Oh, my God," I gasp.

Emme and Bren scramble to her side. I turn around to look at Johnny just in time to watch his eyes roll into the back of his head and his body collide against the ground.

Chapter Twelve

I open and close my right hand, my nervousness and fear agitating Sparky. She's ready to release the full gamut of her power. And if it was up to her, she would have already blown the helicopter we're in straight to hell.

But not before smacking us for being stupid enough to climb in.

My lips press tight as I shake out my hand. This rusty old copter is the last place my lightning and fire need to make an appearance. I need to think happy thoughts if we're going to survive, like lambs prancing along a daisy-covered field or some shit.

I rub my arm when she jerks again. Evidently Sparky wants to roast the lambs over a spit and jab me in the eyes with the damn daisies for even suggesting it.

The loud, non-stop thrum of the engine does nothing to settle me, neither does the disjointed beat of the propellers.

"We're going to die, aren't we?"

"No, Taran," Gemini replies.

"Would you tell me if we were?'"

"Yes," he says.

"Even if it was a brutal kind of death? With like, shattering bones and flying organs?"

He doesn't even blink. "Of course."

My face falls into my hands. Well, my man's honest. I'll give him that.

I take a breath, and then another, trying to settle my nerves, and maybe settle Sparky, too. She's twitching like a dog wagging its tail, standing by the door demanding out. Except dogs, to my knowledge, don't have the power to shoot flames when they pee.

I drop my hands. "How much longer?" I ask.

Bren leans forward from where he sits across from us, his forearms falling to rest against his knees. He rubs his hands together, his light blue irises giving away the alertness behind his stare regardless of the exhaustion ringing dark circles around the orbits. Having torn through his clothing when he *changed*, all he's wearing are sweatpants. Aside from his moppy brown waves and scraggly beard, his skin is entirely exposed, not that he seems to mind. "Ten minutes later than the last time you asked, kid," he answers.

"You can't be serious," I say, convinced time is somehow going backwards.

Gemini's large hand cups over mine. He and Bren have been so intent on watching Johnny, they've barely acknowledge me or Emme. "I know I may be asking the impossible," he begins. "But try and relax."

My stomach leaps into my throat when the helicopter jerks unexpectedly. This isn't the smooth ride we expected, the nice, modern, *safe* ride Tye was to effortlessly provide back to Tahoe. Oh, no. When lightning struck, the world literally moved, and Destiny tried to die, *again*, we thought it best to keep her and Johnny far away from each other.

Johnny groans from his position on the stretcher. I think the thick leather belts pinning him in place are hurting him, neither Gemini nor Bren used much care when strapping him in. But they didn't head my warning or Emme's. To them, Johnny is the enemy. The jury has delivered the verdict and the judges are toying with the idea of gnawing his arms off.

"We have to keep him secure," Gemini insisted. "I don't know what he's capable of and I don't want to find out midair."

I'll give him that one, but seeing Johnny like this is hard. Short of the creepy leather mask, the poor guy looks like a scrawny stand-in for Hannibal Lector in *Silence of the Lambs*. Then again Hannibal did end up peeling that poor sap's face off so who am I to complain?

I push the hair from my eyes, wishing this night would end.

Johnny fainted in Destiny's presence. I was sure he keeled over and died. Hell, Destiny came damn close. Shayna and I performed CPR while Emme attempted to heal her. Emme insisted there was nothing to heal, that her body was shutting down. It wasn't until Gemini threw Johnny over his shoulder and put some distance between him and Destiny that Emme managed to restart her heart.

Tye lost it, yanking her into his arms the moment she opened her eyes and carrying her into the helicopter. "You're either in or out," he growled at us. "But I won't take the Fate." His stare darkened. "And if he comes anywhere near her, I'll feed him his fucking heart."

He didn't give us time to decide. The rotor blades started immediately after he settled Destiny in the rear, leaving Gemini and Koda to figure out a way home.

My fingers dig into the seat as we bounce yet again. This was the best they could do, an old army helicopter belonging to a friend of Aric. And because our luck wasn't bad enough, that old friend was away on business and his wife didn't fly.

The helicopter dips again. My knuckles blanch. I startle when trickles of blue and white smoke drift into the air and the smell of melting plastic wafts into my nose.

"Taran, do *not* set us on fire," Bren tells me.

"I'm not doing this on purpose," I say, groaning when I see my fingerprints singed into the seat.

I rub my hands together, not sure we'll make it back to Squaw Valley before Sparky blows us out of the sky.

The helicopter jerks again, left, then right, and somehow

up.

My stomach twists into knots, I swear to God creating a bow. "How long has Koda had his license?" I ask. It doesn't seem like he took lessons very long.

"Not long enough," Bren mutters.

His intense gaze skips to where Emme is sitting quietly beside me, the severity behind it softening as he takes her in.

The army helicopter isn't one equipped to carry a large squadron into combat. If anything, it was probably used to transport supplies or possibly for surveillance. Each side is fixed with a row of five seats. The center is open and unobscured, and where the wolves placed Johnny. There's plenty of room given our small numbers. But when we boarded, Emme chose to sit with me and Gemini.

At first, I thought she was rattled. Emme's kind and gentle nature makes it hard for her to watch others suffer and I believed she was perhaps remembering those she wasn't able to save. Until I saw her curl inward and realized how much it seemed to hurt her not to be with Bren.

I glance up, noting Gemini scrutinize the way Bren regards her. Like me, he knows something is up. The strain between them is worse each time they're together, thickening the air like tar.

We collectively groan when the helicopter does another odd maneuver that's more like a spiral than anything a helicopter should be able to do.

"Christ," Bren mutters, scratching his beard irritably. "Did Koda actually get his license?"

I expect several loud growls from Koda telling Bren to screw off. Aside from the sound of the blaring engine and whipping blades, there's nothing.

Bren straightens. *"He doesn't have a license?"*

Gemini clears his throat . . . and that's about it.

"No," I say. "Oh, no, no, no, no, no. Tell me you didn't shove us onto a plane with a wolf who doesn't know how to fly." I glance around, half-expecting us to burst into flames and fall from the sky. "I'm serious, tell me he has a license, a permit, something!"

Gemini works his jaw. "Koda took flying lessons at a young age and accrued several hours toward his license. He was considered a natural and a gifted student by his instructor."

"I don't care if he graduated at the top of his class in airplane school or whatever the fuck. Does he have a license or not?" Bren snaps.

"*No*," Gemini grinds out. "His instructor was beheaded during a mission to Indonesia before Koda could take the final exam."

"Of course he was," I say, pulling at the straps of my seatbelt and making it that much tighter. "Of course." My hands slap against my lap. "So then what were all those fly dates he had just recently?"

"Lessons," Gemini grumbles.

"*Lessons?*" I ask. "He was still taking lessons?"

"It was more like a refresher course," Gemini adds when swears shoot from Bren's mouth like fodder. "As I said, he was considered gifted."

"By the guy who lost his head in Indonesia," I remind him, clutching my right arm when she starts to tremble.

Bren's attention bounces from the cockpit back to us when the helicopter dips yet again. "You stuck us ten-thousand feet in the air with some asshole—"

This time Koda does growl: loud, deep, and challenging.

"Your mother," Bren growls back. He veers on Gemini. "Why in the *hell* did you think this was a good idea?"

"I never said this was a good idea," Gemini says, meeting Bren with equal force. "But I trust Koda and we were out of options." He jerks his chin in Johnny's direction, tense with a heaviness I've never witnessed. "We have to get back to the Den. We have to figure this out."

"And we will," Bren replies. "*If we live.*"

Our bitching morphs to groans when the helicopter tips to the side and we bounce several times.

"Sorry, dudes," Shayna calls from the front. "We hit some turbulence."

"I just hope we don't hit the side of the mountain," I

mumble.

"No shit," Bren agrees.

I reach out and touch Emme's hand. Her expression is as pained as mine. Gemini's right, we have to figure out what's happening, and maybe distract ourselves from this hellish ride. "Em, what did you feel when you touched Destiny? Did anything feel out of the ordinary?"

"That's hard to say since I never felt anything like her." She pushes a strand of her blond wavy hair behind her ear and gives it some thought. "Her magic is outrageously strong, but I think she keeps most of it contained, or it's contained for her." She pauses and adds, "The best way to describe it is power trapped in a diamond case."

Gemini and I exchange glances. "Power that's trapped?" I question. She nods. "So she's not fully using all the mojo she has?"

"From what I can tell, no." She presses her lips. "Like I said, I've never felt anything like it."

Wow. I've experienced the magic Destiny does allow through firsthand. I can only imagine what she's capable of at full-strength.

"If she's that strong, perhaps there's hope," Gemini says. "She might recover." His focus glides toward Johnny. "So long as we keep their magic from clashing again."

"If that's the case, shouldn't Koda turn this bitch around instead of heading to the same damn place Destiny is waiting?" Bren asks. "You saw what happened last time. We don't need a repeat performance."

"It should be fine," Gem tells him.

"Should be?" Bren challenges.

Oh, and this is so not a good time to test Gemini. "The Elders are placing Destiny within the confines of the vault," he snaps. "All the objects housed there, in addition to their collective magic, should be enough to keep hers and the Fate's power from connecting." He frowns when he looks at Emme. "What is it?" he asks, lowering his voice.

"I'm not certain Destiny will recover," she admits.

"Why?" I question. "You said so yourself she's

outrageously strong. Maybe she can, I don't know, tap into all that mojo she has stored and allow it to save her."

"I don't think it works like that, at least not from what I felt," Emme explains. "It's as if her power remains, but her body is weakening."

"How so?" Bren asks.

Under his scrutiny, her words slow, and she struggles to explain. "Everything that makes her human, her cells, tissue, and organs aren't functioning," she says. "At least not as they should. I've felt this in my hospice patients before, right before they go into the light. But it shouldn't be happening to Destiny, she wasn't sick or injured." She wrings her hands, appearing at a loss. "It's like her body has decided it doesn't want to live anymore."

"Could he be doing something to her?" Bren asks, motioning toward Johnny.

His voice is terse and Emme doesn't look at him when she replies. "I don't see how. When I touched Johnny, it felt like he was shutting down, too, only not as rapidly as Destiny." She shrugs. "Perhaps males of their kind are stronger."

"As opposed to females in general?" Bren asks. He holds out his palms when Emme lifts her chin, her cheeks flushing pink. "Hey. Just asking."

"What would you know about being strong?" she demands.

It's like a verbal slap across the face. A strong one. Hell, even I jump.

All the muscles along Bren's chest and arms constrict, and his face reddens. "More than you think, doll."

"What the hell?" I ask. My attention drifts between them. Bren mutters something I don't quite hear and Emme averts her gaze. "Seriously, what is it with you guys, lately? You're behaving like bitter exes instead of close friends."

My jaw pops open when both find someplace else to look. "Did you—" I can't even finish my own thought because this is all sorts of messed up. I hold out a hand, forcing the words out. "Are you sleeping together?"

"Not exactly," Bren answers, looking directly at Emme whose face is practically on fire.

"Not exactly?" I ask, my voice shrilled. "How do you 'not exactly' sleep with someone?"

"I kissed her, all right?" Bren says, his face flushing once more. "It was no big deal."

Emme regards him with so much hurt, it takes all I have not to launch myself across Johnny and beat the cockiness right out of Bren.

"You *asshole*," I tell him.

Gemini appears about as thrilled at the news as I am. At the same time, he doesn't seem surprised. "Did you know about this?" I ask.

"I didn't know the details," he admits. "Based on their mutual . . . aromas when they're around each other, we've had our suspicions."

"We?" I ask.

"Aric, Koda, and I," he replies, doing a double-take when he catches sight of my non-too-pleased expression.

"And you didn't tell me."

"Taran, it happens," he says. "When *lone* wolves join a pack, they often become attracted to unmated females during, ah, certain periods."

I think I might actually kill someone. "Are you trying to tell me *Bren is in heat*?" I swallow hard. "With *my sister*?"

"Hey," Bren says, appearing insulted. "*Bren* can hear you."

"No way," I bite out.

He shifts in his seat. "Taran, look."

I shake my head, the tension thickening the muscles along my shoulders making it hard to move. "Don't sit here and tell me all this is you being horny."

He knows what I mean.

"I'm not doing anything," he rumbles.

"Why?" I demand.

His stare flickers to Emme. "I told her it wasn't a good idea."

Emme presses her lips, something she does when she's

trying not to cry. That's when I finally get it. She doesn't just like him, and he's doesn't just want to sleep with her. They're mates. Holy shit, *they're mates.*

And he won't do anything about it!

"Stay away from her," I tell him, my expression and tone as dark as he's ever witnessed.

"Taran," he begins.

"I'm serious, Bren," I say, cutting him off. "If you're not going to man up, you need to keep your fucking distance."

His eyes flash with anger and more emotion than I'm used to. I expect him to argue, he doesn't, and in a way it upsets me more.

"I will," he promises. He bows his head, but not before casting one last look at Emme who's seconds from falling apart.

Lightning crashes in front of the helicopter, rattling it hard and causing the stretcher to bounce in place.

Koda yells from the front. "We're here. But we're not going to make it to the peak." The cabin explodes with a flash as lightning strikes once more. "We have to land on the side of the mountain. Hang on!"

Chapter Thirteen

The helicopter lunges forward, sending the stretcher Johnny is strapped to crashing toward the front. He moans in total misery, his head shaking back and forth.

It's not from the strike. Something is happening to him.

"Gem—" My voice cuts off when I see it, the tattoo, the one of the serpent circling the heart moving along Johnny's chest and constricting.

Johnny screams, the pain he feels morphing into a physical force that pushes us back and pins us against our seats.

The copter dives, swerving into a tailspin. "It's Destiny," I shriek, ramming my eyes shut. "We're too close to her. We have to head someplace else."

"Koda, get us out of here!" Gemini yells to him.

Koda grunts from the cockpit, struggling to level the copter. He evens us out, but it's only for a second. From one breath to the next, the copter thrusts back down. "We can't leave," he hollers. "We land now or off one of the peaks."

Thunder explodes from every direction and we begin to lose ground. Johnny is howling in agony, his body jerking back and forth.

The copter barrels down, then up, as Koda fights to stay in control.

Gemini rips free from his seatbelt. Bren does, too. Gem wraps his body around me and Emme, trying to protect us from the inevitable impact.

Bren shoves him off Emme, his hands gripping the seat on either side of her head. "Listen to me, Emme," he tells her. "I need you to land this helicopter, you hear me? I need you to set it to the ground."

Emme's face is the color of chalk, and I don't think I'm any better. "I can't move what I can't see."

Despite the jerky movements of our ride, Bren smoothly eases closer, speaking low into her ear. "Then let me be your eyes."

I glance at Gemini, who's watching them as intently as I am. Like Gemini is shielding me, Bren is doing the same for Emme, using his body to spare hers.

Jesus.

I look to Gemini, trying to gather my courage and remain strong. He adjusts his position around me and presses a kiss on my forehead. "I love you," he says. "I'm not going to let anything happen to you."

This is where I tell him that I love him, too, and assure him that no matter what, we're going to make it. But the awful jolts and Johnny's pained screams keep me from speaking and the best I can do is wrap my arms around his waist.

I turn my head and watch Bren, hoping he'll do as he claims and help Emme safely land us.

He keeps his hands beside her head and straightens to look out of the window. "I see the ground," he says.

Emme's lids fall closed. "I need more than that, Bren. Give me feet, or yards, something I can picture."

The sky once more illuminates with light. As it fades, Bren speaks. "High enough to sky dive," he answers.

I don't know what that means and practically slump in my seat when Emme nods.

Another stream of lightning follows a long explosion of

thunder. It does something to the air, charging it with enough magic to irritate my skin.

The engine's roars abruptly quiet and the bat of the propellers quickly slow.

"*Taran*—"

I hold out a hand, silencing Shayna, over Johnny's wretched cries. "Emme has us," I manage.

For a moment everything is still, like we're floating, until another flare of lighting detonates and we tip downward, falling side to side like a feather in the wind.

"Tree tops," Bren tells her.

"Okay," Emme says.

"Tree tops," Bren urges. "Steady, Emme, steady—"

We hit something that rebounds us backward. "Straighten us out, Emme," Bren says. "Straighten us out, *now*."

"I'm *trying*," she says, her teeth clenched tight.

We collide into something hard, causing the row of seats across of us to indent inward and a strong wind to seep in.

"Emme, that was a cliff," Bren says, his voice growing panicked. "Go, right, *right*."

Emme loses her fight with the cliff, ramming the side of the copter repeatedly as we spin.

"Hard left," Bren yells. "*Do it now*."

The crashing sound diminishes and we fly blindly through the air.

Gemini cradles my head. I think we're going to die. We start to fall . . . and then we don't.

"More trees—*shit*," Bren says. "Emme, stay with me."

Emme's face is pinched tight, her hands blanching as they grip the arm rests. "I can't."

"Yes, you can. We're almost there." Bren curses. "Hold us—just hold us. The road, leading up, we're almost to it."

"How far?"

"We're hitting the top of the trees," he says, the sound of something smacking the underbelly confirming it. "Lower us. Now."

"Now?" she asks.

"Yes; now!"

If giants were real, and one was holding us, the landing would be the equivalent of him dropping us in search of a less banged up toy to play with. We bump, judder, and lurch, slamming to the ground.

I don't expect to stop so abruptly.

Who am I kidding? I don't expect to live. For the most part, Bren's whole "let me be your eyes" was bullshit. He's freaking *blind* as far as I'm concerned.

But we made it. Yeah, baby, we made it!

I lift my chin to meet Gemini's face. His expression mirrors mine, as if half expecting us to keep moving, falling, and crashing to our deaths. He eases off me, looking outside the window.

"Did we land?" I ask.

"Yes," he answers.

"Are we teetering perilously on the side of a cliff?" I'm not trying to be downer, this is just the kind of luck I've grown accustomed to.

He shakes his head. "No, but we can't stay here." He looks to Emme. "Well done," he tells her.

"You did it, Emme," I agree. I reach to stroke her hair when Bren lifts off her. My hand pauses inches from her face when I take a good look at her.

Her small body is covered with sweat and her nose bleeding profusely. I scramble out of my seatbelt, trying to find something to use to stop the bleeding.

Bren rips the leg of his sweatpants off and presses it against her nose. "You okay?" he asks.

She nods, holding the soft gray fabric against her face. "Yes," she stammers. "A little tired."

And frightened, and feeble, and my God, my poor sister. Her fair skin carries a sickly pallor, made worse by the amount of blood soaking her dress and face. I want to yank her to me, protect her and keep her safe. It's what all of us who know her ever want to do. But as sweet and delicate as Emme appears, she's not weak, nor will she allow herself to appear that way if she can help it.

She looks at me. "I don't think I can hike up the

mountain."

Her legs tremble, giving away the amount of energy she expended. I stroke her hair. "Honey, I don't think you should even walk, at least not yet."

"She won't have to," Gemini says. His nostrils flare from the amount of blood he scents on her. "Let me carry you, Emme," he offers. "You've already done enough."

Bren opens his mouth, ready to argue, but ultimately edges further away from her.

Shayna pops into the compartment with Koda behind her. He brushes off the broken glass covering his arms and shoulders. Lightning flashes behind him, making him appear more ominous and giving me a view of the blood soaking through his white T-shirt.

The front windshield must have shattered, and like our wolves, he used his body to protect Shayna. "You dudes, okay?" she asks.

Her position from the cockpit must have provided one hell of a play-by-play, and she's likely shaken up. But Shayna is very much a 'don't panic unless we're out of weapons and we're about to be eaten' kind of gal. We landed, and despite the lightning and thunder continuing to browbeat the mountain, that's good enough for her. "Time to move, team. Can't stay here all night," she reminds us.

She's right. By now, Johnny is openly weeping in pain. I start toward him when a wave of magic sends me sprawling backward. Gemini catches me, holding me in place.

"What's wrong?" he asks.

My vision sharpens as I feel my irises go white. "It's Destiny," I say, her presence barraging my senses. I jerk my head to the right, expecting her to materialize. "She's coming."

"They can't be together," Gemini snaps. "We have to put some distance between them."

Bren and Koda charge toward Johnny, breaking through the straps and setting him free.

"It hurts," Johnny cries, his moans turning to sobs. "It hurts so much."

Koda throws him over his shoulder, his long legs kicking through the bent metal door and busting it open. Shayna chases after him. I stumble forward, my legs leaving the ground when Gemini sweeps me into his arms.

"Babe, don't," I say. "Get Emme."

"Bren has her," he answers tightly.

As he speaks, Bren races past us, embracing Emme close to his body.

We're in a sprint straight down the mountain, only to cut a sharp left when lightning strikes and demolishes an entire row of trees hugging the road.

Through the long, thick branches of sugar pines hovering over us, I catch a glimpse of the thickening clouds as they gather momentum. I think it's close to dawn, it has to be. But there's no trace of light. Darkness reins, its rule interrupted by the harsh appearance of lightning as the storm reaches another pinnacle.

"Where are we?" I ask.

"Four miles from the peak," Gemini replies.

He leaps down the rough edge, his feet sliding and maneuvering through the sharp rocks and thick vegetation. Koda glances back, making sure Shayna stays close. He and Bren are barefoot, not that you would know it by how fast they're hauling ass.

We reach the next steep, the ground leveling slightly when something passes us, moving like a blur of motion.

"Tye, *no!*" Gemini yells.

A white lion barrels into Koda, knocking him and Johnny across the terrain. Koda's back strikes a tree, the impact ricocheting him off the trunk. As he rolls, he *changes*, into a very pissed and ferocious red wolf.

Gemini's twin wolf rips through his back, passing us and tearing through the ferns and rocks to stand between Koda and Tye.

Bren jets forward, leaving Emme with Shayna who's guarding Johnny's limp form. From one leap to the next, he *changes,* the large paws of his brown wolf digging into the earth and kicking back the soil.

It takes all three wolves to subdue Tye's large lion form. Gemini sets me down between my sisters. I've never seen Tye so out of control, his long fangs snapping and his claws raking in the air, fighting to reach Johnny.

"*Enough*," Gemini growls, stomping forward.

Thunder roars, shaking the ground and sending more lightning to zig-zag across the sky. An explosion of light bursts on either side of us, one yellow and one silver, materializing the two head witches, their long staffs raised high in the air.

The witches run toward us. Genevieve's long black hair sails behind her, mere steps from a witch with long silver hair, her indigo gown blending into the night.

"Taran, move Emme," Genevieve orders.

I don't argue, lifting Emme and trying to coax Shayna out of the way. Her hand is gripping her sword, her gaze set on Tye. "I've never seen him like this," she says.

She didn't like him hurting Koda. None of us did. They're supposed to be friends. Except nothing is normal, not the storm, not Johnny, not anything we've seen.

"Genevieve," I say. "What's happening?"

"Fate and Destiny can't co-exist," she says, mirroring Gemini's exact words. She slams the edge of her staff into the ground, tracing a circle around Johnny's writhing body. On the opposite side, the other witch does the same.

Genevieve steals a glance my way. "The skies are reacting to their magic. If Ines and I don't create a strong enough barrier to encase him, and buy the others time to get Destiny off the mountain, the mountain will split."

"The mountain will *split*?"

"Yes," she replies, moving quickly. "Fate and Destiny should never meet." She looks up and toward the road. "She's coming. She's coming now."

What feels like a tsunami of magic rages down the mountain. Johnny is screaming, but over his screams, and the increasing clamor of thunder and lightning, I hear her.

Destiny's cries fill my ears, the anguish in her sobs palpable. The air shifts, each particle filling with the extent of her hurt.

Tye, now human, slowly rises, his naked skin dripping with sweat. "What are you doing to her?" he roars, his fierce gaze fixed on Johnny.

The wolves growl, snapping their fangs and keeping Tye from Johnny.

Genevieve and Ines begin chanting in their respective languages, their voices raised and their magic pumping into each syllable. But it's not enough. Their words of power only mildly affect the cacophony of energy advancing toward us.

The witches dig their staffs into the ground, yelling over the destruction of the escalating storm. A globe, alternating in sparks of silver and yellow surround Johnny, growing denser with each punch of magic the witches use to reinforce it.

More lightning, more thunder. The storm is closing in, bringing down more trees. Genevieve and Ines are now screaming, putting everything they have into their spell. But they're only two people trying to stop a dam of energy from bursting.

Wicked winds swirl, turning the small space between us into a cyclone of divination, and leaving us in the eye.

Koda *changes* back. "It's not working," he hollers. His long hair smacks against his face. "We have to get our mates out."

Gemini looks to the road. "We can't leave the Fate, nor can we risk drawing him closer to Destiny!" he yells. "Genevieve, we need a stronger blockade around the Fate."

"We're trying!" she counters. Her voice is barely audible, and like Ines, her entire body is quaking.

"*Proteggere!*" Genevieve commands. "*Proteggere!*"

"*Protéger!*" Ines orders. "*Protéger!*"

Protect they mean, nourishing the spell with all their might. They're trying and formidable. They're just not enough.

That tsunami of power I felt approaching amplifies, ready to drop as an army of SUVs career down the mountain.

My right arm shakes uncontrollably, making it hard to keep my feet. Each jolt of lightning that strikes the earth slaps at my power, challenging it and attempting to cast us aside.

Oh, and my arm doesn't like it one bit.

The familiar buzz surges through me, coming to life and increasing in viciousness the closer the strikes land. My arm is angry. *No*, I'm angry. The foreign power I'm feeling more like a threat and an invasion, rather than something natural and welcomed.

I don't think about what I'm doing. I follow my arm's lead, permitting my fear and frustration to soak my magic in wrath. It's now my arm and I challenging the clashing energy, calling it out and making it clear it's not the only thing here with power.

I ball my hand into a fist and raise it, barely keeping the flowing energy tensing my muscles contained. "Power," I whisper, my vision clearing as the potent energy effluxes and comes crashing down. "Give me power!"

All at once the bolts of lightning rampaging the sky thread, forming a flashing cobweb of light that join at the center and become one.

"*Taran!*"

Gemini's voice is the last sound I hear before nature's fury and everything that is Fate and Destiny strikes my arm.

My body crashes to the ground, the world as I know it fading in and out.

Chapter Fourteen

My teeth and skeleton are rattling out of control. Every bone colliding against itself, scrambling my brain and organs into mush.

My body twitches in response to the surplus of power, convulsing, thrashing, taking on a mind of its own.

It takes a long few moments for me to settle—at least, that's what I think—except for my right arm which can't stop quivering.

I'm lying on a bed of sand, that's what it feels like. I can't be sure how I landed on sand and I can't make anything out. My eyelids are unusually heavy, giving me only blurry glimpses of my surroundings.

There's no noise, no sound, no wicked winds beating against my skin and hair. There's only silence that dreaded silence that always accompanies the end of life.

I think I'm dead.

My racing heartbeat threatening to implode within my chest proclaims otherwise. It also calls me a bitch for putting us through whatever the hell I put us through this time.

Somehow, I manage to pry open my eyes. As I watch, the once tumultuous clouds part, revealing the sun in all its morning glory.

For one quick breath, peace is all I see and feel. That tranquility, however, is abruptly obscured by Gemini's face, his expression fierce as he clutches me against him.

He's speaking fast. Not that I can hear him.

"What?" I ask, my voice sounding muffled.

I think he's yelling. That's what it looks like. His lips move slower and his features further tense. Something pops in my right ear and his voice fades in and out.

"God damn . . . crazy . . . the fuck . . . die . . . seriously. . . die . . ."

"What?" I ask again.

He lowers me, standing abruptly and peeling off his shirt.

A bombardment of little popping sounds overtakes my right ear. Emme appears in my line of vision. She takes Gem's shirt and drapes it over me.

"Gemini's angry," she says, her voice barely perceivable. "About you devouring the storm. He's right, Taran. You shouldn't have done that."

"I ate a storm?" I ask, my voice stuttering out of control.

She turns to where he's pacing, and I think swearing, too. "Perhaps it's more accurate to say you devoured Destiny and Johnny's combined magic. Well, at least your arm did." She tucks a strand of her hair when it falls around her cheek. "Whatever happened allowed Destiny to pass. She's off the mountain and headed away from Squaw Valley."

Emme sounds as if she's under water. It's only because I'm straining to hear and reading her lips that I catch as much as I do. "Is she all right?" I manage.

"I don't know," she replies. "She was screaming as she passed. The Elders were trying to shield her like the witches shielded Johnny. It wasn't enough." She folds the shirt around my waist. "But you were. You were everything they needed."

"Dude," Shayna says. She shoves her face in mine as the pressure dulling my left ear eases slightly. "That was the most incredible thing I've ever seen." She thinks about. "Except for the time you set the entire sky on fire. That was pretty cool, too."

She pulls off her shirt and tugs it over my head, leaving her wearing only a sports bra. I don't know why everyone continues to take off their clothes and cover me until I realize I'm naked.

"What the hell?" I ask, scrambling to push up on my elbows.

I fall perfectly still when I realize my legs are bent at the knee and I'm buried in blue ash from my shins down.

Shayna holds out her hands. "You should have seen yourself, T. It's like Thor himself swung his hammer and brought it down on your arm —only there was no, you know, *hammer*. Just lightning. Lots and lots of lightning."

"Uh-huh," I say, grateful I missed the show.

I try wiggling my toes. Turns out I can't. For now, I'm just thankful they're still attached, given Shayna's oh-too descriptive visual of me being nailed into the earth.

Emme ties Gemini's shirt around me like a skirt when I sit up. "You sort of . . . exploded," she explains. "And the blast disintegrated the ground."

The retelling becomes too much for Gemini. He abandons his cursing fit and lifts me in one smooth move, placing me further back and near what resembles a burning shoe. My charred outline remains on the ground. With a trembling hand, I try to toss my hair over my shoulder, except all I feel is bare skin. I gasp, thinking I'm bald.

"It's still there, T," Shayna assures me, her words releasing in spurts of sound. "It's just sticking up a little." She does an arching motion around her head. "Like an afro. But I think Genevieve can fix it and give you back your eyebrows."

"My eyebrows?" I ask, not wanting to believe what came out of her mouth.

"Totally," Shayna adds, nodding. "You fried them and your lashes clean off." She holds out her hands. "But don't worry. I don't think anyone will notice and, on the plus side, you may never need another bikini wax again."

"Oh, God," I whimper, touching my face. All I feel is smooth skin and lots of ash.

I look up to where Genevieve and Ines elegantly wait.

But don't you worry one damn minute, they're fine and still very much have their eyebrows. In fact, both raise theirs when they get a gander of me.

Their beautiful maiden gowns sway in the dying breeze, along with their silky hair. Meanwhile I'm standing in a tube top that barely keeps my breasts in, a ripped T-shirt for a skirt, and the only hair on my body levitating in the air.

"How's it going?" I ask, stepping forward.

"Fine," Ines replies, her French accent thick and just as lovely as her face, even as it fades in and out. "*Et toi?*"

"Oh, I'm dandy. Just missing some hair." I shrug. "It happens, you feel me?"

She nods. Sort of.

Vieve can't stop staring at my forehead. "That was quite a display of power, Sister Taran," she says. I can barely hear her, but I don't think she's whispering. Like my sister and Ines, her voice is most like a muffled and distant echo, its pitch alternating from almost normal, to barely audible.

"Tell me about it," I say. Her eyes widen. "What's wrong? Am I yelling?"

She appears almost afraid to answer, looking to my sisters for guidance. "Ah, yes."

"Oh. Sorry." I stop just in front of her, muttering through my teeth. "You can fix this shit, right?"

"I . . . hope so," she says, casting an apologetic glance in Gemini's direction.

Awesome.

I continue forward, trying to strut and failing miserably. With how bad my arm continues to jerk and twitch, I can't even walk a straight line.

My focus travels to Johnny where he's sitting on the ground. He looks weak, tired, and is breathing fast, but he's no longer screaming in agony, nor does he seem in pain. I'm glad. I don't know him, but it was hard to watch him suffer like he did. And poor Destiny, I can't help thinking she's worse off.

Not that I'm the only one who's thinking of her.

Tye appears ready to charge. If it weren't for the wall

Bren and Koda are making with their colossal bodies, and the way Gemini's twin wolf continues to circle him, Johnny's blood would be dripping from Tye's fangs. Johnny can sense as much, his full attention on Tye.

"You shouldn't have done that," Gemini mutters tightly. I didn't know he was behind me, my hearing still out of sorts. He adjusts my clothes, making sure I'm covered. "You could have been killed."

My hands fall against his skin, leaving blue and white soot marks. I try to wipe it off, only to give up when I make it worse. "I didn't have a choice," I say, hoping I'm keeping my voice soft. I motion to the damaged trees surrounding us. "We were all going to die."

"That doesn't automatically make you the go-to sacrifice." He releases me slowly as if it pains him. I want to reassure him except I don't get a chance. He leaves me and walks to where the wolves await his orders.

I wish we could leave. But as much as we've already faced and fought through, his job isn't done and our situation is far from over.

I hurry behind him, at least I try to. Something is off in my balance, and the world isn't quite as I remembered it.

Mounds of blue and white ash expand across the perimeter, creating a flower with petals extending out in sharp sweeps. My guess is, the way all the bolts intertwined, I was hit with one mighty blow, the residual power branching out of my body and creating the blossom.

Each step I take reminds me of the soft, powder sand along the Caribbean beaches, except instead of white sand, there's ash in swirls of blue and white. It must have been something to see, but it was a whole something else to perform it. I don't think I was unconscious long, just long enough to settle the weather-beaten atmosphere and stop the earth from quaking.

If I had to repeat the process, I'm not positive I would be able to, or if I'd survive. I pretty much followed my arm's instincts and magic, unsure exactly where she'd lead us.

Shayna helps Emme forward until both stand beside me. I

hadn't realized I'd stopped walking. The way the earth continued to sway, I assumed my legs were still moving.

"What happened exactly?" I ask, watching the world pitch from side to side and briefly pondering if it might be me and not it.

"You blew up and everything around you," Shayna tells me. "But whatever you took, you took for the team. The earth rumbled at our feet, but we didn't feel the impact." She gives me the once-over. "I mean, not like you."

"Good," I say, thankful I didn't barbecue the entire mountainside and everyone on it.

Shayna clasps my hand when I take another few steps. It's then I realize I'm headed away from everyone and into the woods. "Are you okay?" she questions.

"Sure. Why do you ask?" I answer, wondering why there are two of her.

Both Shaynas blink back at me. "You're wobbling. Not in a bad way, more like a baby learning to walk." She looks around and behind me. "You might try walking with your legs closed, if you can." She crinkles her nose. "That skirt you have going on wasn't made for squatting, if you know what I mean."

I nod slowly, noting how dizzy the motion makes me. "All right."

"I think you need help," Emme says. The soft touch of her fingers brush against my cheek before I can ask her who she's talking to. "There could be something off in your system."

"Could be," I agree.

"I'm over here, Taran," she says, carefully. "That's a tree you're speaking to."

"Sorry, I didn't notice," I say. And I still don't notice now.

"Oh, I see," Emme says quietly. "You ruptured your eardrums, and you have some ah, bruising at the base of your skull."

Almost immediately, the world rights itself. I feel myself straighten and my balance returns. "Better?" she asks.

"Yes," I reply. I didn't realize how bad I was until she fixed me. I sigh and fuss with my makeshift skirt. "Much better. Thank you."

Gemini frowns in my direction, his voice low as he speaks into his cell phone. He must have heard my conversation with Emme and is likely bothered by how much I tried to mask.

He disconnects, looking to Tye. "Destiny is safe. The Elders have settled her at one of our strongholds."

"How is she?" Tye asks, his glare cutting in Johnny's direction. "'Safe' isn't good enough and doesn't tell me shit."

Tye stands naked, giving us a full view of his muscles and everything else God gave him because Tye is *were* and doesn't give a damn.

"She's sick, Tye," Gemini answers. "Whatever happened left her weak."

My wolf doesn't bother to sugar-coat anything, but I was counting on a little hope.

"Is she in pain?" Tye asks.

"No, not like before. Mostly weak and fragile."

"How fragile?" Tye curses when Gemini doesn't answer. "Just tell me."

The silence between them is almost too much to take. "She's dying, Tye," Gemini tells him. "The Elders don't think she has much time left."

Shayna sucks in a breath. All I can do is cover my mouth.

The color drains from Tye's face. "That's not possible," he says. He glances around as if searching for something. "She was fine yesterday. I talked to her on the phone. She wanted to meet up when she returned—"

Gemini meets him square in the face, silencing him instantly. "I'm sorry," he tells him. "You have the Pack's deepest condolences, and I swear, we'll help you and Destiny anyway we can."

Tye doesn't seem to hear him or understand. Shock riddles his features only to be displaced by an unrelenting fury. "How the fuck is she dying?" Tye asks, his eyes glistening with all the pain he feels on behalf of his dear friend. "She's a Destiny. Destinies don't die. They keep going until another is born to take her place."

"Another did take her place," Ines responds, her tone flat as she scrutinizes Johnny. "Just not in the way any of us could have predicted."

Tye hones in on Johnny. "Bullshit. He's not taking her place," he says, his stone-cold tone, holding everyone in place. "That's not how this is supposed to work."

"How is it supposed to work?"

Emme's words are barely noticeable, the breeze rustling the thick pine needles and the tension stabbing the air drowning out her meek voice.

"Tye, Destiny is our friend," she says, her stare softening as she looks at Tye. She wipes a tear that falls. "None of us want anything to happen to her, and I'm not trying to upset you. I merely want to understand what's happened so I can help, or somehow make this right."

"There is no making this right, Emme," Tye tells her. He regards the witches, the anger he's feeling punching out every syllable. "Is there?"

Genevieve replies, the way she adjusts her hold over her long staff making her appear more regal. "It's with great regret I share what I do," she begins.

"I'll bet it is," Tye says.

She ignores the slight, looking to Ines who nods in a way a doctor would when he tells a new resident to pull the plug.

"The creation of Fate and Destiny are determined by powers and magic beyond ours," Genevieve explains. "And while they share abilities such as their accuracy for predicting the future, that's where their similarities end and where the magic bestowed upon them collides."

"Resulting in all this," I say, motioning to the devastation around us.

"Yes, Taran," she agrees.

For the first time since I've known her she appears at loss. What I wouldn't give for her to know what to do and make everything right.

She adjusts the hold over her staff again. I don't believe

it's a nervous gesture. I think she's preparing to act against Tye, unsure how he'll respond to what she tells him. "Because of the chaos their mutual existence brings, the first born, be it Destiny or Fate is allowed to live. Whoever follows must be killed within the first year of life."

Emme's horror reflects in Shayna's features. Koda stiffens, his need to comfort her warring with his obligation to guard Tye. "But it's not his fault," Shayna says, eyeing Johnny.

He sits on the ground, his arms curled around his legs, trying to stay warm and attempting to shield himself from what's coming. "No," he says. "It's not my fault." His expression is blank as he looks ahead. He's been very quiet, not wanting to risk disturbing the lion in his presence. "I didn't choose to come into this world, and I didn't choose to be what I am." He turns to look at me. "Just like the rest of you. Can't you see, my only crime is being born?"

"No, not your only crime," Tye says.

He's referring back to the witch law, the one that states Johnny has to die.

"It may be a crime to have two of the same or whatever," Shayna says, appearing to struggle with everything happening. "But why does death have to be the penalty? Johnny has gone this long without anything happening to him or Destiny." She shakes her head, causing her long dark ponytail to swing along her back. "I mean, up until they met both were living and okay."

"But the world wasn't," Genevieve reminds her. She looks at Johnny. "You're what? Twenty-two?"

"Twenty," Johnny mumbles, lowering his head.

"And what's happened over these past two decades?" Genevieve questions. "We've had Tsunamis strike the earth, quakes that have leveled cities and buried humans alive, demon lords that found a way into our world, one supernatural war, another just beginning, and the start of an evil even the strongest among us will fall to."

I don't move, listening, remembering.

"Look at all we've faced since the coming of the Fate."

She points to my arm. "Look at all the inconceivable disruptions and betrayals. Our appointed Guardians of the Earth turned against each other, and cast a blow that could have finished us all." Her lips form a firm line when I tense. "All this darkness, we've blamed on simply darkness itself. But now we know the real cause."

"But why is all this happening to Destiny and Johnny now?" Shayna questions, motioning to Johnny with a tilt of her sword. "If this is all real and how it's going to go down, why didn't they react this way sooner?"

"Proximity," Genevieve replies. She turns in Johnny's direction. "I presume you've never been close enough to trigger such a clash?"

Emme interrupts before Johnny can answer. Like me and Shayna, she wants to spare him. "So if they'd never crossed paths, both would be fine and no one would have suffered?"

"I'm afraid it doesn't work that way, Emme," Genevieve responds. "As much as their powers collide, their magic eventually calls to each other, forcing them to meet."

"Oh, my God," I say, rubbing my face. I glance up to see everyone watching me. "Destiny had never heard Johnny's music. But she told us that something about it called to her. She had this strange look on her face when she said it. I should have guessed something was wrong." I glance at Johnny. "I'm sorry. I should have kept them apart."

"It wouldn't have made a difference," Genevieve says. "When their magic calls, they must answer. It's too powerful to resist. They would have found a way to meet."

"All right. They met. But what if we keep them separated?" Emme offers. "If we put enough distance between them, perhaps Destiny can recover."

"Impossible," Ines replies. "The world can only have one Fate or one Destiny, its magic has insisted upon it since the formation of magic itself."

"What if Fate goes and Destiny stays?"

The malice behind Tye's question is so blatant it reeks of poison. The wolves gather around him, closing their circle.

"Uh-uh," he says, pointing at Johnny when he scrambles

back. "You weren't supposed to live, *she was.*"

Tye leaps, *changing*, his large claws protruding and aimed at Johnny. The wolves collide against him, trying to hold him back, their bones crunching from the force of the impact.

Johnny takes off in a sprint. As Shayna and I rush after him, the eagle inked into his shoulders sprouts from his back, growing as it extends and flaps its wings. He separates from Johnny, clutching his arms and lifting him away.

My lightning builds as my arm shoots out, sending a bolt straight into the now immense bird. Johnny screams, and the eagle explodes in a wash of color, dropping Johnny on the hard forest floor.

The small stones and debris dig into my feet. I ignore the sting, anxious to reach him before he attempts his next great escape. We find him trying to crawl away, the skin on his shoulders where the eagle emerged raw and blistering. He's sobbing, but I don't think it's just from pain.

"I'm sorry," I say, knowing I hurt him, and recognizing how much he hurts in return.

"I didn't ask for this," he says, thick tears dripping onto the ground in front of him. "I didn't ask for any of it."

Shayna rubs her nose, trying to beat back the tears. We know how he feels, just like we know there's not a damn thing we can do about it. "I'm sorry," I repeat quietly. "But we can't let you leave."

"Tye," Genevieve says, her voice tense and stern. The wolves have secured him again, and he's returned to his human form. But he's still fighting, making it hard to keep him in place. "It's not in your charge to kill a Fate or a Destiny that duty, as witches, is ours alone."

"But you won't fucking do it, will you, Genevieve?" Tye demands, the skin on his face and neck straining with each word. "You're going to keep him alive now that Destiny's dying because you need a new royal to worship. Even though most of you bitches shunned the one who was always there— *always.* No matter how many God damn times you'd rip her apart the moment she turned her back."

Emme gasps. I don't blame her. This isn't the Tye we've known.

Genevieve raises an elegant brow, ignoring the insult. "Our laws only permit the execution within that first year. Killing him now would be murder and could potentially send the world on a collision course." The small crease along her forehead relaxes when he doesn't appear to budge. "Don't you see, Tye? Fate and Destiny are as much a part of the world as the magic that defines us. Without either, there's no predicting what will happen."

"That's all you care about, isn't it?" he yells. "Some pussy lackey to give you the heads up!"

"Tye, listen," Genevieve urges.

"No, you listen. *He* did this to her!" Tye growls. "He made her sick and he's making her die. If he goes, she'll live."

"We do not know that, young lion," Ines interrupts.

"One way to find out," Tye says, lunging forward.

"You kill me, the tigress and her babies die."

My head whips in Johnny's direction, sparks of fire exploding from my fingertips. "What did you say?"

"You heard me," he says, his reddening face meeting Tye as he answers me. "There's a tigress. Not a *were*, but a woman who becomes one. I've seen her and the wolf she calls her mate in my visions. Those children they're supposed to have, they'll meet their fate with me." He huffs. "You listening? Hurt me and they're the ones who'll pay the price."

"You're lying," Tye accuses.

"Am I?" Johnny fires back. "Why don't you try me and see?"

"Don't," Emme says, veering around her eyes brimming with tears. "Tye, you can't risk anything happen to Celia." He doesn't respond. "Destiny is your friend," she tells him. "But Celia is, too, and there's a great deal riding on her survival."

"No," Tye says. "That's straight out shit and you're all eating it up. He needs to die. Don't you see? It's the only way to save Destiny!"

I'm so out of my mind right now, it's all I can do not to light Tye up like a torch. He lunges forward again, and again, his animal side taking over all reason the man within him knows.

"Don't do it," I plead. "Don't hurt Celia!"

"He won't," Gemini answers. He snatches Tye by the throat, his vicious stare drilling into him. "You ever threaten Celia or her children's safety, I'll kill you myself."

Chapter Fifteen

"Destiny is Tye's mate, isn't she?"

I'm so quiet, I barely hear myself. But Gemini, Celia, and Aric's hearing being what it is, I could probably whisper the words in the bedroom behind us and they'd still hear me.

"Yes," Gemini answers, his eyes on Celia and Aric where they sit across from us.

"I thought they were friends," I add when no one else speaks. "Close friends for sure, but not more than that." I turn to Gemini, my heart so heavy, it's hard to keep talking. "How come his lion never recognized her as his before? They've been friends since before they could walk. They could have been together. Why did it take all this for them to see it?"

By "this", I mean Destiny dying. It's hard to think the words and even harder to say them, and I'm not alone.

"Sometimes, it takes a tragic event for *weres* to recognize their mates," Gemini answers his comment as heavy as his tone.

My butt sinks into the soft cushion of the couch as I cross my legs. The furniture is almost the exact match to the set we have in our living room in Dollar Point. Aric wanted Celia to feel more at home in the Den and had their suite decorated accordingly. He wants her happy. But this isn't home and given what's happened, we're all a long way from happy.

Gemini keeps his arm around me, stroking my arm lightly. I freaked out when I learned Celia and Aric were among those in the caravan of SUVs barreling down the mountain. I should have known he would try to get her to safety. But between Destiny's wretched screams and all of nature threatening to split the world in two, you can say I was a little distracted. Distraction, though, can be a gift. No way could I have pulled off what I did had I known she was in danger.

It didn't take them long to return once they knew the storm had passed and the threat was over. What did take long was settling Tye. Watching the Pack drag him away was tough, but seeing my sister, who just wants to have her baby in peace is harder.

Aric cradles her protectively. His hold is gentle, it always is when it comes to Celia, but the ire darkening his features is too much. I look away, disturbed by the anger and fear it carries, and weepy over the love it holds, too. Like Celia, he wants that chance to hold their child.

Gemini meets his gaze, as second in command, and as his friend. "We're watching Tye closely," he assures him.

Aric clenches his jaw, speaking slowly and carefully. "It may not be enough."

Celia takes in a breath, her hand sliding over his thigh. "You can't kill him, love," she tells him.

"I can if he risks your safety," he tells her.

Like Tye, Aric is thinking more with his beast than with his head. "Aric," I say, cautious not to look at him directly. "You count on the North American Were Council to protect Celia and as an ally. You can't go around threatening the president's son."

"Actually, he can," Gemini responds, doing nothing to ease the tension making me its bitch.

"You're not helping," I sing.

"I'm only stating what's true," Gemini counters. He leans back, extending his arms across the back of the couch. "As

165

one of the lead Guardians to the Earth, and as our president, Omar has an obligation to the greater good first and foremost. In challenging Johnny, Tye risks Celia's life and that of her children, and by extension the world's future. This leaves Omar with a choice to make: Step down and protect his son, or remain where he is and allow us to do whatever it takes to ensure Celia's safety."

"What if he's lying?" We all look at Celia. She's been silent, and sad, and too many things I don't want her to be. But she isn't staying silent now. "Johnny was desperate, he could have lied about my life ending with his. For all we know, that's one of his strengths."

"Did you sniff a lie?" Aric asks.

"No," Gemini replies. "And I've been careful to take in everything he says."

"But we don't know if masking lies is among his abilities," Celia stresses.

"Even if it is, I don't care," Aric tells her. "I'm not taking any chances when it comes to you."

"Neither will we," Gemini assures him. "If it comes down to it, the lion goes."

"The lion?" I repeat, fuming when Gemini and Aric regard me without a trace of doubt or regret. "His name is Tye. He's our friend, or have you forgotten everything he's done for us?"

"A friend wouldn't risk my mate's safety," Aric grinds out. "And regardless of his past deeds, they don't absolve him from any threat against her."

I shake my head. "You *weres* and your laws."

"Do you have a problem with us trying to keep your sister alive?" Aric fires back.

"Easy, *Aric*," Gemini says, meeting him with equal force.

"Actually, I do have a problem. Want to hear it?" I stand and point to Aric, not waiting for a reply. "You're all about black and white, rules that can't be bent or broken. Tye won't risk harming Celia, and if you could reason past your anger and your insane need to protect her, you would see it."

"It may be black and white to you, but it's not to us,"

Aric answers, his voice sharp. "It's what's helped us keep the world safe since the dawn of time."

"You know, all that dawn of time crap is getting really old," I add. "Seriously, enough already. The last thing we need right now is for *were* to be pitted against *were*." I lift my arm. "You saw how well that worked out for us last time."

"Tye, isn't going to hurt me, Aric." Celia's voice is so soft, I don't quite hear it, and it's so distant, I just want to hug her and bring her back. "He's upset, and rightfully distraught. His mate is dying, that means he doesn't have much time either."

She's right. When *weres* lose their mates, most die from the grief by the rise of the next full moon.

"Let him be, and give them space," Celia asks gently. "Please, Aric, allow them to live whatever time they have left in peace."

Aric cups her face. "It's not that I can't sympathize with his anger or his sadness," he tells her. "Believe me, I can. That doesn't mean I can just let it go and hope he'll do the right thing. We don't know what his grief will do to him or how he'll respond because of it." His focus returns to Gemini. "How many are watching him?"

"Enough," Gemini answers. "He's with Destiny now, and my guess is that at least for the moment, that's where he'll stay."

"And where is she?" I ask. Gemini and Aric exchange glances, as if debating whether or not to tell me. "I'd like to see her, she's our friend, too."

"At the house," Gemini answers. "It's the only stronghold we know is still safe."

I play with the edge of my shirt. A quick shower and change in to jeans and a T-shirt were all I had time for. "Good. It's a nice place for her." I blow out a breath and walk toward the kitchen. "It's home."

"Can I see her?" Celia asks. "I want to make sure she's as comfortable as possible."

Seeing that she's dying and no one can help her.

Aric's hand strokes her side. "Soon. I want to make sure

nothing happens over the next few days with Johnny here at the Den. Ines and Genevieve have returned to Europe. We won't be able to get you off the mountain safely without them."

I straighten. "The queen bees are back in Europe? Already?" I ask. "Never mind," I add, motioning like I'm waving a wand. "I get it."

Aric's attention skips briefly my way. "They'll return if I *call* them. But that will only happen if Celia needs to be immediately transported from the Den." He looks at Gemini. "Or if Destiny's and Johnny's power clashes again."

"If I have to be transported, will it be to the lake house?" Celia asks.

My chest clenches. It's the place the Omega secured and where Celia is to give birth.

"No, sweetness," Aric replies. "Being a new stronghold, we can't be sure it hasn't been compromised."

Celia's face falls into her hands, the weight of everything that's happened over these past few months appearing to hit her at once. "So for now, we stay here?"

Aric pulls her against him, kissing her head. "For now."

"You'll stay with me, right?" she asks. "You're not going to leave me to fight whatever is out there?"

It takes him a moment to answer. "I'm not going anywhere," he replies.

"Yet," is what he means. I know Aric, it won't be long until his wolf compels him to find what hunts his mate.

Gemini and I leave them. They need a moment and perhaps we do, too.

We walk into the kitchen. Their quarters are nice. A large apartment better suited for a successful couple living in New York than a supernatural couple hiding away in a mountain fortress. What I'd give for them to be that human couple far away from here, and for their biggest concern to revolve around what trendy restaurant they'd visit that night.

I reach for a bottle of water in the refrigerator and pass it to Gemini. My head is pounding from lack of sleep and stress, and my eyes are so dry they burn. But nothing I feel compares to what Celia is going through. I only wish I could help.

Gemini comes up behind me when all I do is stare at the plastic bottles lining the top shelf, the coldness from the fridge barely perceptible against my beaten down senses. He shuts the door to the refrigerator and leads me to the table, pulling me onto his lap. "Have a drink," he murmurs against my ear, cracking open the bottle I passed him and placing it in my hand. "The magic you conjured expunged a great deal of your energy. You need to take care of yourself and replenish it."

"So I'll be up for whatever crazy crap the day might bring?" I ask, taking a long pull.

He doesn't bother to sugarcoat it. "Yes."

I finish half the bottle and give the rest to him. I think I'm still thirsty, but I can't seem to force it down. Maybe he feels the same. He sets the bottle along the antique gold and granite table. "What are you going to with Johnny?" I ask.

His unflinching gaze fixes on the bottle. "For now he's with us, but there's not much we can do to keep him. He's not our prisoner, and regardless of what happened between him and Destiny, he's committed no crime against the earth."

"I know." My head falls against his shoulder. "Did you see him, how bad he hurt when she was close?" I shudder. "I couldn't stomach watching him suffer."

I frown when he doesn't reply. It's not that I expect him to be disturbed by the memory, my wolf can handle a lot more than me. I just don't expect his silence then. "What are you thinking?" I ask, stroking his light goatee when he doesn't reply. "Do you think he's lying?"

Gemini's hand sweeps along my thigh to my ass, adjusting me so I lay closer against him. "I don't know. Even if he can somehow hide the truth from us, it's hard not to believe him. He was close to death in Destiny's presence." He looks at me. "I could smell it."

"What do you mean?" Although I ask, I'm afraid what he might say. Death in general is creepy, and in the mystical world, it's downright terrifying.

"When something dies, there's a strong aroma that

accompanies that passing," he explains. "We equate it to the soul leaving the body. It's the only time our kind can scent it."

"And you definitely smelled his?" I ask.

"I did." He cups my knee. "But it gets worse."

"It always does," I remind him.

He smiles, but it doesn't last. "I could smell Destiny's soul as they brought her down the mountain. It was everywhere. I'm stunned she's still alive."

I raise my head. "So if you scented it, Tye did, too."

"Exactly. Which is why he reacted so violently." His features gather and edge. "That didn't mean I could allow him to kill Johnny."

"I know."

I look over to where Celia and Aric wait in the living room. The way he holds and speaks to her is precisely what she needs now. That, and a break from all the crazy.

"Let's go," I whisper.

Gemini stands, easing me to the floor and leading me out. "We'll see you guys later," I call, holding out my hand when they start to rise. "Dinner maybe?"

"All right," Celia says, rushing to her feet and to where I'm waiting before we can make our escape.

She hugs me, something she always does. Today it's a little stronger, a little sadder, a little less like the sister I know. I slide my hands across her back, reminded how much the world literally hangs on her shoulders.

The longer I embrace her, the more the pang of sympathy filling my chest becomes too much. Except my tears aren't what my sister needs from me. "We're going to figure this out," I assure her.

"Okay," she says.

"You don't believe me, do you?" I ask.

"Not one word," she admits.

Laughter through tears are one of the many things Ceel and I have shared throughout our lives. Today is no exception. I step away, before she sees the few that trickle down my cheeks, but not before I catch the ones she can't manage to hold in.

The moment we open the door leading out to the hall, the young wolves and cougars on guard appear, their imposing beast forms erasing any trace of my misery. "Alert me of any changes," Gemini orders.

They bow their heads as we pass. They're young, likely students who want to help. Gemini's arm slinks around my waist, his large hand resting in the "girlfriend zone". He's not typically this affectionate unless another male challenges his position, but he is feeling protective.

I'm not feeling protective. I'm mostly being myself. Being all class and not giving a damn what others think, my hand slips into the "boyfriend zone" and I give him a pat. "Something on your mind besides the fate of the world, baby?"

"Yes," he answers. The way his deep voice drops an octave guarantees I'll have a peaceful nap following a very long romp in bed.

"Nice," I say, flicking my incisor with my tongue when I glance up at him.

"We need to talk," he says.

"Talk?" I ask. "Dirty and during?" I give him another pat. "Sounds good to me."

He smirks. "If that's you want."

"Oh, yes. I want," I assure him.

He laughs. "There's something else. Something important I've kept quiet about it for too long."

My hand falls away as we reach our newly appointed quarters at the end of the hall. "What's up?" I ask.

He punches in the code to our keypad, allowing our entry. "I'll explain in the bedroom."

I step inside, no longer sure where this is headed. "Am I going to like it?"

"I want you to," he says, shutting the door behind him.

There's a large framed mirror just inside the foyer, it's a decorative piece. I sneak a look. My long hair is slightly fuller, the long waves continuing to react to the consumption of lightning they were forced to endure mere hours ago. Genevieve assured me it would eventually settle. Based on what I see, "eventually" is long ways away. But I won't complain. Girlfriend did manage to regrow my eyebrows and lashes.

I play with my hair as I step out of sight of the mirror. I'm not wearing makeup, not even a stitch. That's rare for me. I like being all dolled up, although au natural is how Gemini likes me best.

Maybe it's a good thing now, considering the ominous vibe I'm getting from him.

We reach our bedroom, the large California king bed calling to me to huddle beneath the clean white covers. But as I reach the edge, Gemini's hands find my waist, turning me carefully.

He grips my hips, his thumbs rubbing the exposed skin where my low-cut jeans hang and the T-shirt doesn't quite cover. If he was feeling playful he would tease the skin in slow seductive circles or tug the edges of the denim further down. Instead he continues the same languid movements as he wrestles with what to tell me.

"This is bad, isn't it?" I ask.

"It doesn't have to be," he murmurs.

As effortlessly as he says the words, we lose ourselves in each other's stares. It's easy to. In those beautiful dark eyes, I don't need to be so tough, and nothing is as bad it could be.

The moment doesn't last, nor do our stares linger. For what feels like the first time, he's the one who turns away. I'm not sure why until he speaks. "You've always struggled when it comes to us," he says. "Every step in our relationship has been a challenge from the start."

I can't deny that's true. "What's your point?"

My remark makes him smile. I think he's happy, although I also know there's more there. "You love me," he says. "I felt it long before you finally told me. And while we've endured a great deal, our love has remained and sustained us."

"It has," I manage, not wanting to picture my life without him. Been there, done that, and it was hell. That doesn't mean I'm ready for what I think he's about to ask.

"I want us to try for a family," he says.

"Eh?"

"A baby," he says, ignoring my slacking jaw. "I want you to have my child."

"You want to have a baby. With me?"

He smirks. "No, love."

"Oh, good," I say, patting his arm and attempting to walk away. "Glad we had this talk."

He holds tight and his smile warms. "I want to have several with you."

"I'm ready if you are," he adds when I stand there, torn between keeling over and running for my life.

My heart speeds up, and of course, it's not with joy. Holy shit seems more like the appropriate response. "You're not asking me to marry you." Hey, that's where I thought we were going with here, and damn it all, that was bad enough.

His eyebrows arch ever so slightly. "I would, but you've made it clear you're not the marriage type. Your words, not mine," he reminds me.

"You're being serious. About this whole kid thing?" I ask. "What about everything you said about none of us making it. About the world going ka-boom and every one of us blowing up like bits of shrapnel." I point at him. "And what about my vision? The one I told you about with the tiger skull." I don't want to think about what I saw, or how certain I am it belongs to the one tigress I know. I didn't even want to tell him about it, but I did, hoping it would help.

"Your visions give you a warning of what could come. They're not always accurate nor are they as strong as Destiny's."

"That didn't make what I saw any less real," I argue. "Remember all those other visions I had? They were dead on."

"You mean like the one of Celia and Aric holding their son? Yes, I remember the details Aric shared. You gave him and Celia hope, along with the drive to keep fighting."

"I meant the other ones, the not so hopeful ones with demons swarming me. It happened, Gemini. They found me and there was a great deal of swarming."

"But they didn't take you," he reminds me. "You fought through the attack and were spared because you were forewarned. This vision is another warning to be more vigilant so Celia stays safe."

"Did you tell Aric?" I make a face when he shoots me a "What do you think?" look. "No wonder he's so angry."

"We're all on edge because of it. But where Destiny foresees what should come, your premonitions serve to advise us. We'll take them, and use them to help her."

I tap my fingers against his chest. "So even with the skulls and all this crap we've been through over the course of a week, not to mention how stressed you are over us dying a miserable death, you want to talk babies."

"It's because of what's happed that I'm thinking long-term," he says. He falls back onto the bed, pulling me on top of him. "There has to be more than the darkness we're seeing. Take Fate existing with Destiny. It shouldn't be, but it is. The impossible becoming possible, making me think perhaps we will survive it all."

My hand smooths across the fabric of his shirt and my long hair drapes against his shoulder as my legs fall on either side of him in a straddle. "Are you trying to keep me out of trouble by knocking me up?" I ask. I tilt my head in the direction of the door. "You see how well it's working out for Celia. Being confined is driving her insane, whether it's to her benefit or not."

He lifts my hand, playing with it as he watches me closely. By the window, a flock of birds sing, their happy twittering suggesting they're pleased the mountain didn't crack in half. "That's part of it. But not the main reason," he adds quickly when I try to slip away. "Have you seen Aric and Celia, those moments where they're not thinking about the troubles ahead? They're happy, Taran, madly in love with the child that's coming and more in love with each other than I thought possible."

"They are," I say. "But those happy moments are rare."

"No, it only seems that way because the hard times are so

pronounced." He gathers me to him. "They don't have the ideal life they deserve. But we're fighting for the closest thing to it they can have." He pauses. "I think I should remind you, as I often remind myself, this fight isn't just for Aric and Celia. It extends to all of us, *our* happiness, *our* future."

"All right, say we get a chance at a real future," I say, my mind wandering. "A small pocket of something special that allows us to have babies of our own." I lift my chin to better see him. "There's nothing to stop that pocket from being ripped away."

"No, there's not," he agrees. "But with that mentality, man and *were* would have given up long before now."

He's right. That doesn't mean I'm ready to concede.

In the seconds that pass, I allow the steady beat of his heart against my ear to soothe me. "You analyze things constantly," I tell him. "Trying to find reason and logic even when everything is going to hell."

His knuckles dance along my lower back. "That's right."

"But although you're using reasoning to persuade me to make puppies with you, saying all the violence and scary obstacles we've faced aren't enough to give up, that's not why you want them." I smile when he stiffens, regardless of my nervousness. "What's going on?"

"It just feels right, Taran. Every time I'm with you, every time we make love, I want to take that next step with you." He considers his words. "I want us to have a family and grow old together, it's why I fight as hard as I do. I want this for all of us."

When I say nothing more he asks, "Do you want it?"

It's not something we've discussed much, mostly because I've raced away with my arms flailing every time he's brought up the subject of family. But Celia's pregnancy has affected me in ways I wasn't prepared for.

"I don't know," I confess. "I've never pictured myself as a mother. More like the 'fun aunt' the one who'll give them candy, let them stay up past midnight, take them shopping even when their closets are busting with toys and clothes."

He inhales deep, scenting my growing unease. "Seeing

how you were raised, and how painful your childhood was, I understand why you'd choose being an aunt over a mother."

"I always believed it's safer to be an aunt," I admit. "Then you never have to worry what will happen to your children if you're gone." My arm curls round him, seeking the comfort I need when the hurt from my past tugs at my insides. And as easily as that, his warmth and his presence encase me with love. I press a kiss to his chest. "But then you came along."

"And?" he asks.

"You're going to make me say it, aren't you?"

He chuckles, something he hasn't done in too many days. "Yes."

"And my world changed in ways I never counted on." I rub against him, allowing my hips to speak my desire as I kiss his lips. "I like you. A lot."

He sits up, cupping my cheek. "You like me?" he asks, his teeth taking a nibble and giving my lip a pull.

"Mmm-hmm," I admit, grinning as I watch the heat building in his gaze. "I say you're a keeper."

He laughs. "I'll remind you of that next time you're mad at me."

I give his thumb a swirl with my tongue. "Don't give me a reason to get mad and you won't have to remind me," I add, grazing the tip.

His dark eyes turn feral when I angle my head to give his palm a taste. "Don't do anything crazy and I won't give you a reason to be mad."

"Now, babe, when have I ever done anything crazy?"

He looks at me.

"Today?"

His eyebrows raise.

"In the last thirty minutes?"

He unsnaps the top of my jeans. "You've been good these last ten minutes, I'll give you that."

"Good?" I stroke my body along his. "Oh, and here I thought you liked me naughty."

I don't feel my shirt come off. From one moment to the

next, it's lying beside me.

"You want something?" I ask when he unhooks my bra with a twist of his fingers.

"Maybe," he says.

I jerk when his mouth attacks my nipple.

He bands his arm around my waist, holding me in place as he sucks harder. I gasp. Like my shirt, my jeans and my panties are simply gone, disappearing beneath hands that move fast and a strong body that moves faster.

His bare body writhes above mine when he flips me over, each caress and flick of his tongue, inciting me to feel more of him. I spread my legs, permitting him inside me and allowing him to take our pleasure to the next level.

His thrusts come hard and possessive. "I love you," he murmurs, his voice tight when I beg him for more. "I want forever with you."

Through grunts and deep tortured moans, we spend the remainder of the morning making love. It's incredible. It always is. But this time something is different, more of a need to please, rather than simply the desire to.

I suppose we need to remind ourselves that at least for now, we're safe, and in love, and that anything is possible.

We fall back in bed when we're finally sated, having exhausted the multiple positions Gemini threw us in. I rest my head against his shoulder. It's where I'm most comfortable, and where he likes me to sleep. But as my eyes drift closed, I realize how much changed with the talk we had.

He loves me, and now he's ready to love another . . . a smaller more fragile version of us.

Chapter Sixteen

"The Fate wants to see you."

The wolf in human form is huge, imposing, and, what the *fuck* are they feeding these guys? He takes up almost the entire doorway. That doesn't stop him from bowing his head when Gemini walks up behind me.

"Fine," Gemini tells him. "Tell him we'll be there shortly."

The young wolf shakes his head, his shaggy brown hair batting against his forehead and shoulders with how low he keeps his chin. "He says he wants to speak to your mate alone, or he won't speak at all."

I shrug. "All right."

I start to follow when Gemini cuts in front of me. "Where are you going?"

"To speak to Johnny," I reply. I try to inch around him only for him to sidestep in front of me.

"Really?" I ask.

"I know you think he's an innocent kid. He's not."

"You don't like him. I get it. That doesn't mean I can't talk to him." I cross my arms when he doesn't budge. "Gemini, he's not a prisoner and you are not his warden. You

178

heard the prez last night. We have no grounds to keep him."

It was a hell of a conference call, lots of growling and yelling, mostly by Tye. Tye demands a duel between him and Johnny to determine his worth. The witches demanded Tye respect Johnny's position within their kind, as they respect Celia and Omar. I don't think daddykins appreciated the witches placing Celia's importance before his, but ultimately, President Omar Gris de Leon ruled in favor of the wand-wavers, proclaiming Johnny is to be spared from harm at all costs.

"Babe," I press. "We've kept him here long enough. If we continue to treat him like our enemy and captive, we're no longer the good guys, and we risk offending the witches."

I'm not the first person to rise in defense of the witches. But I've been a part of this world long enough to recognize insults to packs, clans, and / or covens aren't easily dismissed by the species it offends. If anything it results in more distrust and paranoia.

Gemini scowls, more taken aback by the "bad guy" reference. "You know what I mean," I stress. "Omar gave us until this afternoon to release Johnny. Let me talk to him while I still can. I'll iron out the details of his departure and maybe get a better fix on him."

"Fine, but I'm going with you. If he speaks, he speaks to us."

Ever try to argue with a wolf? No? Lucky you.

I point at him. "Fine. But try not to be your growly self. You know I only like those sounds in bed."

I strut out the door, passing the wolf who practically becomes one with the wall when Gemini steps into the hall.

Johnny was kept for the past week on the other side of the campus, as far away from Celia as Aric could manage without shoving him into a tent and handing him a marshmallow to roast. I saw him the other day when we took a walk, flanked closely by the pack of snarling *weres* who weren't exactly making it a skip through the park.

Clouds loom over us as we step outside, turning the crisp mountain air colder. I huddle into the long cardigan sweater I pulled on following my shower. The sweater is warm and a lovely shade of "oatmeal", very neutral like my jeans and white shirt, and very unlike the hot pink platforms I'm wearing.

Every woman needs color in her life, even a "weird girl" like me.

"Do you have to wear those?" Gemini asks. He keeps his stare ahead. "I assumed you learned your lesson the last time you chased Fate."

"Hmm," I say. "Are you trying to tell me he'll outwit and outrun you wolves, and that it will be up to little ol' me to catch him?" The collective scoffs from the wolves trailing us are telling enough. They're in their human forms, not that they can't tear something to shreds with their bare hands. "Then don't worry about it," I add. I wrap my arms around Gemini's waist. "Besides, you don't seem to mind the heels when I wear them to bed."

A few wolves glance over their shoulder, trying not to chortle at Gemini's beat red face. "Turn around," I say. "This is a private conversation and considering you spend most of your lives naked and womanless, you have no room to judge."

I adjust my hold over Gemini. "The cute shoes stay."

He slips his arm around my shoulder. "I suppose it's too much to ask for you to be practical."

"In my world, fashion is more important."

"In my world, footwear you can run in keeps you alive."

"I can run in these," I add, sounding insulted.

"Can you climb a tree in them?" the wolf beside me asks. He averts his gaze when Gemini narrows his eyes. I guess the wolf isn't supposed to talk to me too soon after my being in bed with Gemini reference.

That doesn't stop me from answering. "Why would I need to climb a tree?"

"To escape," he mumbles, careful to keep his gaze off me. "You know danger. Human women have been known to do that."

"Sweetheart, I'm not exactly human," I remind him. "And if I'm in danger I'm not climbing a tree. I'm burning it and the whole damn forest down if I have to."

I hop up the stacked stone steps when we reach one of the original structures. This building was always a dorm and used during the time of war to house *were* families fleeing to safety. I try not to think about how fast it will fill back up, especially if the shapeshifters do come a-calling and try to bust down the doors.

"Any word on the shapeshifters?" I ask as we step inside. "Or their nematodes?"

"Neophytes?" he offers.

"Same difference," I say.

He smirks. "No just more chatter linking them as the probable leaders of the Dark Alliance."

I pause as we reach the bottom of the steps. "Like what?"

The wolves turn to face him, scenting the same thing I sense, that we don't know everything.

Gemini crosses his arms. "We were going to brief everyone this afternoon," he says, more to them than me. "The Chinese Imperial coven killed a shapeshifter early yesterday, an old one by the name of Shakur."

My jaw drops. "He went after Genevieve?"

"Not exactly." Gemini doesn't seem to want to answer. "He targeted Ines's daughters. They're teens and not as formidable. He would have succeeded had the Imperials not been guarding them."

"Are the Imperials all right?" I ask.

"Four didn't survive the onslaught. They were too young and not as experienced," he explains, his jaw hardening. "The others were more mature and strong witches in their own right. They were close to destroying him when Ines arrived. She finished him off, then cut out his heart and burned it."

"Why?" I ask. It's not that I'm surprised a head witch would be so brutal, it's more like I recognize her actions as a message.

"Shakur tried to rape and kill her daughters. If it weren't for the Imperials, he would have brutalized them." He watches me carefully. "Burning the heart was a warning meant for his mate."

No wonder I'm just now learning of this. He was trying to spare me from the gruesome details, not his pack.

"The shifter was mated?" I ask.

"Yes."

Except for my lips, I'm not able to move. "That means the mate will seek revenge."

"And make Ines her first target," he replies, finishing for me. "More Imperials have been summoned, in addition to several *were* packs in Europe."

His head jerks up, almost at the same time the wolves growl in the direction of the second level.

My arm twitches as Johnny's magic spills into the foyer. "What is it? I ask.

"Blood," he replies, racing up the steps.

Everyone bolts past me, I don't think I'm even to the fourth step when the door at the far end of the hall is thrown open.

"Son of bitch," I say, my heels stomping as I race forward.

The wolves huddle outside the room which is odd. I expected everyone to storm in and, I don't know, carry out Johnny's broken and limp form. I don't realize what's happening until I move closer and see Gemini with his arm out, keeping everyone back.

A large wolf with a heavy coat of brown fur steps in front of me when I snake my way around the other *weres*. He must have been assigned to guard the room.

Deep creases form around his eyes when he frowns, making it clear I'm not allowed through. I bend and pat him on the head. "You must be new here," I say, my smile as friendly as his scowl. "If you weren't, you would know that's my mate and you don't get to keep me from him."

He exposes his fangs when I straighten. My right arm flares with blue and white flames. "Two things," I tell him. "You're pissing me off and more importantly, you're pissing off Sparky. *Get out of my way.*"

"Let her through," Gemini says, his voice oddly hollow.

The other *weres* rub their arms as if itchy. Something is

off. I reach the door, jerking my chin in the same way I would if I smelled something bad. But there's no bad smell.

It's simply magic.

I move slowly. All the furniture in Johnny's loft has been pushed against the wall, creating a large open space where he sits at the center. He's barely dressed, wearing a pair of jeans and nothing else. Piles of broken glass lie around him, separated according to color, the largest piece, a red one, clutched tightly in his hand.

"What are you doing?" Gemini asks.

"I'll replace the vase," Johnny says.

"That's not what I asked," Gemini growls, more unnerved by the thick and strange magic layering the air than what Johnny has done to the room and to himself.

That's the difference between me and him. Magic aside, this is a disturbing sight. "Are you all right?" I ask, certain Johnny has snapped.

"Would you care if I wasn't?" he asks, smirking.

"I would," I respond truthfully.

My honesty, and I suppose the concern shadowing my features, erases his cockiness, leaving me with the young man I first saw, and all the vulnerability I noticed.

He straightens, exposing his stomach and the blood drenching his torso. The damaged skin where the images of his bandmates once lay, as well as the other tats we destroyed, healed within a few hours. Most witches require healing herbs, or the attention of a mystical healer to tend to their injuries, otherwise they mend at a human's pace. Johnny can heal himself. It's one of his gifts as a Fate. But here he is, covered with blood from injuries he self-inflicted.

At first I think he's cutting and he's more damaged than any of us suspected. I rush into the kitchen and snag a towel, hurrying back to Johnny.

"Taran," Gemini warns, hooking my arm and keeping me in place.

I slip from his hold. "He needs help. I'm not going to stand here and watch him bleed.

I kneel in front of Johnny, noting how he watches me

when I grip his shoulder and press the towel against his stomach. He's shocked I'm being kind to him, or more to the point, that anyone would show him kindness.

"It's okay," Johnny tells me.

I meet his face, growing sad as I take in every speck of his being. Everything about Johnny screams he's endured too much too soon, and all he ever wanted was love. He's screwed up. Be it his life, his lifestyle, or something more, he's nothing but a ball of insecurity and misery, carefully glossed over with tattoos and cloaked beneath the façade of a rock god. "It's really not," I tell him quietly.

He tilts his head, his eyes brimming. I think he's going to cry. Instead he offers me a small smile laced with enough gratitude to warm my soul. "I'm not hurt," he says. "I'm just working."

He places his hand over mine, stiffening at the sound of Gemini's growls. Very carefully, he guides my hand across his torso, using me to help him wipe. I notice cuts, lots of them digging deep. But as he lifts my hand away, I realize they're not just slices across his skin, rather an outline of a bird with long feathers.

Like an animated movie coming to life across a screen, colors of blue, green, red, and gold glisten and spread along his skin, each vibrant tone matching the pieces of the broken glass laid out around Johnny.

The bird turns its head, blinking once before shaking out its long feathers.

"It's a peacock," Johnny tells me. He releases my hand. I was so captivated by the image, I hadn't realized he was still holding me. "Not one like in a zoo or the wild, more like how I see one in my head." He leans back on his heels, exposing the entirety of the image carved into the length of his torso.

The peacock sits up and away from Johnny's stomach, keeping its lower half seated as if nesting. It watches me closely, clicking its small beak several times before its tail feathers fan out in a beautiful spray of gold.

The tips are long enough to tickle Johnny's skin. He chuckles. "Okay, now he's just showing off."

"He's alive?" I ask.

Johnny's smile vanishes. "As much as he can be," he replies. "He's a part of me, my magic, I mean."

"Can you communicate with him?" I scan the remainder of his exposed skin, including the sleeve tattoos inked into his arms.

"Yes," Johnny answers. "But not as much as I'd like to."

"What do you mean?"

The peacock settles back into Johnny's skin, becoming merely another graphic.

Johnny presses his palms into the floor and straightens his legs. "When I was little, I didn't have any friends, and I sure as shit didn't have any fans." His attention falls to the peacock. "People thought I was weird and kept their distance." He huffs. "And my folks kept me plenty far away from other witches. I got lonely and started making friends of my own."

"On your skin?"

"Yeah, mostly," he says, his voice drifting. "It started in grade school. I had trouble learning and understanding so instead of taking notes or whatever, I'd draw on my hand. Drawing was the one thing I was good at. Birds were my favorite. One day, the one I drew on my hand started to move."

He glances up when the door snaps shut. I don't have to guess Gemini asked for privacy and ordered the *weres* to wait downstairs, just like I don't have to guess that he chose to remain.

"Your drawings became your friends," I guess.

"In a way," he says. "I wasn't alone when they were with me and I wasn't the only freak in the room."

"Is that why you have so much ink, so you don't have to be alone?"

His lips press tight. "Something like that."

I think back to the night of the concert, and how his tats fought so hard to save him. "So your bandmates were never real, and because of it, they weren't real werewolves."

All the hurt Johnny carries spills into the air, drenching it with melancholy. "They were real to me, Taran."

We sit in silence for a long while. I want him to speak, but I won't force him to. Whatever he feels or needs to articulate should come freely. I think the world owes him that much.

"When do I get to get out of here?" he finally asks.

I look to where Gemini waits with his arms crossed. "Technically, you're free to go whenever you wish."

"What the fuck is that supposed to mean?" Johnny asks.

"Watch your mouth," Gemini growls at him.

"You're not our prisoner," I explain quickly. "And believe it or not, we don't mean you any harm. But there is a group referred to as the Dark Legion. They're growing in numbers and are targeting our strongest."

"You mean like you?" he asks.

I take another look at the peacock. "More like you," I reply. "If they know about you, they'll find you and either kill you or try to use your power. If you let us, we can protect you."

"I have protection," Johnny says, motioning to his tats. "And a fucking legion of my own. My fans would do anything for me."

"Your fans are human. Neither they nor your magic is enough," Gemini says. "You saw how easily we crushed everything you threw at us and how Taran alone was able to catch you. The Dark Ones won't be as merciful to you or your fans."

"Think of them," I plead. "All those people who adore you could be hurt. You've been hiding out in the open, but that's no longer an option. Not after everything that happened at the concert."

"Why not? The investigators chalked it up to being part of the show," Johnny points out. "I saw it on T.V... But my crew, they're going to know."

"The investigators only claimed the effects were part of your show because that's what we wanted them to believe," Gemini tells him. "As for your crew, they were also taken care of."

His face goes white. "Not like that," I explain quickly. The investigators and everyone backstage was entranced. We have people for situations like this to keep humans from becoming aware of our world."

"People? You mean witches," he scoffs. "Yeah, saw all they're good for."

I place my hand on his knee. As a whole, *weres* don't like their mates demonstrating affection to anyone aside from close family. It's never been an issue for me and Gemini since I'm not the affectionate type. But Johnny is killing me. The experiences he's endured: losing his parents, having no friends, being ostracized by society? I've experienced all of it, and that shit still hurts.

"The shifters are going to find out about you, if they don't already know." I sigh when he won't budge. "They don't care about the human populace or about being discovered. They'll mow down anyone in their path, including your fans."

"Then I'll die with them," he says, the severity in his tone alerting me to the truth behind his statement. "They loved me when no one else would." A tear cuts down his cheek. "You saw them, right? They're the only ones who care whether I live or die."

"They're not the only ones," I whisper. It takes all I have not to cry with him. "Please, Johnny, let us help you."

"No," he says, his voice breaking. "I want my life back." He looks at Gemini. "Just get me out of here, man. You don't ever have to see me again."

Gemini meets him square in the face. "If that's what you want."

"It's what I need," he says, punching out every syllable. He quivers, his respirations increasing. "My parents used to tell me that one day, I'd understand why they kept me away from the mystical world." He laughs without humor. "I didn't get it. I was excited when they told me what I was, thinking I was going to Hogwarts or some shit. I didn't understand why they didn't want me to be a part of it and was *pissed* at them for denying me friends and keeping me away from beings who wouldn't consider me a freak." He looks around. "I get it now. This is fucked up and I want out."

"Fine." Gemini jerks his head in the direction of the door. "Let's go."

Johnny rises a lot faster than I do. I stand slowly, pulling away from Gemini when he tries to help me. "You're letting him leave, just like that, even after seeing what he can do."

"I sent a wolf to inform our Elders of the Fate's abilities before I shut the door," he tells me. "But his magic changes nothing. He's not Pack, he's no *lone* I need to monitor, nor is he a rogue vamp or witch who needs to be accounted for." He looks to Johnny. "He's a Fate, who with or without us, will meet his."

Johnny hurries to the kitchen where he left a T-shirt draped over a stool. It's too big for him, the *were* he borrowed it from far exceeded Johnny's leaner build, making Johnny appear smaller and younger.

"What do you see?" I ask Johnny. "When your predictions come, do you know what's going to happen to you?"

There's no genuineness in his smile, and far too much bitterness. "Yeah. I'm going down as the greatest Fate that ever was. Don't you worry about me."

It's what he claims, but I don't think he means it in the way he intends.

"Can I get a phone? I need to call my manager." He swipes at his face. "Drake thought I was tripping. He didn't understand what I was saying the last time we spoke. I-I-I need to tell him I'm coming back, and that the tour is back on."

"Sure." I reach for my phone in my back pocket and hand it to him, noting how badly he's shaking. "Are you all right?"

"Yeah, and no. I don't know what I'm going to tell him. It looks like I just up and left. He's probably going to lose it on me."

I remembered hearing Johnny on the phone with his manager. He was scared, promising to continue touring regardless that it seemed he was really gunning to quit. I don't know Drake, but I imagine that like his fans, he probably can't get enough of Johnny.

"Were you planning on walking away from the music industry?" I ask.

Johnny looks up from fiddling with my phone. "No. I just wanted to take a break. Stop touring for a while, maybe try acting or take a real vacation, you feel me?" He taps the numbers on my phone. "I've been on the road since Drake discovered me three years ago—Drake, it's Johnny. Sorry, I've been out of touch." He glances my way. "I lost it a little. But I'm okay now. I'm coming back to you, to the hotel. Just wait for me, okay?"

He disconnects. "He wasn't there. Do you mind if I hang onto your phone for a while?"

"No, but I do," Gemini answers for me. "We'll provide you with a secure line." He shoots me a look, warning me it's a done deal and not to bother arguing. "I'll be the one taking you back to your people. Where do you want to go?"

"Take me to Santa Barbara," Johnny orders. His voice lowers when he catches Gemini's non-too-pleased expression. "Please," he adds. "He's at the Belmond."

"You're sure?" Gemini asks.

"Positive," Johnny answers. "It's been a few days, but Drake wouldn't just leave me. I'm his only client." He shrugs. "He booked the top floor for us for a week."

In other words, Drake wouldn't leave without his meal ticket.

Gemini reaches for his phone, tapping an icon with a moon on it. "I need a private plane chartered for the Fate . . . Santa Barbara." He shifts his stare on me. "As soon as possible."

He disconnects, motioning me to follow him out.

"Wait, where are you going?" Johnny asks, hurrying to catch up with us.

"Nowhere you need to be," Gem tells him. "Wait here until I come for you."

"I thought you said I wasn't a prisoner," Johnny calls after him.

"You're not, I just need a moment with my mate," Gemini replies. He throws open the door where about four imposing and snarling *weres* wait. "My pack doesn't like the aroma of your magic, and the scent of blood has them on edge. I'd encourage you to stay on your own accord."

"I can wait here," Johnny stammers.

Gemini slams the door behind him. He continues forward, his movements so quick, I have to run after him. "You weren't very nice to him," I say.

Gemini stalks forward. "He's lucky I didn't throw him against the Goddamn wall giving the way he was looking at you."

I roll my eyes. Now I get it. I snag his wrist and pull him into a small lounge, shutting the door behind me. "You're being ridiculous—"

I squeak when Gemini hauls me against his hard body, the passion surging within him stirring my own. I wrap my arms around his neck. I want to kiss him, but the fierceness he greets me with turns my caress more soothing than sexy.

"Taran," he says, his tone severe. "I don't like the Fate and I don't trust him."

I tilt my head. "Because you think he's hitting on me, or because of something else?"

He turns his gaze in the direction we came from. "I'm not sure, maybe both. What worries me most is that your magic is different when you're around him." He looks at me then. "It clashes with his in one way, but in another, it seems to compliment it. I can't explain it. All I can tell you is my wolves warn against it."

Chapter Seventeen

I didn't like what Gemini had to say about my magic and Johnny's clashing. I didn't like what he had to say about them complimenting each other either. It doesn't seem right, considering we're so different. Or maybe that's what I want to believe.

I turn the wheel, gently guiding Gemini's SUV along each curve in the road. I'm so lost in my thoughts, I don't realize how close I am to Tahoe until the highway leading to Squaw Valley ends and the one running parallel to Tahoe begins.

My gaze flickers to my arm as the road evens out. There's a definite pull when I'm around Johnny. I just didn't attribute it the same way Gemini did.

I began sensing magic more strongly when we first moved to Tahoe, so as much as Johnny's magic felt different, it didn't surprise me to feel it once I realized what he was. What did surprise me was how easily he mesmerized me with his singing and power, and how the ache from his past stirred the ache I've tried too many times to forget. My sisters and I are immune to vampiric hypnoses and suggestions. None of us, however, seem immune to Johnny's draw.

It wasn't until Gem told me how unnerved his wolves were by Johnny's mojo that I took more care to try to understand it. This isn't simply my lover being jealous and protective. He's leery, very much as he would be in the presence of another predator.

My right arm gives a shudder as I remember that surge of power that filled the foyer when we entered the dorm. In making himself bleed, maybe he also bled out an extra dose of his magic.

"Are you agreeing or disagreeing?" I ask Sparky when she twitches again.

She doesn't respond, but I suppose that's a good thing. I'm weird enough. The last thing I need is my hand turning into a talking sock puppet, minus the sock.

I rub the back of my neck, trying to ease some of the stress from the day. It's close to dinner. Soon the sun will turn in and allow the moon to take charge. I never expected to arrive this late and planned to leave for home immediately following lunch. But then Johnny happened.

Spell-wielding or not, it was hard to find him as I did. I didn't feel right taking off until the plane was secured and Johnny was escorted from the Den. I couldn't abandon him, knowing how intimidated he is by the Pack. Being the odd guy out takes on a whole new meaning around beasts with fangs and claws just waiting for you to make one wrong move.

"Poor sap," I mutter.

Despite the day, and the last few, my mood lifts when the sign for Dollar Point comes into view. I'm almost home. But as I catch my first sight of Tahoe, and how the swirls of orange and pink sky cast light along the lake's gentle waves, my smile vanishes.

"Destiny isn't well, T." Those were Shayna's exact words when I called to make sure it was okay to visit. "But it would mean the world to her if you came by."

Jesus. How could I refuse?

I pull into my neighborhood, a small cul-de-sac with a few homes. Most of our neighbors are young professionals, here for the serenity the lake offers and the night life just a short drive away. Most things they've seen, they've been "encouraged" to forget through magic, for their safety, but more so for their sanity.

Two SUVs are parked directly in front of the house, and two more are stationed close to the path that leads to the lake. Mrs. Mancuso is sweeping her walkway. I nod in the direction of the stiff middle finger she waves at me. Oh, yes, it's good to be home.

"*Pace*," I say, whispering the word that allows me safe passage through the wards and into the garage. My body cools as I feel the wall of protection part. It's only then do I hit the garage door opener and drive through.

The double wide door creaks open loudly, in the way it has since we first moved in. The sound brings me comfort and I'll take all it gives me. This isn't going to be a fun visit. I only hope that I can somehow offer comfort, and that I don't yet have to say goodbye.

The door leading into the laundry room opens as I slip out of my ride and near the steps. A few *weres* I don't know pile out in human form.

"The mate," the one in the lead tells the others.

They nod, understanding. "I'm Taran," I clarify, offering a wave.

Their gazes shift to my arm and back to me. "We'll be outside guarding the perimeter, mate to Gemini."

Oh, yes, *weres* are all about the warm and fuzzies. "Thanks," I say, beaming. "Glad we had this time to bond."

I hop up the stairs. It's warm in the laundry room with the dryer on, the clothes spinning gently as I step into the kitchen.

I'm surprised to find Bren there.

With Emme.

And enough tension between them to spackle tile.

He leans back into the kitchen chair, threading his hands behind his head, watching Emme prepare a tray of food, and overall acting very mate-like.

"Emme is Bren's mate," I insisted the other night over

dinner.

"He can't be," Aric replied, not bothering to look up from his food.

"Why? Because you don't think he's good enough for her?" I countered.

He looked up then. "That, and because he's been a *lone* all his life."

"He's not a *lone*. He's part of the Pack," I reminded him. *"Your pack."*

"No, we welcomed him into the Pack," Gemini clarified. "But his *lone* tendencies have kept him from fully committing to being one of us." His expression sharpened. "It's these same innate tendencies that will keep his wolf from recognizing and committing to his mate, *if* he even has one."

"Bullshit," I said, and I'm saying it now.

The strain between them reminds me of the time when Gemini and I broke up, how awful it was, and how far away he seemed even when we stood mere inches apart. Yet as much as I hate what's happening with them, and to them, it doesn't compare to the despair competing for space in the room.

Death lurks close. I feel him. And there's nothing I can do to kick his ass out.

"Hey," I say.

I wasn't sure Emme realized I was waiting by the door, not with the way she kept her head down and her full attention on preparing the tray. She covers a hot bowl of soup with a lid, and arranges a cloth napkin and a spoon carefully beside it, taking her time to make sure everything is just right. It's only when she finishes that she walks toward me and hugs me gently.

"Hi," she says.

I hold her against me, worried I'll somehow hurt her, even though I realize she's not as delicate as she appears. "I didn't know you were here," I admit. "I thought Shayna and Koda were watching Destiny today."

"They were, but they've been here a lot. I told them I'd take over her care and stay the night. This way, they can get a break, too."

"You've been here a lot, too," I remind her. "Just as much as Shayna and Koda."

"It's all right. I want to be," she whispers. "No one else comes, but us." She lifts away from me so I can see her face and all the sympathy it carries. "She doesn't say much. But she always seems happy to see me."

How could she not be? Emme is like an angel you'd want welcoming you into heaven. At least, she's who I'd want for me.

I play with her hair, praying heaven won't claim Emme before me. I'd gladly go first. The world is kinder with her here, more soft, and maybe more innocent, too. "Can I see her?" I ask.

"That would mean a lot to her," she says, reciting Shayna's almost exact words.

I glance at Bren who's unusually quiet. "You okay?" I ask.

"As good as I can be, considering all this shit," he says.

"I know what you mean," I mutter.

He pushes out of his seat and lifts the tray, easily balancing everything with one hand. "I can take that," Emme says, not that she looks at him when she says it.

"I got it," Bren says, his tone making it clear there's no sense in arguing. "I'm not sure what kind of mood you'll find Tye in, and I'm not taking any chances."

"He hasn't left her side," Emme adds, her attention darting briefly to Bren.

"Of course not," I say, casting them one hell of a look. "They're mates. Together is how they belong."

A small line forms between Emme's brows when she frowns. She may not know what I'm talking about, but Bren does, and that shit needs to come from him.

He looks at me as Emme turns to fill a glass of iced tea. "You know what I mean," I mouth.

He straightens to his full height. "You're wrong," he replies.

"What?" Emme asks, glancing up.

She lowers the pitcher of iced tea back on the counter when all Bren and I do is glare at each other. The Lord is testing me because I'm ready to knock this wolf out. Except now isn't the time to zap some sense into him.

Bren marches ahead of us, his stance as rigid as the strain surging between Emme and him.

I should say something, again, now is not the time to rip into him. So I take in my surroundings, allowing the familiarity of my home to settle me.

It hasn't been that long since I was last here, but already it's too long. God, how I wish things would get back to normal, at least normal for us. I miss the days where my sisters and I would sit at the table and have tea. It's something we all used to enjoy. We'd talk about everything or nothing at all, laugh at something goofy Shayna said, something raunchy Bren did, or the plans we had with our wolves.

I took it for granted, and didn't realize how much I look forward to it. Life's like that. The simple things are often the ones we most want back.

The heels of my hot pink shoes barely make a sound against the dark hardwood floors as I cross the kitchen, despite how each step feels more leaden than the last.

"I wish Destiny would stay in my room," I say quietly.

Emme pauses behind Bren as he reaches for the door leading to the basement. "I told her you'd offered," she explains. "But she said she didn't want to die in your room and have you think it was haunted. Especially if you and Gemini were having 'relations.'" Her face reddens. "Those are her words, not mine."

I laugh a little, and so does Emme, no matter that anything surrounding "relations" always cause her cheeks to redden. It's such a Destiny thing to say, and am I ever going to miss her saying them.

Bren opens the door and hops down the steps, the ease and speed in which he moves (even with his hands full!) a great deal more graceful than what I manage in my shoes. He stops halfway down, his spine stiffening. "You want me to help you or something?"

I grip the railing, thinking he's talking to me. "I'm all right," I say. "I just need to go slow."

"I meant Emme," he says, turning back. "But I can help you, too, I guess."

Emme is in flats and a soft pink maxi dress. If she wanted to, she could probably swing from a vine in the clothes she's wearing as opposed to the ensemble I chose to strut around in. So, yeah, what in the *hell* is up with him? He's not just some horny wolf like Gemini and Aric claim. It's more like the *lone* and the man in him are fighting fang and claw not to see what's in front of him. Or should I say, *who's* in front of him.

"I'm fine, Bren," Emme says, her voice mimicking the confusion I'm feeling.

"I'm just saying, I don't mind carrying you or some shit," he says.

He stomps ahead. I do, too, catching Emme's arm. "Did you kiss him again?" I mouth, not wanting Bren's super-hearing to pick up on what I'm asking. I do a double-take at the sight of Emme's blush.

"No." She glances in the direction he disappeared. "I think he's trying to be a gentleman."

I'm not sure if she's trying to mean what she says or if she actually believes it. All I know is that there's more here than either are saying, and likely more they're doing.

I release her arm slowly when I hear Bren address Tye.

"Taran's here," he says. "And Emme has food for Destiny."

I know Tye is upset, and too many other horrible emotions to name, and because of it, I've tried to prepare myself for how I'd find them. But I'm still not ready.

I step down. To our right is our game room with a pool table, large sectional, and a flat screen fixed to the wall. To our left is the bar area. In front of the bar, a full-sized bed has been placed, the electronic kind used in hospitals to elevate the foot and head of the bed.

Destiny's upper body is positioned sitting up, with pillows propped behind her head and under her arms to keep her supported. Strands of her long dark hair fall free from her lopsided bun, making her appear haggard while the white of her zebra print pajamas further highlights her pallor.

Tye waits beside her, the small cushioned chair he's sitting in barely enough to hold his large body. He's hunched over with his head bowed and his hands clasped together. I think he's praying. It's not until I get a close look at the way his hands tremble that I realize he's only barely containing his rage.

Destiny blinks her eyes partially open, her lids heavy with apparent weakness and exhaustion.

"Hi, Taran," she says, her voice so frail I barely hear it.

I swallow the building lump in my throat and smile. "Hey, Des. How's it going, girl?"

She glances at Tye. "It's going," she replies, struggling to form her words. But then she smiles, and it's all I can do not to cry.

Bren holds out his hand, keeping me back when I try to approach.

"Tye?" Bren calls. "The girls want to get closer to Destiny. They'll serve the food."

Tye rubs his face hard. "It's up to her," he says, answering as if Bren asked a question. He drops his hands away. "Des, you want to eat? Emme has that noodle soup you like."

He likely smelled it even with the lid in place. Her smile lifts a little more. "You want me to, don't you?"

"It'll be good for you," he tells her, his expression worn.

Poor guy looks like hell. His eyes are sunken from lack of sleep and he's lost a tremendous amount of his bulk. Tye was always extraordinary. But that strength that used to flare like a lighthouse has been swallowed by a sea of torment. He hurts because she does. If that's not real love, if that's not what it means to be mated, I'll never know what is.

It takes her a moment to reply, and I'm sure she's drifted off to sleep. She nods, in a way that's barely perceivable, the motion draining her of her strength.

Bren gestures Emme forward with a tilt of his head. She lifts the tray from Bren's hand and carefully places it across

Destiny's lap.

"I can help you eat," she offers.

"That might be better," Destiny says. At least that's what it sounds like. I'm straining to hear.

Emme lifts the cloth napkin. "Here, sweetie," she says. "Why don't we place this around your neck to spare your pretty clothes from any food that may drip."

She pauses when Tye stiffens and an ungodly glare shoots in her direction.

Bren hauls Emme behind him, stepping into Tye's line of vision, his features as fierce. "You know Emme would never hurt her," Bren tells him, his voice gruff.

"I know," Tye says, his comment sounding forced and too close to a growl. "I just . . ." He takes a breath, spitting out a row of swears.

Emme edges around Bren and carefully walks to Tye's side of the bed. She reaches for him, only to have Bren snap his hand over her wrist and yank her back behind him. His response is so quick, I barely registered it. He didn't hurt her, if anything he seemed to use more care than usual. But it's as if his touch is too much for her and she shrinks away.

"Bren, let her go," I say, meaning it in more ways than one. God damn it, if he's not willing to do anything about their connection, the least he can do is not string her along.

My lightning cracks and sparks fly above my head when his hold becomes more shielding. "Bren," I warn.

"He's not going to hurt me," Emme says, keeping her face away from Bren and fixed on Tye.

I'm not sure who she's referring to, it's hard to tell with both *weres* so on edge. She slips from Bren's hold. But just when I start to think she meant Bren, Tye is who she addresses.

"Tye," she says, easing slowly around the bed. "I can help soothe you, if you let me." She pauses a few feet from him. "Will you let me?"

He swallows hard, though says nothing. Emme takes his response as a yes and falls to her knees in front of him, assuming a passive and less threatening stance. Using the same gentle movements she used with Destiny, Emme takes Tye's hands in hers, her gentle yellow light sheathing him and causing him to collapse forward. He sways in place, fighting to keep his balance. But then slowly, his spine curls and his head gently lowers, pressing against Emme's.

She sighs, keeping her eyes closed as her small body bears his weight and her healing *touch* shoulders his emotions.

Tye looks ready to break down, and the way Emme rubs her forehead against his, she's ready to let him. It's a beautiful sight, drawing a brittle yet grateful smile from Destiny. I turn away, trying to stay strong. It's only then I catch how much it seems to tear Bren apart.

His knuckles crack as his hands ball into fists. I clasp his wrists, my jaw falling open with how rigid he appears. "Hey," I say, keeping my voice as soft as possible. "Stop it, okay? She's only trying to help him."

His chest rises and falls, his breaths labored. "I don't want him to hurt her," he bites out.

"He won't," I say. I should be annoyed by how he's acting. More than anything, I'm stunned.

I release him as Emme's light recedes, watching Bren closely as I step toward her and Tye.

"Thank you," Tye says. "I didn't realize how bad it was."

Emme can't heal a broken heart, but her light is as gentle as she is, allowing her to soothe spirits and give them some reprieve.

She cups his shoulder. "Why don't you take a moment?" she suggests carefully. "You could use a break."

Tye doesn't move. "Please, listen to Emme," Destiny says, dragging out each word. "I'm worried about you."

"*She's* worried about *me*," Tye mumbles.

"Tye, please," Destiny says, what little energy she has leaving her quickly.

His bruised gaze meets hers, watching her as she returns to asleep. He waits for her to respond, to open her eyes. When she doesn't, it's as if the last bit of hope he has vanishes.

"I'll be outside," Tye says.

For all Emme's light seemed to help, it was only temporary. He storms away, angry, and likely hurting more than before.

I should let him be. I don't of course, not in the condition he's in. I follow him out through the sliding glass doors. He doesn't bother shutting it, knowing I'm behind him. I close it using care not to make a sound and watch him as he stomps to the edge of our property.

He stares out in the directions of the thick woods. I take my time to reach him, that horrible feeling of dread following me closely and threatening to permanently engrave itself into my soul.

Tye is enduring so much, his beast is likely going wild. So when I reach him, I don't dare stand behind him. I stand beside him, crossing my arms and waiting for him to speak.

"Do you want to know how many of the witch elite have come to see their shining star?"

I already know the answer. He doesn't have to tell me.

"Not a one. You and your sisters are the only ones who visit. Even Celia in those small moments she's allowed off the damn mountain, this is where she chooses to be, with her. With my girl."

"We like her," I say.

He presses his lips, keeping his focus ahead, not that he likely sees anything in front of him. "She likes you, too. Always has."

I know he means it, and it breaks my heart a little more.

He scoffs, his mind switching to those who haven't been as nice. "The witches always whispered about her being odd for a Destiny," he tells me. "I'd hear them, in the other room as a kid when me and Des used to play on the floor with our toys. 'She's not a traditional Destiny,' they'd say, alluding to how the previous ones were so tall and striking. But that didn't stop them from associating with her. Oh, no, because no matter what she looked like or how she dressed, Des still was the one, the sole witch gifted with power beyond belief." He turns his chin in my direction. "Something her parents reminded everyone, every chance they got."

I've heard stories of her parents, both heavyweights in the mystical world and oozing with money. Her mother used to model, I think, and her father reigns as one of the most compelling warlocks in existence. I've never met them, nor do I want to.

"Have her parents been by?" I ask. I'm not trying to rile him further, but that's all I manage to do.

"No. They called once," he says, holding out a finger. "Telling her that she was better than this and a true Destiny wouldn't be taken so easily. What kind of horseshit is that? They might as well have called her a loser like all those other bitches eluded to her entire life." He turns his attention back toward the woods. "It's why she dresses the way she does. She knew she wouldn't fit in and decided to have a little fun." His voice fades. "She was always like that, you know. Looking forward instead of paying attention to what was said behind her."

"She's a good person, strong," I smile. "And a freak of nature, but aren't we all?"

Tye meets me with a frown, only to chuckle at the sight of my smile. It's a rare feat, being able to laugh even as another piece of you splinters away. I guess that's why I've always liked Tye.

"Yeah, aren't we all," he admits.

The sliding glass doors open and Bren charges out, appearing worse for wear. He holds his hand out as we start forward. "It's fine." He strips out of his shirt. "But I need a good long run and so do you." His attention shoots from Tye to me. "Destiny just finished eating and wants a bath. Emme says she needs your help washing her."

"Sure. No problem." I pat Tye's shoulder when he hesitates. "Go with Bren," I insist. "Destiny could probably use a little girl time."

I walk away, hoping he doesn't follow or know why Destiny wants to get cleaned up.

Her time is coming faster than any of us are ready for, and she knows it.

I hurry to the door, whispering the power word that

unlocks the wards and keeping my stare forward so Tye can't catch what I'm thinking in my features.

Holy shit, I don't want Destiny to die. But I can't dismiss what I see, or what I feel being around her. It's like this vat of power, once filled to the brim is slowly being emptied.

As I close the door, Bren's large wolf form disappears into the woods, a white lion racing behind him.

Emme stands at the foot of Destiny's bed, her arms filled with fresh linens and her eyes swimming with tears. "I set up a shower chair, will you help me?"

"Anything you want, Emme," I reply. "Just let me know what she needs."

She places the fresh sheets and blankets on the bar and hurries into the bathroom. There's not a lot of space in there, just a standing shower, a small sink, and toilet. But it's enough.

I reach Destiny and pull back the sheets. She doesn't move and I'm worried she's asleep until her lids flutter. "Are you sure you're up for this?" I ask, concerned that the exertion maybe too much.

"I want to look nice . . ." she croaks. "For Tye."

Of course she does, he's been her one true friend, and will be her forever mate.

I try to smile, but there's that awful ache again, casting a sting along my eyes. "Let's help you out of your clothes, all right? We'll change your bed and give you something fun to wear."

"Taran," she says, her voice excruciatingly feeble. "I can't see anymore."

I cover my mouth as a strange film sweeps across her once bright irises. "You're blind?"

"No." The skin along her neck pulls as if she's trying to swallow, but isn't quite able to. "My visions are gone. I can't bring one up . . . I've tried . . . I need to see . . . need to warn you."

"Warn us about what?" I ask.

"About the babies." Each syllable she manages is sluggish, making her hard to understand.

I lean in close, trying to hear her and understand, too. "The babies?" I repeat. My stomach churns. I think I know where she's going. "Celia's babies?"

I jerk up when she coughs, worried she's choking only to find her laughing, or at least trying to laugh. "No, Taran. Your babies. Yours and Gemini's."

I stop moving.

The small amount of humor she manages dwindles, leaving only a barely there grin. "You and your sisters have always been special. It's only fitting your children will be special, too."

She's delirious. She must mean Shayna and Koda's kids, maybe Emme's too —

"Don't fight what's coming," she says in her same dull and listless tone. "You've always stood by Celia, and when it's time for her children to meet their fate, your sons and daughters will stand by them, too."

This time, I'm the one struggling to speak. "Are they going to be all right?" I stammer. "All of them?"

There's no hesitation, despite her slow speech. "No."

"What's going to happen to them?" I ask. She doesn't answer, that odd film in her eyes obscuring them further.

"Destiny," I say, my voice growing louder. "Tell me what's going to happen to our children."

"I don't know," she says, trembling. "Their destiny dies with me . . . and their fate belongs to Johnny."

Her last words drain her and she falls asleep. I look to where Emme stands with her mouth covered. "She has to mean your children, and Shayna's."

I shake my head slowly, silencing her. "No, she meant yours, too."

Our attention returns to Destiny, waiting for her to tell us more. When she does nothing more than breathe in that same shallow way, I adjust the blankets around her, trying to keep her warm.

"Don't," she says, her eyes remaining closed. "I want to look pretty." Her lids lift. "Will you help me look pretty?"

Tears blur my vision. "Whatever you want, Destiny."

We take our time. I wash her hair as Emme cleans her body. I know that as a hospice nurse, Emme has cared for the dying, and bathed those who've passed so they looked presentable for their families. I just don't know *how* she's done it.

Emme wraps Destiny in the bath towels she ran through the dryer. "I don't want her to get cold," she says, hurrying to dry her legs.

"I know," I say, as feeble as Destiny is, a chill could push her further toward death's door. I reach for another towel and swap it out for one that's already cooling.

By the time Bren and Tye return, Destiny is lying in a freshly made bed and wearing a blue nightie and robe I brought down from my bedroom. I never knew how long or thick her hair was until I blew it out with a wide-barrel rolling brush, leaving the ends to fall in a cascade of silky waves.

"Hi, Tye," she says, her lips shiny and pink from the gloss I applied.

I added a little blush, too, and a few swipes of mascara. It helps, just not enough to mask her declining health.

"Hey, Des," he says.

"She looks beautiful," Emme tells me quietly.

"She was always beautiful," Tye replies.

He walks to her slowly, resuming his watch on the chair and taking her hand gingerly in his. The devastation in his features when she greets him with a smile is too much, and I have to look away, swiping the tears that come.

My phone rings, I hurry outside, not wanting to disturb their moment.

Gemini's face flashes across the screen as I answer. "Hello?"

"Are you all right?" The way he asks, assures me he has bad news to share.

"I'm with Destiny," I reply. What sounds like digging and flinging dirt, fills the other end of the line. That, and the sound of Johnny weeping.

"Babe?" I ask. "What's happened?"

"We made it to Santa Barbara," he tells me.

"And?" I press, sensing the hesitation and heaviness in his voice.

"We encountered something we weren't expecting." He pauses. "Johnny's manager is dead, so are all the members of his staff. We're burying the pieces now . . ."

Chapter Eighteen

Johnny shakes uncontrollably, pretty much the same way he's been shaking since I picked him and Gemini up at the airport. I thought for certain he'd ask for Emme. He knows she can heal even rattled emotions, but instead of requesting her presence, he begged for mine.

I'm sitting in the back of Gemini's SUV with Johnny, something Gemini didn't take too kindly to. I get it, and ordinarily, I'd prefer to sit with my man. But I can't leave Johnny. Not like this.

He reaches for the pack of cigarettes in his back pocket. Most are crushed, but he manages to retrieve one that was somehow spared. With a trembling hand, he lifts it to his mouth.

"Can I get a light?" he asks, stuttering.

"No," Gemini replies from the front.

"Beings with supernatural senses don't like smoke," I explain. "It bothers their noses and makes them cranky."

As if to validate my point, Bren turns around from his spot in the passenger seat and shoots him a nasty glare.

"Please," Johnny says. "Look, I'm not exactly keeping it together back here."

Ordinarily, I'd take the wolves' side. This time I don't. This past week, Johnny has experienced pain on multiple levels, and despite the agony he endured in Destiny's presence, nothing compares to how bad he looks now.

"Just let him have a few drags," I say.

Gemini's dark eyes flicker to the rearview mirror. "Fine," he says, more for me than Johnny.

The brisk air that flows during the early hours in Tahoe sweeps in as Gemini rolls down the rear window as far as it will go. Johnny extends his hand, and with a small flick of my wrist, I light his cigarette.

He inhales deep like a seasoned smoker, releasing a small stream that transforms into a white bird with fluttering wings. It turns its small head briefly to look at Johnny before flying swiftly away.

His motions calm him, and he takes another drag. Again, another bird forms, this one smaller, the tail dissolving into three smaller birds that follow the leader out.

He flicks the ashes as Tahoe comes into view, the rising sun just a blip of light across a horizon filled with gentle waves. The road inclines and Johnny takes another drag, once more another white bird takes shape within the smoke, stretching out its wings and soaring into the air.

"What are they?" I ask.

"Huh?" Johnny asks, appearing lost in his own thoughts. "Oh. Doves," he says, turning around to speak to me. "I'm saying goodbye, you know? To my people." He returns his focus outside. "I won't get another chance to, will I?"

"No," I say. That's one of the things about the human and supernatural worlds, as much as they interact, they continue to be separate entities with different rules. They can't know about us, and given everything we spare them from, they wouldn't want to anyway.

"Who was the first dove for?"

I only ask because he seems to want to talk about what happened. Johnny grins, the smile excruciatingly split between bitterness and joy. "My manager." He laughs. "For the most part, Drake could be a real asshole. 'You can't eat

208

that shit, Johnny,' he'd tell me. 'People won't pay to see a fat bastard.'" He shakes out his hand when he sees the disgust on my face. "It gets better. My personal favorite was, 'You have to stay fuckable, for the women and the men. Make them want you and you'll never go to bed alone, even long after your balls shrink and gray.'"

"You're right," I say. "He was an asshole. God rest his soul."

Johnny laughs again, like before, it's with that same stoic humor that reveals another layer of pain. "Yeah, but you know what? He helped me. He was the one who hooked me up with the right people and put money in my pockets." He returns the cigarette to his lips and takes another puff, creating another dove who doesn't appear as ready to leave him. It circles his head twice, its wings flapping fretfully before it sweeps out of the window and takes to the sky. "Without Drake, I'd still be on the street, starving and begging for change."

That didn't give him the right to mistreat you.

It's what I want to say, but I don't. Regardless of how he was treated, Johnny loved Drake, and mourns him. I let him because he needs to.

I lean against my seat, the motion reminding me how long it's been since I last lay in my bed, and how one more night has passed without me sleeping.

I stayed with Destiny following Gemini's call. It's not like I could sleep after learning what happened, nor could I bring myself to leave her.

She'll be gone soon. No more feathers, no more funky zebra and polka dot prints, no more glow-in-the-dark booty shorts.

I left the house in tears, struggling to come to terms with her impending death. As I waited for Gemini and Johnny's plane to land, I cried even more. I couldn't help thinking about how unfair life is, not just to beings who are different like Destiny, but to those like Johnny who only appear to have it all.

"What about the other dove?" I ask, forcing myself back

to reality. "The one with the little chicks?"

A cobweb of red lines crawl across Johnny's sclerae. I think he's going to cry again, but the tears don't come. For now, the well has run dry. "That was my publicist, Jude. She was nice, smart." He swallows hard. "She had three kids, used to talk about them all the time."

"Oh, God," I say.

"They're grown," he adds, his voice hollow. "Nena, her youngest daughter just graduated law school." He shrugs. "Still, she won't get to tell her mama goodbye so I did it for her." He rolls the cigarette between his fingers. "Starlight was the third. She was Jude's assistant and was always stressed out, worried she'd say the wrong things, but always managing to say the right ones."

"She sounds sweet."

"She was," he agrees. "She was from the south, Mississippi, I think." He chuckles. "Always called me, 'sir', no matter how many times I told her not to and that I was too young for that shit." His voice fades further away. "Paulo was the last bird. He was my stylist. If I was gay, I probably would have dated him. I'm not, so we settled on being best friends." His smile dwindles. "He was a great guy, the first person to tell me it was going to be okay, even when it wasn't."

He flicks the cigarette out of the window, something I hate that people do. But I can't call him out, not when he's falling apart.

"How will anyone know they're gone?" he asks.

Gemini answers, like me, he's been listening closely. "There was enough blood on the scene to suspect foul play. The police will rule it a homicide and the appropriate people will be notified."

"What about the shapeshifters? Any chance they'll be arrested?" he asks.

Once more I'm reminded how little Johnny knows about this world. "Shapeshifters aren't exactly human," I explain. "They're born witches and they can resume their human forms if they choose, or as they die. For the most part, they maintain the form they feel most powerful in, usually a predator or something that can do a lot of damage."

"You mean something killer, like a dragon?"

"Dragons were never real, kid," Bren says from the front. Like Gemini, he doesn't trust Johnny, but at least he keeps his voice fairly neutral.

I grab onto the armrest when Gemini makes a sharp turn and takes the highway leading to Squaw Valley. "As much as they can command any form, they're limited to creatures that exist or existed in the past," I explain.

"Like dinosaurs?"

"Yes." Although there's nothing to smile about, I manage, my sense of pride getting the best of me. "My sister once took on a pterodactyl." I give it some thought. "And a wooly mammoth."

"Whoa. They sound incredible," he says.

The wolves don't outwardly growl, but they come close. "That's not how I'd describe them," I say, my tone dissolving Johnny's awe. "They're monsters who make hundreds of blood sacrifices in order to command the power of hell within them."

"By killing vamps?" he asks, sounding confused.

"You're associating blood sacrifices with those who drink it," I interpret. "That's not how things work."

Bren cuts me off, appearing annoyed. "Vamps don't count as sacrifices. They don't have souls. Humans do and are easy prey which is why they're the ones often targeted."

"What about you?" Johnny asks me. "Can they come after you?"

"They've tried. Weres, witches, and beings of magic like me all have souls, and because of our magic, we're more worthy sacrifices. But we don't go down easy, not like humans."

He grips the seat in front of him, struggling to steady his breathing. "So Drake, Jude, all my friends weren't just killed. Those shifters sacrificed their souls to gain more power?"

"Not exactly," I reply. "Their souls were sacrificed to move one step closer toward their goal of becoming shifters. But shifters aren't stupid, and if they're part of the evil that's rising, we're in a lot of trouble. What happened to your friends is just the start."

"So no justice, for Drake, Jude, Paulo—anyone of them?"

"Not necessarily," Gemini responds for me. "Actual shifters didn't kill them, their neophytes did. I could tell by the type of magic littering the room. We have *weres* in the responding police force. If they can find them, they'll take care of them."

"By locking them up? Bullshit," Johnny states. "It's not like they can just take away their wands and be done with it."

"I never said the *weres* would arrest them," Gemini replies. "I only said they would be taken care of."

"Oh," Johnny answers, Gemini's frankness hitting him all at once. He reaches for another cigarette. Gemini notices, but doesn't stop him.

The cigarette is partially broken. Johnny breaks off the damaged tip and extends what he salvaged toward me. "Please," he asks.

My fire flickers from my fingertips and the tip ignites in blue and white. Johnny inhales, creating another bird. "How do you do that?" I ask.

"I'm an artist," he replies simply.

"How do you do that?" Gemini asks, albeit a little more harshly.

Johnny pauses, bouncing in his seat when Gemini rolls through a large pothole. I think he's toying with the idea of not answering, if so, the glare Bren tosses over his shoulder changes his mind rather quickly. "I will some of myself into whatever I create," he replies. "Be it my tats, a painting, or my music."

"So when you sing . . ."

"I will myself to sound good, and for those who feel pain to feel my pain, too" he adds, his mind appearing to wander.

I think back to the rough and tumble crowd of people who attended his concert. I mostly dismissed them as delinquents and offenders, and they probably were. But sometimes the toughest people become that way not because they're born predators, but because they were preyed upon. I'll give Johnny this, he knew just the right crowd to lure in.

I pretend not to care or notice the effect his music had on me, my attention trailing to the road and to the thickening forest edging closer to the asphalt. "What happens when you draw?" I ask.

"Anything I create gets a piece of me," he states. "The longer it's with me, the stronger and more real it becomes."

Which explains why he has so many tattoos. In keeping them close, they absorb more of his power. "Is that why your bandmates could speak to me. They were with you a long time?"

"Yeah."

I turn in time to catch the way his gaze skims down my body. He's not leering, but he has taken an interest in me.

"I inked my boys in when I realized how much of me went into my lyrics, and how society throwaways like me seemed to connect to it." He blows out a stream of smoke from the side of his mouth, sending a flock of tiny white birds to disappear into the wind. "I needed a band, you feel me? People who could stand by me and make me Johnny Fate."

"How did you teach them to play?" Gemini asks. His voice is even, and anyone else listening might not pick up on his anger. I do. But then no one knows him like me.

Johnny tenses as he often does when the wolves address them. "I willed them to learn."

"That's not good enough," Gemini says, picking up on something I don't. "From what I've learned, you don't play an instrument, and I don't think your power would allow you to play one just because you wanted to." He eases off the accelerator as he rounds the bend, keeping his stare ahead and his attention very much on Johnny. "How did you do it?"

"I watched a lot of music videos," Johnny admits. "And stuffed whatever I felt in each note into my boys."

Gemini doesn't respond, seemingly satisfied with his response.

"They seemed so human," I say, recalling their imposing forms. "At least from afar."

Johnny puts his cigarette out on the sole of his boot. Instead of flicking the butt out of the window, he shoves what's left into the front pocket of his jeans and reaches for another one. This one is broken, too. As much as I don't like the amount he's smoking, I want to keep him talking, and light the next before he can ask.

"My boys were with me for a few years," he says, his mind once more wandering.

"Right," I say carefully. "But how did they go from your skin to performing for hours on stage?"

"They became entities of themselves," he replies, appearing to withdraw. "Even though they were mostly figures of what I needed them to be." He drags his fingers through his bleached white bangs, pushing them away from his eyes. "I used to let them walk around after the shows so they'd be more visible. One morning, I woke up and they were standing by my bed, watching me." He laughs. "Scared the shit out of me and two women lying next to me . . ." He frowns when he catches my surprise. "What? I'm rock star, Taran. Did you expect me to be a virgin?"

"It's not that, you're just *young*." I shake my head. "I don't like you doing that."

"Doing what? Having sex? Don't you and—"

"I would be very careful with the words you say next," Gemini warns.

It takes Johnny a moment to speak. "I'm legal," he says. "And so are they. Every time I take someone to bed, my people make sure of it."

"That doesn't make it okay. You're being exploited," I tell him frankly. "And used."

He scoffs. "What else is new?" He does a double-take when I look at him. "Taran, I'm not this guy who's spent the past two decades being worshiped, but I am the guy who gave all those assholes who mistreated me the ultimate fuck you by taking the stage and owning it. You think girls liked me back then? Most of them laughed when I tried to talk to them. They're not laughing now, are they? No, all of them are lining up for a chance to screw me."

I cross my arms. "Yet when they leave you're back to being all alone."

Johnny rams his mouth shut. "Tell me more about your band," I say when he quiets.

I think he's pissed and done talking, but then it's like he can't seem to stop. "My boys were becoming more," he says. "Who knows, maybe with time, they would have had families of their own."

"Doubt it," Bren mutters.

"You don't know me, werewolf," Johnny snaps.

Bren turns around, smiling. But that's Bren, big grin on his face right until he cracks your skull open and flings your brains over his shoulder. "True. But I do know you're not God. You don't get to decide what lives, what becomes, kid. No matter what kind of fucking power you have."

Johnny doesn't like what Bren has to say. "Pull the car over."

"Johnny, calm down," I say.

"Pull the car over now!" Johnny orders.

Gemini veers off the road, slamming down on the brake. "Fine, get out."

"Wait, *what*?" I ask.

Johnny scowls and throws the door open. He doesn't jump out, not right away. He wants us to stop him, to know someone cares.

Apparently the two "someones" in the front don't.

He leaps out and slams the door shut, hurrying out of the way when another SUV jets up the highway and almost hits him.

"I can't believe you're just letting him leave!" I yell.

"I can't believe you haven't killed him yet," Bren says to Gemini. He links his fingers behind his head. "Hey. Do you want to head to O'Malley's? I hear they offer an all you can eat breakfast for nine bucks."

"Seriously?" I ask.

"Okay, maybe it's ten," Bren adds.

Johnny leaps over the guardrail and stomps into the woods. I glare at Gemini, seething. "You're going to let him go, just like that?"

"The Fate doesn't belong to us," he says, keeping calm.

He doesn't like us fighting in front of others and it reflects in his tone. Well, that's too damn bad because I'm raring to go. "His name is Johnny," I remind him. "And don't pull that he's not one of us crap. Neither am I and look at how *magical* things are between us."

Bren laughs and it takes all I have not to zap the shit out of him.

Gemini isn't laughing, he turns around, gripping the side of Bren's seat. "Don't compare what he is, to who you are. I don't trust him. Where he could have used his power toward something good he used it only to better himself. Don't you see? He became that renowned idol he always wanted to be." His grip tightens. "You never would have used your powers like that."

"You're wrong."

He rights himself, realizing I'm telling the truth.

"My childhood sucked, you know it did. Too many times we went without, and more times than not we hurt. If I had Johnny's power, especially at his age, I would have jumped at the opportunity to save us."

I fling open the door and throw it closed behind me. I don't usually allow my emotions to get the best of me— scratch that, I do all the time—but it's not often I allow my deep-seeded memories to poke through. They bring out misery I tried to forget and always result in vicious tears.

I place my hand over the guard rail and swing my legs over. I'm still wearing my hot-pink shoes. In my defense, my only mission was to pick up Gemini and Johnny from the airport.

The long thin heels pierce through the sand and mud along the rocky terrain. I stretch out my hands, trying to balance as I maneuver down the small incline. I don't want to cry buckets over my pathetic upbringing, I've done it enough. But a tear escapes even though I order it back home and demand it stop being a little bitch.

I blame my exhaustion and time with Destiny for being

overly sensitive, until I sense Johnny and his sadness. He's crying too. I don't hear him, or see him right away. I feel him. The same melancholy pull that first drew me tugs at my heartstrings. I suppose Johnny doesn't have to create anything to be heard. He simply has to be.

I find him near the small section of woods where the highway loops around. He looks from side to side, appearing torn over which way to go.

"Right takes you back where you came, left takes you down the mountain. Straight takes you across the road and into deeper woods." He starts to head straight. "Uh-uh. That's not someplace you want to be, even during the day."

He looks at me, his eyes red and swollen. "Are there demons in there? Creatures or some other shit?"

"Probably," I admit, taking a seat on a large boulder. "But I was referring to the black bears and rattlers. Either way, something's going to take a bite."

He looks down at the dirt and edges away. Maybe he sees something. Maybe he doesn't. Regardless, escaping into the throes of Squaw Valley doesn't sound as promising as it once did.

He walks toward me and takes a seat, the way the boulder slants putting us at almost eye level. He reaches into his back pocket for his cigarettes, but quickly changes his mind.

"He hates me," he says. "They all do."

The wolves, he means.

I put my left hand over his and give it a squeeze. Between his palpable sadness and the amount of empathy he inspires, I can't help myself. "It's not that they hate you. *Weres* just perceive strangers as a threat or prey until they get to know you and their beasts decide for them."

"Are you saying your boyfriend will like me once he gets to know me?" He rolls his eyes. "I doubt that."

I doubt it, too, but I don't admit it aloud. Despite all his tears and fragility, Gemini considers Johnny a predator and recognizes the harm he can potentially cause. I recognize it, too. I just don't have an inner beast prowling within me, constantly toying with the notion of gnawing Johnny's limbs off.

"I had a plan," Johnny says. "Go back to my people and back to my life." He looks out toward the highway. "But that was before."

He releases my hand. I think he's ready to bolt. But too many thoughts appear to race through his mind. "What's going to happen to me, Taran? If Destiny dies, will the witches claim me as their new Messiah?"

"It looks that way," I reply. I stretch out my foot and roll the ankle. "As much as she didn't look the part, Destiny was queen in the witch world. But where most queens are admired, most saw her as strange. They respected the position more than they ever respected her."

"Do you think they'll respect me? If the time comes and they absorb me into their covens or whatever, do you think it will be okay?"

"I think you have the potential to become the rock star of your kind, just as you were in the world you created for yourself."

He doesn't smile. Probably because I'm not smiling either. "Is that such a bad thing?" he asks.

"Johnny, your life may have been glamour and glitz on the surface, but it came with a lot of shit few saw. Your manager, your fans, someone always wanted something from you. That won't change if you take Destiny's place."

"You think the witches will use me?"

I shake my head. "No. I know they will."

He releases a long, defeated breath.

"Genevieve isn't so bad," I say, trying to add a little light to all the gloom I painted. "We're not friends, but she's tried to rule her best according to witch law and ultimately sides with the greater good."

"Can I trust her?"

"I don't know," I admit. "She and Ines lead the strongest covens. But their loyalty isn't to their Lessers or any of their kind. It's to their ways." I sigh. "And their ways may not necessarily be in your best interest."

"Am I getting another Drake?"

"No, you're getting another two," I answer him truthfully.

I lick my lips, they're dry and taste salty. Having not slept and barely eating is taking its toll. That doesn't stop me from telling Johnny what he needs to hear. "Gemini told me *weres* have always warred with those who threaten the earth. Yet despite the light they cast, evil continues to lurk in the shadows, growing fiercer and more formidable." He watches me, paying close attention. "The witches and vamps sense it, too, and all agree matters have worsened over these past two decades."

"Because of me being born?" He huffs. "That's not my fault. I didn't choose to come into the world, and I sure as hell didn't cause all this darkness."

"I know."

It's all I say. Although it wasn't his intent, his presence caused a shift in the mystical world, and ultimately in the world itself. I almost had a heart-attack when I learned Johnny's birthday. It was the exact day my sister was inflicted with a magical illness, and mere days from the first time she assumed her tigress form. Now look at her, pregnant with the first child destined to change the world. I can't dismiss it as a coincidence. Not with all the subsequent turmoil surrounding Johnny's presence.

"Things are bad," I say, trying to spare him to some extent. "But it's because they are that we need all the help we can get." I motion behind me. "You may not be a *were*, but you are a witch. When . . . if Destiny dies, you'll take her place and inherit her stardom."

"But you don't want me to," he concludes.

"That's not true. What I want is for you to keep your eyes open and realize there's always a price for fame and glory."

He slumps forward, weighed down with all the stress he feels. "What happens to me now?"

"If you'd like, we can summon the witches and let them know you wish to join them. But after the attack against Ines, it might be some time before they can come for you and ensure your safety."

"Then where will I go in the meantime?" he asks. "I don't want to go back to the cave."

"Den," I correct, the reference lifting my mood only slightly.

"Whatever. They hate me, Taran, and I'm not exactly crazy about them."

A thought occurs to me. It's not perfect but . . . "I know where you can go," I say, reaching for my phone.

A small avalanche of rocks rolls a few feet away. I glance up to find Gemini and Bren looking none-too-pleased as I send my final text to confirm our arrival.

"I spoke with our Elders," Gemini says. "Our Pack has acquired a suite for you at the Falcon Lodge. For your safety, you'll be watched at all times."

Johnny beams, but it's not because of Gemini's offer.

He flings his arm around me. It's then I know we're both in trouble. "Thanks, but no thanks," he says. "Taran just hooked me up with the vampires . . ."

Chapter Nineteen

I'm not sure what Gemini took more offense to, Johnny's arm around me, or me running to the vamps. Either way, Bren had to rip him off Johnny.

I glance in the back seat where he continues to tremble. "You scared him," I accuse.

"Is he still alive?" Gemini asks. He doesn't wait for me to answer. "Then you should be thanking me instead of criticizing."

He stomps on the gas as we take the mile-long road leading to Misha's front gate. The colossal stone wall to my right with gargoyle heads protruding every few feet is all part of his property. Celia lived here for a time, and I haven't returned since the four-penis demon incident, but considering what's happening, this is the best place for Johnny to be.

"Are they nice?" Johnny asks.

"No," we answer at once.

"Wait? They're not nice?"

"No," we reply, like he didn't hear us the first time.

Bren chuckles. "But they are entertaining." He clasps Johnny's shoulder. "So long as they don't see you as prey and recognize you as their equal." He gives Johnny the onceover.

"Yeah, good luck with that, kid."

I turn and face the front, returning my hand to Gemini's thigh. As annoyed as I am, it helps settle him, which is why I'm riding shotgun and putting as much space as I can between me and Johnny. I shouldn't have been so affectionate with Johnny—not because he didn't deserve kindness, but because in returning it, he crossed the line and insulted my matehood with Gemini.

"He didn't know," I remind Gemini quietly.

"He knows now," he responds, not bothering to muffle his speech.

"You're making a big deal over nothing. He probably considers me the older sister he never had." I whisper my words so low, I don't quite catch them over the roar of the engine as he careens down the road.

"You keep saying that," he replies, again not whispering. "But I'm not blind to how he looks at you or how he seeks your touch."

"It's a comfort thing," I argue, keeping my voice down. "He's lonely."

"The only thing he's lonely for is you in his bed," he snarls. "Next time he touches you, he'll have to draw his arms back on with his toes."

I turn around and offer an apologetic smile. "He doesn't mean that," I say.

Johnny pales, and tucks in his legs into him. "I think he does."

Okay. He does. I give Gemini's thigh another squeeze, hoping to remind him of better times and my promise to never leave him.

As I speak to Johnny, I keep my stare ahead. "About the vamps," I begin. "They're not going to attack or mess with you."

"Unless they see you as prey," Bren repeats.

My shoulders slump. "Bren, as Misha's guest, he'll be fine." I face Johnny. "That doesn't mean you shouldn't stay on guard. They'll test you, and with Misha out of the country, they'll want to make sure you're worthy of his presence and not a threat to their master."

"Misha's not there?" Bren asks.

"No," I say. "He's flying back from Transylvania with his bride. He'll be here later tonight."

"His bride," Gemini repeats slowly.

I throw out a hand. "Believe me, I know. I could barely believe it when Edith Anne told me. Celia mentioned a while back that he'd travelled to Transylvania looking for the future Mrs. Aleksandr. Initially she laughed thinking the vamps were making a joke. Well the joke is on us because turns out, he found the lucky gal."

"Why is this the first we're hearing of this?" Gemini asks.

I tilt my head. "I think Aric knew."

"That's not what I mean," he says, removing his foot off the accelerator and allowing the SUV to coast. "He overheard the conversation between Celia and the she-vamp. But as much as that's what Misha claimed, none of us believed him." He tosses a look my way. "If you recall the period when he left, it was the same time Celia was returning home to be with Aric."

And right around the time they became engaged.

"So you thought he was reacting to Celia and Aric's relationship," I determine.

"Exactly. We dismissed it as smoke that would eventually clear. We never thought it would become this." He gives me the side-eye. "Are you certain the leeches were telling the truth?"

I can't sniff a lie, that doesn't mean I can't pick up on one. "I don't see why they'd lie, aside from trying to screw with me. But the info I received was pretty detailed. Like I mentioned, he apparently took his time searching for the one."

My fingers draw invisible circles along his jeans when I catch the concern spreading along his features. "What's the big deal? I'd think you'd be happy, or at least happy he's moving on and giving up on Celia."

"What do you know about the woman?"

His question surprises me. "Nothing," I admit. "Just that

there is one and he's set on marrying her. I'll be honest, I can't see Misha settling down."

"Babe," I press when he doesn't appear to settle. "Why do you care who he's with?"

"Because Misha never does anything without getting something in return." He stops a few feet from the gates leading in, using the last few moments of privacy to further elaborate. "As a master, he could impregnate a female if he willed it to happen."

This is yet another WTF moment. "He can *will* his sperm to procreate?"

"Yes," Gemini answers, as if sperm-commanding was the most natural thing in the world. "For a long time, there were rumors that he and Ileana Vodianova had made an agreement to conceive. Do you remember her?"

As the most powerful she-vamp in the world, Ileana is a little hard to forget. She's stunning, the kind of woman you don't want to take your eyes off and not simply because of her beauty. She's as lethal as her perfect smile and could probably kill me with it.

"I take it she can order her eggs to accept the sperm?" He nods. Of course she can. "But they didn't, right? I mean, I would have remembered that birth announcement."

"No, and for that we're grateful." He huffs. "Nothing good would have come from that union."

If I'm being honest, I like Misha. He was there for Celia when death came knocking and she threw open the door. Still, I'm not stupid to think he's innocent or that he doesn't have an agenda. Being good to Celia doesn't necessarily make him a good guy.

Gemini quiets, not wanting to say more, at least not in front of Johnny. "Anyway," I continue. "After Uri was attacked, he didn't want to take any chances with his girlfriend's safety and returned to Transylvania intent on bringing her back to the compound."

"Is she human?" he asks me.

"I didn't ask," I admit. "Although I probably should have. Mostly, I was too shocked by the news." I shrug. "I guess I'll find out in a few hours."

"You're staying?" Johnny asks, perking up.

"You're *staying*?" Gemini asks, growling. It's not really a question, more like an annoyed statement.

"Just long enough to get you settled and meet Misha's lady friend," I tell Johnny, keeping my attention on Gemini. I stroke his shoulder. "I promise, it'll just be you and me tonight."

Every now and then, I piss off my wolf to the point that my gentle touches and soothing voice do jack shit. This is one of those moments. My wolf is *not* pleased.

"I thought you'd be happy." He looks at me, knowing I'm lying. "All right, perhaps happy is too strong a word. Just look at it this way, I'll get the goods on the future missus. If there's anything crazy or creepy going on, you'll be the first to know."

"Can't the wolves stay, too?" Johnny asks. "We can all party with the vampires."

"What?" he asks when Gemini snarls a curse and Bren all but laughs in his face.

"We're not there to party," I tell him. "And trust me when I say it's not in anyone's best interest to have the wolves hang with Misha's undead peeps." I don't add that I'm also tired of scrubbing fur and vamp blood off my cute clothes. Poor guy is freaked out enough.

Gemini eases off the brake, stopping directly in front of the wrought iron gates. A deep voice booms from the closest gargoyle head. "Who dares invade the House of Aleksandr!"

Gemini rolls his eyes. "Just open the damn gates, Hank," I call out, knowing he can hear me through the glass.

"Fine," he grumbles.

Gemini barrels down the wide slate driveway the moment the gates part. I do a double-take when I find Johnny cowering in the corner, clutching the arm rest. "Don't do that," I tell him.

He glances from side to side. "I'm not doing anything."

"Yes, you are," I insist. "You're demonstrating fear."

"I'm not demonstrating. I'm fucking swimming in it. Did

you hear that guy? The one in the gargoyle head? He sounded possessed!"

"That's just Hank," I tell him.

"Hank?" He allows his legs to slide to the floor. "So Hank is all right? He won't hurt me?"

Bren laughs. "Are you kidding? He would totally rip out your kidneys."

"*Bren*," I warn.

His blue eyes brim with humor. "Well, he would," he mumbles.

"It doesn't matter," I offer quickly.

"*It doesn't matter?*" Johnny asks, his voice shrilled. "These are my kidneys we're talking about." He glances out of the window and tries to unlock the door. It's a stupid thing to do. The meticulously kept landscape may create the impression of a tranquil and safe environment, except vampire guards lurk in the shadows, protecting the compound. Johnny was safer on the mountain with the bears and the potential demon infestation.

"Johnny, get a hold of yourself," I tell him.

"You said I'd be safe here," he reminds me. "That this was a good place to be until the witches came for me."

"You will be safe," I say. "The vamps won't harm you unless provoked or in defense of their master. That doesn't mean they won't try to screw with you."

I groan when he curls inward. "You can't behave this way in front of the vamps. They'll eat you alive—" I hold out my hand when he pales. "Sorry, they won't actually eat you. But they sure as hell won't respect you."

My pep talk does nothing. If anything, he's close to hysterics and I can't have that.

I point at him. "You're the Fate," I remind him. "You have to walk into that compound like you're the baddest mother fucker in the room."

"Just don't verbalize it," Gemini adds.

"Oh, yeah," Bren agrees. "Totally don't verbalize that shit." He nudges Johnny. "Unless you want to kiss those kidneys goodbye."

"Will you stop it," I tell him when sweat pours down Johnny's face. "You're not helping."

An idea sparks in my head. "Think about what it was like to walk out on stage, or attend an event where everyone knew who you were. Were you scared?"

"No, but my fans worshipped me." He glances at Bren. "They weren't threatening to tear out my organs."

"That's not the only reason," I say. "You weren't scared because you were Johnny Fate. You're still Johnny Fate. But instead of being a rock god, you're the new god in Witchville."

I'm trying to make him feel better, but the words are hard to say. The only reason he's getting the title is because Destiny is losing the crown. I suppose that's why my voice softens and Johnny seems to cling to my every word. "Believe you're strong and formidable, and they will, too."

I angle my body back toward the front as Gemini pulls onto the long circular drive. He parks directly in front of the stone steps leading up to the two-story double doors. On both sides of each step waits a vampire dressed in a designer black suit. They're all newly made, deadly, and waiting for one false move.

"Remember what I said," I tell Johnny. I swing open the door. "Come on, it's show time."

I step out, my head high and my shoulders back. Unlike Johnny, the vamps don't scare me. "Hank here?" I ask.

The female vamp at the top hops down in the time it takes me to reach the base of the steps. She smiles with all the warmth of a cobra. "He's coming," she says.

Yes, he is, and does he ever know how to make an appearance. A human, dressed like a scantily dressed Little Bo-Peep races down the steps, giggling and glancing back to make sure she's being followed.

And is she ever! Hank, the naughty sheep, is steadily in pursuit. I know it's him despite that he's only wearing a black speedo and a rubber sheep mask.

It's not a gift. I'd recognize that eight-pack anywhere.

He stops in front of me, peeling off his mask, his sweat-soaked hair glued to his face as if camera-ready for some kind of athletic photo shoot. "Look who's here," he tells me. "My favorite weird sister."

"And look at you!" I say. "My favorite—never mind. I hate all of you."

He looks past me, ignoring the slight. "That him?"

I glance over my shoulder to where Gemini stands beside Johnny. To his credit, he tried to help Johnny appear respected by opening his door. I'm not sure it helped given Johnny's slacked jaw appearance and how he seems ready to move back into the "cave."

I turn to Hank, nodding. "Yes. That is the mighty Fate."

"Mighty?" he asks. He smirks when I nod. "More like puny. You serious about what he is? He looks like some Justin Bieber impersonator minus the height and pubes. Shit, Taran, he could pass for twelve."

"Appearances can be deceiving," I remind him, waving an arm at what's left of his costume. "And royalty knows no age limit. Don't forget, King Tut became Pharaoh at nine."

He huffs. "And died at nineteen."

Bren leans against the SUV with his arms crossed. He dances his eyebrows at the she-vamp who greeted me. "Cast your eyes elsewhere, mongrel," she snaps at him.

Bren chuckles and opens his arms. "Baby, you know you can't wait to have some of this."

She hisses, more because he's right based on the once-over she gives him. I'm ready to hiss, too. It's like he's trying to prove there's nothing between him and Emme.

Hank motions to Johnny. "The tough-guy Fate going to wait by your boyfriend all day?"

And because he doesn't look like enough of a pussy, Johnny takes a step closer to Gemini. Gemini stiffens. It's taking everything he has not to roll his eyes.

I clear my throat. "You may call him Johnny if you win his favor, otherwise you're only permitted to address him as the Fate."

Hank barks out a laugh. "You're kidding, right?" He turns to the other vamps. "Did you hear that shit?" he asks.

Hank stops laughing and leaps away when I light up in a funnel of blue and white flames. "The fuck, Taran?" he says.

The vampires bare their fangs, inching back with their nails elongating. They may be immune to sunshine, but unless they're a master, they're not immune to fire.

"Do you dare question the Fate's power?" I demand.

Hank blinks back at me. "Are you seriously challenging me?"

"You're damn right I am," I reply, adding another notch to my already scorching flame.

Sometimes, a gal has to be the one with the balls in the room, especially when Fate's have all but shriveled up.

"Listen, and listen well," I command. "The Fate is under my protection and that of the Squaw Valley Den Pack. As the most revered and powerful witch among all covens, he is not to be harmed, and as a guest of your master, he is to be welcomed as family and friend without prejudice." Heat flares as streams of blue and white swirl around me. "You will show him the reverence he deserves or you will suffer our collective wrath. Permit him through, bow as he passes, and for hell's sake get him something to eat."

With a snap of my fingers, I switch off my fire. Gemini and Bren flank my sides, their arms loose and ready to act. I turn to address Johnny.

"Are you ready, your highness?" I ask.

At first I'm sure he's ready to scramble back inside the SUV and beg us to save him. But then he shuts the door, mimicking my strong posture and lifting a chin stiff with determination. "I am."

He has to stop himself from saying thank you. It's a good start. What he does next, is even better.

The tattoos along his arms come to life with each step he takes. The vines and leaves of his jungle sleeve snake and move in a makeshift breeze. A leopard stalks through the bright green vegetation, yawning to expose his fangs, the glint in his eyes sparkling as he looks in my direction.

At the same time, lava boils between the cracks in the earth of his Mordor-themed sleeve, spouting smoke as he reaches the first vamp. But when he passes Hank, it's all I can do not to fist-bump him.

The leopard extends out of Johnny's arm and takes a swipe at Hank. Hank jumps out of the way, narrowly avoiding getting clawed in the face.

"That was a warning," Johnny tells him. "Please, for your sake, don't upset my guards."

Bren makes this odd choking sound, trying to keep from laughing. I'm worried he'll give Johnny away, but that's not how Hank takes it.

Like the other vamps, Hank's focus is on Johnny's ever moving tattoos, enthralled by the way the leopard shrinks in size and withdraws into Johnny's skin.

"The Fate is welcomed to the entire east wing," he mutters, watching the leopard stalk through his jungle home.

"No," I say.

"No?" Hank jerks his head up. "Why not?"

"The Fate prefers privacy at all costs," I tell him. "He respectfully requests use of the guesthouse during his stay."

"It's smaller," Hank tells me, speaking slowly as if I'm not aware.

"I know, and I'm telling you, it's what the Fate prefers," I repeat. The less the vamps have access to him, the longer Johnny will be able to pull off this façade.

Hank looks at Johnny, his features quizzical and questioning.

"I like my privacy," Johnny concurs." He lifts his arms slightly. "We all do."

Hank's stare returns briefly to Johnny's tats. With a jerk of his chin, he motions to the vampire opposite him.

"It will be just a moment," Hank tells Johnny. "My apologies, young Fate."

Again, Johnny has to stop himself from saying thank you. But he does nod regally, just as he damn well should.

"This way," Hank says, leading him forward.

I keep my arms behind my back, hoping Johnny will follow Hank and not remain glued to my side. He does, hesitating only briefly.

Gemini turns to me, lifting my chin and planting one hell of a sexy kiss on my lips. It's his way of reminding the vamps who linger that I'm his and also under *were* protection.

It's also his way of telling me my aggression made him hot.

"Tonight?" he asks.

"Tonight," I promise.

Bren knocks me affectionately on the shoulder and hops down the steps. "Way to show them who's boss, Taran."

I wait for Gemini to return to his vehicle and drive away before following the remaining vampires inside.

So far, so good. The thing is, nothing is ever at it seems in the House of Aleksandr.

Chapter Twenty

Ever wake up, feeling like there's someone watching you sleep?

Ever have that someone watching you sleep dressed like a naughty Catholic schoolgirl? Welcome to my world.

Agnes Concepción looms over me, eyeing me with interest. And when I mean interest, I mean she's focused on my jugular and licking her lips. I jump and scramble to the opposite side of the sage couch. "What the hell, Agnes?"

She hops off the armrest where she was crouched, her movements smooth and feline. "The master has returned and would like you and the Fate to join him for dinner." She adjusts her tiny librarian glasses. "But first he requests a private audience with you."

"With me?" I rub my eyes and look in the direction of the bedroom.

"Yes, with you," Agnes says, already annoyed.

Except for the flames dancing in the fireplace, the rest of the living room is dark which does nothing to squelch Agnes's spooky vibe. She's smiling, and still very fascinated with my neck.

"What time is it?" I ask.

"Almost nine."

"Nine?" I hadn't planned to fall asleep, let alone sleep the day away. But following a breakfast fit for a Fate and his nanny, Johnny passed out in the bedroom, and I suppose I passed out on the couch. I reach for the phone on the coffee table, cursing when I realize I missed several texts from Gemini.

Agnes huffs. "Are you coming?"

"I have to text Gemini first," I reply, tapping my screen.

"It is an insult to keep the master waiting." She hisses when my fingertips continue to fly across the screen. "Do you want me to drag you there?"

I glance up. "Do you want me to set you on fire, or for my boyfriend to show up here with his pack and drop kick your front gate open?" I return to my message. "Don't get your thong in a bunch. I'll be with you in a second."

She turns away in a huff. "Just so you know, Celia is my favorite."

"I'm sure she'll sleep better at night knowing that, Agnes," I mumble. I know she hears me, even as she slams the door shut behind her.

You were sleeping? Gemini replies in a text.

Yes, sorry, I respond.

It's only because I didn't sense you were upset that I'm not already there, he texts back.

I don't have to be there to know he's growling. *You were going to bust down the gates, weren't you?*

No.

Liar.

He replies with a sneer emoji followed by a bat and little trickles of blood. Second in Command or not, my mate is damn cute, even when he's threatening to tear a vampire apart.

I'll make it up to you later, I write. *Off to meet Lady Aleksandr.*

Be careful, he answers.

I freshen up in the bathroom and knock on Johnny's door. I'm not sure what kind of hours a rock star keeps, but he stirs when I open the door. "Hey, you all right?"

He nods and rubs his eyes. "Yeah, a little disoriented, but okay."

I lean against the doorway. "Misha invited us for dinner, but he wants to meet with me privately first. Why don't you get a shower and clean up? The vamps will come for you when it's time."

He seems like he's having a hard time moving. I'm not certain why until he meets me with those same sad eyes. "They're still dead, aren't they? Drake and everyone, that wasn't a dream, was it?"

I glance down at the floor, wishing I could tell him otherwise. "No, Johnny, it wasn't a dream."

He nods in that heavy way he does when the world seems like too much. I start toward him, but then he swings his legs over the bed and marches into the bathroom.

I walk to the door and press my hand against the frame. I want to say more, and somehow bring him comfort. Yet when the shower goes on, I determine he's already heard enough.

I leave him to his thoughts, and likely his sorrow, and step out of the guesthouse. The grounds are massive, surrounded by gardens most would kill for, not realizing how much blood was spilled to maintain them. I don't mean the gardeners', although knowing the naughty Catholics, I'm sure they've had a taste. I mean everyone the vamps have mowed down over centuries to gain power and expand their wealth.

A few years ago, when I was awesomely naïve, I used to think vampires were the Mafioso of the mystical world, in retrospect, there's so much to these immortals, including what they've endured for eternal beauty and what they're capable of doing to maintain their positions among the elite. These creatures aren't dumb, they're alarmingly cunning and cutthroat.

We rightfully feared them, except when Celia inadvertently returned Misha's soul, one vampire in a sea spilling with blood emerged, baring the longest and most lethal fangs of all, and ultimately giving her his heart.

Vampires don't have souls, at least, they're not supposed

to. Balancing life and death as he does, Misha will one day be unstoppable. So I don't necessarily flounce into the massive 33,000 square foot, three story structure known as The House of Aleksandr. I strut with caution.

"Hello?" I announce. "Anyone home?"

"*Merde.*"

I try not to roll my eyes, a hard feat in the presence of these vampires.

Chef rushes around the French-inspired kitchen slaving away. I'd always envisioned chefs as full-figured people, dressed in white uniforms, black pants, and funny hats. That's before I met Chef. He has the shirt, the pants, and hell, the funny hat, too. But Chef looks more Gucci model than gold-medalist cook.

The black pants hug an ass so tight you could throw marbles against it and they would crack. Oh, and that white shirt is close to splitting from his overly muscular chest. Wisps of curly black hair escape the funny hat, and if he'd eat half the magnificent meals he prepared we'd need the jaws of life to extract him.

To his benefit, Chef prefers to dine on people. Not that he particularly likes anyone. He rarely speaks, unless you count all the swearing he does in French.

"*Merde,*" he shouts again.

I take a seat at the counter. "Hey, Chef," I say. "Thank you for breakfast—"

He stops in the middle of banging his pots and pans to point a knife at me. "I only prepare such things for you," he says in a thick and overly dramatic French accent. "Tonight you will dine on lamb stuffed with lentils."

"Okay, if you insist. Where's Misha?"

"In zee solarium."

He whips around, just to swear at the lamb stretched across the counter. He probably needs a nap, or perhaps a virgin to munch on.

I walk through the house and into the grand foyer, my steps the only sound. I'm wondering where the hell everyone is when the familiar feel of vampire magic has me glancing up.

What looks like Misha's entire keep waits along the open hall on the second floor. I rest my hand on the railing. "What are you guys doing up there?"

They exchange glances, not that anyone bothers answering. I start to climb when their hands shoot out, waving madly and clearly telling me to stay put.

Sweet, child-like laughter drifts from the solarium. I glimpse toward it and then back at the vampires. "Misha's fiancée has a kid?" I ask.

Panic spreads like fire among them and they try to shush me. Apparently, I'm not supposed to mention the kid.

"The master's expecting you in the solarium," Agnes mutters through her teeth.

"Okay," I say, slowly, wondering what the hell has them on edge this time.

I cross the wide foyer, feeling the vamps' stares burning holes into my back. Again, the little girl laughs. I stop at the entrance to the solarium.

"Hey, Misha."

His name doesn't quite make it out of my throat. He turns from where he was speaking with a young woman on the couch. I glance around, expecting, I don't know, his fiancée. The only other person present is a very stone-faced woman dressed in black, watching them from her spot in the corner.

The girl stands when Misha does. "Good evening, Taran," he says.

"Hey," I say again, my attention returning to the young woman.

She's wearing a blue sundress, very conservative and simple yet likely very expensive. Her skin is olive like mine and her long black hair hangs to her waist. Dark, almost black eyes blink back at me warily. She's tall for her age, at least five feet six inches, and stunning. When she's all grown up, she'll be gorgeous. But she isn't a woman yet, and she has no business standing this close to Misha.

I frown and walk toward them, wondering why someone so young is hanging at the supernatural equivalent of the

Playboy Mansion.

"You look rested, my dear," Misha says to me. A few strands that escape his clip fall to brush against his charcoal silk dress shirt. "And lovely as always."

The sweet-looking girl furrows her eyebrows. She didn't like the "my dear" comment and she sure as hell doesn't like him referring to me as lovely.

I don't like the additional step she takes toward Misha. "I'm Taran," I tell her. "Who are you?"

Misha smiles. "Allow me to introduce you to Breasha. She is to bear my son."

A breeze smacks against my face as Misha's vampires appear at once. Vampires always come to the aid of their master, and I have theirs by the throat.

Misha straightens, easily breaking away from me. I grab him by the collar and force him nose to nose with me, ignoring the escalating hisses from the vampires.

"Are you crazy?" I glance at Breasha. "She's a child!"

Breasha, who initially covered her face in horror brings down her hands, glaring at me with tremendous indignation. "I am fifteen," she tells me in a thick Eastern European accent.

Misha's shaking body forces my attention back on him. The bastard is straight up laughing. He rights himself in one easy move, leaving me holding the collar from his silk shirt.

"My son will not be born for another decade," he says, like that's supposed to excuse this.

"Or perhaps sooner," Breasha adds hopefully.

I blink back at them, allowing the remains of Misha's collar to fall to the floor. "Please tell me you're not claiming this little girl as yours," I demand, my temper rising.

Misha stops laughing and steps toward me, his expression absent of humor. No way. No freaking way is he doing this. "Celia is going to lose her shit when I tell her you're hitting the middle schools for dates."

"I am *not* hitting the middle schools—"

"I hope she shows up here and stakes your ass, you creepy bastard."

"Taran, you will not tell her anything—"

"Oh, yes, I will." I turn away and storm toward the exit. Jeffrey– a newly *turned* vamp—steps in my path. "The master is not done speaking with you."

I scream, my knees buckling when his hand clamps down on my shoulder. That same hand sizzles to a crisp when I release my lightning and shoot it across the length of his arm.

Jeffrey shrieks, as does Breasha, and the creepy woman dressed in black, when he smokes.

He wobbles backward, collapsing and kicking his feet in agony.

Misha, bless his heart, is kind enough to haul him up by the face. "I thought I made it clear the Wird sisters are not to be harmed," he tells him, his voice calm and deadly.

Breasha and her guardian's screams are only slightly overpowered by Jeffrey's howls. Misha's fingers dig deep, crunching the bones and caving in Jeffrey's face.

"Misha, let him go," I say.

He holds tight, not bothering to look at me. "No. He must answer for the insult."

For touching me as Misha's guest, and for threatening the mate of the Second in Command to the Pack. I understand the rules. It doesn't make Jeffrey's re-death easier to stomach.

Horrible plopping—Jeffery's brains hitting the slate floor, I presume—precede the eruption of ash. I'm not watching, my concentration so fixated on the giant windows, I start to singe the glass. Jeffrey, being as young as he is, doesn't need his heart destroyed to die, not with the force of his master bearing down upon him.

Instant silence is followed by two very hard thuds. I cringe, knowing no one bothered catching the future Mrs. Aleksandr or her escort when they fainted.

I lurch away, gagging at the lingering smell of Jeffrey's cooking brains. Misha catches up to me in the garden. One minute I'm alone, the next he's in front of me with his arms crossed.

"What the hell were you thinking?" I ask, glaring.

"I told you. Jeffrey must be punished for the disrespect

he showed you," he replies coolly.

I throw my hands out. "I meant Breasha. Damn it, Misha. She's practically a little girl."

"I'm aware of what she is, as well as how it appears. Don't think I haven't given her age any thought." He watches me closely. "I'm a patient vampire, at almost three-hundred years of age, and with an eternity still ahead of me, years have become mere breaths to take. It's for this reason, and more, I'm in no rush. My plan is to wait until Breasha is well into womanhood before I ask she bear my son."

My heart thuds in sickening beats. "And how long will you wait to ask if you can deflower her?"

Misha's gray eyes flash with anger, only to soften when he regards my features. "I don't take women against their will," he tells me. "If you must know, I've never bedded anyone younger than twenty-seven." His eyes flash for a different reason. "Although I would have made the exception for your sister."

Yeah, you would have. "Celia isn't an option, Misha. She never was."

He quiets, and I do, too, yet not for long. "You're expecting her to bear your children."

"A son," he clarifies. "But only if she wants to."

He takes a seat on one of the wrought iron benches. "Perhaps we should discuss the matter," he says. He sprawls across the bench, one leg bent, the other stretched.

One of his arms rests against the back, the other dangles loosely at his side. His shirt is ruined, the collar appearing chewed off and the expensive fabric is likely splattered with brain bits. He should look ridiculous, but I don't think Misha ever could.

"What happens if she doesn't want to have your kid? Who will bear your son then?"

"I have other options," he replies casually.

"You mean, Ileana."

His sudden stillness is response enough. "What do you know about that?" he questions.

"Just that it wouldn't be a good match. She's . . ."

"Powerful," he answers for me.

"That's what it all comes down to, doesn't it? Getting more and being more. It's why Johnny is here."

He raises a perfect brow. "Need I remind you, you're the one who asked me to keep him."

"I asked you to keep him safe on behalf of the Alliance," I counter.

He motions in the direction of the guesthouse. "And I have."

"Yes, just for the chance to one-up the witches." I knew he wouldn't give up an opportunity to influence Johnny, or for Johnny to owe him a favor. Misha considers his interactions with other supernaturals like a game of chess and will always seek the right moment to hump the queen.

He flashes a fang, not bothering to deny it.

"About your future kiddos," I begin. "What makes you so sure you'll produce a son over a daughter?"

He shrugs. "I'll simply will it to happen."

"Oh, yes, I heard about your semen."

"My what?" he asks, chuckling.

"You know what I mean." I shift my weight to one hip. "Why the sudden interest in family?" I ask. "Is your biological clock ticking or something?"

Misha's smile fades. "There comes a point when every being becomes aware of his own immortality. As I am one of few vampires capable of creating a legacy, I feel obliged to do so."

"Sounds like it's more than a sense of obligation to me," I say carefully, watching how his focus sweeps across my face.

"Perhaps," he agrees, his voice and his stare growing distant.

I almost ask if Celia has anything to do with this. But that's a can of worms better left sealed and buried. He wanted children with Celia. He wanted Celia, period. Her relationship with Aric never discouraged him, but her pregnancy . . . that affected him in ways I never imagined.

"Why does it trouble you to know that I've chosen

children with another?" he asks, affirming my thoughts.

"Because if you're going to have babies, Misha, have them the right way. Not like this."

"Like how?"

"With a young woman you'll never love."

"You assume a great deal," he tells me.

"Then don't let me. Explain yourself. Why her? What's so special about this girl?"

"Her lineage," he answers simply.

"Her lineage?" I look back to the house, trying to pick up on something other than vampire. "Don't tell me she's a witch."

"No, not a witch," he replies, appearing amused.

"Then what is she?" Although I ask, I'm no longer sure I want to know.

Misha leans back in his seat and brushes a strand of his loose hair behind his ear, only for the soft breeze to sweep it back against his cheek. A small smile forms around his perfect lips. "She is a direct descendant of Vlad Dracula."

"The Impaler," I clarify. "The original master of all the masters?"

"Yes."

I glance up as if I can somehow see her from where I stand. I can't. That might be a good thing because holy shit, I think Misha has lost his damn mind.

"She's not a vampire," I say.

"No."

"So then why . . . What's the point?"

"Breasha is of royal blood."

"So?"

"She has been educated in the best schools."

"And?"

"Her family history is impeccable."

"I still don't get it."

Misha stares back at me as if questioning my intelligence. Typically, only his vampires look at me that way. I scowl at him. "She's the most suitable choice," he explains as if I'm missing the obvious.

"Because of who her great-great-great-great granddaddy was?" I ask.

"No, because of her blood. Any child I bear with her will be unstoppable."

He abruptly stops speaking, clutching his heart and curling in agony.

I hurry to him, cupping his shoulder. "Misha, what is it-"

I leap back when his fangs elongate and his savage gaze meet mine. The earth shifts, not shakes, not rumbles, it shifts. First left, then right, knocking me on my ass.

"Taran!"

Johnny stands a few feet away, his tattoos swirling and travelling across his arms and around his body, the tailspin of movement and energy punching through the air like angry fists. But it's Misha, roaring in pain that lures my focus back to him. His shirt falls away in pieces from the surge of vampiric magic coursing through him.

At once the world erupts in gold, blue, and white and I'm thrown across the garden.

Chapter Twenty-One

Rows of skulls erupt from ground, their mouths opening and closing as if crying out in pain. Alternating flames of blue and gold burn their faces, the heat singeing and cracking through the dense bone.

"Taran!" Johnny is yelling from afar. I can't hear what he's saying. I only know he's scared and in trouble.

"Taran!"

The vampires are screaming for me.

"For fuck's sake," Agnes pleads. "You have to help the master."

I can't see her, or Johnny, or any of the vampires. I only feel them, lingering close while their voices screech further away.

Around me, the earth burns, roasting the skulls and releasing a sickening aroma that makes me cough. I'm perched on my hands and knees, my fingers digging into the barren wasteland the garden has become.

I whip around at the sound of Misha howling in agony. He's on his knees, beating the flames overtaking a giant tiger with his bare hands. His efforts and despair are pointless, she's dying, her roars mercilessly raking against my ears.

"No!" I scream, racing forward.

It's Celia, it has to be by the way Misha is losing it. I struggle to reach them, every step I manage taking them further away from me.

Misha's cries turn wretched and his magic responds in turn, sending another burst of his power coursing through me. My arm reacts to the invasion of energy, flailing madly and throwing me against an invisible wall.

The scene breaks apart before I can gather my senses, the inferno and heat surrounding me replaced with large snow drifts and a cruel wind that sails my hair behind me. As I watch, Misha's clothes dissolve. He collapses into a drift, naked and unmoving.

I lurch forward, cursing when I strike the wall and can't find my way around it.

Misha is dying, I sense it even from where I stand. I pound my fists against the walls, calling forth fire that fails to come. Images of the skulls appear and fade. I don't know if they're real. I don't care if they are. I only see Misha, his long, wet hair and limbs strewn across the frozen ground.

He's half the man he was moments ago, his frame lanky and emaciated. His chest heaves as a pool of blood forms beneath him, trickling and tainting the otherwise pure white surroundings. I think he's trying to rise, or breathe. It's only when I stop pounding the clear wall that I realize he's crying.

My hands slide along the invisible barrier keeping me from him, each ragged breath and sob that breaks through his throat like a shard of glass that pierces my heart.

His torment is more than I can take. I'm not certain what happened to him until the long tail of a whip soars past me and the tip cracks across Misha's back.

A man dressed in fur spouts angry words in Russian as he sends the whip soaring again and again, slicing through the muscles along Misha's back and exposing the bones.

"What are you doing?" I scream at him.

He ignores me, pulling back the whip and bringing it viciously down.

"You're killing him," I shriek.

"Stop it!"

My palms slap against the invisible divider.

"*Stop it!*"

I curse, begging the man to show Misha mercy.

He won't listen. Instead he shakes out his hand, now sore and swollen from the strength he used to hurt Misha, and passes the whip to another man.

This other man, he's not tired, and more than eager to take over his comrade's task. Snow falls in wet clumps as he lifts the whip and strikes Misha's broken body.

A streak of blood splatters against my face with the next lash. Somehow it breaks through the invisible space keeping me in. I run forward, tripping over a long skirt I shouldn't be wearing and falling beside Misha.

My long dark hair is now blond and streaked with gray, the force of my fall spilling it from of the head scarf I'm wearing and draping it over my wrinkled and battered hands. My mouth moves, speaking words in Russian I shouldn't be able to say.

The first man swings back his leg, kicking me hard in the stomach, his heavy boot-clad foot cracking a rib. I roll over, gasping for breath as he straddles me.

I beat my fists against his chest, thinking he means to rape me, until his fist comes down in an arc and crashes against my sternum.

I didn't know he had a knife. I caught the glint of the blade as it came down and buried deep into my chest.

Pain unlike any I ever felt spreads along my limbs and warm fluid spills from my mouth. The next stab that comes dulls the ache by half. The third, I don't feel at all. All I feel is my body bouncing off the ground as he continues to pound the knife into my chest.

His strikes are now more annoying than anything, after all, my time to die has come.

My head rolls to the side, meeting Misha's tormented features. Tears stream down his eyes and fluid trickles against his dry, cracked lips.

Still, he screams, his hand reaching out. "Mama. *Mama!*"

I sob into my hands as I return to my prison behind that invisible wall. Misha crawls to his mother, his fingers barely grazing her outstretched palm when the first attacker casts his final blow.

The heel of his boot comes down, crashing into Misha's head. Misha crumbles, his bloody fingers falling just beside his dear mother's grasp.

The men say something I don't understand. Neither bother looking back as they mount their horses. I swallow hard, unable to stop crying even long after they gallop away.

This is a memory from Misha's past, triggered by his pain at watching Celia burn. It's what my mind reasons. But just because it occurred long ago, doesn't make it less horrific or easy to witness. No, this is one of those memories that will haunt me the remainder of my days.

The snow thickens, obscuring him as he lies naked beside his dead mother. But I know they're still here, abandoned like garbage and their bodies left to rot.

I wipe my eyes as another set of riders arrive. I can't see them well through the thickening snowfall. That doesn't mean I don't recognize the man in the lead.

Even then, Uri loved his capes. He motions to the men on either side of him to Misha. They dismount, hurrying to wrap him in the fur blanket Uri throws them.

Uri slides from his steed and carefully removes his thick gloves, watching Misha with interest. His fangs elongate as he hands his gloves to another servant and kneels beside Misha.

The servant at Misha's head pries Misha's mouth open, and as quick as a blade, Uri's incisor cuts through his wrist. Using great care, Uri presses the large gash he made into his skin over Misha's mouth.

I didn't understand the other men when they spoke in Russian. But I understand Uri. Maybe because Misha wants me to.

"Drink, young fighter, young champion, young prince," Uri tells him. "Live for me and you shall have your revenge."

Misha doesn't react, at least not at first. Then I see it, his lips seeking out the edges of Uri's wound. He fastens his mouth against Uri's skin, suckling hard and consuming Uri's blood like a deeply parched man taking his first drink.

Uri loves young beautiful men. I'm not surprised he chose Misha to save. What surprises me is the way he strokes Misha's head as he nourishes him. Not as a lover, but as the son he always claimed him to be.

Misha's head falls to the side as Uri pulls away his now healed wrist, his chest rising and falling with purpose even while his eyes remained closed. I don't expect Uri to coddle him, and he doesn't disappoint. He slips his gloves back into place, appearing to fuss with them so they lay just right while his servants drape Misha's limp body over a horse.

Uri doesn't wait for the man tasked with leading Misha's horse to follow. He gallops away, his beautiful stallion kicking snow behind them.

I suppose he doesn't have to wait. He knows Misha will live.

Just as he knows he'll have his revenge.

"Taran!"

"*Taran!*"

Something hard smacks my face and I'm back in the garden struggling to keep my feet.

Agnes grips my shoulders. "You have to help the master," she says, tears streaking down her face.

I turn to where the vampires surround Misha, his gaze feral and his claws lashing out at anyone who nears him. Ash erupts as he takes one down, and another, and another.

"Hank!" I yell when Misha just barely misses him.

He turns around, his face panicked. "He doesn't see us, Taran. It's like he's blind to us."

More ash streams through the air as another of his family dies, followed by the she-vamp who greeted us when we arrived.

"Celia," I stammer. "We have to call Celia."

"We've tried, God damn it," Hank hollers. "You've been unconscious for almost twenty minutes. We've been calling her non-stop, but the fucking mutts won't let us talk to her."

I whip out my phone from my back pocket and search my

favorite's list, immediately tapping Celia's number. The line goes to voicemail as another vampire wails and ash erupts in a cloud.

"Celia, it's Taran. Misha needs you. You have to come."

My phone falls out of my hand when Misha lunges at me. Agnes shoves me out of the way, up the incline, and toward the house. The others tackle him, trying to subdue him and forcing him in the direction of the guesthouse.

More ash, and now blood. Misha is out of his mind with grief and rage.

"Celia needs to be here," I say. "He needs to know she's still alive."

"What?" Agnes asks. "Why would he think she's dead?"

They didn't see the vision I had. They didn't see her die. But Misha did. Just like he saw his mother murdered.

Growls erupt as well as hisses, the anger behind them startling my already fragile nerves. My vision sharpens as the amount of supernatural magic around me intensifies. I think it's Johnny, but then I see *her*.

Celia storms across the garden flanked by a small army of werewolves in beast form.

"Stand down," she bites out through her teeth, the severity in her tone and stance making me and Agnes back the hell up.

I think she's speaking to the werewolves, but it's the vampires who give her and the wolves ample berth. Her eyes widen when she sees Misha close to the path that leads to the lake.

The cluster of vampires struggling to restrain Misha back away when he falls eerily still. Like a statue, he remains unmoving, his long, deadly nails draped at his sides and his wild gaze focused on Celia.

"Oh, my God, Misha," she rasps.

She hurries forward only to be intercepted by a white wolf with patches of silver and black peppering his back.

"I'm not arguing with you," Celia snarls at him. "I'm telling you, you need to get out of my way."

The wolf *changes*, leaving an immense male looming

over her, his dark skin slick with sweat. "Aric won't like this," he practically barks at her. "You're not supposed to be here."

"My mate will understand," Celia tells him.

I'm not entirely sure that's true. At the very least, Aric might snap someone in half. I just hope that someone isn't me.

Celia whips around when Agnes lurches forward, her nails out and her fangs exposed. "I told you to stand down," Celia snaps.

"The master is in trouble," Hank shouts, storming to Agnes's side. "If these mongrels keep you from helping him, truce or not, they're not leaving here alive."

I'm ready for Hank's head to come to a rolling stop at my feet. But instead of using brute force, sympathy splays along my sister's beautiful face. He's scared, but she is, too.

"Hank, trust me," she says, speaking quietly.

I'm glad she's calm. I'm not. Not with the way the wolves form a ring around her, their haunches tightening as the vamps close in, and not when whatever humanity Celia returned to Misha drifts further away.

I push my way toward Celia, only to be wrenched back by Hank.

"Taran, stay where you are," Celia tells me.

And maybe less blood will splatter on your cute clothes, she doesn't add.

The wolf, the naked one who stands over her frowns. "Aric will understand," she repeats.

He sniffs, trying to uncover her lies. But Celia isn't lying.

Whatever he scents in her makes him nod in the direction of the wolves. "Let her pass," he orders.

"Hank," Celia states, not that she needs to say more.

"You heard her," Hank commands. "Stand down."

The vamps withdraw, giving Celia enough space to easily step through.

I race after her.

Okay. Maybe more like stumble and stagger after her, trying to avoid the multitude of skulls fading in and out at my feet.

Misha's memory left me drained and disturbed. My energy isn't anywhere near where I need it to be, making me vulnerable despite that vulnerable is the last thing I need to be.

Misha slumps to his knees at Celia's approach. Like me, he's exhausted, and struggling, and . . . *inhuman.*

"Celia," I say, my eyes rounding. "I think his soul is gone."

"No," she says.

I try to grab her, but she slips from my grasp. "I'm serious," I stammer. "I don't feel it."

"I do," she answers quietly.

She lowers herself in front of him. I more or less flop, trying not to curse when my knee crashes against a rock buried beneath the soil.

If I'm being honest, I can't exactly feel Misha's soul. What I do feel is all the wrath and strength that comes with it. It's different then, his entire form void of anything close to human.

I'm re-thinking allowing Celia to save the day and am pretty damn sure we're about to die. "This isn't a good idea," I tell her. "He could hurt you. The vamps need to hold him or something."

"No," Celia replies, keeping her voice gentle. "I don't want anyone to touch him."

"Celia," I beg.

Her hand snaps over my wrist when I try to inch forward. "Taran, I told you to stay put," she reminds me.

She tilts her head, her compassion almost palpable as she takes in Misha's beaten-down form. Very carefully, she releases my hand. "Misha, it's Celia," she tells him, her voice sweet, tranquil, and surprisingly absent of fear. "Can you hear me?"

Misha lifts his head. I almost sigh with relief until his seething stare latches onto Celia and his fangs lengthen.

Celia's palm shoots out, keeping everyone in place, including me. "Don't anyone move."

Her command and the surety in her tone are the only reason I don't erupt like a tornado of fire. Holy God, I'll kill him if he harms her.

"What's wrong with him?" I ask, barely breathing.

"He's in pain," she explains, watching him closely.

"Will he attack?" I manage.

"Yes."

"*Yes?*" I glance between them. "Then why the hell are you kneeling this close to him?"

She bats her hands, trying to shush me. "Misha, it's Celia," she says again.

"I know who you are," he responds, his voice unearthly.

"You should," she says. "We're friends."

Her response makes him pause. "I *called* to you," he says, continuing to watch her like he isn't sure she's really there.

"Yes. I heard your voice whispering in my head," she replies. "I'll always hear you when you need me to." She smiles softly, as if Misha's voice doesn't sound possessed and he doesn't seem ready to peel our flesh from our gnawed-off bones.

"Do you hurt?" she asks gently.

His stare falls to her belly. There's no hiding her pregnancy from the world, not anymore, and especially not from Misha. "Yes," he responds, his eerie baritone growing more forceful.

I clutch my arm against me. Right now, Sparky trusts Misha almost as much as I do. She quivers, shaking me and my words. "Celia," I warn. "You have to move away from him."

"It's all right," she says.

I think she's speaking to me until she reaches out and cups Misha's shoulder. "They're gone," she assures him.

Misha's gray eyes turn cold and deadly. "All of them?"

"Yes."

"By my hands?" he questions.

She nods. By now, she's hurting for him. "Yes, just as Uri promised."

He doesn't seem satisfied. "What about her?"

Celia strokes the ends of his hair, very much in that motherly way she always touched Emme's when she was sick or scared. "She's at peace. No one will ever hurt her again. I promise."

"I want to kill them," Misha growls.

Celia's eyes well with tears, her expression changing in a way that startles me. It's not quite angry, not quite vicious. It's simply in tune with those who seek and acquire revenge in blood.

This expression doesn't belong on my beautiful sister's face, not with the compassion and kindness she frequently demonstrates in our presence. But here it is, despite how the prospect of becoming a mother has softened her further.

I suppose revenge is yet one more thing that connects her to Misha. Like him, she knows it well.

"You killed them a long time ago," she reminds him.

"All of them?" Misha asks, before she finishes the last word.

"Yes," she tells him. "They're gone, and now I need you to come back to me." She inches closer, wrapping her arm around Misha's neck and resting her cheek against his shoulder.

I don't like his fangs this close to her throat. Not when he's taken his share of her blood before. Yet as much as he likely remembers her taste, and what it did to him, the moment she sinks into his embrace, his eyes close and his fangs withdraw.

"Please, Misha," she tells him quietly. "Leave your past where it belongs and come back to me."

Misha's breaths, so pained and shallow before quicken. I don't move, too busy gawking and scared out of my mind that he'll turn on her.

If he bites a pregnant mate, *especially* the alpha's pregnant mate, any truce forged will be forgotten and the vamps and *weres* will be at war. I think Celia's counting on Misha to remember this, but I think she's counting on their friendship more.

I fall back onto my heels close to where the faded images of the skulls continue to flash in and out. One by one, they sink into the ground, the lush sod swallowing them whole.

Celia doesn't seem to notice them. Her full attention remains on Misha as she continues to speak softly, reassuring him that he's safe and those who have harmed him are now long dead.

It takes a few minutes, and a few more, before Celia releases him and he opens his eyes.

Sweat drenches his skin, causing his long hair to stick to his face. Celia strokes the loose and messy strands behind his shoulder. "Are you back?" she asks him gently.

Vamps aren't creatures you're gentle with. It's too easy for them to misinterpret kindness as weakness and target you as dinner. I almost remind Celia of this, but she and Misha have always shared a bond no one else can comprehend.

"Yes," he says. He swipes his face, a gesture that seems foreign on someone so refined.

"What happened?" she asks.

"I don't know. My magic, Taran's, and the Fate's reacted."

"The Fate?" she questions.

"Here," Agnes calls.

Tim, one of Misha's bodyguards, is carrying Johnny with his arm draped over his shoulders. Johnny's tattoos appeared to have settled back into their original spots. But like Misha, Johnny has seen better days.

Celia's brows knit, her attention back on Misha. "Where did the magic take you?"

His attention falls to her belly. "Nowhere good. Nowhere safe."

My vision sharpens further. I don't have to turn around to know who's here, but I do anyway now that I know Celia is safe.

Gemini's jaw is set tight. Aric stands just in front of him, the rage surrounding him accelerating like a dangerous landslide as he takes in Misha's close proximity to Celia,

Celia and Misha rise as one, with Celia edging slightly in

front of Misha. "I had to come, love," she tells Aric. "I couldn't leave him hurting like this."

Aric doesn't respond with words, reaching for her hand and pulling her protectively behind him. Celia doesn't fight him, knowing the closer she is, the easier it will be to soothe him.

"We have to talk, wolf," Misha tells him.

"About you keeping your distance from my wife and mate?" Aric replies, his timbre low and fierce. "Good. You've used up any favors you think she might owe you."

"She owes me nothing," Misha responds. "The only debt that remains is one I owe her."

Aric doesn't take his comment any better. Misha doesn't care, his stance growing more severe. "This isn't about me and Celia. It's about her future and that of your children," he says, his features hardening as they hone in on me.

I can practically hear Aric's muscles stretch when his gaze drifts in my direction.

"The skulls are a warning, Aric," I tell him. "Something is coming after Celia."

"What skulls?" Aric asks.

At first I think he's distracted by Misha's presence. But nothing gets past this wolf. I frown and point to the remaining skull as it disappears into the ground. "All of them," I reply.

Gemini takes point beside me, appearing as thrilled with Misha as Aric.

"Taran," Celia says. "There are no skulls."

Chapter Twenty-Two

We don't leave vamp camp. None of us even move, the tension and fear over what may be coming cementing us in place.

"I saw them, too, Master," Hank says, falling to his knees in front of Misha. "The skulls were everywhere and burning in flames."

It's only then Misha tears his gaze from Celia. "What else did you see?"

Hank glances up, appearing afraid to answer. Misha lost control over his magic and mind the moment Johnny appeared. Johnny's power must have somehow clashed with Misha's magic, and I suppose mine as well, stirring that vision I had at the concert when I first met Johnny, and causing Misha to completely lose his shit.

The pain at watching Celia die, and not being able to save her, too closely mimicked his mother's death. Jesus, how could he not remember that moment then?

"I saw the tiger," Hank answers. "But nothing past that."

"What tiger?" Agnes adds, her breath catching when she looks to Celia.

"There was a tiger on fire," Hank says, his hands

clenching. "The master tried to save her."

"Her?" Aric asks.

I rub my eyes, remembering Misha's howls and how he futilely beat the flames with his hands.

"It looked female," Hank mutters, more afraid to tell Misha than Aric. "But it was hard to know for sure."

Misha scans the area, his attention skipping over every one of his vampires. They all shake their heads, allowing Agnes to answer for them. "We only saw the burning skulls, Master." She lifts her chin. "But Hank was closest to you. It could be the reason he witnessed more than we did."

Aric doesn't move, neither does Celia. Gemini stalks forward, menace spilling from him like blood from a fresh kill. "Misha tried to save her," I reiterate. "I saw him."

"And did he?" Aric asks.

The words are hard to say. "No. Her skulls were among those burning."

"Was it me?"

Celia asks the one question none of us dare ask.

"I don't know," Misha answers.

Aric's focus jerks to me. "I can't be sure either," I answer.

"She's a golden tigress," Aric points out. "Her markings are distinct. How can you not know?"

"The flames had already stripped her of her fur when I reached her," Misha answers.

A bomb could have fallen from the sky and destroyed everything around us, and the aftermath still wouldn't have been as quiet as we are now.

"I'm not sure Misha was there," I say.

"What do you mean?" Aric asks frowning. "He told you he was and you saw him."

"I know, but . . ." I cover my face, it's only then I feel the bruise forming where Agnes slapped me awake. I release my hands slowly. "With the exception of me lifting the skull, this vision was almost exactly the same as the one I had at the concert. Everything was on fire and the entire area reduced to nothing but flames and ash. But it's like Misha didn't belong there. I put him there." I meet his face. "Or maybe his magic did. Did you feel the flames, or the heat?"

He doesn't immediately answer, appearing to give it a great deal of thought. "No. I couldn't feel her."

"You mean Celia," Aric states.

He and Misha stare each other down. It's not in challenge. It's because neither want to believe that was really her.

"It could have been another tiger," Edith Anne interjects. She kicks at the ground. "Even without fur the master would have known if she was pregnant."

Her words cut off and she withdraws at the sight of Misha's glare. Edith isn't an easy vampire to like. She's selfish and spoiled. But in her own way, she likes Celia and is trying to offer us hope.

"My apologies, Master." She turns to face Celia, her expression one I can't read and one I don't recognize on her. "None of us want Celia to die."

"She wasn't pregnant," Misha says. "That I'm certain of."

Celia edges away. "Good," she says. "At least the baby was safe."

Which means her babies will live even if she doesn't.

I veer away, swiping my tears and march to where Johnny sits on one of the benches. "Did you see the flames? The skulls, everything?"

He looks to Misha, horror riddling his features. "I saw everything," he says, making it clear he saw more of Misha than he intended.

"Call the grandmaster, the head witches, and Omar," Misha orders. A vamp takes off toward the house. Misha stops in front of Aric who is seconds away from destroying the entire compound. "The Alliance needs to be informed." His focus drops to Celia. "It's the only way we can prevent this madness."

He storms away. I follow, or at least try to, practically running to keep up with him. "The vamps didn't see the snow," I mutter, trying to speak in code.

257

"No," he says.

"Why?"

Misha's long hair sweeps over his shoulder with how hard he turns around to speak to me. "I will never allow them to see me in a moment of weakness."

"But then why did I . . ."

His stare falls to my arm. "The magic in your arm is ancient, so is mine, and in a way so is the Fate's, since fate and destiny have always existed. They don't like each other." He frowns, picking up on something I don't. "Or perhaps they do."

Gemini said my magic and Johnny's both compliments and clashes. I suppose there's always room for one more, and this space seems reserved for Misha.

"So whose future did we see?" I grab Misha's arm when he doesn't answer. It's a stupid question given his volatile state. Gemini knows it, shoving himself between us and hauling me back. "Whose future?" I demand, trying to break free of my lover's hold.

Misha's shoulders rise and fall, anger and the heat of the moment summoning his aggressive nature. Somehow, he keeps it together. "It's yours, Taran, and Celia's. You saw me. I couldn't help her because I wasn't there to help."

He walks away. The vampires scrambling after him as he disappears inside the house.

The conference call goes well. And when I say well, I'm lying. The best I can say is no one died, and no one's killed each other. Yet.

Johnny sits to my right, with Agnes on his opposite side. Like the rest of us, he's ill at ease, waiting for the leaders to pass their ruling. To his credit, he's not openly showing weakness. If anything, he's showing his strength. His tats crawl along his skin, exactly as they did before our collective power went boom and I saw some shit we'll never unsee.

The peacock Johnny drew on his stomach shakes out his

feathers as he parades around the room, his form massive upon leaving Johnny's skin. He passes the row of vamps lining the wall who creep away from it. They're not afraid of the bird, they're afraid of the power behind it. So are the wolves who growl as it struts by.

Omar, the president of the North American Were Council watches it with interest from the giant screen directly in front of us. "As president, I hereby offer the Fate our full protection and declare him a national treasure."

Genevieve and Ines seethe from their screen to the left, the silver and gold light streaming from their amulets indicative of their anger and disdain.

Johnny straightens. "What does that mean?" he asks me over Ines's reply that Johnny isn't the *weres'* to claim.

I lean toward him yet it's Gemini who replies, his voice terse. "That you're under our protection should you agree to join the Pack."

"I'm not a *were*," he says, sounding confused.

"No," Gemini agrees. "It's an official title granted only once before." His attention darts to Celia, who became a national treasure only after Destiny declared her and Aric's children as the ones who would save us all.

Aric isn't happy, neither are the witches. "Let it be known that as Alpha and Leader I'm against any declaration that puts my mate at risk."

"Your mate is still under our protection, I assure you." It's what Omar says, but he doesn't bother looking at Aric when he says it. No, his admiration is too busy skipping between Johnny and that damn peacock.

"The Fate belongs among the witches," Ines insists, her anger building.

"I believe you have enough problems," Omar adds casually. "The shapeshifters are coming for you, witch. Burning the heart branded a target into your back, and into those you most cherish. Take this time to prepare for the inevitable counter-strike." He smiles. "We'll see to the Fate."

Uri laughs from the screen poised in front of Misha. It's the type of laugh that has nothing to do with humor and everything to do with superiority. Somehow, he feels he has the upper hand. "The Fate will do better with those who show him respect." He smiles in Johnny's direction. "And those more accustomed to the lavish lifestyle he leads. May I be the first to welcome you into our family, young Fate?"

Ines snaps, screaming at Uri and Omar in French. Growls erupt from Omar, and Aric. Like the rest of us, Aric recognizes that Celia and their children will be the ones ultimately   screwed. The peacock shoots forward, the plumage from his gold feathers vanishing in colorful spurts as he reforms into Johnny's skin. No one notices, the collective group at each other's throats when Johnny storms out.

Gemini clasps my hand when I rise. He knows I'm going after Johnny. "I can't leave," he says, jerking his chin in Aric's direction. "Our pack needs to show a united front, even if our president won't."

"I know," I reply. Like me, Gemini narrows his stare on Omar. Omar notices and smiles. He's not afraid of us, except maybe he should be.

"You need to stand by Aric and Celia," I say, pressing a kiss to his temple and slipping from his hold. "I need to . . . I don't know what I need. I just need to get the hell away from everyone before I burn this shit down."

I stomp away, furious. These supposed leaders have their own agendas, their own needs to fill. I understand it, but like Aric, my priority is Celia's safety, not who gets to claim a super power like Johnny.

Since the incident on the mountain, I feel Johnny more, his feelings and turmoil of emotions, but most of all his growing power. Each moment Destiny comes closer to death, I sense Johnny getting that much closer to becoming omnipotent.

I'm sad for both of them, for Destiny who's dying far too young, and for Johnny who's too young to bear the title Fate brings.

I pass the library, nodding to Hank and Agnes who wait by the large lead glass window. They seem angry, likely having heard every bit of the conversation next door, as well as sensing Misha's frustration.

"You headed out?" Hank asks.

"Soon," I say, hoping it's true.

My stare falls to my feet as I continue forward, my hot pink shoes the only bright spot in the dark hall.

Although I shouldn't, I smile softly when I sense Johnny's magic pulling me toward the solarium. It's familiar and welcoming, drawing me to him and away from the escalating voices.

Breasha and her guardian are long gone, tucked away and protected from the chaos. I'm still not crazy about Misha's arrangement with her. But I trust Misha enough to do the right thing. If not for me, for Celia, who counts on him when it matters, and who can somehow see beyond the omniscient master he's quickly becoming.

With a sigh that does nothing to release my stress, I step into the solarium.

The entire glass ceiling reveals a canvas of midnight blue and gleaming stars. It's perfect, very unlike this less than perfect night.

Johnny paces near the wall of glass that gives a view of the lake, his tats snaking across his arms and back. Like him, every image he created is agitated. And like him, they're probably worried what's to become of them all.

I take a seat along the ridge of a giant planter, glimpsing at the canopy of Flame Mimosas branching out over my head. They partially obscure my view of the sky, not that I mind. Both are different yet neither is less beautiful.

Water trickling from the stone fountain at the center and Johnny's nervous steps are the only sounds in the room.

"What's going to happen to me, Taran?" he asks, stopping suddenly.

"What do you want to happen?" I offer a sympathetic smile. "Besides for all this to go away?"

"I want to feel safe," he replies, his voice cracking. "I don't want anything to hurt me."

I glance behind me, hoping no one is close. The last thing

Johnny needs now is to be perceived as weak or as another pawn any of the elite can move around as they wish. I don't see anyone, but this is Misha's home. He has eyes and ears everywhere.

My first thought is to shush Johnny, but the damage is done, and whatever he's feeling, he needs to feel for the sake of his sanity.

"The *weres* don't like me, do they?" he asks. "I don't mean just Gemini's pack. I mean all of them."

It's not the first time he's questioned how the *weres* feel about him. "It's not dislike," I say. "It's what their animal instincts feel when they're around you. They sense that you're capable of more than perhaps you're aware of. That unknown strength makes them leery and leads to distrust." I cross my legs. "Keep in mind, belonging to a Pack is all about protecting your own. If they don't know what you can do, they can't guard against it."

"They don't have to worry about me."

As much as I like Johnny, he's dead wrong.

"Look," I say. "The offer to join the Pack is a generous one. You'll be protected and allowed all the benefits the title of national treasure affords."

"Will I ever be one of them?"

"You'll be as much of *were* as we are," I reply truthfully.

"So I'll never belong?"

"No," I answer just as bluntly.

Johnny rubs his hands, the worry and thoughts troubling his mind drawing deep lines along his forehead. "The witches might not make it," he says. "That's what Omar was trying to tell Ines, wasn't it? That she's nothing more than a snack waiting to be eaten."

"Ines and Genevieve are the strongest of your kind. Neither will go down without a fight."

"That's not what I'm asking," he tells me. He digs through his jeans for a pack of cigarettes and a lighter. No doubt gifts from the vamps. He lights up, taking a drag. "They may be tough, like you claim, and like I saw when we were on that mountain. But shifters are stronger."

The puff he releases turns into a dragon with large wings. He flies around the room, releasing gray smoke in long, swirly streams.

I watch it disappear, speaking slowly. "The shifters are the strongest of all the supernaturals," I agree, trying to act and speak casually and failing miserably at both. "It takes many of us just to bring one down."

"How many?" he asks.

"Too many," I say. "Lives are lost each time we fight them. Look at the Imperials. They're the Wonder Women of their kind and even they died protecting Ines and her family."

"Are the vampires as easily defeated?"

I frown. "That wasn't an easy defeat, Johnny. It only seems that way because shifters are absurdly strong."

"That's not what I mean." He looks in the direction of the exit when I nod. "From what I've seen, vamps are stronger than witches. Take Misha. He packs a serious punch. I felt it when our magic met. He can take on a shifter. I know he can."

"Misha is lethal, but he can't take down a shifter alone." It's what I say, although after everything I saw and felt in the garden when our collective magic slapped us around, I'm no longer certain that's true.

Between him and Johnny, it was Misha's strength that struck me the hardest. For the most part, we've spoken of Misha's mounting superiority in whispers, and how one day, no preternatural will be able to touch him. I think it's because we're afraid to admit the truth.

He's already beyond what we worried he'd become.

"Why does he still submit to Uri?" Johnny asks, his thoughts mimicking mine. "He's already stronger than his master. I don't have to know Uri to see it."

The air stills around us, thick with tension and fear. That's when I'm certain we're not alone. I try to silence Johnny, but he knows, and doesn't care who hears him.

"It's a respect thing," I say, hoping he leaves it at that.

"Or because Misha feels he owes Uri for letting him have his revenge."

"It's not as easy as you're making it," I insist, wishing he hadn't seen Misha's vulnerable side.

Johnny blows out another puff of smoke, this time a winged stallion. "Yeah it is."

I rise, brushing off my jeans. "You're wrong. Misha loves Uri, and Uri thinks of him as son." It's true, I think. Mostly though, I'm speaking to those listening just outside this room. They need reassurance that the relationship between their master and grandmaster remains strong.

"Let me ask you this," he says. "If you were me, who would you stay with?"

"The *weres*," I reply.

He snorts, his reaction making him choke on his smoke. "No, Taran. If *you* were *me*, who would you stay with to keep you safe."

"The vamps." I don't hesitate. "Uri's right. Their lifestyle is more what you're used to. But Johnny, despite what you've seen, the *weres* are the heart of this world, and their strength and magic is what makes it beat."

He watches me closely, trying to gauge whether I'm lying. For a long time he simply stands there, playing with his lighter as he ponders his next move.

"I think I know what I have to do," he finally says.

From his jungle-sleeve tattoo, a beautiful blue butterfly emerges, fluttering through the open window and disappearing into the night. I frown. "What are you doing?"

Tears shimmer his eyes. "Saying goodbye to the life I knew, and hello to the one that will help me survive."

He mashes out his cigarette on the side of the cement planter and flicks the butt to the side. Without a glance back, he marches toward the foyer.

I think it's a power play and part of his newly elected "I don't give a damn" persona. Still, I lift the butt, trying to find a place to dump it.

Agnes steps from behind the fountain. She was here the whole time.

"I'll take it," she says, holding out her hand. Her stare flickers toward the doorway where Johnny stands. "He's waiting for you."

I follow Johnny as he returns to the conference room, his arrival causing an immediate silence. Like I taught him, his head is high and his shoulders are squared.

His tats move across his skin in a show of dominance as he steps between the large screens. For the first time, I can't sense his fear. But I know it's there, and somehow, worse than before.

"I've made a decision," he says, speaking over Omar when he tries to greet him. He meets Uri in the face, something I would hesitate to do even in front of a monitor.

"I choose the vamps," Johnny announces, speaking quickly when the entire room erupts with noise. "But I have conditions."

Uri leans back into his seat, appearing impressed. "What are they?" he asks.

Ines storms off-screen. "Don't do this," Genevieve says, affronted and angry. "That isn't where you belong."

Johnny ignores her, speaking to Uri as if only he matters. "One last concert for my fans, and for my people who didn't make it. Only I want the *weres* to guard me and for Misha to come for me once it's over."

"Where?" Uri asks.

"Why do you want us guarding you?" Aric asks. He rises slowly as does Gemini. "If you're choosing the vamps, why not let them watch you?"

Johnny looks at Gemini. "I want Taran with me. I know you won't let her go unless you're there, too."

That much is true.

"Where do you wish this concert to be?" Uri asks. He doesn't like the attention on anyone but him and is pissed Aric momentarily stole his spotlight.

"Orangeburg County, in South Carolina. There's a new arena. One of the last few times I talked to Drake, he said that's where I needed to be." He huffs. "Thirty-thousand capacity. Go big or go home, right?"

"If that's what you want, you shall have it, young Fate," Uri tells him, looking as pleased as a cat with a screeching canary in its mouth.

Johnny meets my face, and for the briefest moment, I feel his heart shatter. "It's what I want," he says. "I think it's time we all embrace our fate."

Chapter Twenty-Three

I step out of Johnny's dressing room, smiling when I see Gemini. He's in charge of Johnny's security, something he insisted upon when I insisted on going.

Johnny wants me with him, and whether we say it or not, I think this is our last goodbye.

"Hi, babe," I say, laughing when his scowl remains firmly in place. "What's wrong?" I hang tight to my phone and turn slowly, causing the skirt of my strapless pink chiffon dress to flutter. "I'm wearing practical shoes and everything."

It's true. I ditched the dagger pumps I'd planned to wear for sparkly ballerina flats.

He pulls me against him. Oh, and there's that smile I like. "I'd rather have you alone with me, and far away from here."

I wrap my arms around his neck when he bends to kiss me. "Ever have hot sex backstage at a concert?" I ask. He shakes his head slowly, his face warming with desire. "Do you want to?"

"Very much," he replies, grazing his teeth along my neck. He stops at my ear, giving the lobe a tug. "But not until I'm sure we're safe."

My impish demeanor dissolves. "Do you think the

shifters will come for him?"

"I don't know," he admits. "Chatter surrounding the neophytes has been minimal and limited to the countries within South America. That doesn't mean we can assume they won't appear. Stay alert so we can wake up safe in each other's arms."

He kisses me again, easing away only when the local pack approaches. "We'll be outside, guarding the perimeter. If there's any trouble, or even if you suspect there might be, call me."

"I will," I promise.

I watch him march down the corridor that leads toward the exit and away from the screaming crowd shouting Johnny's name. It didn't take long for the vamps to organize the show, a week tops, I think. And it took less than twenty minutes for every seat to sell out. It's one hell of a way to go out, but I suppose this is what Johnny needed.

This arena was erected in what seemed like the middle of nowhere. It's a massive colosseum with several elevated tiers and where the newly formed football team will play their first game come fall. The farmer who owned the land must have made out like a king. And from what the local pack told us, he still has the potential to make more. More builders are bidding on the wooded acres surrounding the arena, hoping to put in a mall, and possibly erect a small town to bring more businesses to the area.

I consider how much the area residents will make with just Johnny's show alone when the door to his dressing room cracks open.

My smile appears when the man of the hour steps out, wearing black leather pants, boots, and a vest. His long bleached hair, on top of his head, drapes over the side against his cheek. He looks almost exactly as he did when I first saw him, except for the little bit of innocence he seemed to lose along the way.

"Ready?" I ask.

"I guess I have to be," he says, forcing a smile I wish he didn't have to.

All at once, he's surrounded by his people, a brand-new set of sharks dying to get a piece of him. They don't yet realize that it's those with real fangs who get to keep him.

The *weres* assigned to him follow, close enough to guard all the while trying to shield themselves from the loud obnoxious intro Johnny's new band delivers. When we're almost to the stage they disperse, rushing to guard the entrances and spare their sensitive hearing.

A woman with a headset approaches, like the rest of the human staff, they seemed to want to keep their distance from the *weres*. "Johnny wants to talk to you before he takes the stage," she tells me.

"Sure."

She clutches my arm when I start forward, gripping me hard and meeting me with a nasty glower. "You need to hurry," she insists. "We have a schedule to keep and thirty-thousand people to please."

I shrug her off. "And you need to keep your hands off me."

"You obviously don't know who I am," she informs me.

"No, sweetheart, you don't know who I am." I motion to where the *weres* vanished. "You might be afraid of them, but trust me when I say they're a lot nicer than me."

I push past her, maybe a little too harshly seeing how she staggers back. If this is the kind of people Johnny surrounds himself with, is it a wonder he was ready for a break? The thought makes me sad, so does his future. I worry what will happen to him, and hope he's strong enough to face what's coming.

Unlike Destiny.

Shayna, Emme, and I stopped in to see her before we left Tahoe. If I thought she looked bad before, nothing compared to how we found her. She looked dead. I thought she was by how Tye openly wept at her side. But then she opened her eyes and thanked us for being her friends.

I swallow back the memory, and every speck of sadness I felt when we said our goodbyes. I don't want that same future for Johnny. I want him to live the long life he deserves.

The crew hurries past me as I wipe my eyes and hop up the stairs leading backstage. Each worker speaks fast and moves faster, distracted by their tasks and the last-minute details to make Johnny shine.

From the other side of the stage, Shayna waves. Koda nods, releasing her cautiously and disappearing into the shadows. Like Gemini, Emme, and Bren, he'll be guarding the perimeter. I hope we don't need them, but if we do, they're the team I want to have our backs.

Johnny peeks out to the arena from his spot behind the curtain. I smile, hoping he'll return it. As he lets the curtain fall back in place, he does. It's not much of a grin, but it's there and I'm happy to see it.

He walks to me slowly, pulling me into a tight embrace. "Thanks, Taran," he says, speaking slowly. "For everything."

I'm not what anyone would call a "hugger". I make the exception for my family and my lover. That's it. Even when Celia and Aric went through what they went through—and I saw how broken Aric seemed, how lost he was without her, I couldn't bring myself to hug him. For the most part, I wanted to punch him in the nose.

Johnny is different. He's not family, but I'll be damned if I want to let him go. He straightens as he carefully releases me, chuckling when he sees my face.

His gaze softens when I stroke the long blond strands away from his eyes. "I'm going to be all right, mama bear," he tells me. He looks in the direction of the stage. "No matter what comes, I'm ready for it."

"I know you are," I tell him.

The guitar soloist currently blasting away reaches a crescendo, his rapid movements across the strings slowing as he scales down the melody. The crowd goes wild, their collective screaming deafening.

They know who's ready to take the stage.

At once, the lights go out, taking the shrieks and hollers for Johnny up another notch. With a deep breath he squares his shoulders, leaving me and stepping into the darkness.

Thousands of feet stomp at once, rumbling the floor and

adding to the cacophony of noise. But the moment the spotlight flashes on, and Johnny lights up like a burst of lava from a dormant volcano, the noise is too much and my hands slam over my ears.

The screams pain me, threatening to burst my eardrums. It's only temporary, the agony receding as Johnny drags out the note from the first word he sings.

"Angels.
Angels walk among us.
Holding us when we fall.
Protecting against those who maul our bleeding souls."

Each verse takes a life of its own, breathing air into the wounded crowd, and giving my heartstrings a pull. Be it magic, or simply Johnny, his talent is unmatched.

I wrap my arms around myself and bow my head. He called me mama bear. I'm not his mama, that's for damn sure. But between the way he fires my need to protect, and how I feel every time I see Celia stroke her pregnant belly, I'm starting to think that maybe being a mama is a fear I should no longer shy away from.

I think of Gemini, and how he held me last night as we slept.

Maybe it's time to try a new adventure.

My focus returns to Johnny, the light reflecting like a halo against his skin. It's amazing to see the way the darkness surrounds him while he stands untouched in the light. He turns back to me and offers me a wink. I smile, flattered.

My phone buzzes in my hand. I expect it to be Gemini, only for Tye's face to encompass the entire screen.

A horrible chill runs down my spine. "Hello?"

Static fills the line.

"Hello?" I repeat, plugging my opposite ear.

Tye speaks fast, but I can't understand what he's saying. The line isn't clear and his speech is garbled.

"Tye, *Tye*? . . . I can't hear you. Slow down."

I make out only a few words, and I hate every one.

"Dead . . . Destiny is . . . Celia's children . . ."

"Destiny is dead?" I ask. I cover my mouth, waiting for

him to clarify, but the call drops.

I ring him back, only for it to go straight to voice mail. My hand is shaking as I phone Gemini, speaking quickly when he answers. "I think Destiny is dead."

"What?"

I edge away from the curtain. "Tye just called me. He was upset. The connection was bad and I couldn't make out what he was saying. He said something about Celia's children and Destiny being dead."

He shouts orders to his wolves canvasing the perimeter. "Taran, I need you to stay with Johnny, something's wrong."

My thoughts become a muddled mess, thinking Destiny's demise has started a chain of events that no one could have predicted. "What do you see?" I ask him.

"Nothing. But Destiny can't be dead. None of my *weres* guarding her have called."

"Then call them!" I yell.

"We're trying." There's a pause as a slew of voices speak to Gemini at once. He curses and switches back to me. "No one is getting through, Taran, the texts go unanswered. Someone picks up the line, but no one can hear what they're saying."

"What if something attacked them—"

"Then they would be fighting, not answering their phones or trying to make calls. Something is happening. I'm coming for you and Johnny now—"

My phone buzzes again, signaling another call. "It's Tye," I say to Gemini. "I'll call you back."

"All right, just stay with Johnny. I'm on my way."

I switch over to Tye's call. Again, nothing but white noise. "I can't hear you," I yell into the phone. "Tell me what's happening."

My back slams into the wall and I drop my phone, inundated by an onslaught of magic that paralyzes me.

Destiny appears in my line of vision, her voice hollow and echoing from every direction, and her image a staccato of movement.

"Taran, hear me," she says.

Glimpses of the backstage intermix with glimpses of Destiny. "Taran, hear me," she says, her voice growing weaker.

"I hear you," I say, fighting through the overstimulation of imagery.

She's in her bed, the one in our basement, her long black hair contrasting deeply against her pale white skin and the ivory robe she's wearing. She's almost dead, I know she is.

Her breaths are harsh, labored, every word she expresses appearing to rob her of life. "Fate doesn't get to decide if Celia's children will rid the world of evil," she says. "It's destiny."

"What?" I ask. I want to presume she's delirious, and losing herself as she fades into the light. But there's a reason she's reaching out to me so close to death, and I'll be damned if I don't pay attention.

"Destiny, tell me what's happening," I plead.

The barrage of images separating my reality from my connection to her dwindles and I start to see more of the dark curtains swaying in front of me. "Uh-uh, girl," I tell her, spitting each syllable out through my teeth. "Don't you leave me now."

A flash of her face appears and she slowly blinks her eyes open. "That's it, baby," I say. "Show me what you've got."

Johnny's singing fades, as do my surroundings, leaving only Destiny. "Fate doesn't get to decide if Celia's children will rid the world of evil," she repeats. "It's destiny."

"Okay, I heard you," I say carefully. "Now tell me what you mean."

Tears swim in her eyes, releasing one by one. "Evil has known about you and your sisters since the dawn of creation, and long before it first cursed your family." More tears fall, her weakness overtaking her, but her anger pushing her forward.

I'm crying, too, for what she's enduring and how much it hurts her to speak. "What has evil known?" I press.

Almost at once, her tears dry up, her stare determined

even as the rest of her body betrays her. "That your children will rise against it." She swallows hard. "Fate knows it, too . . He's been leeching my power in order to kill them all."

I feel myself rise from the position on the floor, the slow thuds of my heartbeat speeding up and growing pronounced.

"Johnny is leeching your power?" I manage. I turn in the direction of where I think the stage is, but all I see is Destiny.

"Yes," Destiny says, her remaining strength quickly leaving her. "You *have* to kill Johnny, Taran. In order for your children to face their destiny, their fate with death must be destroyed."

I barely believe what she's saying, my insides sinking into the floor. But I'm listening. God damn it, I have to. "Johnny is their fate with death?" I stammer.

"Yes," she answers.

And then she's gone.

Chapter Twenty-Four

When I was a little girl, I used to have nightmares about my parents dying. I used to dream of dark caskets being lowered deep into the ground. I couldn't see them, but I knew it was them.

"Don't cry," Daddy used to say as he held me. "It was only a dream."

Until it wasn't.

I blink my eyes against my bleak surroundings, staring at the pull ropes and heavy curtains for what seems like too long. What happened to my parents was a nightmare that came true, all because long ago, when the world first began, Evil and Good decided to battle it out, and Good determined we would stand among its warriors.

I turn in the direction of the stage, my lightning cracking against my fingers as my balled hands open wide. Too many times I've wished for my daddy to hold me again, to wrap me in his protection and love, to assure me that all the bad was just a dream and only good awaited now.

Except this isn't a nightmare. It's my fucking reality where I have to choose between a young man's life and children yet to be born.

It should be an easy choice. I've known Johnny a handful of weeks. These are my children I'm speaking of, *our children*, mine, Shayna's, Emme's, and Celia's. *Celia* who is already carrying the *fate* of the future in her womb—

Fate.

There's a word.

No, there's a person.

God help me. No matter how easy this choice should be, it's not.

I step on stage. Johnny's fans are so mesmerized by his melodious voice, they don't notice me. They don't even notice the *call* of wolves, surrounding the arena. From every side a wolf is howling, alerting their kind it's time to fight.

Something is wrong. Gemini called it.

And it's up to me to make it right.

"T!" Shayna yells from the other side of stage, the swords she holds in each hand elongating. "Shifters and neophytes are invading the arena, we have to get Johnny out of here . . ."

I stop noticing her, my focus completely on Johnny as my lightning charges and the spark within me surges like a wicked storm. One strike, that's all it will take given the gamut of electrical energy crackling the air and readying to unleash.

But while Johnny's fans don't see me, he does.

His face is turned in my direction, his features sullen as thick tears soak my skin.

"The devil comes out to play," he sings.

The peacock tat on his belly comes to life, much to the "oo's" and "ah's" of Johnny's audience.

"Sometimes he needs to stay," Johnny sings.

The peacock looks at me and spreads its wings. What appear to be rocks roll from the eyes of the feathers as it shakes them out.

"To hear my will and help me be."

They stop at my feet. I see them. I do. But I see my target more.

Johnny finishes the melody, drawing out the last two

words. "And to give your lives to *protect me.*"

The rocks at my feet tip from side to side, tilting up, revealing empty eye sockets and missing teeth.

Skulls.

Just like in my damn visions.

Fuck you, Johnny Fate.

They clatter across the stage as more fall away from the tail feathers. They could be bombs, or something more. It doesn't matter, they won't be enough to stop me.

Bottom line, our babies are the ones who need to stay. Fate, his ass needs to go.

"This is how it's going to be?" Johnny asks, his betrayed tone resonating across the arena. Ironic, seeing he's the one betraying us.

"This is how it has to be," I reply. My stare falls to his chest as the tat of the serpent circling the heart comes alive. It constricts the heart, holding it in place when it quivers and opening its maw wide.

Long fangs pierce the center, puncturing deep and making it bleed.

I fall backward, clenching my head when Destiny screams.

My hands slip through my hair and smack against the floor when the truth hits me at once. Destiny is the heart. Fate is the serpent.

I get it now, and does that shit ever make me move fast.

I scramble to my feet as the rafters shake above us, matching the increasing clamor from the skulls. I kick the skulls out of my way as a man dressed in black robes leaps on stage. I presume he's a neophyte. I also presume he needs to die.

The strobe of light he carries expands in his hand, bleaching his wrinkled face and dark eyes as he spits out a curse. Shayna leaps in front of him, just missing the charge of lightning I send sailing, and slices his head off with her sword.

The strobe crashes against the stadium floor, exploding in a flood of power that flings her across the stage and tosses me against the far wall.

I don't stop moving, my lightning shooting toward Johnny. I scream when it collides against the fans who throw themselves in its path.

Johnny is using his magic to seduce and lure his fans. Everyone in the audience is clamoring up on stage to shield him, climbing all over each other in their desperation to protect him.

I lose him in the crowd overtaking the stage, calling my fire when bodies in black armor form and rise beneath the skulls.

Shayna rushes to my side, ramming her sword into the eye socket of the warrior who lunges.

Her sword smokes and the skull splits in half. She yanks out the blade, gasping as the magic eats away at the metal. "What are they?" she asks, pushing her power into the blade so it mends and sharpens.

"Whatever Johnny wants them to be." My lightning strikes, taking out the next few warriors who advance, as well as another human rushing to fight for Johnny.

"Damn it!" I yell.

"T, we can't attack, not without killing the humans," Shayna pleads. "They'll die for him."

"We don't have a choice," I say, tears dribbling down my cheeks. "Johnny has been draining Destiny's power." I lash out, jolting another warrior who charges and stunning a woman with long black hair. My lightning electrifies the piercings along her bottom lip, burning her mouth. I sob as she falls to the floor screaming.

"T, *I can't*," Shayna says, watching the woman clutching her face writhe in agony.

"Shayna, we have to." I take a breath, trying to keep it together as I send more lightning soaring across the tightening expanse. "Destiny says if Johnny doesn't die, our kids will meet their fate with death."

Her face goes white. "*Our kids?*"

"Our babies, Shayna," I rasp. "Just like we've stood by Celia, our children will stand with hers."

She hesitates for just a moment before slashing her sword across the shoulders of three more warriors. Their bodies slump, their heads rolling away from them, and still more come.

I scan the arena, watching helplessly as Johnny's fans lead him further away and Koda's howl reverberates in the distance. "Where are the wolves?"

"With the shifters, T. There's at least two and a whole army of neophytes." She brings down her sword on the head of another warrior. The skull cracks and the body slumps, but these things are everywhere and drawing closer.

"We need to take out Johnny!" I holler over the growing chaos.

He's almost to the door and all we're doing is backing further away from him.

She slices the limbs off the warrior, trying to grab her. "We also need to get these people out of here."

My lightning explodes two more skulls, their remains falling against a small man with a long beard. She's right. We have to get the humans out. I just don't know how.

The doors leading to the food court bust free from their metal frames when an elephant-sized grizzly bear demolishes its way through. Pack wolves cling to it, trying to bring it down. I know it's a shifter, its immense size and the way it mows through the fans continuing to rush toward Johnny, proclaim it loud and clear.

The *weres* fighting it are not alone. Emme races in behind Bren's large wolf form. Even from this distance she sees us, and her eyes lock on me. It's the only warning I receive before she lifts me and Shayna with her *force* and hurls us at the arena floor.

Shayna howls, her high-pitched battle cry and the light reflecting from her spinning swords alerting everyone in the vicinity that she's coming, she's ready, and to get the hell out of her way unless they're prepared to die.

From the moment my feet leave the floor, I'm screaming my mother-fucking head off.

Emme has bad aim. Horrible aim. Dear God, I'm going

to die.

The floor packed with people comes at me at full speed. I crash into a beefy guy with way too many piercings, but just enough bulge to keep me from landing spread eagle with a splat.

Shayna descends doing some sort of flippy thing, housing her swords the minute her feet connect with the concrete, and reaching for her toothpicks.

I peel myself off the pleasantly plump guy, jerking my foot when he snags my ankle. "Don't hurt Johnny!" he yells at me.

"Fuck off," I yell at him.

I zap him with a jolt of lightning and crawl away, hurrying to my feet and taking point behind Shayna as those rising to protect Johnny close in.

Shayna converts the toothpicks into needles. They leave her hands faster than I can blink, clearing a path through the crowd herding Johnny closer toward the exit. Men and women rush by me, clutching their faces and trying to pull them out. I whirl out of their way, not wanting any part of them. It's a disturbing sight and damn effective, the pain Shayna inflicts just enough to distract them from their quest and break Johnny's spell.

I try to reduce the amount of lightning I release, but it's damn hard to concentrate on lessening my power amidst the escalating chaos surrounding us.

Bellows erupt and bits of ceiling rain down when the *weres* slam the giant grizzly into the base of the stage. They're trying to keep the shifter away from the humans. Except the humans are everywhere.

And so are the neophytes.

Black smoke appears in swirl and a woman in dark robes materializes, her long staff aimed at Shayna.

I light her up with a siphon of flames, the intensity so strong sparks spray against the mob clustered around Johnny. It doesn't do much damage, just enough to snag their attention and snap them free of Johnny's hold.

I race around the burning witch, fighting against the

panicked and shrieking people now trying to escape. Something hard hits me in the back of the head, knocking me down. I cut my hand on something sharp. Blood drips from my palm as I try to push up on my knees.

My nose is bleeding, too. I'm not sure why. Something doesn't feel right and I can't see well, my vision is fading in and out.

A foot connects with my face, the impact tossing me back to the floor. Blood pours out of my mouth and nose. I try to rise and put one foot under me when something else bangs into my shoulder.

People are everywhere. They ram me, kicking and trampling me. I curl inward, cocooning myself in my fire. It's just enough to keep people off me and gives me a moment to gather my senses. I'm hurt and my stomach churns with nausea.

Except I can't just fucking lay here.

I force myself to my feet, my stomach lurching when I push forward. Shayna is battling it out with another neophyte, dodging her curses as she reaches for her dagger. She flings her blade, puncturing the neophyte's skull. I'm almost to them when the witch I set on fire grabs me, her eyes fierce and her skin only partially burned.

She yanks me to her, her fingers digging into my throat. "We will kill you," she spits out, ignoring the swirls of my blue and white flames crisscrossing like ribbons across her face. "All of you."

My fire has no effect on me and it's only barely touching her. The protection wards around her body are strong and her hands are killing me. I gasp, choking as she clamps down.

Oh, and Sparky doesn't like that one bit.

My right hand shoots out, snatching her by the throat and lifting her off the ground. I feel her neck crunch beneath my grasp as my fire builds and anger consumes me. She trembles, releasing me to smack at my hand. As I watch, the protection wards she built around herself break down. Her skin sizzles, crackling off in pieces.

"Burn, bitch," I tell her. "*Burn.*"

Like a missle ignited in blue and white flames, my arm launches her. She soars into the second tier, the impact splitting the first few rows and caving in the second level.

Yet it's Johnny who screams.

I stagger, the dizziness and pain I feel making it hard to keep my feet. Someone runs into me, then another someone, the collection of howls, shrieks, and sounds of destruction across the arena disorienting me further.

"Taran!"

I fall into Gemini's arms. He cradles me and moves fast. I shiver as cold air strikes my face, the agony stabbing through my veins dulling and confusing my thoughts.

Behind us, something wails in torment and vicious growls erupt. Flesh tears and death fills the night. I think a wolf is dead, but then Gemini yells, "Take him down, *now*."

I want to ask him what's happening, but I struggle to form words. My body grows colder as my pain tucks the rest of the world away from me. I make out some words and sounds. Except I can't see anything, my vision completely blurred.

"We have to kill Johnny," I manage. "And Misha has to stay away."

I try to tell him that Johnny is the one who'll hurt our babies, that he's sacrificing his fans to save himself, and plans to sacrifice Misha. It's why Johnny wanted the *weres* to guard him, their magic makes them heartier tributes, and why he requested Misha to retrieve him. As the strongest vampire, Misha was the ultimate prize Johnny needed.

I think I tell Gemini. My lips move, but I can't be sure I actually speak.

He seems to understand. So does Emme.

Her light streams across my cooling skin, easing the pain and sharpening my vision back into focus. My shoulders jerk when something in my face snaps and my ribs fasten into place. Based on what seeps out, my nose was bashed in. I swipe at it irritably as Gemini wrenches me to my feet.

Like me, he's covered with blood. All the wolves are, their dense fur coated in crimson. The shifter is dead. I catch sight of his naked human body lying across the field, beside a *were* who didn't make it.

We're far from the arena. I can see it from the edge of the forest where we stand. Blue and white flames eat through the roof and the left side is partially collapsed.

"What happened?" I say, stunned by how quickly my fire has overtaken the building.

"Your arm's magic and Johnny's clashed when you obliterated that witch." Gemini swallows hard. "I think it knew you were dying and reacted in turn, destroying part of the building and attempting to kill him."

"And did I?" I ask, thinking back to the way Johnny screamed.

"No. He's more powerful than we ever gave him credit for."

After robbing Destiny of her magic and life, of course he is.

I glance around. The humans are gone, but even from where we stand, I hear them sobbing. Somewhere along the highway, a shit-ton of paramedics and firetrucks blast their horns.

People are hurt, many of them dead. Not that we're better off.

Another enormous shifter stalks forward, this one a panther, licking her blood-soaked chops as she trails an army of neophytes and Johnny's skull warriors."

Chapter Twenty-Five

The neophytes chant as one, their dark magic building along with their spell.

"Where are our witches?" I ask, the vile magic coating my tongue with its filth.

"En route," Gemini says, crouching as his twin wolf snarls at his side. "They're not as quick as Genevieve or Ines."

"Figures," I mumble.

"We're out of *weres*," Gemini adds, his voice tight.

"Uh-huh," I agree, my voice cracking as my inner heat gains momentum.

Gemini keeps his focus straight in front of him, growling when two wolves race ahead. They slam into an invisible barrier, writhing and whimpering in agony.

"What are you doing?" he yells when I start forward.

I frown, my gaze skipping from where he's clasping me by the shoulder, back to his face. "The same thing I always do, baby. Getting ready to burn shit down."

I whirl, a pipeline of spinning flames striking the witch in the center.

He detonates in chunks, that's right, chunks. I was more

careful with the amount of magic I used indoors. But we're outside now, and no way are these bastards getting away with this.

The writhing wolves shake off their stupor, charging with Gemini and the remaining *weres.*

"Keep them off me," I yell. "I'm going after Johnny. Emme, launch me!"

I stand tall, my left arm bent at my side and my right arm up a la Supergirl.

Emme stops running, glancing back at me. "Are you sure?"

"Yes, the nematodes are here to collect Johnny. We can't let that happen." I resume my Supergirl pose.

"They're neophytes, Taran."

I slap my hands down. "Like I give a shit, Emme."

She cuts me off with a very irritated throw.

Screw Supergirl. Once more I'm screaming, and flailing, and certain I'm going to die.

The one shoe I managed to hang onto flies off and I land in Gemini's arms. Apparently, he "went long."

"Put me down," I insist.

"Not now," he bites out.

I look behind us. The panther has left the fight and is gunning for us.

Gemini swears, grounding to a halt as a wall of skull warriors appear, blocking our path. He plants me down and from one leap to the next *changes* into his massive wolf form.

I don't quite have my bearings when his fangs clamp down on a warrior's head. He breaks through the skull, flinging the body toward the encroaching panther.

My feet are swept from under me when a warrior snatches me up by the waist. I scream, with rage and all the power boiling its way through me, forcing him to drop me when he bursts into flames.

I land on my knees, my fingers digging into the soil as the ancient magic that makes up my arm takes over and encases my body in an armor of flames.

The panther reaches me, her large paw slapping me aside

when her fangs fail to bite through my fire. I roll, the pain her strike causes combined with my accelerating magic scorching the earth and singeing a path across the field.

My body and the earth beneath me tremble. The same thing that happened in Egypt. My arm knows we're in trouble and is reacting to the threat, feeding my flame with mystical kindling and an extra-large dose of otherworldly gasoline.

"Power," I whisper, getting a high from the wickedly addicting heat coursing through me. "Give me, *power*."

"Oh, *shit*," Bren says behind me.

"Everyone run!" Gemini yells.

The absurd mix of mayhem and mysticism fusing within me peaks, and in one colossal moment it erupts, colliding against everything in the vicinity.

My head jerks up as a mushroom cloud of blue and white spreads along the sky, cloaking the atmosphere as far as I can see. The release should feel good and leave me begging for more. Yet as I find what looks like an ocean of fire eating away at the field, all I feel is out of control.

I stand and walk forward, the heat rising from my core creating ripples in the air as flaming skulls rain from the sky. I kick them out of my way when they land in front of me, my bare feet searing them and leaving marks. Their bodies are gone. Now they're left to burn along with the barren wasteland the area has become.

I expected them to burst into color like all of Johnny's tattoos. But these were different than the rest, maybe because he's become so much more than he was.

My hands ball into fists as I think about everything he did. I know I'm moving toward him. I feel him. He's no longer far away.

It's only when I reach the skull of the panther that I stop, bending to lift it, just as I had lifted the other feline skull in my vision.

This isn't my sister. It's the shifter. My fire killed her as she shrank in size to return to her original human shell.

This time when I cry, it's from relief. My sister doesn't die. She'll have her chance to have her babies. I drop the skull. Provided Johnny meets his own damn fate.

The knowledge gives me strength and propels me ahead, my quick steps turning into a sprint when I feel Johnny's magic build.

I find him in the parking lot by a large Dodge Ram, clutching his belly as he shoves his way inside the cabin. Maybe I couldn't destroy the skulls, but I did succeed in causing him a lot of pain.

Johnny yells to the fan trailing him to start the vehicle. The man, he doesn't look good. His skin is horribly blistered and his face is smeared with soot. He teeters back and forth, struggling to reach the truck. He must have been trapped in the arena when it caught fire, along with everyone else trying to protect Johnny.

If the others look anything like this man, they didn't make it. They died for Johnny, not that he'll ever care.

His eyes widen when he sees me. He shuts the door and scrambles into the driver's seat.

I launch a fireball from my arm, nailing the truck and sending it rolling across the lot. It crashes into the side of Johnny's tour bus, igniting the image of his face on fire.

Legs kick at the splintered windshield, banging frantically against the glass. Something clasps my shoulder, brutally clamping down. I don't turn around. I ignite, my body a conduit of flames that expand out.

I turn enough to see the last of Johnny's skull warriors disintegrate to ash. But at the sound of breaking glass, my attention is all on Johnny.

He crawls out from the busted windshield, bleeding from the multitude of cuts raking his skin and holding tight to his stomach from the damage I did to his skulls.

Except I'm not done with him yet.

I charge after him, tackling him when he tries to run away. We fall hard against the asphalt where I proceed to beat the unholy shit out of him.

I'll be the first one to admit that I can't fight. But hell hath no fury like Taran Wird pissed off. I punch him in the head, kicking him repeatedly, and bringing down my elbow hard into his chest.

His hands snatch at the air, trying to catch my wrists as he yells at me to stop.

He gains the upper hand, rolling on top of me and pinning me in place. "I don't want to hurt you," he spits out. "Not you!"

My chest rises and falls in quick succession, my lungs desperate for air from all the energy I've expunged. "No, you just want to hurt my sister," I grind out.

His features scrunch, his voice pained. "That's not true. I would never hurt anyone you loved. The neophytes told me they'd leave you alone, that you and your family would get out in one piece."

"They're liars!" I scream at him. "And so are you!" My eyes burn with vicious tears. "Destiny told me, she's *saw* it. Remember Destiny?" My gaze flickers to the tattoo of the serpent puncturing the heart. "She never did anything to you and you fucking murdered her!"

"It's not murder, it's survival!" Fluid pools in his mouth and he begins to sob. "I want to live, Taran. I want to be safe. It's all I've ever wanted to do."

He looks up at the inferno the area has become. "I didn't choose to be a Fate, Taran. It chose me. All I've ever wanted was a normal life—to be a normal guy, not this freak." He keeps his stare ahead. "But here I am, with vampires, *weres*, and witches all wanting me and none of them able to save me. It's the reason I sent my messenger to find the one group of preternaturals who could."

His messenger? My eyes widen. "The butterfly tat," I say. "You set it free to find the shifters—God damn it, even after they killed your friends?"

"I didn't want to, I *had* to. They're the strongest, you said it yourself." He grabs my shoulders, shaking me hard. "Can't you see? This is my chance, Taran. My one chance to survive this shit."

He's playing at my sympathy. I know what it's like to be weird and hated for it. I know what it's like to beg God and the Powers that Be to give us a normal existence so we can have homes, and husbands, and babies. But that's not our reality. For good or for bad, this is what we are.

Johnny breaks down. "I just want to live," he tells me. "Just let me live."

"*No.*"

My hand shoots out, my nails digging into the flesh of his chest. Johnny screams, spilling lava from his Mordor tat straight into my arm.

I expect pain, loads of it. Except all I feel is magic.

Like a volcano meeting a super nova of energy, our magic pummels each other, both ancient powers battling it out to see which bitch rules best.

The earth quakes beneath us, splitting the ground, but the Grim Reaper will golf with my decapitated head before I let Johnny go.

I clamp down on my teeth, scraping my nails further in. Through the smoke and our burning surroundings, I see Destiny, her image appearing in a strobe of scattered pictures.

Tye is on top of her, his large palms pressing into her chest as he performs CPR. He's begging her not to leave, to come back to him, crying out that he can't live without her.

My head spins from the diapason of energy streaming from my hand. Combine it with the heat surging around me, and relentless rumbles from the cracking earth, I can't even focus.

The titillation of noise, power, and visuals is too much to take. I don't know anything. What my magic is doing. What Johnny is doing to fight back. All I know is I can't let go.

A fist comes down on my face. Then another.

I ignore the instinct to protect my head, keeping my hand in place and sinking my fingers deeper.

I think I'm losing when the visual of Destiny and Tye fades, becoming lighter. I make out things here and there: the wolves guarding her closing in, the one in front telling Tye to leave her, and how the wolf staggers back when Tye shrugs him off.

Tye's compressions quicken. He's not giving up on her, and I won't either.

My nails pierce bone when the vision slips further away. "Burn, baby," I gasp. "*Burn.*"

The next blow to my face stirs an additional spark inside me, causing it to intensify and gifting it with the incandescent glow and heat I need.

Like Velcro being ripped from its source, my fingers tear off Johnny's skin.

Destiny screams.

And so does Johnny.

What happens next is hard to say. I'm no longer me. I'm one of many atoms in a bomb that goes *boom.*

I soar into the atmosphere, my limbs listless and weak, jolting when my back strikes a sharp rock and I roll down an incline raging with fire.

I don't know how to stop. But my mate does. He appears, the brutal way he snatches hold of my arm, slapping me awake.

"Hang on," he yells. "I have you."

The earth is quaking, the remains of the burning arena falling away into the giant crater I'm currently dangling over.

"Oh, *shit,*" I say.

Gemini holds me with one hand, using the other and his bare feet to scale the side of the rumbling wall.

Chunks of dirt fall like hail, pelting our heads and crumbling against our faces. But I refuse to look down. No way in hell do I want any part of that inferno.

Shayna pokes her head out from the ledge. "*Dude!*" she says.

Koda appears, so does Bren, reaching for Gemini as he nears the top and yanking us out.

"Time to get the fuck out, peeps," Bren says, tossing Emme over his shoulder and darting toward a nearby grove.

Gemini hauls me into his arms and races away, placing me down in a small clearing only when the trembles at our feet subside.

Everything behind us is on fire, everything. Good thing we have that arena size crater sucking it all in.

"Did I do that?" I ask.

"Yup," Bren answers.

With the exception of me and my sisters, whose clothes hang in pieces, all the *weres* are naked, not that I see much.

Everyone is covered in soot and coughing. Including me. "What exactly happened?" I ask.

Shayna and Emme exchange glances. "You sorta blew everything up," Shayna tells me. "Again."

I point to the hole. "But how did I create that? That's . . . *huge.*"

Gemini shakes his head as if he can't believe it himself. "Your power and Johnny's had it out. From what we could see the impact broke through the ground and struck a fault line, empowering it with magic and creating the crater." He frowns, looking out across the hot mess. "The witches are bespelling the first responders and survivors." He tilts his head, listening closely, not that I hear a damn thing. "They're inferring the fire started within the arena after the earthquake struck due to defective wiring."

I look back at the swirls of blue, white, and gold, my power intermixing with Johnny's, I suppose. It must have been something to see the colossal amount of energy it took to feed the fault line, and to watch nature respond so brutally in return.

But it was something else entirely to experience it, and to be the cause.

I watch the flames eating their way into the sky a while longer before I speak. "Destiny's dead."

The quiet that stretches out among us is almost more than I can take. Bren huffs. "Yeah. That's what it looked like."

I raise my chin. "You saw what happened to her?"

It's Gemini who answers. "We all did. The magic that unleashed when you fought Johnny debilitated us. We couldn't do or see much past the visions." He looks at me. "They were yours, weren't they? The ones of Destiny in bed with Tye fighting to revive her?"

"Not completely. I think she wanted me to see, so I did. With how bad she was hurting, it was the only way she could communicate."

I remember how dizzy the strobing images made me, and how hard it was to differentiate between the here and now and what was happening in Tahoe. Tears fill Shayna's and Emme's eyes, except I'm the one who cries first.

"The tattoo was what Johnny used to drain her," I say. "The one of the snake piercing the heart."

"Destiny was our heart," Shayna says, repeating my exact thoughts. The realization causes her tears to run faster and all at once, she breaks down.

"She was," I agree. I sniff, trying uselessly to keep it together. "I just don't think any of us knew it until it was too late."

Koda gathers Shayna into his arms when she cries into her hands. Like the rest of us, his body was battered, and while his wolf has healed him, it can't protect him from Shayna's sorrow. He holds her, hurting because she does.

Gemini pulls me to him. "I just don't understand how he did it," I say, my misery making it hard to speak.

He sighs. "Destiny never knew of him. But the Fate always knew her. I think he baited her with his music, calling to her when he finally believed he could take her."

"But he seemed so shocked when he first saw her," I say. "Like he was seeing something he didn't know existed."

"I think you're wrong," he tells me gently, his knuckles passing gently across my skin. "If anything, I think he was shocked to see you, and your sisters. He wasn't expecting anything like you."

I ease away from him, just enough to see his face. "So all that screaming and suffering on the mountain wasn't real on his part?"

He strokes my hair, appearing sad. "It was. Except where she hurt because her magic was leaving her, my guess is he was in pain due to the gamut of energy being fed into his body." He releases my strands. "He probably spent years nourishing the tattoo so he could take Destiny's power when they finally met. I just don't think he expected what leeching that power would cost him."

"We should have let Tye kill him when he had the

chance," Bren mutters. He spreads his arms out. "Look at all this shit, all these dead humans, the rest of us coming close to biting it. It could have ended before it began."

Gemini frowns. "I don't agree. The amount of energy passing from Destiny into Fate was colossal. If Tye had killed him then, it would have erupted and destroyed us all."

"Instead it only killed poor Destiny," I say.

Emme edges beside me when I wipe my face. "Here," she says. "Let me heal you."

Gemini releases me and steps toward the other *weres* to give us space. Like the rest of us, they look aggrieved.

"I'm all right," I mumble. I'm not a masochist, but I feel like one then. I should have saved her. I should have done more. But I don't think I was enough.

No matter how hard we fought, none of us were enough to save her.

I stare out in the direction of the fiery pit, pondering all the things that went wrong.

"Taran," Emme says. "I don't think you realize how hurt you are."

Maybe I don't. Maybe I don't want to.

I'm having trouble breathing. Mostly though, I'm numb. Johnny was a victim of chance. Like me and my sisters, these powers were shoved upon him whether he wanted them or not. The thing is, we stopped being victims and decided to do something good with all the shit we were handed. Johnny didn't, he continued to play the victim only to become the aggressor, attacking an innocent and killing her slowly.

My breath releases in painful bursts. I can't imagine how much Destiny suffered, not just since meeting Johnny, but in the last few moments of her life. It must have been torture, and yet she used what remained of her strength to help us.

Oh, Destiny, how I would love to see you bouncing along in your zebra prints one last time.

"Taran," Emme pleads.

"Emme, I'm fine," I tell her.

"No, you're not," Gemini answers gruffly, evidently articulating what everyone is thinking based on the way their stares hone in on my face. He storms to my side. "You almost died, twice, and your face and body reflect it. Just let Emme heal you."

I raise my hands to my face, wincing when the numbing lifts and the pain sharpens. My skin is swollen. "All right," I say.

It doesn't take long for Emme to heal me, everything snapping into place rather viciously once she gets going. She cringes, glancing away even as her fingers slip tenderly away from my face.

Gemini takes the phone Emme hands him when she finishes and calls the Den. He's communicating with another *were* to arrange our flight home when Shayna's phone rings.

She reaches into her back pocket, her motions slow, reflecting her exhaustion. "Hello?" Her eyes widen, her head whipping from me, to Emme, and then to Koda whose gaze is just as wide. "Dude, are you serious?"

"What is it?" I ask, hurrying forward.

She looks directly at me. "It's Destiny. She's alive."

My body whips around as I feel a penetrating and familiar pull. From the flames and smoke near the crater, an immense peacock emerges, clutching Johnny's limp form.

Gemini barks out orders, alerting the pack to follow.

But he's too late.

The peacock disappears into the horizon, taking Fate with him.

Chapter Twenty-Six

There were days so bad, I wasn't sure how we'd survive, and nights we couldn't sleep because we were fighting for our lives. Yesterday and last night were one of those moments. Maybe that's why there aren't any tears left to cry.

The air was so dense with regret and worry it was hard to breathe, much less sleep.

I barely spoke the entire flight back to Tahoe, listening as the Alliance elite scrambled to find Johnny. Each word spoken was another icepick to the heart, spreading the numbness taking me over.

Gemini opens the passenger side door to his black SUV, allowing me through. And although he climbs inside and cranks the engine, he doesn't immediately pull away. Instead he greets me with one of those sweet, outrageously sexy kisses he gives me when we're alone and have no place to go.

It surprises me, given all the shit the last twenty hours have brought. That doesn't mean I don't welcome it and take every bit of love it carries.

He pulls away as I begin to relax, and strokes my face. "You need to sleep," he tells me.

He's worn. But his two wolves will keep him going for

days. I don't have a beast to energize me, and only now recognize how exhausted I am. "Okay, but with you, in our bed, and in our real home."

"Then that's what we'll do," he says, pressing another gentle kiss across my lips.

He pulls away, the SUV splashing through the large puddles created during last night's rainfall. I might have burned a good part of South Carolina to ash, but Tahoe is freshly cleansed from last night's storm.

As we near the end of the tarmac I catch sight of Emme and Bren. His head is bowed as he speaks to her quietly. She's wearing his old biker jacket, the long sleeves dangling past her hands. But it's her small smile that gives me pause.

There's something special between them. I'm just not sure he's ready to see or feel it, no matter how much she needs him to.

As Gemini pulls away from the airport and onto the main road, my thoughts return to Johnny. But how I wish I could will those thoughts away.

"All those people killed in the stadium were blood sacrifices," I say. "Weren't they?"

Gemini rubs his jaw, the longer whiskers of his goatee sliding between his fingers. It's not an irritated gesture, not like it sometimes is. Like me, he's in deep thought. "That's what it seemed like," he agrees.

"So Johnny will become one of them, won't he?" I swallow back the anger and maybe more sadness than I should. "He'll be the next big shapeshifter."

"Maybe," he says.

"Maybe?" I question. "He's a witch and killed all those people. He could have sacrificed them on behalf of a dark deity. Babe, he would have done whatever it took to save his own ass."

"It's not as easy as that, Taran. Before becoming shifters, dark witches spend their lives delving in arts laced with evil and ill intent." He curses. "As much as I didn't like Johnny, he wasn't evil. Those feelings he had for you were genuine, and came from someplace good. Good isn't something dark witches are capable of, and neither is anything that resembles friendship."

"Then what will he become?" I ask.

"I don't know," he says, his SUV barreling down the road. "It's obvious he made a deal with them. The neophytes and shifters wouldn't have arrived in the numbers that they did just to kill or kidnap him. Johnny summoned them, and based on the information we gathered during the debriefing, it was when you stepped onto the stage to kill him."

"That makes sense." I look up at him. "You know he'll go to the shifters, right? After everything he did, there's no other supernatural group who will take him."

"No, evil is all he has now," Gemini says. "There, he'll either be used, emerge as a neophyte, or become something more."

"Either way more powerful," I conclude.

"I don't know about that." The corner of his mouth lifts with something that appears too much like pride. "Taran, no matter how powerful he was, you inflicted immeasurable damage." He motions to my arm. "We still don't know what your arm's power is capable of. But Johnny does, and now he fears you because of it." He steals a glance my way. "Just as I saw those visions Destiny presented us, I could sense his fear. He was afraid of you. He knew he'd die at your hands."

"But he didn't."

"No," he says, his voice certain. "But one day he will. Fate now knows you'll be the one to kill him."

Guilt fills me. "If that's true, why didn't I kill him? Why did I hesitate?"

"You hesitated because you're human, my love." He reaches for my hand and kisses it. "It's one of your best qualities and what keeps me from fully surrendering to my beasts." He smiles softly. "I wouldn't be the man I am without you."

"Don't be nice," I say, my voice trembling. "I don't deserve it."

"You do. You may not have killed Fate this time, but you saved Destiny."

At least I can take comfort in that.

I lean my head against his shoulder when he puts his arm around me. "Do you want to stop someplace to eat?"

"No." I rub my eyes. "Let's go home. I want to check on Destiny, and make sure she's all right. Then we'll eat. Then we'll sleep."

"Whatever you'd like, Taran."

We don't say much on the short drive back. But what we say is enough, returning to a sense of normal I cling to with everything I have.

Apparently, normal is a pussy and doesn't belong in our world. Gemini straightens and I right myself as a plethora of magic bangs into our chests when we reach Dollar Point.

"Fate," he growls.

"Uh-uh," I say, my heart bursting with enough joy to taste. "It's Destiny, she's interacting with the magic from the Lake."

Gemini floors it. As the Lake comes into view, I see them, millions of sparkles spreading across the water and flowing in the direction of our home. He peels into our neighborhood, swerving to a stop in front of our house.

The wolves, the ones who are supposed to be guarding her, stand along our front lawn, watching in awe as the black and silver sparkles swirl like shimmering fireworks.

One of the wolves jogs toward us when he sees us hurry out. "It's Destiny," he says. "She's become something stronger." He shakes out his hands as if he can sense the power she emits. "I've never felt anything like her."

The world is held in a delicate balance, and now that Fate has changed, so will Destiny, evening the odds. I don't wait. I race up the wooden porch steps and into the house, out of my mind with joy and bearing a smile as large as life.

That smile drops when I find Destiny and Tye going at it like horny gorillas on my dining room table.

Tye's jeans and boxers are down to his ankles, exposing an ass only partially obstructed by a pair of zebra-stripe clad legs crisscrossed over his back. He pumps away, growling deep as hot pink plumage floats away from whatever ungodly headpiece Destiny is wearing.

I don't stick around to see it. I walk out, slamming the door shut behind me.

Gemini pauses at the top of the steps, frowning. "Are they coming?"

"That's what it sounds like," I reply.

His eyes round as he stares at the door, hearing something I'm more than glad to miss. I shudder as I reach the bottom of the steps, and shudder a little more when another visual of them fills my mind. Son of a bitch, we eat Thanksgiving dinner on that table!

Gemini jogs after me when I stomp down the walkway and cut into the path leading to the Lake.

He's laughing so hard, he's gripping his sides. "You think this is funny?" I ask. I rub my eyes, but some things you just can't unsee.

"Oh, hell yes." He hauls me to him by the waist. "It's what mates do, Taran. After everything they've been through, they deserve to make up for their time lost. As do we."

"I know, but why do they have to make up that time all over our dining room table?"

He shrugs. "Probably because they've already defiled the kitchen."

"Oh, gawd," I say, wondering where the hell else I'll be finding feathers.

I relax into his chest, lifting my chin when he finally finishes laughing. "Now what?" I ask. "Where do we go from here?"

He adjusts his hold, keeping me close, his embrace and the gentle way he regards me speaking beyond the words that come. "Now, we make our own destiny."

Reader's Guide to the Magical World of The Weird Girls Series

acute bloodlust A condition that occurs when a vampire goes too long without consuming blood. Increases the vampire's thirst to lethal levels. It is remedied by feeding the vampire.

Call The ability of one supernatural creature to reach out to another, through either thoughts or sounds. A vampire can pass his or her *call* by transferring a bit of magic into the receiving being's skin.

Change To transform from one being to another, typically from human to beast, and back again.

chronic bloodlust A condition caused by a curse placed on a vampire. It makes the vampire's thirst for blood insatiable and drives the vampire to insanity. The vampire grows in size from gluttony and assumes deformed features. There is no cure.

claim The method by which a werebeast consummates the union with his or her mate.

clan A group of werebeasts led by an Alpha. The types of clans differ depending on species. Werewolf clans are called "packs." Werelions belong to "prides."

Creatura The offspring of a demon lord and a werebeast.

dantem animam A soul giver. A rare being capable of returning a master vampire's soul. A master with a soul is more powerful than any other vampire in existence, as he or she is balancing life and death at once.

dark ones Creatures considered to be pure evil, such as shape-shifters or demons.

demon A creature residing in hell. Only the strongest demons may leave to stalk on earth, but their time is limited; the power of good compels them to return.

demon child The spawn of a demon lord and a mortal female. Demon children are of limited intelligence and rely predominantly on their predatory instincts.

demon lords (*demonkin*) The offspring of a witch mother and a demon. Powerful, cunning, and deadly. Unlike demons, whose time on earth is limited, demon lords may remain on earth indefinitely.

den A school where young werebeasts train and learn to fight in order to help protect the earth from mystical evil.

Elder One of the governors of a werebeast clan. Each clan is led by three Elders: an Alpha, a Beta, and an Omega. The Alpha is the supreme leader. The Beta is the second in command. The Omega settles disputes between them and has the ability to calm by releasing bits of his or her harmonized soul, or through a sense of humor muddled with magic. He possesses rare gifts and is often volatile, selfish, and of questionable loyalty.

force Emme Wird's ability to move objects with her mind.

gold The metallic element; it was cursed long ago and has damaging effects on werebeasts, vampires, and the dark ones. Supernatural creatures cannot hold gold without feeling the poisonous effects of the curse. A bullet dipped in gold will explode a supernatural creature's heart like a bomb. Gold against open skin has a searing effect.

grandmaster The master of a master vampire. Grandmasters are among the earth's most powerful creatures. Grandmasters can recognize whether the human he or she *turned* is a master upon creation. Grandmasters usually kill any master vampires they create to consume their power. Some choose to let the masters live until they become a threat, or until they've gained greater strength and therefore more consumable power.

keep Beings a master vampire controls and is responsible for, such as those he or she has *turned* vampire, or a human he or she regularly feeds from. One master can acquire another's keep by destroying the master the keep belongs to.

Leader A pureblood werebeast in charge of delegating and planning attacks against the evils that threaten the earth.

Lesser witch Title given to a witch of weak power and who has not yet mastered control of her magic. Unlike their Superior counterparts, they aren't given talismans or staffs to amplify their magic because their control over their power is limited.

Lone A werebeast who doesn't belong to a clan, and therefore is not obligated to protect the earth from supernatural evil. Considered of lower class by those with clans.

master vampire A vampire with the ability to *turn* a human vampire. Upon their creation, masters are usually killed by their grandmaster for power. Masters are immune to fire and to sunlight born of magic, and typically carry tremendous power. Only a master or another lethal preternatural can kill a master vampire. If one master kills another, the surviving vampire acquires his or her power, wealth, and keep.

mate The being a werebeast will love and share a soul with for eternity.

Misericordia A plea for mercy in a duel.

moon sickness The werebeast equivalent of bloodlust. Brought on by a curse from a powerful enchantress. Causes excruciating pain. Attacks a werebeast's central nervous system, making the werebeast stronger and violent, and driving the werebeast to kill. No known cure exists.

mortem provocatio A fight to the death.

North American *Were* Council The governing body of *weres* in North America, led by a president and several council members.

potestatem bonum "The power of good." That which encloses the earth and keeps demons from remaining among the living.

Purebloods (aka *pures*) Werebeasts from generations of *were*-only family members. Considered royalty among werebeasts, they carry the responsibilities of their species. The mating between two purebloods is the only way to guarantee the conception of a *were* child.

rogue witch a witch without a coven. Must be accounted for as rogue witches tend to go one of two ways without a coven: dark or insane.

shape-shifter Evil, immortal creatures who can take any form. They are born witches, then spend years seeking innocents to sacrifice to a dark deity. When the deity deems the offerings sufficient, the witch casts a baneful spell to surrender his or her magic and humanity in exchange for immortality and the power of hell at their fingertips. Shape-shifters can command any form and are the deadliest and strongest of all mystical creatures.

Shift Celia's ability to break down her body into minute particles. Her gift allows her to travel beneath and across soil, concrete, and rock. Celia can also *shift* a limited number of beings. Disadvantages include not being able to breathe or see until she surfaces.

solis natus magicae The proper term for sunlight born of magic, created by a wielder of spells. Considered "pure" light. Capable of destroying non-master vampires and demons. In large quantities may also kill shape-shifters. Renders the wielder helpless once fired.

Superior Witch A witch of tremendous power and magic who assumes a leadership role among the coven. Wears a talisman around her neck or carries staff with a precious stone at its center to help amplify her magic.

Surface Celia's ability to reemerge from a shift.

susceptor animae A being capable of taking one's soul, such as a vampire.

Trudhilde Radinka (aka *Destiny*) A female born once every century from the union of two witches who possesses rare talents and the aptitude to predict the future. Considered among the elite of the mystical world.

turn To transform a human into a werebeast or vampire. Werebeasts *turn* by piercing the heart of a human with their fangs and transferring a part of their essence. Vampires pierce through the skull and into the brain to transfer a taste of their magic. Werebeasts risk their lives during the *turning* process, as they are gifting a part of their souls. Should the transfer fail, both the werebeast and human die. Vampires risk nothing since they're not losing their souls, but rather taking another's and releasing it from the human's body.

vampire A being who consumes the blood of mortals to survive. Beautiful and alluring, vampires will never appear to age past thirty years. Vampires are immune to sunlight unless it is created by magic. They are also immune to objects of faith such as crucifixes. Vampires may be killed by the destruction of their hearts, decapitation, or fire. Master vampires or vampires several centuries old must have both their hearts and heads removed or their bodies completely destroyed.

vampire clans Families of vampires led by master vampires. Masters can control, communicate, and punish their keep through mental telepathy.

velum A veil conjured by magic.

virtutem lucis "The power of light." The goodness found within each mortal. That which combats the darkness.

Warrior A werebeast possessing profound skill or fighting ability. Only the elite among *weres* are granted the title of Warrior. Warriors are duty-bound to protect their Leaders and their Leaders' mates at all costs.

werebeast A supernatural predator with the ability to *change* from human to beast. Werebeasts are considered the Guardians of the Earth against mystical evil. Werebeasts will achieve their first *change* within six months to a year following birth. The younger they are when they first *change,* the more powerful they will be. Werebeasts also possess the ability to heal their wounds. They can live until the first full moon following their one hundredth birthday. Werebeasts may be killed by destruction of their hearts, decapitation, or if their bodies are completely destroyed. The only time a *were* can partially *change* is when he or she attempts to *turn* a human. A *turned* human will achieve his or her first *change* by the next full moon.

witch A being born with the power to wield magic. They worship the earth and nature. Pure witches will not take part in blood sacrifices. They cultivate the land to grow plants for their potions and use staffs and talismans to amplify their magic. To cross a witch is to feel the collective wrath of her coven.

witch fire Orange flames encased by magic, used to assassinate an enemy. Witch fire explodes like multiple grenades when the intended victim nears the spell. Flames will continue to burn until the target has been eliminated.

zombie Typically human bodies raised from the dead by a necromancer witch. It's illegal to raise or keep a zombie and is among the deadliest sins in the supernatural world. Their diet consists of other dead things such as roadkill and decaying animal.

This book contains an excerpt from *Sealed with a Curse* the first full-length novel in The Weird Girls Urban Fantasy Romance series by Cecy Robson. This excerpt has been set for this edition only and may not reflect the final content of the final novel.

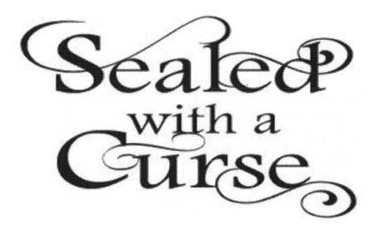

A Weird Girls Novel

by Cecy Robson

Chapter One

Sacramento, California

The courthouse doors crashed open as I led my three sisters into the large foyer. I didn't mean to push so hard, but hell, I was mad and worried about being eaten. The cool spring breeze slapped at my back as I stepped inside, yet it did little to cool my temper or my nerves.

My nose scented the vampires before my eyes caught them emerging from the shadows. There were six of them, wearing dark suits, Ray-Bans, and obnoxious little grins. Two bolted the doors tight behind us, while the others frisked us for weapons.

I can't believe we we're in vampire court. So much for avoiding the perilous world of the supernatural.

Emme trembled beside me. She had every right to be scared. We were strong, but our combined abilities couldn't trump a roomful of bloodsucking beasts. "Celia," she whispered, her voice shaking. "Maybe we shouldn't have come."

Like we had a choice. "Just stay close to me, Emme." My

muscles tensed as the vampire's hands swept the length of my body and through my long curls. I didn't like him touching me, and neither did my inner tigress. My fingers itched with the need to protrude my claws.

When he finally released me, I stepped closer to Emme while I scanned the foyer for a possible escape route. Next to me, the vampire searching Taran got a little daring with his pat-down. But he was messing with the wrong sister.

"If you touch my ass one more time, fang boy, I swear to God I'll light you on fire." The vampire quickly removed his hands when a spark of blue flame ignited from Taran's fingertips.

Shayna, conversely, flashed a lively smile when the vampire searching her found her toothpicks. Her grin widened when he returned her seemingly harmless little sticks, unaware of how deadly they were in her hands. "Thanks, dude." She shoved the box back into the pocket of her slacks.

"They're clear." The guard grinned at Emme and licked his lips. "This way." He motioned her to follow. Emme cowered. Taran showed no fear and plowed ahead. She tossed her dark, wavy hair and strutted into the courtroom like the diva she was, wearing a tiny white mini dress that contrasted with her deep olive skin. I didn't fail to notice the guards' gazes glued to Taran's shapely figure. Nor did I miss when their incisors lengthened, ready to bite.

I urged Emme and Shayna forward. "Go. I'll watch your backs." I whipped around to snarl at the guards. The vampires' smiles faltered when they saw *my* fangs protrude. Like most beings, they probably didn't know what I was, but they seemed to recognize that I was potentially lethal, despite my petite frame.

I followed my sisters into the large courtroom. The place reminded me of a picture I'd seen of the Salem witch trials. Rows of dark wood pews lined the center aisle, and wide rustic planks comprised the floor. Unlike the photo I recalled, every window was boarded shut, and paintings of vampires hung on every inch of available wall space. One particular image epitomized the vampire stereotype perfectly. It showed a male vampire entwined with two naked women on a bed of roses and jewels. The women appeared completely enamored of the vampire, even while blood dripped from their necks.

The vampire spectators scrutinized us as we approached along the center aisle. Many had accessorized their expensive attire with diamond jewelry and watches that probably cost more than my car. Their glares told me they didn't appreciate my cotton T-shirt, peasant skirt, and flip-flops. I was twenty-five years old; it's not like I didn't know how to dress. But, hell, other fabrics and shoes were way more expensive to replace when I *changed* into my other form.

I spotted our accuser as we stalked our way to the front of the assembly. Even in a courtroom crammed with young and sexy vampires, Misha Aleksandr stood out. His tall, muscular frame filled his fitted suit, and his long blond hair brushed against his shoulders. Death, it seemed, looked damn good. Yet it wasn't his height or his wealth or even his striking features that captivated me. He possessed a fierce presence that commanded the room. Misha Aleksandr was a force to be reckoned with, but, strangely enough, so was I.

Misha had "requested" our presence in Sacramento after charging us with the murder of one of his family members. We had two choices: appear in court or be hunted for the rest of our lives. The whole situation sucked. We'd stayed hidden from the supernatural world for so long. Now not only had we been forced into the limelight, but we also faced the possibility of dying some twisted, Rob Zombie–inspired death.

Of course, God forbid that would make Taran shut her trap. She leaned in close to me. "Celia, how about I gather some magic-borne sunlight and fry these assholes?" she whispered in Spanish.

A few of the vampires behind us muttered and hissed, causing uproar among the rest. If they didn't like us before, they sure as hell hated us then.

Shayna laughed nervously, but maintained her perky demeanor. "I think some of them understand the lingo, dude."

I recognized Taran's desire to burn the vamps to blood

and ash, but I didn't agree with it. Conjuring such power would leave her drained and vulnerable, easy prey for the master vampires, who would be immune to her sunlight. Besides, we were already in trouble with one master for killing his keep. We didn't need to be hunted by the entire leeching species.

The procession halted in a strangely wide-open area before a raised dais. There were no chairs or tables, nothing we could use as weapons against the judges or the angry mob amassed behind us.

My eyes focused on one of the boarded windows. The light honey-colored wood frame didn't match the darker boards. I guessed the last defendant had tried to escape. Judging from the claw marks running from beneath the frame to where I stood, he, she, or *it* hadn't made it.

I looked up from the deeply scratched floor to find Misha's intense gaze on me. We locked eyes, predator to predator, neither of us the type to back down. *You're trying to intimidate the wrong gal, pretty boy. I don't scare easily.*

Shayna slapped her hand over her face and shook her head, her long black ponytail waving behind her. "For Pete's sake, Celia, can't you be a little friendlier?" She flashed Misha a grin that made her blue eyes sparkle. "How's it going, dude?"

Shayna said "dude" a lot, ever since dating some idiot claiming to be a professional surfer. The term fit her sunny personality and eventually grew on us.

Misha didn't appear taken by her charm. He eyed her as if she'd asked him to make her a garlic pizza in the shape of a cross. I laughed; I couldn't help it. *Leave it to Shayna to try to befriend the guy who'll probably suck us dry by sundown.*

At the sound of my chuckle, Misha regarded me slowly. His head tilted slightly as his full lips curved into a sensual smile. I would have preferred a vicious stare—I knew how to deal with those. For a moment, I thought he'd somehow made my clothes disappear and I was standing there like the bleeding hoochies in that awful painting.

The judges' sudden arrival gave me an excuse to glance

away. There were four, each wearing a formal robe of red velvet with an elaborate powdered wig. They were probably several centuries old, but like all vampires, they didn't appear a day over thirty. Their splendor easily surpassed the beauty of any mere mortal. I guessed the whole "sucky, sucky, me love you all night" lifestyle paid off for them.

The judges regally assumed their places on the raised dais. Behind them hung a giant plasma screen, which appeared out of place in this century-old building. Did they plan to watch a movie while they decided how best to disembowel us?

A female judge motioned Misha forward with a Queen Elizabeth hand wave. A long, thick scar angled from the corner of her left jaw across her throat. Someone had tried to behead her. To scar a vampire like that, the culprit had likely used a gold blade reinforced with lethal magic. Apparently, even that blade hadn't been enough. I gathered she commanded the fang-fest Parliament, since her marble nameplate read, CHIEF JUSTICE ANTOINETTE MALIKA. Judge Malika didn't strike me as the warm and cuddly sort. Her lips were pursed into a tight line and her elongating fangs locked over her lower lip. I only hoped she'd snacked before her arrival.

At a nod from Judge Malika, Misha began. "Members of the High Court, I thank you for your audience." A Russian accent underscored his deep voice. "I hereby charge Celia, Taran, Shayna, and Emme Wird with the murder of my family member, David Geller."

"Wird? More like *Weird*," a vamp in the audience mumbled. The smaller vamp next to him adjusted his bow tie nervously when I snarled.

Oh, yeah, like we've never heard that before, jerk.

The sole male judge slapped a heavy leather-bound book on the long table and whipped out a feather quill. "Celia Wird. State your position."

Position?

I exchanged glances with my sisters; they didn't seem to know what Captain Pointy Teeth meant either. Taran shrugged. "Who gives a shit? Just say something."

I waved a hand. "Um. Registered nurse?"

Judging by his "please don't make me eat you before the proceedings" scowl, and the snickering behind us, I hadn't provided him with the appropriate response.

He enunciated every word carefully and slowly so as to not further confuse my obviously feeble and inferior mind. "Position in the supernatural world."

"We've tried to avoid your world." I gave Taran the evil eye. "For the most part. But if you must know, I'm a tigress."

"Weretigress," he said as he wrote.

"I'm not a *were*," I interjected defensively.

He huffed. "Can you *change* into a tigress or not?"

"Well, yes. But that doesn't make me a *were*."

The vamps behind us buzzed with feverish whispers while the judges' eyes narrowed suspiciously. Not knowing what we were made them nervous. A nervous vamp was a dangerous vamp. And the room was bursting with them.

"What I mean is, unlike a *were*, I can *change* parts of my body without turning into my beast completely." And unlike anything else on earth, I could also *shift*—disappear under and across solid ground and resurface unscathed. But they didn't need to know that little tidbit. Nor did they need to know I couldn't heal my injuries. If it weren't for Emme's unique ability to heal herself and others, my sisters and I would have died long ago.

"Fascinating," he said in a way that clearly meant I wasn't. The feather quill didn't come with an eraser. And the judge obviously didn't appreciate my making him mess up his book. He dipped his pen into his little inkwell and scribbled out what he'd just written before addressing Taran. "Taran Wird, position?"

"I can release magic into the forms of fire and lightning—"

"Very well, witch." The vamp scrawled.

"I'm not a witch, asshole."

The judge threw his plume on the table, agitated. Judge Malika fixed her frown on Taran. "What did you say?"

Nobody flashed a vixen grin better than Taran. "I said, 'I'm not a witch. Ass. Hole.'"

Emme whimpered, ready to hurl from the stress. Shayna giggled and threw an arm around Taran. "She's just kidding, dude!"

No. Taran didn't kid. Hell, she didn't even know any knock-knock jokes. She shrugged off Shayna, unwilling to back down. She wouldn't listen to Shayna. But she would listen to me.

"Just answer the question, Taran."

The muscles on Taran's jaw tightened, but she did as I asked. "I make fire, light—"

"Fire-breather." Captain Personality wrote quickly.

"I'm not a—"

He cut her off. "Shayna Wird?"

"Well, dude, I throw knives—"

"Knife thrower," he said, ready to get this little meet-and-greet over and done with.

Shayna did throw knives. That was true. She could also transform pieces of wood into razor-sharp weapons and manipulate alloys. All she needed was metal somewhere on her body and a little focus. For her safety, though, "knife thrower" seemed less threatening.

"And you, Emme Wird?"

"Um. Ah. I can move things with my mind—"

"Gypsy," the half-wit interpreted.

I supposed "telekinetic" was too big a word for this idiot. Then again, unlike typical telekinetics, Emme could do more than bend a few forks. I sighed. *Tigress, fire-breather, knife thrower, and Gypsy.* We sounded like the headliners for a freak show. All we needed was a bearded lady. I sighed. *That's what happens when you're the bizarre products of a back-fired curse.*

Misha glanced at us quickly before stepping forward once more. "I will present Mr. Hank Miller and Mr. Timothy Brown as witnesses—" Taran exhaled dramatically and twirled her hair like she was bored. Misha glared at her before finishing. "I do not doubt justice will be served."

Judge Zhahara Nadim, who resembled more of an Egyptian queen than someone who should be stuffed into a powdered wig, surprised me by leering at Misha like she wanted his head for a lawn ornament. I didn't know what he'd done to piss her off; yet knowing we weren't the only ones hated brought me a strange sense of comfort. She narrowed her eyes at Misha, like all predators do before they strike, and called forward someone named "Destiny." I didn't know Destiny, but I knew she was no vampire the moment she strutted onto the dais.

I tried to remain impassive. However, I really wanted to run away screaming. Short of sporting a few tails and some extra digits, Destiny was the freakiest thing I'd ever seen. Not only did she lack the allure all vampires possessed, but her fashion sense bordered on disastrous. She wore black patterned tights, white strappy sandals, and a hideous black-and-white polka-dot turtleneck. I guessed she sought to draw attention from her lime green zebra-print miniskirt. And, my God, her makeup was abominable. Black kohl outlined her bright fuchsia lips, and mint green shadow ringed her eyes.

"This is a perfect example of why I don't wear makeup," I told Taran.

Taran stepped forward with her hands on her hips. "How the hell is *she* a witness? I didn't see her at the club that night! And Lord knows she would've stuck out."

Emme trembled beside me. "Taran, please don't get us killed!"

I gave my youngest sister's hand a squeeze. "Steady, Emme."

Judge Malika called Misha's two witnesses forward. "Mr. Miller and Mr. Brown, which of you gentlemen would like to go first?"

Both "gentlemen" took one gander at Destiny and scrambled away from her. It was never a good sign when something scared a vampire. Hank, the bigger of the two vamps, shoved Tim forward.

"You may begin," Judge Malika commanded. "Just concentrate on what you saw that night. Destiny?"

The four judges swiftly donned protective ear wear, like construction workers used, just as a guard flipped a switch next to the flat-screen. At first I thought the judges toyed with us. Even with heightened senses, how could they hear the testimony through those ridiculous ear guards? Before I could protest, Destiny enthusiastically approached Tim and grabbed his head. Tim's immediate bloodcurdling screams caused the rest of us to cover our ears. Every hair on my body stood at attention. What freaked me out was that he wasn't the one on trial.

Emme's fair freckled skin blanched so severely, I feared she'd pass out. Shayna stood frozen with her jaw open while Taran and I exchanged "oh, shit" glances. I was about to start the "let's get the hell out of here" ball rolling when images from Tim's mind appeared on the screen. I couldn't believe my eyes. Complete with sound effects, we relived the night of David's murder. Misha straightened when he saw David soar out of Taran's window in flames, but otherwise he did not react. Nor did Misha blink when what remained of David burst into ashes on our lawn. Still, I sensed his fury. The image moved to a close-up of Hank's shocked face and finished with the four of us scowling down at the blood and ash.

Destiny abruptly released the sobbing Tim, who collapsed on the floor. Mucus oozed from his nose and mouth. I didn't even know vamps were capable of such body fluids.

At last, Taran finally seemed to understand the deep shittiness of our situation. "Son of a bitch," she whispered.

Hank gawked at Tim before addressing the judges. "If it pleases the court, I swear on my honor I witnessed exactly what Tim Brown did about David Geller's murder. My version would be of no further benefit."

Malika shrugged indifferently. "Very well, you're excused." She turned toward us while Hank hurried back to his seat. "As you just saw, we have ways to expose the truth. Destiny is able to extract memories, but she cannot alter them. Likewise, during Destiny's time with you, you will be unable to change what you saw. You'll only review what has already come to pass."

I frowned. "How do we know you're telling us the truth?"

Malika peered down her nose at me. "What choice do you have? Now, which of you is first?"

Photo by Kate Gledhill of Kate Gledhill Photography

Cecy Robson is an author of contemporary romance, young adult adventure, and award-winning urban fantasy. A double RITA® 2016 finalist for Once Pure and Once Kissed, and a published author of more than sixteen titles, you can typically find her on her laptop writing her stories or stumbling blindly in search of caffeine.

For more, visit my Website:

www.cecyrobson.com

For exclusive information and more, join my Newsletter:

http://eepurl.com/4ASmj

Made in the USA
Monee, IL
02 October 2020